THE
APPLE
FALLS
FROM
THE
APPLE
TREE

THE APPLE FALLS FROM THE APPLE TREE

stories by

Helen Papanikolas

Swallow Press / Ohio University Press // Athens

01 00 99 98 97   5 4 3 2

Swallow Press/Ohio University Press books are printed on acid-free paper ∞

Book design by Chiquita Babb

Library of Congress Cataloging-in-Publication Data

Papanikolas, Helen Zeese.
  The apple falls from the apple tree : stories / by Helen
Papanikolas.
    p. cm.
   ISBN 0-8040-0993-7 (clothbound : alk. paper). — ISBN
0-8040-0994-5 (pbk. : alk. paper)
    1. Utah—Social life and customs—Fiction. 2. Greek Americans—
Utah—Fiction. 3. Immigrants—Utah—Fiction. I. Title.
PS3566.A612A87 1996
813'.54—dc20   96-13264
                                                  CIP

"Great king of heav'n" 1848–1931 © 1948 LDS
Music: Leroy J. Robertson © 1948 LDS

"O God the Eternal Father" Text: William W. Phelps. Included
in the first LDS hymnbook, 1835.
Music: Felix Mendelssohn

For my sisters, Josephine, Sophie, Demetra,
who is gone, and my girlhood friends of the
Athena and Demeter clubs.

CONTENTS

THE
APPLE
FALLS
FROM
THE
APPLE
TREE

COUNTY
HOSPITAL
1939

The young woman got off on Main Street and waited almost fifteen minutes with a group of unsmiling, silent people to transfer to her second streetcar. Above the few small buildings of the western city the sky had become a soft gray color. Although Kallie was hungry and her feet hurt from the long day spent standing on the laboratory's cement floor, the dove-gray color soothed her. She boarded a streetcar that was almost empty. Now, in the Depression, people walked miles to save the fare.

When she got off at her corner, the sky had deepened to a steel color. She walked the block and a half to her house, wondering what she would find there. The dining room light was on. Her mother turned it on only when she had visitors. Kallie stopped for a moment, then went on to the purple brick bungalow her parents had bought in the middle 'twenties, when times had been prosperous. She thought of walking to the side of the house, quietly opening the door, and creeping to her bedroom where she would shut the door, lie on the bed, and pretend she was sick. She knew it would not work. Her mother had ears like a night animal. Also, her mother did not believe in women lying down in the daytime; she would carry on that Kallie had insulted her visitors. The women's talk came from behind the door in high-pitched Greek visiting voices.

Kallie turned the knob and opened the door to a familiar scene. Overweight Mrs. Hadjis and gaunt Mrs. Kerasou were sitting on the blue brocade sofa under an enlarged family photograph: Kallie's seated parents, her father's big head topped with bushy gray hair; her mother sitting primly with folded hands on a black dress, in mourning for her village parents; her two older sisters and their husbands; her brother Bill standing next to her father; and Kallie standing at the side of her mother. Both visitors were in black for dead husbands. Kallie's friend Dea called them the "twin blackbirds" when she was in a bad mood and Mrs. Happy Hadjis and Mrs. Cherry (Kerasou derived from the Greek word cherries) when she was in good spirits.

"Kaliope! Kaliope!" the women screeched in unison. Kallie walked over to them smiling politely, bowed, and shook hands with them. She asked after their health in the correct polite Greek her mother had drilled into her and her older sisters from the time they could speak.

Good cooking scents were in the room, yet Kallie knew what was coming. "You're a little late," her mother said, looking at her with sharp dark eyes, her deeply wrinkled forehead furrowing even more. "We've been waiting for you to take the ladies home."

Immediately Mrs. Hadjis began protesting, opening and closing her mouth like a little beak in her fat face. While continuing to smile, Kallie thought of them in their mourning clothes and their little beaks, yes, as Dea said, like two blackbirds. "We told your mother," Mrs. Hadjis insisted, "we'd take the streetcar, but she wouldn't listen." Mrs. Hadjis's fat arms were encased in black silk that smelled of old sweat.

"No, she wouldn't think of it. Would not think of it," Mrs. Kerasou said mournfully. Puffs of brown wrinkled skin fell in pouches below her eyes, so dark they looked black. Kallie had been taking Mrs. Kerasou home ever since she learned to drive. Mrs. Kerasou waited comfortably until Kallie came home from the hospital. Mrs. Kerasou's husband had been killed in a mine explosion fifteen years previously, but she still expected sympathy and special privileges. She usually contrived to come alone and leave with a bulging brown paper sack Kallie's mother unobtrusively placed next to her purse on a crocheted bedspread. "My black Fate. My black Fate," Mrs. Kerasou would intone, moving back and forth against the car seat, her arms folded under sagging breasts.

"Any time you're ready," Kallie's mother said, "Kaliope will take you." But the women sat.

Kallie excused herself and walked through the adjoining dining room with a glance at the big oak table which was covered with one of her mother's embroidered dowry cloths. On it were the remains of the afternoon *kafé,* as her mother called it: coffee cups and dishes with cake crumbs, apple parings, and walnut shells. In the kitchen her father was seated at the table attempting to eat quietly, an impossibility: he drew in the lemon soup with a whistling sound. He nodded. "The *karakakses* are still here," he said with a humph, making Kallie smile. *Karakakses,* magpies. The women were like blackbirds to him too. His thick gray hair bristled out like the United Mine Union president, John L. Lewis's. Two American customers who came into his store regularly called him "John L." Her father laughed, but even though he admired John L. Lewis, he was a Republican.

Kallie gave a conspiratorial nod: the visitors should not know what he was doing. It was one of her mother's Greek notions of propriety that visitors must not feel they were obstructing the routine of the house. Kallie cut a piece of bread and began eating quickly before she was summoned. The bread stuck in her throat. "Kaliope," her mother called and Kallie hurriedly filled a glass with water and drank it to force down the bread. She gulped and her mother called again, "Kaliope" in a light, almost playful tone that angered Kallie even more than her mother's sharp eyes.

Kallie hurried into the living room and said, "I'll get the car out and then I'll come in for you ladies."

"No, no," Mrs. Kerasou said, her usual insincere objection, and stood up. Her black dress, grayed from many washings, hung down to her ankles like a sack. "We'll come out. You're doing enough as it is. We told your mother but she—" Mrs. Kerasou shrugged her wide shoulders.

Mrs. Hadjis moved from side to side until her buttocks reached the edge of the sofa. Then, laughing and struggling, she grasped the arm of the sofa with one hand and a cushion with the other and, breathing heavily, stood up. "I should have helped you, Mrs. Katerini," Kallie's mother said with a dark glance at Kallie. The women had known each other since they had come to America as picture brides for strangers more than thirty years ago, but they continued to address each other with the proper title of "Mrs." before their given names. Sometimes it amused Kallie. She walked out of the house quickly, down the long driveway, and lifted the heavy wooden overhead garage door. Carefully she backed out her father's immaculate dark green Hudson, which he had bought in 1929, just before the Wall Street crash. Her mother helped the women onto the back seat. "Come soon," she said. "Come soon and we will say it all with our *kafé*." Mrs. Kerasou took in a deep sorrowful breath. "If God wants," she said. Mrs. Hadjis thanked Kallie's mother inordinately and waved again and again until Kallie backed into the street and turned southward. Her mother kept waving.

"You're such a good daughter," Mrs. Kerasou said. "I wish I had had a daughter, but God gave me sons. Not that they're not good boys. Oh yes, they are good, good sons. Considering what Fate dealt them. A father killed in his prime. Achh. Achh."

"Of course," Kallie said, remembering the day she had come home from the university to find Mrs. Kerasou weeping as she told Kallie's mother that her oldest son had ruined the family's reputation. He had married an *Americanidha*. Her mother had said that now Mrs. Kerasou had something more to add to her list of Fate's injustices.

"I have good children too," Mrs. Hadjis said, slightly doubtful, and then began a complete inventory of each of her eight children's situations, how big or small the older ones' houses were, who was attending the university, and Sam, of course, her youngest, was the best dancer of all. "At the church *horoesperidhes* no one can lead the circle like my *Semmy*. He is a real *leventis*." Mrs. Hadjis laughed after every prounouncement.

"How are your grandchildren, Mrs. Kerasou?" Kallie asked. She did not want to hear about Mrs. Hadjis's Sammy, who had told her friend Dea that the Greeks who came to America were fools not to have continued the dowry system. He was looking for a wife with property. "You, you," Dea had screamed. "You make me sick. You squat to pee!" Kallie was shocked that Dea would talk like that.

Sammy had laughed. "I thought I could get a rise out of you."

In the deepening gloom Kallie drove toward the railroad district, where the three-domed Greek church rose surrounded by old pioneer houses, several boardinghouses, a service station, an Italian importing business, one small grocery store, and a shoe repair shop. Mrs. Kerasou's rundown brick house was one of a row in a narrow alley. As the car came to a stop, Mrs. Kerasou leaned toward the back of Kallie's seat. "Kaliope," she said with some excitement, dispensing with her funereal tone, "did you hear about that Koulerakis who shot his brother-in-law? You know, down where the coal mines are?" Mrs. Kerasou knew all the accidents and crises of the Greeks.

"Yes, I did, Mrs. Kerasou."

"Is he going to live? The brother-in-law?"

"I don't know anything about it."

"Oh, I thought maybe you did, being you're like a doctor."

Kallie opened the car door and helped Mrs. Kerasou out of the car and up the three steps to her house. Through the two small glass panes near the top of the door, Kallie looked in: in the barren living room, three of the Kerasou sons were sitting on the linoleum floor in front of a small radio, laughing. "I guess they're good and hungry," Mrs. Kerasou said as she opened the door.

Mrs. Hadjis on the back seat began a long monologue about her ailments: what her doctor said; what she read in the doctor's advice column in the New York Greek newspaper daily; what her niece who lived in Chicago said about her mother-in-law who had the same problems. Kallie remembered that Mrs. Hadjis had told her mother that Dea smoked. "You know, Kaliope, and forgive me for saying this, but when I go to the toilet to do the thick business, it comes out like rabbit pellets. What's wrong? Is it a bad sign?"

"No, just eat more fruits and vegetables."

"You could be right. Now that I'm all alone, I just eat what's available. A little cheese, some olives. But that's strange. Like rabbit pellets."

Mrs. Hadjis lived ten miles beyond the county hospital. As Kallie drove past it with Mrs. Hadjis enumerating her ailments, the dimly lighted hospital looked quiet and peaceful to her. "Next time we visit your mother, you must play the piano for us," Mrs. Hadjis said at her door. "Those songs you play remind me of our sweet country. Oh, how I love to hear"—and she began singing "My Thessaloniki, no matter how far I go, I will never forget you." She broke off to be hospitable. "Come in, Kaliope. I'll serve you a *Couka Coula*."

The two insisted back and forth, Mrs. Hadjis that she should come in and Kallie that she should not. When she returned home, the sky was black. She could hardly pull down the garage door. Her father was seated next to the radio with his head turned sideways, close to the staccato voice of H. V. Kaltenborn, the news announcer. Her mother had the table set for her in the kitchen and hovered over her, urging her to eat a little more soup, more salad. Kallie ate in silence, hating her mother's attempts at appeasement.

"Here's a dish of *rizoghallo*," her mother said as Kallie finished, and placed a bowl of rice pudding before her.

"I don't want any *rizoghallo*," Kallie said with a push of the bowl. It had taken her years to realize her mother cooked special desserts for her children when she had punished them earlier or forced them to do something against their will.

"Have it later then," her mother said in a resigned voice.

"I don't know why you feel you have to provide your friends with rides home! They have children! Why don't they telephone their children to come for them?"

"It wouldn't be hospitable." Her mother stood with her arms folded in front of her apron.

"What's going on in there?" Kallie's father called out.

"Nothing much," her mother said and quietly closed the kitchen door.

"You don't care that I've been working all day and then I have to drive your friends to their houses! Mrs. Kerasou's boys were listening to the radio and she couldn't get in the door fast enough to serve them their dinner!"

Kallie's mother was looking at the floor; her head bent to one side patiently. "Be quiet," she said. "Don't let your father hear us."

"And that Mrs. Hadjis! She lives all the way in Midvale. Why doesn't she have the sense to go visiting early and take the streetcar before it gets dark?"

"Yes, well."

"And what kind of stupid women are they anyway? Mrs. Kerasou asks me if Koulerakis's brother-in-law is going to live as if I'm God. And Mrs. Hadjis had to talk about going to the bathroom! Why do you have them for friends anyway?"

"In America we take what's available," her mother said angrily. "And don't put your nose up in the air."

"You never ask Vasilis to take the women home! It's always me! He can do anything he wants! You think because he's a boy it's all right. I can't even go to the hospital dance! Everyone who works there is going, everyone but me." Kallie hurried out of the room, well aware that she had not scraped her dishes and piled them in the sink. She took a bath and said the Lord's Prayer before an icon of the Virgin and Child that was set on a shelf in the hall. A hanging red glass globe with a burning taper inside lighted the icon with a dazzling shine. She went to bed early, leaving the door partially open.

By then she had finished being angry with Mrs. Hadjis and Mrs. Kerasou. She thought of the odd look on her mother's face when she had mentioned the hospital dance and felt a little pleased. What the look meant eluded her. It was, and she hated to admit it, as if her mother were sad for her. The icon's glow came through the half-open door and projected oddly shaped silhouettes on the ceiling.

She thought of the morning and the hospital. She wondered why the intern whom people called the Rabbit had killed himself. The Rabbit had hurried, almost running, down halls, into wards, out again, hurrying, hurrying, the stethoscope in his pocket flying. He was a doctor with years of studying behind him. Doctors were important.

Women wanted to marry them. Why would he kill himself? A new intern had come to take his place and she might see him tomorrow. Long after the last streetcar stopped running, she was awake. She heard her brother bump his car onto the driveway and her mother hissing at him in the closed kitchen.

The next morning her mother was demanding that Bill get up and drive Kallie to work. He sleepily grunted, "All right. In a minute."

"Get up now!" her mother shouted as Kallie quickly made a peanut butter sandwich and put it and a banana into her purse. The morning was cold and she slipped on her white jacket. Quietly she left the house and walked to the streetcar stop. At the transfer corner, the streetcar was late and she kept looking at her wristwatch and thinking of Mrs. Dauber's displeased eyes if she were not seated at the microscope by eight. Eight to four-thirty were the hours Mrs. Dauber, the senior medical technologist, had assigned her.

She was on time. As she stepped down from the streetcar, she glanced at the hospital. She felt proud that she was employed there and after four months had become part of it. The bright blue of the sky gave a sharpness to the pale yellow brick of the three-story hospital and the buildings next to it: the nurses' dormitory, the squat TB Ward, and the Infirmary. In front of the buildings the clear air heightened the colors of the grass and mounded circles of tall red canna lilies encircled with blue lobelia and miniature marigolds.

She had eased into the quick flow of the hospital, learning the names of the town doctors, the interns, residents, and the student nurses, girls from farms and small towns out in the western sagebrush desert. The personnel fascinated her, from the head orderly, Kirk, and his collection of lowly younger men, who owed their jobs to the county commissioner, Obert Baldwin, to the matronly superintendent of nurses. She was learning the histories of the chronically ill patients in the TB and Infirmary buildings and in Outpatient. With their worried, pained faces they too had become part of the hospital's incessant activity, so different from the gray world of her immigrant house.

As she walked up the new cement steps, a government WPA project, she hoped no one would bring up the Harvest Dance. She hurried over the wooden floors to the black barred elevator cage that rose with a metallic grating and often stuck between floors. Instead of opening the elevator gates she went up dull gray marble stairs. The hospital had been built in 1912, only twenty-seven years ago, but it looked dark and decrepit. The wooden floors creaked and echoed. Doors leading to rooms and wards had been painted so many times that gouges showed the successive layers. Perhaps white at one time, the walls were grayed. Yet for all that, there was something comforting about it for Kallie.

A dry odor was in the still air. Kallie had become aware the first day she came to the hospital that odors were quickly taken care of. The superintendent of nurses would not allow them to persist. This kept nurses scurrying: every patient who had not had a bowel movement that day was summarily given an enema. Behind screens women and men complained.

On the landing of the second floor, the superintendent, a white-faced woman, who reminded Kallie of the stout women in *New Yorker* cartoons, was standing at a nurses' station down the hall. Student nurses encircled the superintendent, holding their hands crossed in front of them. Kallie had bought a subscription to the *New Yorker* with her first paycheck.

She went on to the third floor, past Surgery's swinging doors, and down the hall to the laboratory. She stopped a moment at the door. It had become a habit. The second day she had come to work, she walked in and faced a horror: a leg, severed near the pelvis, protruded from a long pan on the table. It was white, almost hairless. A fourteen-year-old boy, running away from home, had lost his hold while trying to climb a moving freight train.

Mrs. Dauber was not in the laboratory, a long, narrow room with three walls made of windows that reached from the floor to the ceiling. On the black wooden table, almost the length of the room and set against the east wall of windows, a Bunsen burner flamed silently, the bright blue center encircled with a yellow plume. Years of spilled acids and chemicals had scarred and pitted the table. Lined at the back were glass beakers of all sizes, test tubes in jars, and brown bottles with stained labels. At the front Mrs. Dauber had begun several liver and kidney tests.

A smell of formaldehyde and balsam came from the specimen room next to the laboratory. It was L-shaped, between the laboratory and Surgery and no larger than a utility closet. The room had two doors, one opened onto the hall, the other into the laboratory. In it Dr. Roberts examined the pieces of grayed and bloody organs taken from anesthetized patients and dead bodies and then came into the laboratory to look at slides made from their tissues. The formaldehyde caused the inside of Kallie's nose to swell. She had closed the door on the first day she had come to work, but when Mrs. Dauber returned from Outpatient she said, "I keep that door open," with a stress on the word *open*.

A row of Outpatient charts, each with a glass slide smeared with a discharge, had been set near the edge of the table. A lone bottle of urine was placed over a pink request slip. Kallie read the name on the slip and immediately put a drop of urine on a glass slide, turned on the microscope light, and looked through the lens. The circle of vision was choked with white and red blood cells and clusters of beaded staphylococci. She breathed in deeply and wrote down the findings.

With meticulous attention she then began staining the slides. She picked up each one with a pair of tongs, passed it over the Bunsen flame, placed it on a wire rack on the drainboard, and stained it. A burnished bronze appeared, a beautiful color she liked. The once-white porcelain sink and drainboard were entirely streaked with brilliant purple gentian violet and safranine red dyes. The colors reminded Kallie of the experimental paintings she had seen in *Art News* magazine in the city library one Sunday afternoon when she didn't know what to do with herself. She had become bored with going to movies with Dea and had she stayed home to read, she almost certainly would have quarreled with her mother about some old-country thing or another.

Kallie placed a slide under the microscope. There was no need to search carefully for the gonococci. They were abundantly present in the distorted white cells. She wrote her findings in the correspondingly worn Outpatient chart and looked at the name again — her university biology professor. Kallie held to her parents' old-country respect for educated people. It was inconceivable to her that the biology professor had become a puffed-faced alcoholic sitting squeezed on the benches of Outpatient with hundreds of others. Many of them had always been poor; some had been accountants, schoolteachers, carpenters, and had never known poverty until the Depression. The professor had avoided her eyes, pretended he did not know her when he had come to the lab for a glucose test on Diabetic Clinic day. She remembered that at the university students called him a "pansy," a "fruit," a "queer."

The telephone rang. Kallie picked it up quickly, hoping it was not a call from Emergency. "Kallie?" Dea's voice was harsh in her ear, as if her mouth were close to the telephone so that Mr. Pappas sitting at the far end of the counter would not hear her.

"Dea!" Kallie said, almost in reproof. Kallie had told Dea the telephone had to be free for calls from Emergency. She looked over her shoulder at the door.

"I'll only keep you a second. I was just wondering if you heard that Mary Yiannos got engaged."

"No. Who to?"

"Some fellow from Wyoming. I thought maybe you had heard something."

"No. I better hang up before you-know-who comes in."

"Okay." Dea's voice faded in disappointment.

Kallie hoped Dea wasn't hurt at being cut off abruptly. Dea was her closest friend. She glanced at her wristwatch, hurriedly began placing the blue-stained glass slides under the microscope lens, and moved them about looking for bacteria. The slides had been brought up from GU, the Genito-Urinary clinic in Outpatient, a half-hour earlier. She wanted to finish them before Dr. Roberts arrived and might need the microscope.

When her vision blurred from her intense concentration, Kallie looked out the windows and down on the back yard of the hospital. A pale yellow brick interns' and residents' quarters had been built on top the low boiler building. Around it stood a blackened cement incinerator, various corrugated tin sheds, the gray wooden laundry, and a greenhouse with dirty, whitened glass. No one facing the front of the clean, orderly buildings would know they existed.

She could spare no more than a few moments from the microscope. The laboratory had only one. A request for another microscope had gone unheeded because of the Depression. At least, so Mrs. Dauber had answered one of the residents. Kirk, the head orderly, told Kallie soon after she was hired: "I asked McMillan. He's the purchasin' agent and he says she never did ask for one. She don't want another microscope." Kirk had been injured in an automobile accident. He walked with his tall, thin body leaning backwards and his long legs thrust forward.

If Mrs. Dauber had wanted another microscope, Dr. Roberts would have seen that she got it. When residents working in Emergency ordered a blood typing, Mrs. Dauber could have done it at another microscope instead of having Kallie stop her work. Also, when Dr. Roberts looked at the specimen slides, Kallie had to get up and work on something else. It had been a puzzle to Kallie at first because Mrs. Dauber seemed to work quickly and efficiently. Now, after several months in the laboratory with the silent woman whose mouth was grimly set, Kallie knew Mrs. Dauber did not want another microscope because it would have confined her. She wanted to be free, to be out of the lab, to push the rattling electrocardiogram and metabolism machines to the wards and Outpatient clinics. Kallie thought Mrs. Dauber must have become silent as a child, teased over her short stick-like leg. She remembered a boy in grade school who had been called "cripple" and who had barely limped, nothing like Mrs. Dauber.

The resident on Surgery, Dr. Harlow, walked in, slumped on the chair next to the microscope table, and said in a twang, "God, what a day this is going to be." Kallie gave him a commiserating nod. She liked having the interns and residents sit back in the chair, legs crossed, as if they had found the lab a pleasant place to spend their few moments of leisure. Behind his glasses, Dr. Harlow's eyes looked small, but Kallie had noticed one day when he was cleaning the lenses that they were large and blue. Dr. Harlow took out a hand-rolled cigarette from his hospital jacket and began smoking. Kallie glanced at him; he was looking off, thinking.

One Saturday Kallie and Dea had taken their nieces to the park to ride the merry-go-round. Dr. Harlow and his wife had been standing by the fence of the little lake, watching the ducks. He looked down at his wife fondly and said something. She raised her head and smiled. Kallie thought she had witnessed an intensely intimate scene, but Dea said, "I'll bet she doesn't even realize how lucky she is." Enviously they gazed at the two. "Got to get going," Dr. Harlow said and his long gait vanished.

The Bunsen burner's flame flickered each time Kallie stood up and took exactly two steps toward the big sink. Someone came into the specimen room, then the refrigerator squeaked open. Bottles of blood were kept there as well as purple fruit juice, which the interns and residents depleted over the weekend. Kirk had told Kallie they mixed the fruit juice with the alcohol that was kept in the cupboard over the sink. Every Monday Mrs. Dauber checked the cupboard and refrigerator to make certain there was enough alcohol for the tests and fruit juice for the blood donors. Almost everything Kallie had learned about the hospital had come from Kirk. He couldn't tell her enough in his laconic monotone.

Kallie lifted her head and listened to approaching footsteps, but it was not Mrs. Dauber's characteristic walk — the built-up shoe on her right withered leg making rubbing sounds over the floor. She looked back into the microscope and became aware that a figure had sat down on the chair next to the table. "Good morning," the low voice said. Kallie knew who it was before lifting her head, Dr. Ben Lowe. They smiled at each other. Kallie had noticed that Dr. Lowe never sat down when Mrs. Dauber was in the room. Other residents and interns often came into the lab to smoke after finishing in Surgery, but Dr. Lowe did not smoke. Kirk had told Kallie that Dr. Lowe's parents sent him a big package twice a month and included a carton of cigarettes among the cookies and candies. The interns and residents waited eagerly for the packages because otherwise they would have to resort to their cigarette-rolling machine. The interns made fifteen and the residents twenty-five dollars a month.

Dr. Ben Lowe was a slender man of twenty-eight with a narrow face, bright black eyes, and full mouth. Although he shaved closely, a faintly black shadow lay over his chin. An innate dignity made him seem handsome to Kallie. She was conscious of people's dignity or lack of it; her father had it. She thought of him wearing a long white apron tied at his waist, filling the shelves of his small grocery and pharmacy store. He expected Bill to become a pharmacist, to take over when the old druggist retired. Kallie knew it would not happen, at least not as her father thought it would. Her father did not know that Bill had failed his advanced chemistry class.

"Have you tested the Fairfield boy's urine yet?" Dr. Lowe had been born in America, but there was an inflection to his words. Kallie knew it came from his family's speaking Chinese in their house. Many of her generation, the children of Greek immigrants, had a similar speech pattern, the consonants pronounced hard.

"Yes. It's four plus albumin, numerous blood cells."

Dr. Lowe made a *ts* sound with his tongue against his large teeth. "We're trying that new sulpha drug on him." He looked up at the smoky ceiling and frowned slightly, pulling down one eyebrow that slightly altered his smooth, unlined face. "Would you test his hemoglobin today? I didn't make out a slip, but I think it's a good idea."

"I'll do it as soon as I finish the Outpatient urines—when they come up."

"Doyle," Dr. Lowe said with a soft, amused snort and they nodded and smiled at the name of the Outpatient orderly, perennially cheerful even when being lectured about having a low IQ. Dr. Lowe lifted his right palm and passed it down his cheek. A large oval jade stone on his ring finger slipped to one side.

"I've got to have this ring made smaller." Dr. Lowe smiled ruefully. "I've lost weight running around this hospital."

"It's a beautiful ring. Is it a family heirloom?" Kallie would not have been so familiar with any of the other young doctors. She smiled at his nod. "Have you been rushed today?" she asked, looking through the microscope as she talked, remembering the pathologist would be coming soon.

"I took Dr. Benson's shift in Emergency last night." Dr. Lowe never used a surname without a title.

Rapid footsteps pattered toward the laboratory. A student nurse came in, wearing the regulation uniform, a blue-and-white striped full skirt with a white starched bibbed apron over it. A white nurse's cap, without the pin that was awarded at the end of the first year of training, topped a flounce of red-dyed hair. The "Bottle Red Head," Kirk called her. Her skin was a transclucent white with minute blue veins visible at her temples. When she smiled widely, small, even white teeth showed. She was a pretty girl, several years younger, Kallie thought, than she was.

"Dr. Lowe!"

Dr. Lowe looked at the student nurse a moment and then said, smiling, emphasizing each word. "Yes, Miss Ivy Madsen."

"It's not much fun on OB now that you're gone."

Kallie looked up. Dr. Lowe shook his head and opened his eyes wide in mock wonder. "I never thought there was much fun going on in OB."

"Well, it was better when you were there." Ivy Madsen handed Kallie a request slip and looked about the laboratory as if searching for some reason to remain longer. She sighed. "I wish I could sit in a chair instead of running my legs off." She arched her eyebrows and sniffed.

Dr. Lowe gave her an indulgent smile. "It's a good way to get exercise."

"Oh, I can think of better ways to get exercise."

Dr. Lowe said nothing for a moment, then pursed his lips. "I can't find time for anything else." He stood up. "I better go get my lunch before there's nothing left."

"Oh, sure," Ivy said with a shrug of one shoulder, "all you doctors, you get steak, but what do we get at the nurses' dining room? End of the month, the money's gone, and they feed us squash and gravy. I'm so sick of it. I would give *anything* for a good restaurant meal." She sniffed again prettily.

Dr. Lowe waved a goodbye and left the room with Ivy chattering at him: "Nobody cares about us nurses. We're the bottom of the totem pole."

Kallie looked out the window, annoyed with Ivy for following Dr. Lowe. If the Warden, as Kirk called the nurses' superintendent, saw the resident and nurse together, there would be trouble: "No fraternizing on the wards." Kirk could imitate the superintendent's mannish voice perfectly.

Kallie looked down into the back-yard jumble of the hospital, thought of Ivy flirting with Dr. Lowe, then looked back at the slides. Ivy was a poor Idaho farm girl. Kallie had seen a tube of toothpaste in her apron pocket one day when the student nurse had leaned over to lift up the telephone at the side of the microscope. Kallie had thought: Ivy was afraid someone would use the toothpaste if she left it in the dormitory. She had looked about secretively. "I'll only be a minute. I'll hang up if old Dauber walks in."

Kallie had two more slides to examine when Kirk came into the room, walking as if he were a puppet on strings, sat down, and lighted a cigarette. "You seen Doyle?"

Without lifting her head Kallie said, "He brought up the slides and blood samples from Outpatient but not the urines."

"Oh, that kid." Kirk smoked leisurely, gazing off. His eyes were a pale gray, his face long, his body as thin as most patients in the TB Ward. "Well that's what you git for havin' to put up with FOBs. I haven't seen hide nor hair of him since I sent him to take some drugs over to TB and the Vegetable Bin. I'll git on him to bring up the urines pronto. If I c'n find him."

Kirk was himself an FOB, Friend of Baldwin, the commissioner in charge of the hospital. The FOBs were expected to get out the vote for the commissioner every four years. Kirk pretended he was not one of them. Kallie finished the slides, wrote on pink slips, and clipped them to the worn patients' charts. She noticed on one of them, under *Doctor's Comments: Patient says he pisses like a steer.* Smiling, she was about to show it to Kirk but checked herself. It would be all over the hospital by the end of the day and the patient would be the butt of jokes.

Kirk lifted his deceptively benign face. He looked at the blue sky above the nurses' dormitory. "I sure like Indian summer," he said. "The best time of the year. Now if it would only last for the Harvest Dance, it would sure pick up everybody's spirits."

"Are you going to the dance, Kirk?" Kallie blinked in surprise for mentioning the dance.

"Yeah, my wife likes to go. Course I can't dance with my bum back, but the orderlies know they better dance with Hazel if they know what's good for them." He laughed, showing crooked, tobacco-stained teeth. "You goin'?"

"I haven't decided yet." A pang struck her in the chest. Even if someone asked her she couldn't go. Her parents would not let her. She hated her mother's, "What's the matter with these Americans? Throwing their daughters to the dogs." Her friend Dea had been foolish enough to argue about it with her mother. "You think the first thing people do when they go out is jump behind a bush and . . ." She hadn't finished because her mother slapped her hard and intoned an old proverb: "'When the ant sprouts wings, it's lost.'"

Dea had sobbed: she was twenty-three years old and if there wasn't this awful Depression she would get on a train, go somewhere far from her mother and all the old Greeks, and get a job. Kallie had quarreled too with her mother about dating—when her father was not in the house. "It won't be the man who pushes the baby buggy," her mother had said ominously and then told her several stories about village girls who had got into trouble and whose brothers had to kill them and the babies.

"It's savage! It's—it's—and you people are supposed to be Christians!"

"Yes, and you're one of us, so don't say 'you people.'"

"This is America, not Greece," she had shouted as she hurried out of the room so she would not have to hear more hated words.

Kallie stood up and began pouring stomach juices from small brown cardboard cartons into test tubes. She lifted her upper lip in distaste. Mrs. Dauber usually tested the specimens for acid, as well as doing the stool and sputum specimens. Kallie was surprised when she first began working in the laboratory that Mrs. Dauber did not seem to mind. Without the urine samples Doyle should have brought, Kallie had to busy herself.

"Well," Kirk said, standing up with his body leaning backward, "I'm gonna find Doyle and tell him if he disappears one more time, he's not gonna graduate." Kirk, walking jerkily, chortled all the way down the hall. Doyle, the tall, handsome blond orderly, did not look retarded and Kallie was relieved when he told her, "I'm gonna git my diploma purty soon. Soon's I git operated on." He meant he could permanently leave the Training School after having his tubes cut. Kallie was glad that this big child could not then become a father. Some parents of the battered children in Pediatrics laughed and talked like children themselves.

Someone was running toward the laboratory with a jingling of glass in synchrony with heavy footsteps. Doyle appeared out of breath holding a cardboard box. "You know why I'm late? I'm late 'cause the druggist he ask me to take some medicines over to TB an' the Vegetable Bin an' I stopped to talk to this guy that's a relation of mine. Some kind of relation. I better hurry. Kirk's mad at me."

Kallie helped him take thirty or more bottles out of the box: a pickle bottle with the label still on it; a pint jar with dark brown urine; many small jars of different shapes, two with wax paper over the tops held in place with rubber bands. The odor was nauseating. If her mother could see these bottles of urine, the brown cartons of sputum and feces: "For this we sent you to the university?" Her mother had a horror of body fluids. A nurse who washed people and emptied bed pans was a debased woman to her. Kallie told her mother she only examined blood, which was almost true.

"Look!" Doyle held up a small pear-shaped bottle with a minute opening. "I wonder how he got the piss in this here bottle!" Doyle laughed and Kallie shook her head in agreement: he was repeating what someone else must have said.

"It's a hair oil bottle. We tell them not to use hair oil bottles, but they do it anyway."

"Oh," Doyle said and picking up the empty box ran down the hall. *The Vegetable Bin,* he'd said: someone long ago had given the name to Infirmary on the far corner of the hospital grounds. All of the patients, the very old, the paralyzed, the maimed, knew they were lifelong residents of the Vegetable Bin. Even now, after four months in the laboratory, the bright red canna lilies on the raised mounds in front of the Infirmary building were pretty but incongruous to Kallie.

Kallie washed her hands, took her purse from the drawer under the microscope, and went out to the fire escape to eat her lunch, the sandwich and banana. Nurses were walking toward the dormitory and Dr. Lowe and Dr. Harlow were on their way to their quarters. Dr. Harlow gave a sudden loud laugh and slapped Dr. Lowe on his thin shoulders. Kallie smiled. The camaraderie among the interns and residents made her happy.

The hospital was without a cafeteria. The nurses ate in their dormitory; the interns, residents, and staff doctors in the quarters above the heating plant; and the maids and orderlies in the kitchen. Kallie had decided Mrs. Dauber did not eat lunch at all. She had never seen her with a lunch sack or leave the building at noon.

Kallie sat on the fire escape every day except Thursday to eat her sandwich. On Thursdays Madeline Peterson, who worked for Dr. Roberts in his uptown laboratory, came to sketch cancer lesions for him and she and Kallie ate in the drugstore across the street. Madeline had once drawn two gallstones in beige hues, not pocked and irregular as Kallie had seen them in jars of formaldehyde in the pathology class at the university, but smooth, round, on a straight surface, each with an elongated shadow. Madeline had painted them not for Dr. Roberts, but for herself. They were beautiful. No one would guess they were gallstones. Kallie wished she had the painting for her own.

She thought of lingering on the fire escape. The autumn day was finely cool, the great granite-topped mountains in the distance rose from a blue haze, and the acrid scent of burning leaves was in the air. Where, she wondered, would she eat when autumn deepened and it would be too cold to sit on the fire escape. Reluctantly she stood up and returned to the laboratory. She lined up a long row of test tubes in upright racks and poured urine from the bottles into them. She was testing each one with litmus paper when she heard the dragging of Mrs. Dauber's shoe and the creak of the metabolism machine being wheeled toward the laboratory.

The metabolism machine bumped loudly as it was pushed against a wall in the specimen room. Mrs. Dauber limped into the laboratory and without a word began looking at slender glass tubes and writing down their sedimentation rates. She was a pale woman in her late forties. A deep frown descended from the middle of her forehead to the bridge of her small nose. Her ashen hair was thin and slightly waved. When she spoke to Kallie, her light greenish eyes with their stark, small pupils looked as if they were piercing her. Throughout the day Mrs. Dauber wore a blue sweater over her uniform, even in the morning when the laboratory was often hot from the sun on the tall glass windows.

Mrs. Dauber turned, glanced through the pile of charts next to the microscope, and went into the specimen room. In a moment the pathologist's spry steps clipped over the cement floor and then his high stool scraped over it. "We have two autopsies scheduled for tomorrow, Dr. Roberts."

Kallie listened while she worked at the black wooden table: something, almost a sweetness, was in Mrs. Dauber's voice when she spoke to Dr. Roberts. Their voices came to her with a tone of two people who had worked together for years and knew each other well.

When they had practiced doing venipunctures on each other in pathology class, Dr. Roberts had supervised while Madeline prepared to insert a needle into Kallie's arm. He had said, "Dark people have thicker skins." The needle went in easily. Madeline, who didn't know exactly all the different bloods in her veins, was darker than she. Dr. Roberts had said nothing earlier when Kallie nervously, because he was watching, had done a venipuncture on Madeline.

Kallie lifted the white metal tray in which she kept syringes, pipettes, cotton, hydrochloric acid, and alcohol. She felt light, expectant: she might catch a glimpse of the new intern. Kirk had said he was dark, maybe a foreigner. Down the hall outside Surgery the short town doctor called Stormy Simmons was shouting at a thin man with longish black hair and several days' beard. "Who the hell do you think you are, Fairfield? Your wife was scheduled for a cauterization on Monday and you bring her in today expecting *me* to take care of her!" The doctor's little paunch, like a round watermelon, moved up and down under his white surgeon's gown. Stormy Simmons had to stand on a stepstool to work. "Hang on to my heels," he would say whenever he had an obese woman lying mounded on the operating table.

"I had car trouble," Fairfield said with no expression on his dour face. His black eyes looked steadily down at the little doctor.

"What the hell business have you got with a car? People on welfare should take the streetcar! Get tokens from the social workers! This is the last time I'm going to give you the time of day!" The doctor flailed his arms about, shouting, too wrought up to see the glittering hate in Fairfield's eyes.

Kallie hurried past them, holding the tray handle tightly, through the swinging doors and into a bisecting hallway. She passed the few private rooms, which Kirk had told her were set aside for the FOBs. At a nurses' station on the second floor, two first-year students, one of them Ivy, were seated writing. A woman doctor was standing at the side of the desk reading a chart. She was a large woman with gray hair cut short, just above her ear lobes. Besides a retired Chinese gynecologist, she was the only woman doctor in the city. As Kallie passed the gynecologist, she said, "Good morning, Dr. Murphy," even though she was uncertain that the doctor knew her. The doctor answered with a pleasant "hello." Ivy looked up mischieviously and gave Kallie a little wave with curled fingers as if they shared a secret. Kallie glanced at her quizzically and walked on.

Kallie had begun greeting Dr. Murphy from the day she came out of Pediatrics at the same time the doctor walked out of OB. By the time Kallie had reached the OB nurses' station, Dr. Murphy was walking down the stairs. Two nurses were seated at the desk. One of the nurses said, "Well, by hell, I'll stand up for a man doctor, but I'll be damned if I'll stand up for a woman!"

In the Pediatrics Ward two rows of cribs were separated by a narrow pathway. Kallie looked down the left row, against a row of windows. Little children sat, their widened eyes on her tray, or slept curled up. When a two-year-old child saw she was not coming toward him, he stood up and put out his hands. "Oh, Jackie, I'm too busy to talk to you today." Jackie slumped down and cried soundlessly. Kallie went over to him and through the crib rungs stroked his head.

A four-year-old boy was standing up in his crib waiting for her. He was one of the Fairfields, one of the many children of the man she had just seen looking dangerously down at Stormy Simmons. The Fairfield clan had a shelf of fat records all to themselves. The boy Marlow had been in the Pediatrics Ward regularly from the time he was born. He had learned the inevitable: it did no good to cry. No one ever came to see him and each time he was ready to leave the hospital, he remained days longer because his parents would not come for him. They had no telephone and the postcards the social workers sent were ignored. One of the hospital's two social workers would then angrily drive the boy to his house and come back with the usual story of the filthy Fairfields. Marlow's father was upstairs, but that did not mean Fairfield would visit his son, nor that he would go to Infirmary and look in on his toothless, paralyzed father.

Kallie said, "Hi, Marlow," and set her tray on a small table.

Marlow looked at her with muddy, slitted eyes inside swollen lids. "Why's his hands like that?" he asked and pointed to the black child in the adjacent crib. The three-year-old child looked at his dark hands.

"There's nothing wrong with them," Kallie said. She knew Marlow meant the black hands and pink palms. "They're just hands." She smiled at the black child who gazed at her with large eyes. "Now give me your finger, Marlow, and I'll do this so quickly you'll hardly notice it."

Marlow put out his small hand. Kallie pricked his middle finger and drew blood into the pipette from the small droplet. Next she pressed an alcohol-moist cotton ball on the puncture. The blood was a pale red. With one hand she picked up the tray, with the other she reached out and patted Marlow's head and then the black child's. She left them with Marlow staring at the black boy.

As she passed the OB nurses' station, Ivy whispered loudly, "Miss Poulos, don't you think Dr. Lowe's cute?"

Kallie stopped, her head jerked. "I never thought of him as cute. I think he's dignified."

The other student nurse, big and plain, guffawed. "Rich guys don't have to be cute. Especially rich Chinks."

"Oh, you!" Ivy said and the two giggled. They were often together, pretty Ivy and big Elmina, whose round face was mottled and broken out into red scabs. Elmina was noted for being alert to men patients' touching their genitals and demanding that they stop.

Kallie hurried down the hall to the men's Medical Ward. The patients in two long rows separated by a wide space were mostly awake. Three beds were hidden by screens. Two of the men were talking to each other. Weber, big faced, peering at her suspiciously behind thick horn-rimmed eyeglasses, had caused, Kirk said, a "big ruckus" when he was brought into Emergency a week previously. Kirk had had to call all the orderlies to pin him down. The other patient, Delaney, was a cheerful big-nosed man with bright blue eyes. "Here she comes," Delaney said, smiling, showing his clacking dentures, "out to drain what little blood we got left." Kallie nodded good humoredly as she set her tray on the bedside cabinet. "Not me?" Delaney said, pretending to be incredulous.

"Yes, you," Kallie answered and proceeded to draw blood from Delaney's vein while he looked on with prideful interest. "You tell me what the hell I'm in here for when you find out," Delaney said and waved his thanks. At the door Kallie stepped aside for the new intern. She held her breath. He was about Dr. Lowe's build and dark complexioned; he could, she thought, be of immigrant background. His name might tell her. She hoped Kirk would learn more about him, but she did not want to say anything to him, afraid he might take her question as a sign of interest. Kirk had said, "You can't git a word out of him. You'd have to use a pair of pliers."

Noises and flurries of activity came from Surgery Ward. The operations were finished and staff doctors and residents were seated or standing looking through charts. Nurses stood nearby, waiting for instructions. With her shoulder Kallie pushed open the swinging doors leading to the hall outside Surgery. Behind Surgery's closed doors voices and the metallic clicking of instruments came.

There was no time to think the rest of the day. Doyle brought up slides from the Dermatology and Cancer clinics. Kallie stained and examined them, then prepared slides from bacteria growing on agar plates. Mrs. Dauber was out most of the afternoon doing electrocardiograms in the Cardiac Clinic. Kallie worked fast. She and Mrs. Dauber took care of the laboratory tests for the entire hospital. There must be an FOB who could be hired, but Kallie had become certain as the weeks passed that Mrs. Dauber did not want anyone else. She didn't want Kallie either. If she could have done it all herself, she would have. Kallie understood that; she also liked to work alone. Madeline's chirping in laboratory classes at the university had annoyed her and she had often wanted to tell her to be quiet.

Kallie was looking at blood slides for leukemia when Luther Meeks came in with his smell of rabbits, hay, and alfalfa. Kallie moved her eyes sideways from the microscope and saw some kind of green mash around the soles of Luther's old boots, which laced up almost to his knees. Her gaze went up the old fashioned breeches and plaid shirt to Luther's head. Luther's hair stuck out, oily, long in need of cutting. His face was dark and deeply grooved on either side of his thin mouth. He always had a day or two's growth of whiskers, and squinted. "I've gotta take time off and get some glasses," he said one day when Kallie asked him about an illegible name on his list.

"Well, here's the dope," he said loudly and handed Kallie a sheet of paper with a brown stain at one end. Kallie took the paper from the side to avoid the stain. "Every single one's positive," he said gleefully. "Damn them all."

Luther Meeks was forty-four years old. It was easy to know his age if a person knew the day the famous scientist Louis Pasteur died. Luther said he was born the day Pasteur died and the great man's genius had been passed on to him. He had first read about Pasteur in his high school biology class. It came to him like a streak of lightning, he said, when he saw the date of Pasteur's death. He left school and got to work breeding rabbits and experimenting on them. To support himself, he performed pregnancy tests on the rabbits.

"You got my TB samples?" Luther had not taken the trouble to learn Kallie's name.

"Yes. At the end of the table, next to the centrifuge. That's where we always keep them for you." It was Kallie's regular answer to him. With a preoccupied air Luther asked the same question each time he came to the laboratory. She thought of Luther innoculating the cringing rabbits with tuberculosis sputum.

"Where's the boss woman?"

"In Outpatient, doing EKGs."

"Okay. I'll take my loot and go about my business." Luther picked up the cardboard box with his big red hands and taking long, clumping steps walked out of the laboratory. His loud voice came outside Surgery. "Well, how's the boss woman today?"

For a minute or so Luther and Mrs. Dauber talked. Luther complained about a doctor who hadn't paid him what he should have. Kallie went to the centrifuge machine and placed vials of blood into it. She looked down the hall. Luther was waving his right hand in circles, the cardboard box in the crook of his left elbow, and Mrs. Dauber with arms crossed over her sweater was nodding, her face relaxed and even pleasant. Luther said he read in the *American Medical Association* journal about some experiment with molds. "Well, hell! I always knew there was somethin' good about molds." Kallie turned on the centrifuge machine and the whirring shut out Luther's talk.

In late afternoon Kallie covered the microscope, washed and rinsed the test tubes and beakers, and walked down the hall. It was the only time of day when the hospital was quiet, just before the patients were brought their evening meal. They were served at four-thirty, so that the kitchen help could go home. The patients would not eat again until morning. The kitchen staff came in at seven, but another hour or so would pass before their trays came up the elevator. It bothered Kallie. She herself often got up in the middle of night to drink a glass of milk because she was hungry.

A low sing-song noise came from the Psychiatric Ward, barely audible. No one was seated at the nurses' stations. The long dim corridor would remain unlighted for another hour as an economy measure. Early dusk had settled over it, shadowing the dingy walls and doors with their many coats of dulled paint. At the end of the hall the one narrow window was tinted a faint pink, which meant a sunset. The hospital was peaceful to Kallie after the long day. Then she remembered Ivy and Dr. Lowe and the new intern.

As she reached the marble staircase, a song came from the second floor, from the women's Medical Ward. A black woman was singing a spiritual. Kallie stood on the steps listening. The old woman's gangrenous leg had been amputated on a previous hospital stay. All the way to the operating room she had insisted that she wanted her leg buried "so I'll be whole in Heaven." When she awoke from the anesthetic and asked about her leg, Kirk was sent to the incinerator to retrieve it, just in time.

For several moments Kallie stood on the stairs. The new intern came down the steps. She looked at him, but he went by. The peace was gone. From the basement trays clacked as they were put on trolleys. Voices rose up the elevator shaft. Footsteps sounded on the floor above her and beneath her. She walked down to the first floor and out the side door. She breathed in deeply as she looked at the bright orange sky.

Bill was not at the curb in front of the nurses' dormitory. Her father had taken from his savings to buy the gray coupe: her mother would make it up with her frugal ways. Yet Kallie had not expected Bill to be there. He would have his excuses at the dinner table. Her father would say, "I bought that second car not just for you, donkey," and her mother would say, "Are you taking American girls out and you can't bring your own sister home? In Greece brothers watch out for their sisters." Kallie would say nothing, maybe look hurt.

To the north the orange sunset was swept with gold and magenta clouds. Kallie hoped the streetcar would be late. From childhood she had stood motionless watching sunsets change before her eyes. Then Elsie Martin, the supervisor on Isolation, came out of the grocery store across the street carrying two large bags and hurried toward her. Elsie Martin's face was flushed and her blonde hair hung limply. Some of her early prettiness was still visible. "Let me help you," Kallie said and took one of the grocery bags.

"Oh, thanks a lot. I was late getting off my shift and had to buy some groceries. I haven't got a thing in the house. I was so afraid I'd miss the streetcar and then have to wait a half hour for the next one. And my kids and Jack are so hungry by the time I get home. It makes me so nervous."

"Do you have to transfer?"

"No, thank God, but I live on the Avenues and there are so many stops in that part of town. Almost every corner someone gets on or off." Elsie Martin craned her neck looking for the streetcar.

Kallie asked if there were many patients in Isolation and after a moment of frowning and looking down the street, Elsie Martin answered absently, "Twelve," then her face relaxing with relief, she said, "Here it comes!"

They sat behind the driver and put the sacks between them. Kallie glanced at the waning sunset as the streetcar rattled on. The sky was changing subtly; the colors fading to pastels, yet glorious in their way. Several people were on the streetcar, but only Elsie Martin talked. "You know Jack, my husband," she said, looking at Kallie earnestly and began telling Kallie what she had already heard from Kirk, "Jack's in a wheelchair. Three years ago he and some of his buddies took some tires. It was winter and had just snowed. And they went up to this hill and got inside the tires and rolled down the hill. Only Jack crashed into a tree. He's been in a wheelchair ever since. I don't know why they had to act like little boys and get in tires and roll down the hill. It's been so hard. The children—I've got two—aren't old enough to really take care of themselves. And Jack loses his temper with them. And they're always hungry, all three of them. Like little birds waiting to get fed. I'm always so tired. And as if I haven't enough to do, I was made head of the committee for the Harvest Dance."

Kallie broke into her monologue. "Who would do a thing like that?"

Elsie Martin tightened a corner of her pale mouth. "I think I know," she said and her eyelids drooped with fatigue. Then she was silent until Kallie got off at Main Street.

Kallie walked across the street to wait for another streetcar. She glanced a moment into a store window at the mannequins exquisitely dressed in the latest fashions. At the adjacent bookstore she looked at a display to see what she would buy with her next paycheck. She had recently been drawn to novels about big cities. Authors like James T. Farrell glamorized the crowded streets, the tall buildings, the tenements. As she stood there next to a woman she recognized, a department store clerk with black-dyed hair, holding a paper bag with delicatessen packages, she suddenly turned down the street. She could not go home immediately to the quiet house, her father at his radio, her mother energetically working in the kitchen, giving her orders.

Dea sat on a high stool behind the American Candy Store's big bronze cash register and for a moment her dark eyes brightened as Kallie walked in. Dea was wearing a black silk dress with a small white collar.

The black color had caused a horrendous outburst from her mother: "Only women in mourning wear black! Who died that you go buy a black dress?"

"In America clerks wear black." Dea had described the scene to Kallie, laughing, "She hasn't noticed *yet* that many clerks wear navy blue." Dea had been in a good mood after winning out for once over her mother. She looked stately in her fashionable black dress that actresses like Kay Francis and Barbara Stanwyck wore in movies.

Kallie sat at the counter next to the cash register. Dea emptied ice cubes into a glass, pushed the lever for Coca Cola syrup, added fizzed water, and placed it on the counter for Kallie. It was a standing order from the owner Mr. Pappas that Kallie should be served a Coca Cola whenever she came into the American. Kallie watched Dea. Her profile was the classical kind seen in books on antiquity and gave her a somewhat undeservedly haughty air. She had to defend Dea when girls said she was stuck-up. They didn't know her. Her father was awful, a barking tyrant. Her mother was full of village superstitions: all through grade school Dea wore a blue bead pinned under her collar to ward off the evil eye. Dea had tried many schemes to make enough money to move away. She had entered numerous limerick contests, but never won any of them. For a while she thought of writing something for *True Story* magazine, but she could think of nothing that would equal what the magazine accepted for publication. One story told of a girl who was afraid to accept a marriage proposal because the man would see the scars made on her back by her stepfather's cat-o'-nine-tails.

In front of the glass cabinets that displayed pyramids of assorted chocolates, Mrs. Kerasou's fifteen-year-old son was mopping the white hexagonal-tiled floor with great sweeps of a grayed mop. Taki had been born a few months after the mine explosion that had killed his father. He raised his hand and said, "Hi!" He smiled so readily.

Kallie renewed her disgust with Mrs. Kerasou. Still, Taki, her youngest child, smiled a great deal, laughed almost as much as Dea when she got into one of those hysterical moods where she thought everything was funny, even when it wasn't.

The American was quiet; the fans in the pressed-tin ceiling whirred softly. At the other end of the counter Mr. Pappas was talking to Jim Monoyos, who was sipping a cup of coffee. Jim Monoyos was a city detective who had risen in the Greek community's estimation during Prohibition. He would telephone the whiskey makers in Greek Town when the Feds were coming.

"They're talking church politics," Dea said. "You'd think that was the most important event in the world." Both men called out to Kallie and because no one else was in the candy store, they asked about her father in Greek. "They're thinking of bringing Harilao for the church's twenty-fifth anniversary," Dea said, her gaze still fixed on the two men. "Some of the church board say he charges too much to come all the way from New York with those other two musicians."

Kallie said, "But he can really play the *lyra* like no one else." Yet nausea began foaming in her stomach. She wanted to hear Harilao play the old Greek folksongs, but not in the smoke-filled church basement. Girls she had known when she had lived in Greek Town would be dressed up, laughing self-consciously with each other. Young men they had known in Greek school would lounge against the wall across the room and talk about them. Some of the girls would dance with each other.

That's when the world had turned bleak, in the church basement. American girls were going to junior proms and senior hops. They were going out on dates to movies and to A&W drive-ins where they sat in cars and short-skirted waitresses brought hamburgers and root beers on trays that fitted into the rolled-down windows. She, Dea, and their Greek school friends went to the smoky church basement and danced to the old Greek folk songs. After hours of Greek dances, American records were put on a Victrola. Once in a while a boy crossed over and asked one of the girls for a dance. The black-dressed mothers looked on, sharp eyed, looking to see how much space there was between their bodies.

Before this she and Dea had been innocent children, walking to Greek school after public school. They held hands unless they had quarreled earlier. On the way they stopped at the bakery and looked earnestly into its windows, then on to the various candy stores and gazed at displays of chocolate treasures. How they had yearned for a cookie or a candy bar during Lent; how they had counted the days when they would take communion in preparation for the Resurrection on Great Saturday midnight and then be able to eat all the forbidden foods of Lent.

In the low-ceilinged church basement the floor had been darkly stained with roast lamb grease. Kallie and Dea sat at long tables used for celebrations and wrote notes to each other, drew caricatures of teachers, giggled, learned the alphabet, succeeded in reading three primers, and memorized poems to recite on the March Twenty-Fifth celebration commemorating the Greek revolt against the Turkish rulers.

For one celebration Kallie and Dea had memorized poems extolling the *klefts,* the Greek guerrillas who fought the Turks. Their older sisters dressed them in pastel georgette dresses and put ribbons across their heads with little bunches of cloth flowers above their ears. "Now, don't be scared," their sisters told them. Kallie and Dea spoke their poems, standing in front of American and Greek flags while their parents, seated on folding chairs, nodded approvingly. The parents went home and the sisters took them, happy with relief and pleased with themselves, to the American for nut sundaes.

Their sisters had competed over them. "Dea's hair is naturally curly," Koula would say and Nitsa would say something like, "Well, Kallie's is thick and fine and she can wear it all kinds of ways." Nitsa tried to work Kallie's hair in one of those ways but had to give up. Dea and Kallie sometimes talked about their sisters and laughed.

"Did you find out anything more about Mary Yiannos's engagement?"

"No. Anything new with you?" Dea asked in a dispirited voice.

Kallie wished she hadn't come. "Except for a new intern, but I don't know anything about him. Oh, but I had the great pleasure of taking your favorite people, Mrs. Happy Hadjis and Mrs. Cherry home yesterday." She smiled thinly. "Anything new with you?"

"New?" Dea scoffed. "Just that Solly Stratigos with his toothpick and poor English came in again. I can't understand how a person can go all though the university and still say 'he don't' and 'he come.' It makes me mad—people like him getting to go to the U."

Dea and Kallie looked out the doorway. Dea's brother had his law office on the sixth floor of a building across the street. One day Kallie and Dea had gone there with some papers Mr. Pappas wanted delivered. They walked up to the sixth floor because Dea was afraid of elevators. Wherever they went, she always looked for stairways. Dea's brother smiled, sitting behind a big desk, and didn't stand up. Kallie could not tell if Dea was embarrassed by his bad manners.

All the plans made by Dea's mother had gone awry, except for marrying her oldest daughter Koula to a prosperous immigrant. Koula had always stood up when one or the other of her brothers came into the room and given him her chair, but Dea refused. When the family was leaving for a name-day visit or for church and a son had not come home in time for dinner, Dea's mother told Koula or Dea to remain behind to reheat and serve the food. Koula had done so dutifully, but Dea was sulky and silent. Her mother called her *movoris,* stubborn.

Dea was on the honor roll all through high school, but had to work as a cashier for her godfather to put her brother Tom through law school. Kallie had a secret longing, which she had never mentioned to Dea: she wanted to return to the university, take advanced piano lessons, and learn music theory. She had to watch herself and not blurt it out. Dea would rage that at least she had gone to the university. Kallie's hidden wish was fading; she had fought to go to the university and had a job that paid sixty dollars a month, higher than schoolteachers. Piano lessons? Her parents would look at her as if she were a crazy fool. What could she do with more piano lessons? Sit on your eggs, they would tell her. Kallie could see no way she could return to the university in the Depression.

Dea's dark gaze remained on the door, but no one was there. Her eyes widened in anger. "I'm so mad! Today some American—he owns the shoe store down the street—he asked me if I knew Tony Doullas. Tony Doullas, that old-time bootlegger! I'm supposed to know Tony Doullas just because he's Greek."

"I know," Kallie said and looked at Taki, who was whistling a cowboy tune while he mopped. "Red River Valley," Kallie thought and for a moment looked at him, puzzled. He was so poor and his mother was a mess. Yet he was always whistling or playing his harmonica on the street, going home after work. Kallie thought that maybe it didn't bother him so much because he was a boy. Dea corrected his English assignments. "I'm not sure I can go to a movie this weekend," Kallie said.

"Oh, no," Dea objected. Dea loved movies even more than Kallie, especially what were called "screwball comedies," in which beautifully dressed women like Rosalind Russell with important jobs got the better of brash, handsome men. They took turns choosing which movies to attend. Dea often chose Broadway musicals, Jeannette MacDonald and Nelson Eddy films, but she wasn't sure about stars like platinum blonde Jean Harlow, who wore slinky white satin dresses that graphically showed she wore no brassiere or girdle. They both admired Katherine Hepburn, who was always very rich, lived in mansions with marble entrances and ancestor portraits on the walls, and disregarded custom. Kallie's first choice was a drama like *Winterset,* about Sacco and Venzetti, probably innocent, who were executed as foreign anarchists. At least once a week on Saturday or Sunday they watched a movie eating popcorn in the cool dark movie theater, half filled with patrons. Then they went out to the gray streets where men sold apples on corners.

"That Solly hinted about a movie. Wouldn't come right out and ask me."

"Maybe he thought they wouldn't let you," Kallie said. *They,* the parents.

Dea gave a short laugh. "Mrs. 'A' Number One said—"

Kallie interrupted, "You mean Mrs. 'A' Noombeer One." They laughed discreetly as their mothers had drummed into them from childhood not to make a show of themselves and draw people's attention. Mrs. "A" Noombeer One's husband owned a small, dreary cafe with the logo on the celluloid menu card: *"A" Number One Cafe.* His wife considered herself the Greek community's best cook and said so often. "I'm the best cook," she would say with deep satisfaction, and add in English, "'A' Noombeer One Cook."

Dea said, "The great cook was visiting my mother and she said the Stratigoses had a big fight. She was out hanging up her wash and heard every word. Solly's mother carried on that if he didn't marry a Greek girl, it would kill her."

"He's at least likeable. Not like those two sisters of his, with their noses in the air."

Dea's eyes glistened. "If you think he's so likeable, why don't you go out with him?"

"He didn't ask me. He asked you."

"You wouldn't go out with him even if you could."

Kallie looked toward Mr. Pappas and Mr. Monoyos, deep in conversation, accenting their words with shrugs and flamboyant hand gestures. "Oh, Dea."

"I didn't mean it."

They used to quarrel often when they were younger, usually over which songs would make the Hit Parade. They knew they were too old now to listen to the radio and screech over the Hit Parade, too old to eat popcorn and their sisters' homemade fudge. "What's wrong with you girls?" Dea's mother demanded one evening. "You've got food to eat, a roof over your heads. What more do you want?"

"Wouldn't it be awful to marry into that family," Kallie said, shaking her head at the preposterous thought. "Imagine Mrs. Stratigos for a mother-in-law."

"Yeah. She looked at the sheets the day after her precious Stevie married Stella and said there wasn't enough blood on them."

"Why didn't they stay in their villages where they belong?"

Dea looked at the cash register. Her face was drawn downward with early signs of aging. She was almost two years older than Kallie. They had gone to the same grade school and were in the same class because Dea had been sent home two years in a row until she learned to speak English. Everything bothered her now. "What in the world were they thinking of? Sending us Greek kids to American school without knowing one word of English! Didn't it occur to them we'd have a terrible time not knowing what was going on? All that baloney about keeping up the Greek language and our mothers never did learn enough English to communicate with the gas man."

Kallie would not say that her mother had learned enough English to travel all over the city on streetcars and could telephone stores to order C.O.D. articles she saw in the newspaper. Kallie nodded good-bye to Mr. Pappas and Jim Monoyos.

"Do you have to go? It's so dead around here lately. Anyway, what are you doing this weekend that you can't go to a movie?"

"I'll probably have to help Nitsa. Cooking for Jim's name day."

"Oh, God."

Kallie sighed. "Last year on St. Demetrios, I know at least two hundred people came by. My mother was so ashamed she said this year we'd have to make twice as much food."

"Just think having to serve all those people you wouldn't be caught dead with. If you could just invite the people you wanted instead of having open house and all the *sara* and *mara* come trooping in."

"Tradition," Kallie said with mock loftiness.

"In this Depression yet. My mother skimps all year to have roast lamb, baklava, the works. It makes me sick."

"We used to think name days were fun."

"We didn't know any better." Dea smiled wistfully. "Remember how we used to bite our lips so we wouldn't laugh out loud at those old Greeks and some of the funny things they'd say. We'd run into a back bedroom and explode."

"And your mother would come in and threaten us."

On the streetcar Kallie realized she was hungry and was eager to be home. "Hello, Papa," she said to her father, who was sitting in his big plush chair and leaning toward the radio in the ornate cabinet bought just before the stock market crash. A burned-out cigar with a thick gray ash lay in an ashtray on the coffee table alongside a circle of empty flowered ceramic boxes. Without turning his head, he nodded. At his side, neatly folded, were the local newspaper and the Greek-language daily from New York.

Kallie stood for a moment in the center of the living room. On top of the radio cabinet, pictures of her two sisters' small children surrounded a glass bowl of hard candies, which Kallie's mother bought pounds of at after-Christmas sales. More photographs of the children in baptismal dress, of the two wedding parties, and several small ones of relatives in Greece were set on the fireplace mantel and the upright piano in an alcove. Her father leaned his head closer to the radio. He was engrossed in the news. His business, Greek church politics, and the news were his great interests.

"Oh, you came, Kaliope," her mother said softly in Greek to avoid interferring with the news. "Why are you late?"

"I stopped by to see Dea."

Her mother twitched her lips. Since Mrs. Hadjis had told her that Dea smoked, her mother was silent whenever her name was mentioned. Who could have tattled on Dea? She was careful where she smoked. What silly trouble it was for her, washing out her mouth and brushing her teeth before she went home. At least the cigarette smoke on her clothes could be explained by working in the American. No doubt it was one of Mrs. Hadjis's sons who had caught her smoking and ran to tell his mother. Probably the youngest, who rolled his shirt sleeves up tightly on his upper arm and was never without a pack of cigarettes in his pocket, but it was all right for him to smoke, of course it was all right—he was a male.

Kallie's mother wiped her hands on a gingham apron and with the back of her arm brushed back a strand of gray hair from her wrinkled forehead. "Where's Vasilis, Kaliope? Didn't he pick you up?"

"No, he didn't pick me up." Kallie waited. When her mother called her Kaliope in that strung-out *Kal-i-o-pee,* she knew an errand or task awaited her. Yet she didn't like her mother's calling her by the diminutive *Lyopie,* which sounded like something greasy.

"Come in the kitchen. I've got a pan of stew for Antigone."

"I'm so tired," Kallie said as she followed her mother into the kitchen. "Why can't Pete stop by?"

"He works."

"So do I work," Kallie said sharply, but she wanted to see her sister Antigone's children.

"Yes, I know," her mother said in a mollified tone and Kallie waited. A cardboard box was on the drainboard; inside was a ring of crumpled newspapers. Her mother placed the pan of stew in the center. There were two such boxes. Kallie's mother had devised them with the nests of newspapers to forestall her husband's rage at food being spilled in his immaculate Hudson. Kallie looked for the second box. It was under the kitchen table.

"I thought," her mother said without looking at Kallie, "that as long as you were out, you could also take some stew to Nitsa."

"Why? Is Nitsa sick?"

"No, but I made plenty and as long as you were taking the car out it would —"

Kallie broke in. "I'm not taking any food to Nitsa."

Her mother sighed. "Anyway, Nitsa always has food cooked, no matter how she feels."

Again her mother sighed and, leading the way, opened the door, and walked heavily down the three cement steps and to the garage, saying, "Now, you tell Antigone I'll come by in the morning so she can get her groceries. I don't want her to take the baby out. Those colds can turn into *pounta.*" *Pounta,* pneumonia, was one of her mother's many fears. Kallie hated the Greek demotic word *pounta.* Her mother usually used the proper word: *peripnevmonia.*

Now her stomach pained with hunger. She drove carefully through the dusk, farther into the outskirts to streets of small brick houses. Even before she got out of the car, she heard the baby's shrieks. They penetrated through the walls of the house. She had never in Nursery heard a small baby with such a loud voice. The door was unlocked and Kallie opened it while balancing the cardbard box on her hip. The radio was broadcasting a baseball game, loud, competing in the small living room with the baby's screams. Pete was sitting on a rust-colored plush sofa, a wedding gift from his mother. It had matted into shiny spots where people sat and where they leaned against the back. He was holding the baby awkwardly while Antigone, disheveled, her face grimacing with worry, was trying to put a teaspoonful of medicine into the little mouth. Three-year-old Tina turned from watching their futile attempts and ran to Kallie. "Aunt Kallie," she squealed and Kallie realized she had brought nothing for her little niece. "I'll bring you a surprise next time, Tina." Pink liquid streamed down the baby's chin as he hiccuped and looked at Kallie from the corner of his watery eyes.

"I can't make him swallow it," Antigone said with a sob. Kallie put the box on the dining room table.

"Here, you take him," Pete said to Antigone, handing her the baby, and sat back with his head leaning towards the baseball noise.

"He's got to have this medicine," Antigone wailed. Her hair, stringy, needing washing, hung over her forehead. "He's been sick three days. He keeps waking up and won't drink water or anything because it hurts his throat."

"I don't like to do this," Kallie said, "but . . . Oh, Pete, please turn the radio off!" Pete turned the dial with a quick hostile look at Kallie. He was already losing his hair and he was only twenty-six. The first time Kallie and Dea noticed that his thick widow's peak was disappearing, it amused them. Dea had never liked him, even though they were cousins. They had grown up in the old immigrant district in row houses behind the church. "He's going to look like his stubby, bald-headed dad in a few years," Dea had said with satisfaction. She would not allow herself to forget that Pete, her cousin, had let a big Italian girl taunt her at recess. He had merely looked on.

"I've seen nurses do it," Kallie said. "I'll pinch his nose and when he opens his mouth to breathe, you put in the spoon. He'll have to swallow it to breathe."

Pete turned with a suspicious frown. "I hope you know what you're doin'."

"We've got to do *something,* Pete." Antigone looked at him with exasperated fatigue.

"Well, okay then."

"Quick," Kallie said and pinched the little nose. Antigone emptied the pink liquid into the open mouth. The baby struggled for breath and swallowed, then gave a shrill cry and squirmed in fury. "Sit down in the rocker and I'll set the table," Kallie said.

"What did you bring?" Antigone sat down, rocked, and patted the howling baby's back.

"Stew."

"Swell." Pete turned on the radio. "Your mother makes real good stew."

Kallie lifted the pan of stew from its nest and taking Tina's hand, they walked through the crowded dining room. Her parents had given Antigone and Pete the dining room set as a wedding present. It was too large for the room. There was hardly enough space for chairs between the table and the bulky buffet that stood against the windows. On either side of the buffet were heavy dark blue brocade drapes. Kallie knew it wasn't so—her mother would not have allowed it— but she thought the draperies were weighed down with dust. It was hard to breathe. She stopped in the kitchen doorway in dismay. Soiled dishes and pans were piled on the drainboard and in the sink.

"Are you hungry, Tina?"

Tina nodded. Her fine light hair needed brushing. Kallie cleared off a space on the oilcloth-covered table and arranged a small serving of the stewed beef and green beans on a plate, buttered a piece of bread, and poured a glass of milk. Tina drank thirstily. *That, that Pete,* Kallie thought, *can't even see to little Tina.* She cut the meat into small pieces.

While Tina ate, looking at her food intently, Kallie began washing dishes and scrubbing the pans that had become encrusted with dried food. Hate for Pete mixed with her own hunger.

"When do we eat?" Pete called.

"When I get this kitchen cleaned up," Kallie said loudly as she wiped the dirty stove top, swept the floor, and looked for whatever more she could do to keep Pete waiting for his dinner. She did not like him. She'd had a feeling that her father did not like Pete either and one night found it was true. She overheard her parents speaking in low tones after Pete and Antigone had eaten dinner with them. She had been walking down the hall toward the living room when their hushed voices stopped her. She was afraid that if she turned back, the wood under the carpet would creak and they would know she was there. She stood still. "I should have tried harder to find her a better husband," her father said, and her mother answered, "You did the best you could. No one better came asking for her." "I should have waited a little longer." "No," her mother said with quiet emphasis, "she was getting too old."

Kallie found a jar of honey in the cupboard and spread it on Tina's bread. Tina swung her legs and ate, making *mmm* sounds of content-ment and looking at Kallie happily. Kallie set the table for Antigone and Pete. Antigone came into the kitchen, pushing back her stringy hair. "He's finally fallen asleep. I look a mess," she said and sat down with a bump.

"Tig, why don't you take a bath while I'm here and if the baby wakes up, I'll take care of him."

"I'm too tired. I'll take one when Mama comes tomorrow morning."

"Grub ready?" Pete said at the door.

"Sit down. I'll serve it. Wait a minute, Tina. Let me wash your sticky hands." Kallie wet a washcloth and wiped the small hands.

"I want to show you my new dolly."

"All right. In just a minute."

Pete laughed as he ate, food bulging out one cheek. "You remem-ber my cousin Gus from Chicago? He saw you that time at the baby's baptism? I got a letter yesterday from him. He asked about you. I'm gonna send him a postcard and tell him 'No dice. You wouldn't want her. She's *educated.*'"

"Oh, Pete. After Kallie brings us stew and cleans the kitchen you have to talk like that."

"Let's look at your doll, Tina."

Tina jumped, sprinting up and down the hall like a fawn and into her small bedroom. Kallie praised the doll and Tina pointed to its mov-able eyelids. Kallie looked into Antigone and Pete's bedroom across the hall. The bed was unmade; Pete's clothes were thrown on a dresser bench and on the floor. A doll was propped against the bench, its long, flexible cotton-stuffed legs and arms askew, its southern-belle taffeta and lace dress crumpled. When the bed was made, the doll was set up-right against pillows Antigone had embroidered for her trousseau. Antigone disliked the doll, but it was given to her by Pete's godmother and she felt it had to be displayed. "Can't you hide it in a closet and take it out when you know she's coming?" Kallie had asked. Antigone had shaken her head. "I can't. I never know when she's going to drop in." Kallie had never told Antigone that one evening when she came to tend the children, she had taken off her coat and laid it on the bed just as

Pete came in. He picked up the doll, pulled its legs over the chest and twisted them behind the head. "How's this position? Pretty good, huh?"

Once again in her father's car with the cardboard box and nest of newspapers ready for another trip, Kallie drove with tight lips. Bill had not yet arrived home, but just as they sat down to dinner he came in, smiling, using his charm Kallie thought, and sat down. "Go wash your hands," their mother said sharply.

"Donkey, I didn't buy the car for you to go carousing," their father boomed out.

On her way to the hospital the next morning Kallie eagerly anticipated eating lunch with Madeline. She would not have to sit on the fire escape that day with her dry sandwich and banana or apple. She liked big-shouldered Madeline who, like Kirk, knew what everyone she came in contact with was doing. Kallie ran up the stairs, rushing to begin the tests so that she could eat lunch without feeling that she had to hurry back to the laboratory. Two pans holding bloody fetuses were on the black table when she walked in. One had ineffectual drinking straws stuck on it, but the final desperate instrument was what? Kallie carried the pans into the specimen room, not looking at the contents.

A thicker pile of pink slips than usual lay on the microscope table. It would be a harried day. Mrs. Dauber was down in the basement autopsy room cutting cadavers while Dr. Roberts lectured to medical students, the interns, and residents. Mrs. Dauber was Dr. Roberts's assistant, although she did not have to do the autopsies. Nothing had been said to the medical technology students in the pathology class about this being one of their duties. An intern could have done the cutting, but Mrs. Dauber was always Dr. Roberts's assistant.

On autopsy days the laboratory work accumulated. That morning bottles from the Diabetic Clinic filled one quarter of the scarred table. Requests for EKGs from the Cardiac and Internal Medicine clinics were more numerous than usual. Kallie had barely put alcohol, cotton balls, and sterilized syringes and needles at the side of the microscope when nine diabetics came to the door of the laboratory and stood there waiting.

At the head of the line was a big-boned man of sixty, stooped and silent. He had been a finish carpenter, he told Kallie on a day when they were the only ones in the lab, but had not found work until Roosevelt's WPA came in with occasional jobs. At the end of the line was a small woman in her late forties with suffering eyes in a prematurely wrinkled face. Kallie gave her a weak smile; it was a bad sign to start the day. Mildred Heaton, she knew, purposely wanted to be last. "Good morning," Kallie said. The carpenter took a step forward. "Will you wait a minute. I'll call you."

Kallie picked up the telephone and asked the switchboard operator to find Kirk and tell him she needed an orderly. She did not want to be alone with the big man. He had fainted the last time she had drawn blood from him. Yet he was there in the same threadbare suit coat and she had to call him to come in. He followed with a sorrowful, downcast glance at her, took off his coat, folded it, and sat down heavily on the chair next to the microscope table. He then placed his folded coat over his knees and rolled up the left sleeve of his faded plaid shirt. To give the orderly time to be found Kallie worked as if in slow motion. With a pair of tongs she picked up a needle and syringe from the sterilizer and laid them on a clean towel. She then read his chart, which was unnecessary. Doyle's footsteps echoed down the hall. She thought: well, he's better than no one.

Doyle burst into the room. "I'm here! What'd yuh want?"

"Stand at the side of the chair and—"

"Yeah," the carpenter said in a low voice, "'cause I might keel over."

"Okay," Doyle said and watched with great interest in his bright blue eyes as the man opened and closed his fist. Doyle's head bent far over while Kallie tied the tourniquet on the man's arm. Kallie was relieved whenever chronic diabetics still had good veins. She inserted the needle, drew out the blood, and glanced at the whitening face. She pulled out the needle and pressed an alcohol-moist cotton ball in the crook of the man's elbow. "Doyle, help Mr. Albright put his head between his knees."

"You betcha," Doyle said and roughly pushed the man's head down while Kallie emptied the blood into a test tube.

"Get your hands off me, goddamn you," the carpenter growled and suddenly Doyle looked afraid and stepped back.

"Should I stay?" Doyle asked Kallie, a look in his eyes as if he had been injured.

"No, and thanks a lot."

Doyle bounded down the hall and Kallie gave the carpenter a paper cupful of purple juice. He drank it in one gulp and angrily loped out of the room.

One after another Kallie called the patients until the last one was seated in the chair. Mildred Heaton sat still while Kallie pressed her index finger on the thin outstretched arm and felt for a suitable vein.

"I know my veins are all collapsed," the small woman said in a crackly voice.

Kallie continued to press while Mildred Heaton opened and closed her fist. Although she had become proficient with venipunctures, apprehension trapped the air in her lungs whenever a patient's veins had narrowed into blue lines. She did not want to ask Mrs. Dauber for help. "All right," she said and pointed the needle into a side vein near the wrist. She took in a deep breath as blood rose in the syringe.

Mildred Heaton held the wet cotton against the needle puncture. Kallie gave her a cup of fruit juice and hoped this time she would not start her old complaint, but she began, "I gave my children away because I couldn't take care of them and I don't know what they think of me. What do they think of me for doing a thing like that?" She raised her grieving eyes to Kallie.

Kallie never had a good answer for Mildred Heaton's question. "They understand," she said, trying to make her words sound strong.

"But what do they think of me?" Mildred Heaton went on in her flat crackly voice that always seemed on the verge of breaking down tearfully. "Their own mother giving them away?"

The telephone rang, a call from Emergency. "I have to go to Emergency," Kallie said and Mildred Heaton nodded, her head bent sideways, as if she knew she was unimportant. Kallie hurried with her tray, past doctors standing outside Surgery, through the swinging doors, and down the three flights of stairs toward Emergency. In her cage the telephone operator lifted her hand and waved. Two men were standing nearby, one of them McMillan, the purchasing agent everyone was afraid of. He did Commissioner Baldwin's dirty work, Kirk said. Could hire and fire. He was wiry, in his mid-fifties, with a hard, dark stare. His oiled hair was combed straight back. "Do you think McMillan's widow's peak is natural or does he shave it or somethin'?" Kirk had asked. The other man was sloppily dressed and wore a white druggist's jacket, a puffy-eyed man with thick purplish lips. He was not allowed to touch the bottles in Pharmacy because of a drug conviction. A young woman filled the prescriptions under his direction. Kirk had said, "Someone else got into that kind of trouble and he'd be out of here like a flash, but he's FOB."

Kallie went on past the superintendent's office. The superintendent sat at her desk talking to the assistant director seated across from her, a small woman with eyes magnified eerily behind metal-rimmed eyeglasses. "They're that way about each other," Kirk had said because, Kallie had learned, he had to say something about everyone.

At the end of the hall, in the small lecture room opposite Emergency, cancer patients were waiting to be displayed to medical students after Dr. Roberts completed the autopsies. Madeline, big, dark-haired, with a perennially cheerful smile, waved to her and mouthed "See you later." Kallie glimpsed a patient with half his face eaten away raw. She grasped her tray tighter and went into the room where a boy of ten lay white and unmoving on a trolley. "Here's what I want done," the resident on Emergency said and placed a pink slip in Kallie's tray. He was a short, sandy-haired man who resembled a shoe salesman in Rorback's department store. Kallie drew out the blood, thinking: the boy is dying. She hurried back to the laboratory. On the stairs Mildred Heaton put out a tentative hand. "I can't stop Mrs. Heaton. It's an emergency." At the door of the laboratory she heard soft laughing. Inside Ivy was pulling on Dr. Lowe's hand. "I've got it!" she said and held the jade ring high. "And you can't have it back until you take me to the Harvest Dance."

Dr. Lowe looked surprised, then pleased. Kallie put the tray down on the black table. Showing her even white teeth and waving the jade ring, Ivy gloated, "Look what I've got!" and with her red hair shimmering ran out of the laboratory. Dr. Lowe stood up. "Well, I better get going," he said as he walked out with an embarrassed smile.

Kallie took out the pink slip. "You can hold your horses," Kirk said, walking in, "the kid's dead."

Kallie looked out the window at the back-yard jumble.

Kirk sat down, took out a cigarette, and lighted it with a kitchen match. He leaned his head toward the doorway. "What was that all about?"

After a moment Kallie said, "What do you mean?" although she knew.

"Madsen runnin' out of here like the cat that caught the canary."

"I don't know, Kirk."

Kirk finished his cigarette without another word and once, when Kallie looked up from the glucose tests, he was looking off, his eyes sullen, as if he knew she were keeping something from him. "Doyle was a big help with one of the diabetic patients," she said, feeling hypocritical but knowing she should stay on good terms with Kirk.

Kirk smiled broadly. A compliment to his orderly was a compliment to him. "He's a good kid. Not smart in the noggin', but a good kid. Well, I see you're way behind, but that's okay, Krista'll do the sink test on them urines."

At noon Kallie walked down to the empty lecture room. Madeline quickly put her drawings into a brown portfolio envelope and they walked across the street to the drugstore. Madeline laughed a great deal while talking. Kallie wondered how she could be so happy after what she had just seen. Madeline was in love with the cancer specialist. She said so herself. She collected his witty sayings to tell Kallie. "This guy had this growth at the end of his penis and told Dr. Ramsey he didn't want his pecker cut off and Dr. Ramsey said, 'Okay. Pretty soon it won't fit where you want it to anyway.'" Madeline peeled into wholehearted laughter and Kallie had to pull her back when the traffic light changed to red.

Kallie liked the crowded drugstore. Greeting cards were vertically slotted on a revolving display just inside the door. Next to it a low three-tiered stand held magazines, most of them well-thumbed. Beyond the magazine stand cosmetics fanned out on two shelves inside a glass case. Whenever Kallie looked at the cosmetics she thought of Pete, who bought Antigone drugstore gifts for her birthday and Christmas, usually toilet water. The bottles accumulated in the cabinet under the bathroom sink. At the back of the store the pharmacist worked, a gray-haired, silent man who looked up whenever voices grew raucous at the front.

There were two vacant stools at the counter. A fat, perspiring man with an old briefcase next to his worn shoes was ordering from the browned celluloid menu card. Two men in their fifties wearing hats stained above the band were drinking coffee and exchanging information about themselves. Next to them a woman with lashes thick with mascara kept turning to look at them. Business cards, hand-written notes, and snapshots were stuck in the wide framed mirror that faced the counter.

While Kallie and Madeline looked at the menu, the waitress chewed on a sandwich vigorously, took a pencil from the straw-colored curls next to her ear and swallowing audibly, asked what they wanted. They always ordered toasted cheese sandwiches, potato chips, and Coca Colas. "I knew that's what you was gonna say," the waitress said, raising her eyebrows, drastically plucked into arched lines.

"Did you get the raise, Madeline?"

"No. That cheapskate Dr. Roberts." She mimicked him: "'Don't you know there's a depression on?'" Then she began talking about her grandmother, who was dying. "But that's life," she said.

They finished their sandwiches and Kallie looked at her wristwatch. "Do you have to hurry back?" Madeline asked.

"There were two autopsies today. So that means twice as much work."

"I'd hate to work under Krista Dauber."

"She never talks to me unless it's something to do with the tests. She won't even say 'Good morning.'"

"Well, I might as well tell you."

"What?" A tremor moved in Kallie's heart.

"You know when you applied for the job? Well, Dr. Roberts asked me if you were a Jew. I said you weren't. You were Greek. He said, 'You're sure? Because Mrs. Dauber won't work with a Jew.'"

Kallie's tongue was paralyzed. Madeline laughed. "I guess Krista Dauber thinks a Greek is as bad as a Jew."

Kallie's tongue would not move.

"She idolizes Adolph Hitler. Some day she'll march in with a Nazi armband. She belongs to that America First Committee." Madeline laughed loudly and the lingering men who had ordered only coffee and the woman looking into the mirror and carefully replenishing the lipstick she'd eaten off looked at her. "Dr. Roberts doesn't like Jews either," Madeline said as an afterthought.

Kallie could not remember saying goodbye to Madeline. As she sat at the microscope, she had to bring her attention back to the lighted circle of bacteria. Madeline's laugh—Kallie's mother would have called her a *Ha-Ha*. Madeline could laugh. She was some kind of American combination—English, Irish, German, and "who knows what else," she had laughingly said. All through the afternoon again and again Kallie had to force herself to stop thinking about what Madeline had told her. An unusual kind of fatigue took the will from her arms, her hands, as if they would not do what she wanted of them.

At three-thirty Kallie was still at the microscope. Mrs. Dauber stood at the table, looked at each urine sample, wrote something on the pink slips, then poured the untested urines into the red, blue, and purple-splashed sink. She left immediately, without speaking to Kallie. After Kallie covered the microscope, finished washing the glass utensils, and cleaned off the black table, she opened the charts and read the pink slips. Mrs. Dauber had scribbled "trace," "few blood cells," "4 plus albumin," and so on.

Kallie stopped at the doorway and gave the laboratory a last look. On the second floor she glanced down the hall to the nurses' station outside OB. Ivy Madsen's friend Elmina was sitting there looking idly ahead. Kallie wondered dismally if it were true what Kirk had told her the first day she had come to work. He had been sitting in the chair next to the microscope table when Elmina brought in pink slips from Outpatient. Kirk had said Elmina had an older sister who was even bigger than she. The sister had been a student nurse on OB when a Mormon polygamist came to see one of his wives, who had given birth two days earlier. In the middle of the day all three disappeared: the polygamist, the new mother, and the big nurse. Kirk said he found out later that the student nurse had married the polygamist and delivered all the babies in his exploding family.

Kirk took bets from around the hospital on when the polygamist would come back for Elmina. "Put a dime in the pot," Kirk had said and brought out a small black book from his shirt pocket. "How much time do you say before the Mormon comes back and carts her off?" Kallie demurred, but Kirk had insisted. "A year," Kallie then said. It was not the dime; it was being goaded, just as she had been goaded to take part in Greek school plays, to go name-day visiting with her mother, to hear portly immigrants get up at the Greek Independence Day celebrations and tell the American-born to keep up the Greek language and customs. Dea's father was the worst of them, a gold chain across his bulging vest, bald, speaking in a thick village dialect with a few purist words thrown in. He had lost his money in the stock market crash of 1929, but he continued to act as if he were the wealthiest Greek in the community and respect was due him. He embarrassed Dea.

Farther down the hall no one was at the station outside Pediatrics. Kallie remembered Dr. Lowe's pleased smile. As she reached the side door of the hospital, she touched her waist; under her palm was a kind of heaviness as though she had eaten something her stomach was having a hard time digesting.

Her brother Bill was sitting in the coupe looking at her darkly. "I've been sitting here for half an hour," he said and angrily thrust the car into reverse. "And some goddamn fool parked too close to me. A guy in a clunker."

"That guy in the clunker at least bought it himself. And why did you come early anyway? Then you take it out on me."

They did not speak during the fifteen-minute drive to their house. Kallie sat as near the door as possible and looked out the window. *You, you egoist,* she spoke silently to herself, *just because girls fall for your looks.* He was handsomer than most handsome young men and she was not as pretty as most pretty girls. As Bill drove into the driveway, bumping the car on purpose, Kallie said angrily, "You're the one who should be taking the streetcar. You think because you're a boy, you have the right to have the car. You don't even need a car. You could walk to the U. I walked to the U for four years, but no, Papa buys this coupe so I won't be standing and waiting for the streetcar and you have a fit because you have to pick me up. *When* you feel like it."

"Oh, bullshit!"

"You wouldn't dare talk like that in front of Mama and Papa! You act so innocent around them you make me sick."

Bill looked at the house. "Oh, come on, Kallie." Now his voice turned debonaire and Kallie waited: she knew that voice. "Listen, I'll take you to the hospital dance if you want."

Kallie turned her head quickly to look at him. "I suppose Mama told you to."

"So what? I don't mind. It could be fun."

"Yes, you might see that nurse you met at the Emory House party," Kallie said, mildly sardonic. It was a mystery to her how student nurses met university students and were invited to dormitory parties.

"Okay?"

"I don't know. You'll probably be bored."

"I will not. Well?"

"All right." Kallie moved against the car door, uncomfortable about going to the dance with her brother, as if he were a date. It passed, and she suppressed the excitement rising in her by looking unconcerned.

When they walked into the house their father was listening to Kaltenborn on the radio and their mother was bustling about in the kitchen. The scent of lentils and hamhocks wafted through the six rooms. An assortment of dishes, a big bowl, and several cookie sheets were piled on the drainboard. The oldest in the family, Nitsa, had been there with her children. Kallie's mother usually baked Greek pastries for Nitsa's three and Antigone's Tina when they came to visit. She gave the children, all under the age of five, pieces of sweet dough to pat and shape and which they more often ate than placed on the cookie sheets. She brushed away Nitsa's and Antigone's attempts to put the house in order: "No, take the children and go home. Have the food ready when Dimitris (or Petros) comes home. We'll wash the dishes." We, meaning Kallie.

Nitsa had married Jim a few days after her high school graduation. His mother had been a tireless visitor until then. "She's trying to fix up a marriage between her Demitris and you." Bill had laughed and looked at Nitsa slyly. "Oh," Nitsa said with a coy shrug and blushed. Then it was Antigone's turn. Their mother had expected Kallie to follow their example: be active in the Daughters of Penelope until one of the Sons of Pericles asked, with someone's prodding, to marry her. That's what her mother wanted, but Kallie had been so insistent about going to the university that her father said, "Let her go." Kallie had overheard her mother recently telling a gathering of her women visitors, offhand, to conceal her pride, that Kallie found out what was wrong with people's blood.

The kitchen table was set. Kallie walked into the hall and maneuvered around Bill, who leaned against the wall and laughed into the telephone. Kallie passed him and went into the bathroom, washed her hands, and returned to the kitchen where she cut bread, filled a pitcher with water, and placed a bottle of red wine on the table. "I'll see if the news is over," she said to her mother and went into the living room. Her father's gray head was turned from her, his ear close to the hurried, clipped radio voice. Kallie stood listening.

Kaltenborn was talking about Hitler's march into Poland. Her father turned his heavy, furrowed face to Kallie. "He's almost finished talking," he said in Greek, with dark village fatalism, and leaned again toward the radio. "Get me my big map," he said and Kallie went to the alcove bookcase and brought the large folded map ordered from the Atlas Company in New York. Its permanent place was on the third shelf, which also held her parents' Greek books. Her father unfolded the map and peered at it. "I need more light," he said and brought the map to the dining room table, where Kallie moved her mother's cut glass fruit bowl holding wax bananas, apples, and pears to make room for it. She looked at the map. In early spring her father had drawn a pencil line around Czechoslovakia. "What are you doing?" Kallie's mother had said. "That German, that Hitler has marched in and taken this country." Her mother had said, "How far is it from *patridha*?" Her father had pointed to Greece.

"Fold it and put it by my chair," he said to Kallie and walked into the kitchen looking at the floor. When Kallie sat down, he was noisily eating lentils and ham, preoccupied, his head close to his plate. Kallie's mother looked at her steadily as if she were responsible for the silence. "Is the baby better, Mama?" Kallie asked quietly.

Her mother nodded vigorously and repeated sayings of the grandchildren. She sighed heavily: to Kallie's mother children innocently grew and too soon entered into the troubles of the world. Her mother spoke precisely; she said herself that she had imitated the village schoolteacher's speech. She was one of the few immigrant women of her generation who knew how to read and write Greek. All of her family's land had been given to the older daughters as dowries, and she, the youngest, had nothing. So her father taught her to read and write. "We'll send you to America to find a husband," he had said, "and you'll have to know how to write us letters." Kallie's own father had finished grade school in the village but retained the dialect's *sh* sounds for *s*'s.

"Your sisters are settled and have good children," her mother said, not meeting Kallie's eyes. Kallie knew her parents thought she was already on her way to being unmarriageable, now that she was almost twenty-two. They never asked her about her work. The idea of her working intimately with the bodily fluids of people was repugnant to them. Kallie had thought so herself, but knew why she had majored in bacteriology. From the time she was in junior high she had loved the microscope. The pattern of life was there under the lens: a leaf with uniform cells like minute green beads all around the edge; a hair with its layers; salt, beautiful crystalline cubes; blood, the red corpuscles, the various white cells with their blue-dyed nuclei, the black granular dots.

"That Hitler is up to no good," her father burst out. Bill tried to look interested. "*Tsekoslovaki* in the spring and now he's in *Polandia*."

"*Polandia*?" her mother said with an alarmed frown. "How close is it to *patridha*?"

"Close enough. And that *bastardelo,* that *macarona* Mussolini has sent his soldiers into *Alvania.*"

"*Alvania,*" she whispered. She had come from a village in the Epirus mountains, near the Albanian border. She was silent. She ate as if out of habit, the spoon into the lentils and up to her mouth, down and up, down and up. She looked at Bill and then to her husband. "Could there be another world war?"

"I don't think so, but," he turned to Bill, his voice light and sarcastic, "why don't you go become a priest so your mother won't start the *mirologhia* from now."

Bill laughed self-consciously at the word for funeral laments. The mother got up from the table and they all knew she was going to her icon to light a fresh taper.

"And that *Rooozvelt,*" her father said shaking his head, "he doesn't understand other people, only *Americanoi.* He could get us involved in a war. The no-good rich donkey."

Kallie said as carefully as she could, "But look what he's done so people aren't starving anymore. All those programs that help people." Her father slapped the table. "In America people don't save. They're never prepared for bad times. The *Repooblican* party is the right party, but I'm afraid *Rooozvelt* will get elected again."

Kallie said nothing. She would be voting for the first time. Her father looked at her for several seconds, then said in a kindly tone of finality, "Don't forget. Our family votes *Repooblican.*"

Kallie cleared the table, seeing herself in the curtained election booth, where she would vote the straight Democratic ticket. After washing the dishes and pans and wiping the stove and drainboard, she took her *New Yorker* magazine into the living room. She sat at one end of the sofa that matched her father's chair. She thought of what Madeline had told her and her face went hot. No, she thought, she would not think of it any more that night. She read a few paragraphs and then looked up from the magazine, thinking about the Harvest Dance and the new intern. She visualized the few skirts, shirts, and blouses in her closet, trying to decide what she would wear. She looked back to the magazine, scanned a few more paragraphs, but didn't know what she had read. She thought of herself and the new intern dancing, dancing, around and around. Her mother had been sitting at the other end of the sofa, darning socks. Kallie realized her mother was looking at her. She closed the magazine and glanced at her father.

He was leaning forward in his chair, his head bent toward the radio. No one ever spoke when the news was on. The announcer repeated Kaltenborn's words: Hitler had invaded Poland. Her father was looking at the imitation Persian carpet. He had been in America five years when Greece went to war against Turkey and Bulgaria in 1912 and Greece called the émigré reservists to return to its army. He and almost two hundred others from Greek Town had boarded a Denver and Rio Grande Western coach and gone back. A few years later, again in the United States, he was about to be drafted into the American army during the World War when the armistice was signed. By then he had had three children.

Kallie looked at her father with new interest. Before her godfather died a few years past—he had been gassed in the war—he told of the two of them, he and her father, and their first years in America, going hungry for days, jumping on freight cars taking them to one unknown place after another, looking for work, turned away because they were foreigners, not "white," laying rails ten hours a day at ten cents an hour. Kallie tried to think of her father as a young man.

Whenever her father looked preoccupied or worried, Kallie became uneasy and wanted him to change back to his quiet, calm self. When she was younger, he often asked her to play old village folk songs on the piano. She had been happy to sit on the round stool and go through the entire book her mother had ordered from the Atlas Company. Sometimes her mother hummed as she played. When she reached high school and girls and boys were attending dances and going on dates, she stopped playing the piano. Looking at her father engrossed with the radio news, she wished he would ask her to play one of the old songs.

Bill walked into the room and set his hat on at a jaunty angle. His father frowned and searched Bill's face. His own face took on a blackish hue when he was suspicious of his son. "Where are you going?" his mother asked, disapproving even before he answered.

"To the library to study."

"To study without a book and a tablet?" his father asked, biting off each word.

"They're in the car," Bill said and looked at Kallie, daring her to contradict him.

Kallie wanted to say something, but she was afraid it would lead to a quarrel and she would not be able to go to the Harvest Dance after all. Her mother, too, had become silent, intent on her darning, as if she were unaware of the voices about her. Kallie gave Bill a long look and at the same time was disgusted with herself. Sometimes she hated Bill.

Bill shut the door and in another minute or so the car backed out of the driveway. Kallie glanced at her father, bent even closer to the radio. Her mother's needle clicked against the wooden darning ball. Her parents had no idea how much Bill drank. University students drank too much; the interns, residents, probably the staff doctors, drank too much. Never did her father have more than one glass of wine with his evening meal. Her mother served visitors wine with dinner and Greek liqueurs afterwards. With cold fright Kallie thought of Bill drunk, in an accident.

She opened the *New Yorker* and finished reading it. She would also subscribe to the *Atlantic* or *Harper's,* even though her mother would nag her: "You should be buying dishes and silverware for your trousseau. What is this silliness in America? Our neighbor laughing that she got married without even a dishtowel to her name. Without shame she said it."

The word *dishtowel* was indelibly coupled for Kallie with Saturday afternoons during her high school days. After she, Nitsa, and Antigone had dusted, vacuumed, polished mirrors, and scrubbed the bathroom, they got "cleaned up," by which they meant taken baths and washed their hair. Every Saturday afternoon they sat on the front porch with their sewing baskets. Nitsa had taught Kallie to do the cross-stitch on a piece of fabric made taut by a small hoop. "Stop looking at the cars going by," Nitsa said at intervals. Kallie never finished the cross-stitch. On Sunday afternoons, after church and dinner, they again sat on the porch, Nitsa and Antigone embroidering and crocheting for their trousseaus. Each of them had hemmed and embroidered a dozen dish-towels, Nitsa's with barnyard animals; Antigone's with little girls in sunbonnets. They had crocheted the edges with different colors of thread. Kallie had wondered why they worked so long and hard on dishtowels, which got dirty so quickly.

Saturdays had not been so bad for Kallie: cars flashed by, people walked past, and sometimes a small airplane flew just above the tree-tops. Also, in the evening they would listen to the Hit Parade on the radio. On Sundays, though, a desolate dryness settled on the porch, whether it was a day of cumulus clouds and bright green grass or hazy with autumn and burnished leaves. Few cars drove by, hardly a person walked on the sidewalk. The house was silent. Her father attended church board meetings and her mother took naps. As if they had been affected by the dry silence, her sisters hardly talked, their heads bent, their fingers diligent. Night seemed long in coming. Once, when her mother gave her little speech about the neighbor marrying without a dishtowel, Kallie said, "She should have embroidered a dozen like Nitsa's and Antigone's." Her mother didn't hear the flip-pant tone and nodded emphatically.

The telephone rang. Kallie hurried down the hall to answer it. Her sister Nitsa asked her to stay with her children while she and her husband Jim attended the AHEPA Lodge dinner dance. Nitsa's mother-in-law had insisted it was her duty to stay with the children, but then she had come down with the flu.

"Kallie, I wish you'd come with us the next time there's a social. Some of the younger men will be there. Solly Stratigos, Mike Raptis, Manny."

"I went once, remember?"

"Oh, that was two years ago. You'd enjoy it now." Nitsa laughed musically. "Jim would be proud to have you see him, now that he's the president."

"Maybe, we'll see," Kallie said, not wanting to remind Nitsa that her husband would then have to take turns dancing with her and Nitsa.

Kallie recalled Nitsa's musical laugh fondly. She had always looked up to her. Nitsa had made it easier for her, had paved the way for her having more freedom than she herself had had—going to movies and the university plays at night, taking her side when she had arguments with their mother, and especially encouraging their parents to let her attend the university. Nitsa had been studious, a good student, but she had never even thought of going to the university herself. She was content with having her own home, three children, giving big name-day parties. Dea's sister Koula, Nitsa's best friend, seemed content too.

Kallie went back to the living room. "Nitsa wants me to watch the children so she and Dimitris can go to the AHEPA dance."

"I suppose they'll wear *tookcedos*," her father said sarcastically. Nitsa had several group pictures on her dining room buffet of Ahepans wearing red fezes and tuxedos. "That's their idea of being *Americanoi*," her father had said. Yet Kallie knew her father not only approved of Jim, but liked him. They played cards after family dinners while the women washed the dishes and put the kitchen in order.

Kallie thought she could buy the *Atlantic* or *Harper's* at a newsstand, then her mother wouldn't know. It would cost more, though. She felt her face harden: no, she would get a subscription. She went to bed and lay looking at the ceiling, lighted dimly by the icon's vigil taper in the hall. She dreamed she was at the Harvest Dance wearing her slip, knowing she had it on, but hoping no one realized what it was, hoping they thought it was a dress.

The next day it was all over the hospital: the nurses, bringing slips to the laboratory, laughed, raised their eyebrows and let their mouths fall open in dramatic disbelief: a Chinese taking a white girl to a dance! Doyle said he was going to the dance to see them. Kirk said, "It's raisin' a hullabaloo." Ivy showed Kallie the jade ring pinned inside the pocket of her starched apron. The news reached the TB Ward and Infirmary. "I hope that nice Chinese doctor don't get into trouble," Mamie Stringham said. Her worried eyes were too big for her thin face. Mamie was thirty-two years old and paralyzed. She looked more like a woman of fifty suffering a painful disease. Her face had set into permanent grimaces and three deep horizontal lines furrowed across her forehead. She had been in Infirmary for seven years sitting crookedly in a wheelchair. While in town, performing on the trapeze with the Tom Mix Circus, she had fallen. The circus moved on. Mamie herself called Infirmary "the Vegetable Bin."

All day Mamie sat at a typewriter donated by a professor in the university's English Department. The professor had been a judge of a story contest sponsored by the *Tribune,* and although Mamie had not won, her story impressed him. It was the spirit of the story, he told her when he brought her the used typewriter. Her story was about her life with the circus. "Everyone thinks Tom Mix is so great," Mamie had told Kallie the first day they met, "like in his movies. Well, he's not great. And he hates children. Can't stand them." She used her right forefinger to punch the keyboard. "It's my only chance. If I could only make a thousand dollars to pay for this certain operation, I might walk again. It's a long shot, but I have to try. It's my only hope." Kallie wondered what kind of operation that would be.

After pricking Mamie's finger to test her hemoglobin—the blood pale, pinkish, Kallie walked quickly down the hall and nodded to the Infirmary matron, gray-haired and big-bosomed, on her patrol, leaning on a heavy gnarled cane. Kirk called the matron "the Madame." He said she had run a house of prostitution in her younger years.

Kallie went into the men's ward, which smelled of urine. The Warden was not so particular about smells in Infirmary. She drew blood from a young man who had been injured by a fall of rocks in a copper mine. He could no longer use his legs. He had been crying when Kallie looked down on him. He tried to return her smile, but moved his head away from her. An old man a few beds down called, "That Chink doctor gonna take that white nurse to the dance?" Kallie said nothing, hurried out of the room and past a small one, where a big, gray-haired Greek sat at the window and looked out.

The old man was allowed to attend church. During a Sunday liturgy a few weeks previously, Kallie saw him seated on the right side, the men's side. When the old-country priest, his skimpy pointed white beard lifted, his rose brocade robe faded, came out of the altar holding the chalice high and called out in imperative Greek, "With the fear of God and with faith draw near," the old man struggled with his cane to join the men lining up for communion. He stood leaning forward in front of the icon screen, patiently waiting. As he inched forward, he made the sign of the cross before each icon: St. Demetrios on his rearing brown horse, the Archangel Gabriel with bluish wings, John the Baptist in animal skins, and Christ in bishop's robes and miter. With his hand shaking he had held the red silk cloth under his chin and, as the priest dipped the spoon into the chalice and placed it into his mouth, his old man's eyes widened.

Kallie had intended to take communion herself that day, but seeing the old man, she would not get up. Her mother nudged her and Kallie looked ahead and shook her head, allowing her mother to think she was "unclean," menstruating. Afterwards her mother ranted at the table. She glared at her husband, but Kallie knew it was for Bill's benefit. "And there he was waiting to take communion! *Now* they run to church! Awful men, fell in with prostitutes and got *skouloumendari* from them. They never stepped in church all their years in America. Now they trot to church!"

The old man could not trot to church or anywhere. He was in the last stage of syphilis; the spirochetes, worm-like, fascinating to watch under the dark-field microscope, swam in the pus under the old man's kneecaps. Kallie avoided taking communion from then on and didn't know what to do about it. It was revulsion; she knew there was no way for spirochetes to get into the wine.

She did not want to use the common spoon. Priests said the wine was holy and could not possibly carry bacteria. She had thought it would be interesting to put a little of the consecrated wine under the microscope, but of course she would never be able to get any. There was holy water, though, that priests gave out on St. John the Baptist's feast day. Her mother kept a small bottle next to the icon. Whenever they were sick, her parents drank a teaspoonful of it. She could place a drop of holy water under the microscope to see if there were any bacteria in it. She never did.

Kallie wished the old man was not a Greek. Americans remembered people like him and Tony Doullas, the bootlegger, and the aging old-time gamblers who lived in third-rate hotels.

As she passed the low-roofed TB Ward, two men standing at a window waved to her: one had been an All-American basketball player and now, according to Kirk, had a big hole in his left lung; the other was a tall thin man with a caved-in chest. His brown eyes were always wide open, shining with avid curiosity about everyone, about everything. He too had a typewriter and wrote stories, but Kallie did not want to ask him if he ever had one published. She would have heard from Kirk if he had.

When she returned to the lab, a pink slip lay next to the microscope, a request for a Wasserman on a psychiatric patient. For several minutes she sat thinking about going into the barred room, then asked the operator to page Kirk. The bells sounded and in a few minutes he was in the laboratory. "What's up?"

"I have to do a Wasserman in the Psychiatric Ward. "

"Okay, let's go." Kirk lifted the telephone receiver. "I'm in Psycho if anyone needs me."

The Psychiatric Ward held four beds. Only patients with physical problems were kept longer than a day or two. Those who passed their physical tests were immediately sent to the state mental hospital. Those with tuberculosis were taken to a barred room in the TB Ward. Others with infectious diseases were assigned to an isolation ward in the state mental institution.

A nurse followed Kallie and Kirk into the ward. Two young men were the only patients, a handsome young Mexican in a straitjacket sitting on a chair, his eyes cloudy, unfocused, and the other, with dirty yellow hair and the scraggly beginnings of a beard, strapped down on a bed. Kallie avoided his cold glaring blue eyes. She wiped the crook of his elbow with alcohol and was about to insert the needle when at a faint sound coming from him she stepped back from his flying sputumn. "All right, goddamn you," Kirk said, swinging side-to-side, and clamped his hands over the boy's mouth while the nurse lay across his body. Kallie's hands trembled slightly. His veins were prominent, like many underweight people's. The blood flowed quickly into the syringe and into the test tube. Kallie wiped the puncture and the nurse applied pressure on it. Kirk removed his hands. "You goddamn shit," he said.

"Goddamn whore," the man screamed at the nurse. "Layin' on me with your big fat body!"

Kirk returned to the laboratory with Kallie, where he washed his hands thoroughly. "If I catch anything from that bugger!" he hissed.

"You won't," Kallie said. "That's not how you get syphilis."

Kirk guffawed. "That's a good one. I'll tell that to Clea," he said, referring to the telephone operator.

Kallie was relieved when Kirk left. She preferred being alone after a bad experience. She heard her fast-beating heart while she placed the blood into four test tubes and into the centrifuge machine. She turned on the machine and while it whirred, looked at a blood slide. Mrs. Dauber came limping into the room, an angry red flushing her pale skin. She threw down a sheaf of papers, went into the specimen room, and banged utensils about. She returned to the laboratory, looked through the Outpatient charts, took one out and opened it. "Where's that slide you claim shows malaria?" she asked with an accusatory glance at Kallie.

"It's the first one, at the top of the row," Kallie said coldly. The centrifuge machine came to a stop and Kallie removed the test tubes. For a moment she thought she might have been wrong about the malaria, but they were there, the abnormal red blood cells and the crescent-shaped ones with pigment concentrated in the center. Kallie began the Wasserman test while Mrs. Dauber took a long time examining the malaria slide. Then Mrs. Dauber turned off the microscope light and walked into the specimen room with a jerkiness Kallie had come to know was an extension of her anger. The slicing machine in the specimen room clicked faintly. Kallie thought: she has her nerve not wanting to work with Jews and Greeks.

She could have gone straight to Nitsa's house after work, eaten there, and helped put the children to bed. Instead she went home to change her clothes: Nitsa's four-year-old son had wrinkled his nose one day when she had come directly from the hospital and told her she smelled. If she had the time, she would also have taken a shower and washed the medicinal odor out of her hair.

"If you want to go with Nitsa, I'll stay with the children," Kallie's mother said tentatively, with a quick glance at her.

"No."

Her mother's voice turned harsh. "If the church had a nunnery in this country, you could go there and become a nun."

"Why should I become a nun? Do you think I believe everything the priest says? And I won't ever take communion out of a spoon everyone else uses!"

Kallie's mother gasped.

In her father's clean Hudson, Kallie wished she hadn't said it out-right. Warm guilt brushed over her skin. But by the time she reached Nitsa's six-room bungalow, she thought she did not care.

The house was quiet and the scent of baked honey-and-nut pastries was warm and inviting. The children were in bed. Nitsa was wearing the long blue lace dress she had worn as Koula's maid-of-honor seven years earlier. It was tight around her waist. She looked happy, her round face powdered, her lips reddened. A new permanent frizzed at her temples.

Nitsa led the way into the immaculate kitchen. A big pan on the drainboard was covered with a dishcloth, embroidered with a rooster and two hens. Nitsa removed the dishcloth. The *baklava* was cut in the traditional diamond shapes. Some women were rolling *baklava* into cigar shapes; Nitsa did not approve. On the table, platters of *kouram-biédhes* were mounded with powdered sugar. "I see you've got a good start for Jim's name day," Kallie said.

"Be sure to taste them. I've left some chicken out for you if you get hungry." Nitsa eyes looked troubled. Not looking at Kallie she said, "I wish you were coming with us."

Kallie said quickly, "I've got a new novel to read. I've been on the waiting list at the library and just got it." None of this was true; she had had the book for more than a week. She reddened.

Jim came to the door. His smooth, full face had been freshly shaved. He had a new haircut and looked bathed and rested. "Well, Kallie, doll," he said, putting on the dark red Ahepa fez with the extra gold-colored embroidery that designated his presidency, "do I look okay?"

"You look very, very nice, Jim."

"This tuxedo is a little tight in the pants, but it's ten years old. What can you expect?"

Nitsa looked at him fondly and said teasingly, "He got it when he was in his *trella*." She brushed off his shoulders.

"My bride," Jim said and gave her an affectionate, playful slap on her hip.

Jim's *trella,* his madness, was the period when he had almost married a Mormon girl. He came out of his *trella,* his mother had said matter-of-factly, when the girl insisted that they be married in the Salt

Lake Temple. Jim's mother had scoffed, "She said they couldn't be together in Heaven if they didn't. Hear that?" It was all right for a man to go through *trella*.

Jim came out of his *trella* and did everything right from then on: found husbands for his sisters from among his friends; when he had run out of friends, he had taken one sister to a national Sons of Pericles convention. As soon as his father died, just before the Wall Street crash, he moved their automobile agency to a better location, and succumbed to his mother's machinations and married Nitsa. He was twelve years older, but his face was boyish. "The best thing I ever did," he told Kallie one day, just before he was to leave for a national AHEPA convention, "was marry Nitsa."

Kallie had said lightly, but meant every word, "Don't try to find a husband for me at the convention."

Jim had looked at her deeply. "You shouldn't be like that. Look at me and Nitsa. You could have a nice home and kids. You know I wouldn't fix you up with any fly-by-night or some goof."

"I know." Kallie smiled warmly. "But please don't."

"Well, I sure appreciate having Nitsa for a wife, even if it was kind of fixed up."

Careful, serious Nitsa, who had taken care of Antigone, Kallie, and Bill as they grew up, knew how to cook, wash, and iron by the time she was nine or ten. She had happily married Jim, *trella* or not. She listened to him raptly when he came home from work and told about the happenings of the day in the automobile agency. At dinner parties she looked across the table with lingering smiles while he talked. Even the superstitions he inherited from his mother didn't bother Nitsa. He would not let her sweep the floor after sundown and he never made a business decision on a Tuesday, the day the holy Greek city Constantinople fell to the Turks.

At the door they turned to Kallie and smiled, a couple who would be stout for sure in a few years. "Lock the door," Nitsa said and took Jim's arm.

Kallie turned the lock and sat on the rose brocade sofa. Soft light from twin lamps on either side of it fell on her open book. At first she liked the silence, liked being alone, but after a half hour, a devastating loneliness struck her and the words on the page looked loathsome to her.

The next day Kirk came into the laboratory to smoke and to give his report. "Someone snitched. The Warden called Madsen on the carpet, told her, she could not, n-o-t, go to the dance with Dr. Lowe. She's gonna be campused for twenty-four hours beginnin' Friday mornin'." He leaned back and looked at the ceiling. "The interns and residents said they wouldn't *let* their wives and girlfriends dance with a Chinese."

Kallie looked into the microscope at a blur of cells and spermatozoa in a drop of urine. When she looked up Kirk was no longer in the room. Someone was speaking to her. She turned, startled. The dark intern was looking down on her. "I'd like you to do this blood count over," he said, handing her a pink slip. "The count you put down would indicate polycythemia and I don't see any symptoms of it."

"I counted it twice," Kallie said with a flutter in her voice.

"Do it again," the intern said preemptorily and walked out.

Now she was afraid. She lifted her tray and hurried down to the men's Medical Ward. Patients looked at her, some smiled. *Cyanotic,* she was remembering from her pathology book, *large spleen, headache, many signs and symptoms of an extremely anemic patient.* "Not again!" Delaney said cheerfully. Weber looked at her as if he knew she had done something wrong. Kallie gave Delaney a quick look, then another. No blue showed around his mouth. Her heart beat faster thinking of the humiliation if she were wrong, of the contempt on Mrs. Dauber's face, of the interns and residents not trusting her work. She smiled stiffly and hurried back to the laboratory. Holding her breath, she put a drop of blood in the glass counting chamber. The field was choked with thousands of blood cells. She breathed out slowly, counted the cells in five squares and multiplied by ten thousand. She put down a number almost identical to the one she had noted before—ten million.

She fantasized the intern would come into the lab, look at the count, linger. She fantasized his asking her to go out with him, and she would, no matter what. She thought of his coming to sit in the lab while she worked. She thought: He might stand up for Dr. Lowe. He could be Dr. Lowe's friend. They could all be friends together.

"Did you do the new count?" the special voice asked. He was standing, looking down on her again.

Kallie handed him the slip. He read the number aloud and with a click of his tongue was gone. Kallie looked down on the disorder of the hospital yard, hidden from the street. She looked at her wristwatch. She had an hour before she could go home. Mechanically she worked with glass tubes and solutions at the black table, but her thoughts flowed back and forth between the Harvest Dance and what was happening to Dr. Lowe. On the streetcar thinking about him, she began to feel a sickness in her stomach. By the time she reached her house, she had decided she would not go to the Harvest Dance.

She could barely eat. At the first two bites of one of her favorites, rice-stuffed tomatoes, she could taste nothing, the smell of olive oil and spices was repulsive. "Why aren't you eating?" her mother asked.

"Just tired."

"Hmp! I don't know about that work of yours." A weariness passed over her mother's face. Her shoulders slumped.

While Kallie washed the dishes, Bill's voice came up the basement stairs. Her mother did what she called her heavy cooking, the legs of lamb, Greek dishes, and pastries for the big family dinners in the basement kitchen. Kallie's father had had a carpenter build the kitchen after the family moved out of Greek Town, when Kallie was eight years old. There was a telephone down there and Kallie overheard Bill asking a girl for a date. "Okay, I'll see you in the library ten sharp," he said and ran up the stairs. He stopped. His eyebrows went up in surprise. "Oh, I didn't know you were here."

"Where else would I be?"

"What time's that dance?"

"I've decided not to go."

"Why?"

"I've lost interest in it."

"Aw, come on."

"What do you care? Anyway, when the time came, you'd act as if you were being pulled by the nose."

"I would not. You said you wanted to go, so let's go."

"I guess Mama forced you. Didn't she? Or is it that nurse you met at the dormitory dance?" He looked worried. Kallie wondered if her parents had threatened to take the car from him and give it to her.

"No, I think it'll be fun. You know, see the people you work with and all that."

His voice had turned youngish, with that cajoling tone he had used when they were children and she took him by the hand to a candy store. He would quickly choose the two allowed candies from the penny-candy display, then keep begging for one more piece until Kallie gave in.

"Mama'll think I did something that made you change your mind. This is your chance."

She knew it was her chance to get out, to be like other girls, and she nodded.

After getting ready for bed, she stopped in the hallway at the icon, crossed herself, said the Lord's Prayer, and asked that They help Dr. Lowe. She decided which skirt and blouse she would wear to the Harvest Dance. She thought of the new intern walking straight towards her, smiling, putting out his hand. They danced around and around. Then they stood against the fence around the pond in the City Park and watched the ducks. He looked down at her smiling.

The evening of the dance, Kallie spent an inordinate amount of time putting on makeup. She used a little more rouge than usual. That very day she had bought an eyelash curler and carefully, her fingers trembling slightly, clamped it on her lashes. She procrastinated and took a long time removing curlers and combing her hair. Bill came to the closed bathroom door. "What's taking you so long?"

She had not been able to eat and had drunk a glass of milk. Her stomach was twisting in its juices. "In a minute," she answered. She came out in a pleated plaid skirt and a long-sleeved white shirt. Bill wore levis and a yellow cowboy shirt. "Have a good time and come home early," their mother said, scrutinizing them, her forehead wrinkling deeply. Their father turned from the radio momentarily to make some kind of sound low in his throat.

In the car Kallie sat still, except for rubbing her wrists. She thought she was a fool going to a dance with her brother, as if he were a date; the dancers would jitterbug and she had never done it, only seen it in movies; and maybe no one would ask her to dance and she would be humiliated in front of everyone, and especially Bill. He was whistling, unaware that she was silent.

Then a slow warmth suffused through her body. A pleasant flurry in her chest turned into a fine thrill: something wonderful could happen that night. The sky was black, beautiful. The air was tranquil, with just a touch of coolness.

They drove into the American Legion Hall's unlighted parking lot. "Well, quite a few cars here," Bill said. He jumped out and Kallie opened her door. Two men were leaning against a car a few feet away; one of them lifted a bottle to his lips, then handed it to the man next to him.

Inside, a few people were standing about in small groups. Kirk's orderlies had arranged haystacks and pumpkins in the corners of the big hall and set up folding chairs against the walls. A punch bowl of pink lemonade, paper cups, and plates filled with store-bought cookies were set on a long table covered with white butcher paper. Orange and black crepe paper streamers floated down from light fixtures. A local band, Red's Hot Dogs, was already on the stage, flanked by banners and flags. Four of the six musicians were Italian Americans. The drummer had been a Greek Town neighbor of Antigone's husband and was the godfather of little Tina. The band leader, Red, came from a large Irish immigrant family; an article in the *Tribune* reported that he was scheduled to play on *Major Bowes Amateur Hour*. Red threw back his curly red hair and lifted his clarinet toward the ceiling in imitation of Benny Goodman.

A few couples began dancing to "Sophisticated Lady." People Kallie saw almost every day were standing by the punch bowl, talking and sipping the pinkish punch and eating cookies. Here and there someone was laughing, in a festive mood. Bill was craning his neck, looking about. "Let's have some punch," Kallie said, her heart beating fast. Bill followed her through the crowd toward Dr. Harlow.

She smiled widely at Dr. Harlow. "Hello, Dr. Harlow."

Dr. Harlow stuffed a cookie into his mouth and said, "These cookies are terrible." His wife pulled him away before Kallie could introduce Bill.

"If that's his wife, he sure can't pick them," Bill said.

"Oh, there's Kirk!" Kallie exclaimed as if she had come to the dance especially to see him and, taking a punch cup in one hand and a cookie in the other, led the way to him.

Kirk was standing a little apart from a group of student nurses and their partners. Kallie wondered again where girls from farms and small towns found men. Kirk was looking over the crowd. Kallie introduced Bill. Kirk reared back his head and said, "Well, I'd introduce you to my wife, but I don't know where the hell she is. She's nuts about dancin'. I drive her to the Coconut Grove and she always finds someone to bring her home." He looked deeply into Bill's eyes. "What do you do? You workin' or goin' to school?"

The band struck up a fast, jerky tune and imediately the dance floor filled with jitterbugging couples. "Go ahead. Let's see you two jitterbug," Kirk said, nodding encouragement.

"Oh, not me," Kallie said.

Doyle grabbed Kallie's elbow. "You wanna jitterbug?"

"I've never done it, Doyle. I don't know how."

"It's easy. You jest move your feet any which way you want."

"Go ahead." Kirk said. "Give the kid a thrill."

"Here, I'll hold this," Bill said and took the punch cup from her.

Doyle leaped to the dance floor and, panicked, Kallie blindly twisted her toes inward and outward as she had seen in the movies. Doyle danced ecstatically, twirling, twisting, eyes closed, bumping into couples, forgetting Kallie completely. Kallie tried to follow him through the crowd, then went back to Kirk and Bill, who were laughing uproariously. She knew her face was red.

As the music stopped, cries and applause echoed in the hall. The next dance was a Broadway Follies song. "Well," Bill said, and Kallie followed him to the floor and they danced. Kallie hoped people did not know Bill was her brother. Several student nurses danced together and Bill eyed them. When they finished Kallie said, "Go ask one of the nurses for a dance. I'll sit with Kirk."

Kirk was sitting on one of the folding chairs with his long thin legs crossed at the knees. "Did yuh see that new intern? I found out his name. It's Llewelyn, Dr. Llewelyn."

"No. Where?" Kallie asked, confused: *Llewelyn* was not an immigrant name.

"Over there with Dr. Harlow and his snotty wife. You know why Harlow married that stuck-up bitch? 'Cause her father's a doctor and he most likely'll take Harlow in with him."

The new intern was smiling and listening to Dr. Harlow. Kallie sat up straight, then relaxed against the back of the chair: she wanted to look calm. Bill was twirling a student nurse in some kind of dance that looked Spanish to Kallie. Each time he danced past Kallie, he was holding the nurse closer to him. After three turns about the hall, she had her head on his shoulder. The resident on Emergency danced stiffly by with his stubby wife, unsmiling. Kallie looked at him with a sad amusement: he danced as if he were patiently performing a duty that would soon end. The dark, dour pharmacist pushed his heavy wife forward, both looking tired and uninterested. Dr. Harlow's wife was talking to another woman with dark-dyed hair and a strained face.

Kallie turned her attention to Kirk and pretended to be carrying on a vivacious conversation with him. When Kirk greeted someone or sent an orderly on an errand, she looked for Dr. Llewelyn. He had stayed in the same place, either alone or with an intern or resident. A few more people had come in, but still too few in the big barren hall. Kallie could not see Bill anywhere. She wished he would come back and dance with her. People could see she had nothing better to do than talk with Kirk, or, really, listen to Kirk. Kirk was telling her a story about an X-ray technician and his helper, who had played a practical joke on an orderly. "They got this here skinny lil' guy down to X-ray and pulled off his pants and put a hose up his ass and filled him up with air. They pumped so much air in him, they busted his gut."

"I hope the X-ray technician got into trouble for that," Kallie said indignantly.

"Oh, hell. It was all hushed up because he was the Warden's nephew."

"What happened to him? You don't mean the X-ray technician who's there now, do you?"

"No, a funny thing happened to the Warden's nephew," Kirk began and gazed off with a faint smile. "At City Park one night, three guys jumped him behind the concession stand. They beat the Jesus out of him. Used brass knuckles. After he got out of the hospital, he disappeared. No one's seen hide nor hair of him since."

Kirk and Kallie looked at each other for a long moment. "Here comes Dr. Llewelyn," Kirk said. "He's a Welshman. His parents got converted to the Mormon church over in Wales."

Kallie turned to see Dr. Llewelyn walking towards her. Suddenly her bladder seemed ready to burst. She leaned forward and put a smile on her face. Dr. Llewelyn looked at her as if he did not know her and went past to the punch table.

"He thinks he's the cock of the walk," Kirk said.

Kallie took out the handkerchief she had tucked into her shirt sleeve and held it to her nose. She knew her face was flaming. "Who is that woman standing with Dr. Harlow's wife at the table?" she asked

"That's Llewelyn's wife. What a doozy he's saddled with. Them guys go marry some secretary or nurse just to put them through medical school."

The hall looked bleak. The haystacks and pumpkins were like a school exhibit, the music frothy. Kirk stood up. "There's the commissioner. Just came in with McMillan. I better go say hello."

Kallie stood up also. The commissioner stood by the punch table with McMillan, the purchasing agent, at his side. Orderlies, supervisors, and several nurses went over to greet him, and he took off his hat with a courtly gesture. McMillan looked over his shoulder at Elsie Martin and said something to her. She answered without looking at him and busied herself with placing more cookies on the plates. The commissioner walked with portly stateliness around the hall, lifting his hat and nodding to his subjects.

"Don't you think it's just mean of the Warden to campus Ivy?"

Kallie turned to look into Elmina's big, scabby face. After a moment of profound fatigue, she said, "It was a mean thing to do to Dr. Lowe."

"Huh?" Elmina scrutinized Kallie's face. "Well, Ivy told me to keep an eagle eye out and tell her everything that's gone on. She was so thrilled about the dance and then old Warden has to campus her."

Kallie looked for Bill. She couldn't breathe. She had to get out of the hall. Bill was nowhere to be seen. "I guess it's true though. Races shouldn't mix," Elmina said. Kallie turned her head. Kirk came back to his seat and Elmina, for all her bulk, skittered away.

"Did yuh see my battle axe?" Kirk said. "Practically kissed the commissioner's hand. Look at her," he said, smiling and shaking his head as his wife, who was nearing fifty and dressed like a teenager, swished by in a short full skirt. "You know she don't have no eyebrows. She draws them on with an eyebrow pencil. The mornin' after our honeymoon, you coulda knocked me over with a feather when I saw her puttin' on her eyebrows."

"I've got to go, Kirk." Kallie hurried past a group of doctors standing with their hands in their pockets. Their wives formed another group nearby and their avid talk trailed after her. Elsie Martin was dancing with McMillan. The air was cold. The parking lot was now lighted dimly by a small globe at one end. She made a path through the cars, wanting only to get away, to be alone. When she came to the coupe, she stopped. Two figures were entwined, Bill almost on top of the nurse. Kallie took a step back, then looked at the hall. With a resolute jerk of the door handle, she pulled it open. Bill, his hair fallen over his eyes, looked at her in shock. Quickly the two disentangled themselves and Kallie stepped aside while the nurse got out awkwardly and, smoothing her hair, ran into the hall.

They spoke not a word all the way to their house. Bill stopped in the driveway. Kallie got out and he drove down to the garage. Their mother was sitting on her usual side of the sofa, crocheting a rose-colored afghan for Tina. She looked up. "Did you have a good time?" Kallie nodded. Her mother's eyes were examining her. Kallie went down the hall, past the icon and burning votive light, and into her bedroom.

The next morning Kirk came into the laboratory almost on Kallie's heels. He wanted to talk about the dance, knew bits of gossip he had gathered between the end of the dance and the morning. Kallie kept her eyes on the microscope. "A purty good shebang," he said and chuckled. "'Cept for Dr. Harlow's wife gittin' mad at him and walkin' out. And then McMillan got Martin from Isolation onto a stack of hay behind the stage curtains and they really went at it pretty good."

Kallie looked at Kirk. "That's rotten of him. She's so afraid of losing her job and her husband's in a wheelchair."

"I know he's in a wheelchair. I'm the one who told you that."

Kallie looked back into the microscope.

"Did you hear what the interns did to that guy they brought up from Emergency Sunday? Guy by the name of Weber. Mean sonofabitch. Called them whorelickers and everythin' else he could think of. They got even with him. Give him a pint of nigger blood over the weekend." Kirk laughed grimly. Kallie did not lift her head from the microscope.

"Boy, you're not in a very good mood today." Kirk got up and shuffled out of the room. At the door he called back. "If you see Doyle, tell him to git his ass down to Outpatient pronto."

"All right."

Each time Kallie heard noises down the hall, she quickly stood up and went to the centrifuge. She opened the lid and pretended to look into it, but she was really glancing into the hall hoping to see Dr. Lowe leaving Surgery. It was Pediatrics surgery that morning. Either he was not on duty or she had missed him.

At lunch time she sat on the fire escape and waited to see him walk toward the residents' quarters. She went back to the laboratory feeling defeated. Several times during the following days she contrived to be in Pediatrics in the morning, when the interns, residents, and staff doctors made their rounds. She was either too early or too late. Ivy Madsen came daily to the laboratory with request slips, bubbly, smiling with those small, even teeth.

Kallie tried to make her voice sound off-hand. "Kirk, I haven't seen Dr. Lowe lately. Is he sick or something?"

"Nah. He's here. Still on Pediatrics."

"I don't see him walking over to the quarters."

"Well, for one thing, he's been goin' across the street to the drug store for lunch at eleven-thirty sharp."

Several voices came from the hall. Kirk got up quickly, gave a wave, and left the room. Dr. Harlow and two interns in their surgeon's white pants and tops, masks hanging about their necks, and knitted skullcaps still on their heads, filed into the laboratory. Dr. Harlow sat down and lighted a cigarette, nodded at Kallie, and continued talking in his twangy voice. "What we've got to be careful about is the guy doesn't develop a secondary infection like what happened to that patient brought up from Emergency last week. You know that Greek guy. Weber."

Kallie lifted her head from the microscope. Her heart beat mercilessly. "Weber is not a Greek name. He's not Greek."

"It says so right on his chart under nationality," Dr. Harlow said, smiling.

"No, he's not," Kallie said and looked back into the microscope.

Dr. Harlow laughed. "Don't be paranoid, Miss Poulos."

"He's not Greek."

When the doctors left, Kallie looked down on the hospital's grimy buildings. Suddenly she realized that Weber's nationality was probably abbreviated as *Gr.* meaning German. She had taken German at the university for her language credit and Weber was a German name. Her brain felt cold with hatred for Dr. Harlow.

At eleven-thirty she left the hospital and crossed the street to the drugstore. Only Dr. Lowe was at the counter. She stopped, looked at the back of his head, and took another step forward. He raised his head and glanced into the mirror behind the counter. For a split moment they looked at each other, then Dr. Lowe turned slightly on the stool until his back was toward her. She turned and walked out of the door, flushed, thinking she was a fool. How had she thought she, of all people, could help Dr. Lowe?

The interns and residents rotated and Dr. Lowe was put on Surgery, but he did not come into the laboratory. He nodded to her once in the hall. She smiled, but he went on. From her chair at the microscope she often saw him walking alone to the interns' and resident's quarters. She wondered if the doctors still took the cigarettes and food his parents sent him. She wondered if Ivy gave back his jade ring.

She rode the streetcar. It was better, she told her mother. There were times when she had to do an emergency test and there was no need for Bill waiting for her. Anyway, there was a big light on the corner where she caught the streetcar. The sunsets were still brilliant, but she could see an almost invisible darkness in them. When she reached

Main Street and had to transfer, she avoided looking into store windows at the lifeless mannequins inside their glass prison. She did not stop at the American Candy Store to see Dea.

One day she realized she had not heard from Dea for ten days or more, but she did not telephone her. After she washed the dishes and placed them in the drainer to dry, she thought she should call. Dea would be wondering. She often complained that if she didn't telephone, they'd never hear from each other. How boring it all was, Kallie thought as she gave the operator Dea's number.

Dea must have been waiting for a call; she answered immediately in a strange, artificially gay voice.

"Dea? You sound so different. What have you been doing?"

"Oh, well, nothing too special." After a pause, Dea continued, "I was just about to call you. Telepathy I guess. What's been going on with you?"

"Same old thing. Work, home. Work, home. What's new with you?"

Dea hesitated. "Kallie, would you go on a double date with Solly and me and Mike Raptis?"

"What? When did this all come about?"

"Solly asked me over a week ago and I didn't know what to say. I think my mother will agree if we double date."

"But after all you said about Solly."

"Kallie, I'm almost twenty-four and all I've got to look forward to is standing behind my godfather's cash register."

"I don't know, Dea. I've hardly ever been around Mike Raptis."

"Well, he's the one who suggested you to Solly."

"I don't know anything about him."

"Oh, Kallie, of course you do." Dea's voice became animated. "He's good looking. He runs his father's business. He went to the university. And you know how the girls moon over him at the church doings."

Kallie did not answer.

"Please, Kallie. *Please.*"

GETTING
READY
FOR
THE
FESTIVAL

The noise in the recreation hall adjoining Saints Constantine and Helen Greek Orthodox Church had reached a crescendo by ten in the morning. Women were working at the long tables that filled the hall, their voices raised in competition to be heard. Men were shouting in the kitchen. From the giant stove an indeterminate smell floated outward, a mixture of hot honey, feta cheese, and fried squid from the previous day's cooking. The exhaust fans had worked ineffectively throughout the years of harried festival cooking and fumes escaped into the hall to float upwards and deepen the film on the fancy chandeliers hanging far too low from the ceiling. The chandeliers and blue carpeting had been the idea of a long past church board. They had proposed these changes to the parish general assembly: the additions would make the hall more inviting and wedding and baptismal receptions would likely be held there instead of in the big hotel ball-rooms. Receptions continued to be held in hotels and the hall contin-ued to look like a hall.

While men banged the giant pans and cauldrons in the kitchen, others in the adjacent basketball court were setting up booths and nail-ing boards in place. In spite of the yearly complaints of hard work, aching feet, and arthritic bones, a camaraderie seized the congregation each year as festival time neared. It was especially true of the men, re-tired, several of them widowers, seldom attending church but enjoy-ing male company and the luncheons prepared by the women's church organization, the Philoptochos. The first words they usually said on arrival was: "What's for lunch?"

On half the long tables women were placing powdered-sugar cook-ies, the *kourambiédhes,* in fluted blue paper muffin liners. Their hands were covered with clear plastic gloves. On the rest of the tables women were filling white liners with baklava. The blue and white colors were the idea of the co-chairman (no chairperson-business for this parish), the Philoptochos president, Irene Psaris. The blue and white of the Greek flag had always been the colors for the festival. Irene had ex-tended the color scheme to the smallest details, including the paper liners.

Irene was stout. Every day during week after week of festival preparation, she wore the same print wash-and-wear dress with but-tons down the front, the big pockets drooping with an assortment of pencils, small notebooks, Kleenex packets, a bottle of Tylenol, sugar in a plastic sandwich bag, and various folded invoices. "You ladies will get sick of this dress," she had said and laughed deeply from her fat-padded depths, "but I'm not going to wear anything good and have to keep taking it to the cleaners all the time. *Dolmadhes,* meat balls, squid. You name it. My hair and dress smell to high heaven. Lefty says he can always tell what we've been cooking the minute I step in the door."

The slender, youngish priest, who was already losing his hair, walked into the hall. Irene stopped him and talked at length while he stood mute. She gesticulated with her plump hands, laughed a little, and finally let him go. From table to table she went, making certain the women had enough pastries to keep busy without lagging. She had designated a woman at each table to bring trays of pastries from the kitchen to keep the women supplied. All the seats were taken at every table except the one, farthest from the kitchen. Only five women were working there. Irene thought: What a real odd bunch.

Irene was supervising an oral history program for the church and thought that after the festival was over and the oral histories commenced, it might be interesting to have those same women sit at the table and have a roundtable discussion. They were a good cross section of the parish: the very old woman from the first wave of immigrants, the much younger woman, who had come to America after World War II, the American-born woman (like Irene herself), and the two young women of the third generation, granddaughters of immigrants. It could be videotaped and shown at one of the church functions. Irene was always thinking of new programs to keep people interested in coming to the Philoptochos meetings.

Irene stopped at the table. "My legs are swollen," she said with a heartfelt sigh. "I've just got to give them a rest." She slumped down on a chair next to Mrs. Tsourakis, a humped woman in her mid-nineties. Two women from among the area's earliest immigrants were still alive and she was one of them. Mrs. Tsourakis lifted her head, looked with age-blued eyes at Ellen, the woman across from her, and said in Greek, "Eleni, bring Irini a cup of coffee while she's resting." Mrs. Tsourakis's lower lip had become loose with age and fell away from her false teeth. Ten years or so ago she had worn a wig for a short time, but now her thin white hair lay flattened over her pink scalp. Ellen tightened a corner of her pale lips and made no move to get up. Her gray hair was short and straight with bangs across her wrinkled forehead. Her hair style had remained unchanged since the early 'fifties.

"Oh, don't bother, Ellen," Irene said with a slap of the air. She and Ellen had grown up together and it didn't seem quite right to her that Ellen should wait on her. "I'll get a cup when I go back to the kitchen." Irene, however, looked pleased. She then noticed that Mrs. Tsourakis was not wearing the plastic gloves she insisted the women use while working with food, but decided it wasn't worth mentioning it: no matter what their age, Greek-born women were stubborn.

Mrs. Tsourakis frowned at Ellen, a signal for her to get up and bring Irene the coffee. Ellen got up slowly and mumbled, "All my life my mother told me what to do. She's dead, but now I've got Mrs. Tsourakis telling me what to do." As she turned toward the kitchen, her husband came to the table, holding his hands up in an effeminate manner. "Where you goin', Ellen? Where's your purse? I need a blank check." Ellen looked at her thin-faced husband stonily. There were times when she felt like yanking his long sharp nose. He looked at the floor next to the chair Ellen had been sitting on and picked up a brown imitation leather purse. As he touched the clasp to open it, Ellen pulled it from him and whispered harshly, "I told you never to look in my purse. And how many times have I told you to keep some blank checks in your wallet?"

While Ellen took out the checkbook, her husband greeted the women at the table. "You know," he began, looking at Vassi, a woman who had come from Greece after the Second World War. Vassi kept her head down and he turned to the two young women at the far end of the table, "I owe a lot to Mrs. Tsourakis here." He put his arm around Mrs. Tsourakis's bony shoulders. "She brought me and Ellen together. Yes sir! I was stationed at the army base here and Mrs. T. brought me home from church one day for a real Greek meal. Me and two other buddies. Ellen and one of her friends were helping her serve. So! That's how it all started."

"Here," Ellen said and slapped several blank checks into her husband's outstretched palm. "I'm sure sorry about your husband," he said in a low, insincerely sorrowful voice to Vassi. She lifted her tight face, white from the wrong shade of powder and stark against her short, black-dyed hair that was brushed back severely. "Eh," she said with a fatalistic shrug and looked back at her work. "Is he any better? What are they doing for him? Chemotherapy?" Vassi looked up again with a dark stare. "Better? No, he'll never be better." With a loud sigh, Ellen's husband nodded goodbye.

Ellen gave her husband a disgusted look and wove heavily between the tables. Her knees were rigidly pressed against each other and her legs splayed outwardly. Mrs. Tsourakis watched her and then looked at Ellen's husband hurrying into the basketball court. She had never had children and when the war started, she brought soldiers home every Sunday from church to eat Greek food. She wondered if Ellen ever thought of that Sunday when she had helped serve food to the three soldiers and was sorry she had been there that day.

Ellen smiled wearily and nodded to the women on her way into the kitchen. In the past few years she had gone from being angry to growing incensed with her daughter's spendthrift habits. The memory of their morning's quarrel weighed down her shoulders. She wished now she hadn't stopped at her daughter's house to bring a bowl of stew for their dinner. The leavings of a party were still on the dining room table, and in the kitchen delicatessen and bakery boxes were thrown on the floor. She should have gone back to her car when the door didn't open immediately. She never could learn to keep quiet about money thrown away. "Well, do you think your life's been so great?" her daughter had said, tying on a robe; day-old makeup smudged her eyes.

At the table Ellen had just left, Irene called out, as if over a chasm, to the two young women, the granddaughters of immigrants, "Chrissie, Tiffany, we're right on schedule." Yes, she was sure, a roundtable discussion with the several generations would actually be historic. "The kids had their last practice last night in their new costumes and did they look nice!" She then repeated what she had said to Mrs. Tsourakis in Greek.

"They don't dance Greek like it should be danced," Mrs. Tsourakis said, without looking up. "All that silly back and forth, back and forth." Irene laughed patronizingly and patted Mrs. Tsourakis on her hump. Mrs. Tsourakis knew far more English than people expected of her. They took for granted that because she had been born in Greece almost a century ago she had to be spoken to in Greek. It was convenient for Mrs. Tsourakis to let them think what they pleased.

On Mrs. Tsourakis's left, Vassi had not looked up when Irene sat down. As the president of the Philoptochos, Irene was accustomed to being acknowledged, but she overlooked this of women who had problems, which included almost everyone in the hall except her. Vassi's eyes, even in repose, had a permanently hostile look; her face had become more thin and tight as her husband's illness progressed. She was trying not to think of him in the nursing home, waiting to die of cancer. She did not want him to die. It was not that she cared so deeply for him, but that she had become used to him. She had a horror of being alone, a horror of being a widow. Since he had been taken to the nursing home, she had had a preview of how life would be without him: the house deathly quiet, no human sigh, no sound of another's breathing in the night. She hated and feared going to bed. She would suddenly be thinking of her twelve-year-old self, hiding in a cave while German soldiers scoured the mountainside for the villagers who had knifed two sentries. She no longer spent all day in the nursing home. Her husband lay drugged, his eyes half open. She now went there after lunch and stayed until evening. She didn't know what to do; when she was away from the nursing home, she was in agony that she should be with him, and when she was there, she lapsed into a drowsiness that was punctuated by sudden starts of wide-awake guilt.

Mrs. Tsourakis knew Vassi was thinking about her husband. She felt close to Vassi and her friend Lexi, who would no doubt be coming soon—she never missed a day of festival preparation. The two women were born in Greece, like her, and even though she had lived in America seventy-eight years, there was a bond with Vassi and Lexi because they too had been born on Greek land. She wanted to say something to Vassi, even merely to ask about her husband. She could not. She was ashamed that she was alive and a man thirty years younger than she was dying. If she spoke, she would draw attention to her great age. She felt she was an abomination to be still alive.

At intervals several men stopped to ask Vassi about her husband. One was American born, the others Greek born. They said words like: *a great guy; life of the party; never said a mean word about anyone.* Vassi knew what they meant: her husband was the likeable one; people always clustered about him at parties.

A woman took a seat next to Vassi and greeted the women: Irene, whom she called "our president," Vassi, and Mrs. Tsourakis. She could not remember Chrissie's and Tiffany's names but gave them a congratulatory nod for their coming to help with the festival, and at the same time thought of her only son, who had been killed in Vietnam: if he were alive he would have married a young woman like them, had children like theirs.

Vassi looked at her with momentary relief. "Aaa, Lexi, I was waiting for you," she said in Greek. The two were in their middle sixties and even though they had been in America fifty years, they spoke Greek when they were together. "How is he?" Lexi asked, a good-natured smile on her plump face. Mrs. Tsourakis was also relieved to see Lexi. She was a soothing woman, quiet yet industrious, an excellent housekeeper, all the qualities Mrs. Tsourakis prized in a woman.

"People keep coming over. It's too much. Maybe I won't come tomorrow to help."

"Yes," Lexi said, "you have to come. You'll feel worse at home."

Vassi shrugged and shook her head. While Irene chattered in her ear, Mrs. Tsourakis remembered when Vassi and Lexi had come as teenage girls after the big war and the Greek civil war that followed. Both had been scrawny and big-eyed from malnutrition. They had come from hamlets in northern Greece where the villagers had eaten every edible green on the mountains and then began eating weeds. Their mothers had died young; Vassi's father had starved to death during the German occupation and Lexi's had been killed by guerrillas in the civil war. Distant relatives had brought them to America. Once they arrived, they had had to learn how to make pastries; they could not remember what sugar was like. Mrs. Tsourakis had taught them herself. Her old thinned lips now transformed into a smile. She remembered how they had sat down at the cleared kitchen table after the pastries were in the oven. They drank demitasses of Turkish coffee while they talked and the scent of hot honey filled the house. Lexi soon became known as one of the best pastry makers in the congregation. In America she had grown plump and smiling; Vassi had remained thin and scowling. Mrs. Tsourakis often wondered about this, how people with bad experiences went on living differently. She was convinced it was mainly the kind of people they came from. As the proverb said: The apple falls from the apple tree.

Lexi pulled on the plastic protectors. Vassi gave her a quick but penetrating glance: when Lexi's husband was dying, she went on day after day never complaining; when he died, she never once said she hated to be alone in her silent house. Why was her face plump, unwrinkled? A son had been killed in Vietnam; her husband, who had been much older, died when she was still in her forties. None of it showed on her face. Why couldn't she be like Lexi?

Ellen said, "Hi, Lexi," and placed the cup of coffee and a packet of Sweet 'n Low in front of Irene. Smiling at being waited on, a tribute to her status, Irene said, "Thanks, Ellen, but I use regular sugar. I can taste the difference." She reached into her right pocket and brought out a plastic sandwich bag half-filled with sugar and tied with a red twist. "I always have my sugar handy. Oh, this does taste good." She turned to Mrs. Tsourakis. "Thanks for thinking about me, Maria," she said in Greek. Mrs. Tsourakis did not like being called by her given name and did not answer her. She thought Irene was a good-hearted gadabout. If she had been born in a village, she would have gone to the well every chance she got. Still, she shouldn't criticize. Irene picked her up for liturgies and for the festival preparations.

Irene had been president of the women's church organization for so long, she looked upon the women as her charges, even those older than she. Vassi and Lexi glanced at each other. They always called Mrs. Tsourakis "Auntie," although she was not related to them, out of respect for her old age. It was a village trait they had not lost in America.

Irene kept sipping and murmuring about how good it was to get off her feet and drink a cup of coffee in peace. "Oh, there's Pat," she said and lifting her hand high waved it back and forth. A tightly girdled woman walked towards the table with a disgruntled look on her dewlapped, carefully powdered and lipsticked face. She had just come from a salon, where she had had her hair freshly tinted in a beige-pink color that was startling against her olive skin. She was wearing a pink linen dress that she pulled at with a hand replete with rings: her small engagement ring, a large diamond given her on her fifteenth wedding anniversary, when her husband had begun to make money, her mother's small diamond, which she had had reset in a circle of little diamonds, and a band of diamonds her husband had given her on their fiftieth wedding anniversary, just before he died.

Pat couldn't wait to tell Ellen what she had read in a magazine at the hairdresser's. They had been friends since they were small girls, and Pat, an Americanization of Panaghiota, her Greek name, wanted to tell Ellen all about it and throw off the shameful words she'd read.

But she could not do it with Mrs. Tsourakis sitting there, even if the old woman wouldn't understand what she was saying. She would have to whisper and that was bad manners. Besides, it was something that would take time, not something to blurt out and get over with. Vassi, poor Vassi with her husband dying, and Lexi who always looked so innocent, they wouldn't know about such horrible things, but the young women at the end of the table, who probably attended restricted movies, might know. They could have read that very magazine. She looked at the two young women, a generation younger than she: their smooth faces, undyed hair, not even much makeup. *Her* grandchildren didn't go to restricted movies. She asked them once, straight out, and they had said no, they didn't.

She could hardly believe that what she had read was actually being published. She usually looked at *Good Housekeeping* or *Ladies Home Journal* while sitting under the dryer, but that morning she had picked up a large glossy magazine she had never seen before. She turned the pages, looking at the latest fashions, and saw a shocking article about orgasms. She read it, flushing, getting more and more angry. Women were to use dildos and vibrators, and something unfamiliar, a word she could not now remember. She knew what dildos were, she had heard about them; but to find them recommended in a supposedly high-class magazine! And that wasn't the worst part. The article suggested using life-sized rubber dolls in the shape of a man with the penis and all, for satisfaction! Didn't these women have children? Where would they store a life-sized rubber toy? What kind of sex-crazy women were they anyway? Trashy women. Trashy, trashy, even if they dressed in those expensive clothes worn by pouty, skinny models. She sat down, next to Ellen, nodded at Mrs. Tsourakis, ignored the young women at the end of the table, acknowledged the greetings of Irene, Vassi, and Lexi, but did not hear what they said, she was so angry. And she didn't know when she would get the opportunity to tell Ellen about the article, probably not until they were all through for the day.

Pat and Ellen were in their mid-seventies; their parents had come from the same village near Sparta, and they themselves had gone to the same public school and afterwards to Greek school together.

When they were young women they had joined the Daughters of Penelope and Pat continued to be much involved in it. Wearing fashionable clothes, she took charge of the annual fashion show and of the dinner dance, where the aging children of immigrants ate heartily and encircled the dance floor dutifully one or two times. That over with they sat in groups; the women clustered together and talked about their children and grandchildren, the men drank Metaxas and reminisced about their youth.

Pat had never been able to convince Ellen to dye her hair, get new clothes, and go on cruises with her. "We'll meet all kinds of interesting people, Ellen."

"But I don't want to meet interesting people. I can't keep up with the ones I know."

"That's a poor attitude. If you want to keep from getting old, you've got to work on it." Once she said, "You need to get away from Spiro. You just get in each other's hair."

"Pat, why don't you leave me alone and give your advice to someone who'll listen to you?"

"Okay, then," Pat had said for the time being. Now looking at Ellen from the corner of her eye, she didn't think she would ever again ask her to go on a cruise: her gray hair style was dated; her legs had become knock-kneed; her clothes were years old. She just wasn't smart looking.

Ellen thought Pat looked silly with her new hair tint. Someday it would turn completely pink. She disapproved of Pat's throwing money away on hairdressers and manicurists. Pat had nothing to do all day; she could just as well wash and set her own hair and manicure her own nails. Besides a waste of money, it was being just plain spoiled. Mrs. Tsourakis felt the same way: Panaghiota was the biggest fool in the entire congregation, always bragging about her children and grandchildren as if no one else had any. Her mother had been that way too.

Pat decided she would stop being angry. Her blood pressure, she had to think about her blood pressure. She glanced at the end of the table at Chrissie and Tiffany. She had known their grandparents, who had come from the Peloponnese, and she knew their American-born parents. They were talking with their heads leaning toward each other, Chrissie, a pretty woman with a small face almost lost in a cascade of bouncy hair, was complaining about the priest who wouldn't listen to the young people's excuses when they were absent from dance practices. "If it was a movie you wanted to see, you'd go even if you had the flu," he'd said to Chrissie's son. Ellen and Pat heard her and nodded to each other. "Just like his grandfather," Pat said. The grandfather, also a priest, used to say to the young people, "The *good time,*" the two words in English, "in America, that's all people care about, the *good time.*" And he was exactly right, Mrs. Tsourakis said to herself. Irene was talking to Vassi and Lexi, or else she would have reprimanded Chrissie and Tiffany—in a nice way of course: she didn't like people criticizing priests.

"Well, Chrissie," Tiffany said, lifting her surgically pretty nose in warning, "we better not complain about him or we'll get another Father Harry." "Oh, God," Chrissie said and lifted her hands in fake horror. Ellen smiled one-sidedly in agreement, but Pat looked at them with a pushing out of her lips. She had invited Father Harry and his petite, worried-looking wife to all her dinner parties. He didn't accept invitations to every party he was invited to, but he always came to hers. She was about to put the two young women in their place by saying, "Father Harry is not stuck-up. If people followed the rules, he always went to the hospitals and nursing homes to visit the sick. It was when they called him up at night or the last minute that he got annoyed." She did not have the chance. A moaning came from behind her chair.

Mrs. Leloudis, a tall thin woman of ninety-three, approached the table, but did not sit down. She continued to moan as she wandered around it. Her grieving eyes looked off and her veined hands were clasped to her flat chest. "Mrs. Flower is back," Chrissie said to Tiffany. Leloudis meant *flower* in village patois, and the old woman was often called Mrs. Flower by women born in America. Greek-born women like Vassi and Lexi, however, didn't see the humor in it.

"Come and sit down," Mrs. Tsourakis said sharply. "Sit down and get busy." "The *varos,* the *varos,*" the burden, the burden, Mrs. Tsourakis said to herself and with shaky hands carefully placed a cookie in a blue paper cup.

Mrs. Tsourakis had been burdened with Mrs. Leloudis for over seven decades, from the time they had both come to America as picture brides for men they had never seen. Mrs. Leloudis had not wanted to come; she had wanted to become a nun, but her father took out a stiletto knife from his cummerbund and told her she would go to America or he would twist the knife in her insides. Mrs. Tsourakis's husband had been the best man at the Leloudis wedding. Two weeks after the wedding, Mr. Leloudis complained to his *koumbaro* that his bride kept a dishcloth tied about her forehead and said she was sick and slept on the sofa. "Am I going to live with a woman the rest of my life with a rag around her head?" Mrs. Tsourakis was dispatched to tell Mrs. Leloudis that husbands had certain rights and she better take off the dishtowel. It was the beginning. Mrs. Leloudis had burdened her, burdened her.

About twenty years ago spiteful Mrs. Karatzanos had told a group of women that Mrs. Leloudis and Mrs. Malakos were lovers. "How can women be lovers?" Mrs. Leloudis asked Mrs. Tsourakis. "How do they do it?" Mrs. Tsourakis exploded. "Leave me alone! Don't bother me any more with your silliness. No more! This is the end!" But the next week Mrs. Leloudis was at her door. Stupid Mrs. Leloudis had children while she herself had not one. Mrs. Tsourakis used to walk the floor and wring her hands over it. Why, she wanted to know, why did God do this to her? Many years later she overheard two educated Greek women from Asia Minor say that many immigrant men in their early years in America had gone to prostitutes, who infected them with disease and made them sterile. It wasn't God after all.

"What's bothering you, Tasia?" Irene asked Mrs. Leloudis, the cup of coffee held to her mouth with plump hands. The other women at the table looked up at the black-dressed wraith and an audible sigh came from one of them.

"It's my cat, my Koutounaki! He's been lost for three days. I looked for him last night until it was too dark to see and again as soon as God lighted the skies. I called and called, but —"

"I'll bet the neighbors liked that," Vassi said in English, as if Mrs. Leloudis wouldn't know what she was saying. Mrs. Leloudis had been in America since 1922, and didn't understand much English even though she watched the television soaps with Koutounaki stretched out at her feet.

"He's never been gone so long!" Mrs. Leloudis wailed. "I just lighted a candle for him and prayed. Oh, my poor Koutounaki. Lost, hungry."

"Watch yourself," Mrs. Tsourakis warned. "Don't make a spectacle of yourself."

The women around the table looked at each other impatiently, the youngest, Chrissie and Tiffany, watched with interest, but did not know enough Greek to understand exactly what was happening. "Doesn't *ghata* mean cat?" Chrissie asked Tiffany, who shrugged her shoulders.

"And my daughter. I asked her to put it in the paper, but she just got angry at me."

"Well, sit down, Tasia," Irene said brusquely, "and I'll take care of it." Mrs. Leloudis's blighted eyes opened excitedly. "All right," Irene said in Greek and took out a small notebook and pencil from her pocket. "What color is the cat and you live near City Park, don't you? And your telephone number?" Irene wrote quickly.

"Koutounaki, that's his name, Koutounaki." Mrs. Leloudis enunciated carefully and described the cat.

"Okay," Irene said in English, then in Greek, "I'll call it in." She read aloud authoritatively: "Lost. Black cat with white face and white paws and tail tip. Vicinity City Park. Answers to the name Koutounaki. Call 477.0101. Reward."

Tiffany and Chrissie tightened their lips to keep their laughter inside and avoided each other's eyes. The other women looked at Mrs. Leloudis with annoyance. The old woman got up with a remarkably sprightly jump. "Thank you. Thank you, Irini. May you live a thousand years. I'll go home now and look for him some more."

"If he's a boy cat, he's probably found what all men are looking for," Vassi said sourly.

"Oh, no, he's not like that. Not my Koutounaki," Mrs. Leloudis said.

"How're you going to get home, Tasia?" Irene asked. "Will your daughter come for you?"

"No, I don't want to bother her. I better get a *texi*. Will you call one for me? And I'll go outside and wait."

"You might be out there for an hour," Mrs. Tsourakis said, but Mrs. Leloudis had pulled her purse, coat, and paper sack off a chair and hurried as fast as her arthritic feet would go. "Watch yourself. You'll fall again," Mrs. Tsourakis called angrily.

"Her family's in shambles," Pat scoffed, "and she can't think of anything but her Koutounaki."

"Oh, let the poor old woman be," Irene, the perennial peacemaker as well as the perennial president of the Philoptochos said in a kindly voice. She reached out and tapped the arm of a bald man struggling past with a garbage can. "Pete, on your way back go to the office and call a taxi." "Sure thing, General," he answered and Irene giggled.

"Well," Vassi said, speaking English with the faint accent she would have if she lived in America another fifty years, "poor old Mrs. Leloudis. Her granddaughter's husband left her and she's pregnant again and Mrs. Leloudis is crying over her Koutounaki." She shook her head.

Lexi chuckled and said in English. "In my village we had a woman who had one more baby she didn't want. She already had six. The neighbors came to visit her and she cried and cried and they all gave her advice on how not to get pregnant again. Then one neighbor said, 'There's only one sure way. At night when you're ready for bed, we'll come and tie your legs together.'" The women laughed merrily except for Tiffany and Chrissie. "Sometimes I don't get that Greek humor," Chrissie said.

"Talking about children," Ellen said, "did you see the obituaries today. Chris Hamoulis died."

Pat: "Can you imagine! He had ten kids."

Vassi: "Well, what did you expect? The donkey married a Mormon and then he got converted. So now let her raise them. See how she likes it."

Mrs. Tsourakis showed no interest in the conversation. She lifted her head up, like a turtle from its shell. "Irini, I don't know what's going to happen when your generation is gone. Who's going to come down here and work like slaves to cook and serve and stand on their feet like us? Look," she waved her old hand toward Tiffany and

Chrissie. The women looked at the youngish, healthy women, their hair cut in the latest fashion, wearing stylish denim skirts and crisp, long-sleeved shirts. "Only two of the young women helping us. How will they pay the priest? How will they keep up the church?"

"That's not our worry," Vassi said. "We'll be gone by then." She pulled in her thin mouth until it disappeared. The children came into the nursing home for a few minutes to see their dying father, then out again, because they knew she would be there, every day for hours at a time. They had sacrificed for those children, her husband and she. They wanted them to have a good life. All the tests done to him lying helpless, his eyes on hers, resigned, knowing the doctors would do what they wanted anyway. At first one of the three children would come and wait with her outside the rooms where the horrors went on, then they came less often. They knew she would be there.

Mrs. Tsourakis was saying, "Oh, how it was when we first started. Everyone helped. Everyone made beautiful embroidered and crocheted linens. Now what do they have? Fishermen's caps from Greece and a few aprons. And those tops with Greek flags and sayings on them. In the *Depresh* we helped so many families when the fathers were out of work. The widows with small children. Our dues were ten cents a month, but with that and potatoes and onions we got from Mr. Papadiamantiou and every once in a while lambs from the sheepmen, we kept the families going. We sewed. We made over used clothes. We didn't waste anything."

Ellen was quiet: she had worn someone's hand-me-downs. She often wondered whose. The heavy black coat she had just bought on sale would last another twenty years until she died. Her daughter didn't like it. She could tell. Her daughter, all dressed up in the newest fads. Always entertaining. If you could call it that, picking things up at the delicatessen and the bakery. Spending money right and left. The children couldn't have one good coat, no, they had to have two. They couldn't go to public school; they had to go to a private school.

Vassi burst out in Greek, "If you'd lived through the war with those macaroni-eaters and those goose-stepping Germans taking every animal, every stalk of wheat, you'd think this *Depression* you people talk about was Paradise."

"Yes, yes, Vassi," Mrs. Tsourakis said sadly and looked back at her work. The priest walked by wearing an apron. Vassi turned to Lexi and said in Greek. "Do you know how it offends me to see a man, and especially a priest, wearing an apron?"

Lexi smiled placidly. "Eh, this is America."

Andy Karambis, the co-chairman of the festival, arrived at the table. A carpenter's apron full of tools was tied around his thick waist. Vassi handed him a blue paper cup. "Have a *kourambié,* Andy," she said.

While Andy devoured the pastry, Irene frowned at Vassi: she had made a cardinal rule that only broken cookies could be eaten. "What's up, Andy?" she said.

Andy chewed judiciously, looking off through brown bulging eyes, his thick lips edged with powdered sugar. "Boy, there's so much butter in these, they stick to the roof of your mouth."

Irene laughed. "No margarine for us. We're not that Americanized."

"I need you to look at the booths, Irene. I think we should move the cooking demonstration."

Irene got up, pressing her palms on the table to support herself. "I don't know about that, Andy. I think I took everything into consideration."

"Come and see what I mean."

Tiffany said, "One minute, Irene. What are we going to have for lunch today?"

"Lasagna, and all kinds of salads and things."

"I made a big salad with shrimp," Lexi said. "You know, lots of people don't eat much meat anymore. My granddaughter brought it. Her car's in the garage and I told her, 'You can take my car if you drive me to church and carry in the salad.'" Lexi's kindly face sagged. She remembered her granddaughter's sullen look as she carried the big bowl into the kitchen and then swept by the table without even a hello to Vassi, whom she'd known from the time she was a baby, and Mrs. Tsourakis, who was old and deserved respect. Her granddaughter had two children and wanted to divorce her husband, someone she'd chosen when no one else liked him. The poor little children, two of them, sweet and silent.

"I think Irene's put on weight, don't you?' Ellen said, leaning her head toward Pat. They craned their necks watching Irene and Andy make their way to the basketball court.

"She sure has." Pat nodded vigorously. "When she's with Lefty, she looks much older. Like she could be his mother. She ought to lose about twenty pounds." Pat's thighs rubbed together when she walked.

"You're right," Ellen said and Pat looked as if she had been caught at being disloyal. Irene was her son's godmother.

Lexi, the community's first-rate pastry maker, smiled. "What was that remark Irene made about the butter? It's a good thing we didn't use her mother's recipe for the *kourambiédhes*. Her mother made good *baklava,* but her *kourambiédhes* were no good."

Ellen turned to Pat. "Has Neena said anything more about the"— she was about to say *imports*—"about Roula and the boyfriend?"

The women were silent, making as little noise with the paper muffin cups as possible. This Neena knew everything. She seldom left her house and spent the days telephoning friends and acquaintances for gossip and then dispatching it.

Pat lifted her shoulders and gave her beige-pink head a shake of false sorrow that set her dewlaps aquiver. "She said it was her son who caught them in bed."

The women set off an orchestra of sounds, sharp intakes of breath, hissing, tsk-tsking. "Is his wife going to divorce him? What did Neena say?" Ellen asked.

"No. She's not. She said she's got four children and he had to help raise them. She said men do those kind of things."

Ellen and Pat looked at each other. "They look like us," Ellen said in a low voice, "but when it comes right down to it, they're still Greeks from Greece."

Mrs. Tsourakis kept working, shaking her head slightly: she could believe an American-born woman would carry on with her husband's best friend, but a Greek-born woman! That's what America did to people. "The world is ruined," she proclaimed in a loud but shaky voice.

"There's just no manners anymore," Pat said. "Yesterday I was sitting in the Marriott Coffee Shop. Not some fast food place or anything like that. I was having lunch with my cousin Dena. And at the next table there were these three women, about thirty-five years old. Not kids. I had ordered the crab Louis and I was just putting my fork into it when these women were talking. In a loud voice too. And one of them said, 'I won't take any of that shit from him.' There I was with this beautiful salad with sliced avocado on top and these awful women were using the s word, not once either. I could hardly eat a mouthful and I wouldn't have, but I was so hungry and I had a doctor's appointment."

"You should have got up," Vassi said, "gone over to her and said, 'I hope you like the shit you're eating.'"

"Oh, Vassi," Lexi said.

"Listen, if you don't make a noise," Vassi said and spoke a proverb in Greek, then looked at Chrissie and Tifanny and translated it into English: "'If you want the bell to be heard, then ring it.'"

"I wonder if Mrs. Leloudis got home all right," Mrs. Tsourakis said. "The *texi* drivers always cheat her."

Lexi sighed. "It's the bad language everywhere. The movies, the television, everywhere."

"The Vietnam war did it," Pat said. "Well, I won't put up with it. I tell my grandkids if they want presents from me Christmas, and Easter, and on their birthdays, they just better not use that kind of language around me. But they're good kids, all of them."

Lexi thought of her own granddaughter's sullen face. Tiffany and Chrissie gave each other sidelong glances. "Nize kids," Mrs. Tsourakis said. Lexi began softly, sadly, "I remember when I was growing up. The respect we had to show to all older people. Stand up when they came into a room. Speak to them in the proper way or we'd really get it later. Oh, there were so many things hanging over our heads. Especially us girls."

"It's better that way than the way kids are today," Vassi said. "You could be sick in a hospital or a nursing home and they come in for two minutes and leave. You can't depend on them for real help."

"You remember how we used to spend weeks getting ready for name days?" Ellen said rapidly. "Making everything from scratch? That's not for these young people. Oh, no! Money means nothing to them. They stop at one of these fancy places and pick up a bowl of wild rice and lentil salad with walnuts. Thirty-five dollars to serve eight! You could make it for three! Maybe less. And then they stop at the bakery and get fancy breads and cakes! Even chickens and turkeys already roasted! They don't save a penny! They get a little spot on their clothes and off to the cleaners! So when they have to live on their Social Security, we'll see! We'll see how they like it." Ellen's face was flaming.

Mrs. Tsourakis could not believe what she was hearing. These women, except for that awful Panaghiota, did not come right out and say so but they were criticizing their children. Their mothers were dead and they forgot what they had been taught: "Never let anyone know what goes on in the house. Everything must be kept within the four walls. People must never know our messes." When she was a little girl she had innocently said something to a friend about her older sister's one leg being a little shorter than the other. Her mother had padded the inside of her sister's shoe with folded flannel so it wouldn't be noticed. She had been beaten so badly she was in bed a month. "You miserable child!" her mother had screamed at her, "how will we marry her off? What goes on in the house must never go beyond the four walls." She remembered to this day her mother's shrilling and blazing eyes. She looked at Chrissie and Tiffany—what kind of names were those? In America young people found their own husbands or wives.

"We've spoiled them. That's what we've done," Lexi said. "Now it's like we have to pay them to do some little thing for us. And then they marry and expect that person to treat them like they were treated at home. The next thing you know they talk about divorce."

Vassi: "You can talk yourself blue in the face and finally you have to give up. Let them marry and have some one else fight with them."

Ellen: "You do and do. You go without. And for what?"

Mrs. Tsourakis said sharply: "Don't expect anything and you won't be disappointed."

"It's this sex! Sex!" Pat shook her head and her cheeks shimmered. "Everywhere you look. You can't even pick up a magazine and it's on every page. Awful, dirty things people do! It makes a person want to throw up!"

Vassi shook her head angrily. "With the Greeks the family came first. Everybody looked up to the mother and father. Respected them. Always thought first of them! Now the young people are just like the Americans. They think of themselves first!"

"Someday they'll come crying! They won't have money and nowhere to get it! Then they'll think back and remember how they squandered their money! They'll see!" Ellen breathed audibly.

Mrs. Tsourakis raised her head slightly, her wrinkled eyelids lifted, and her veiled bluish eyes looked alarmed. "Watch what you're doing, Eleni. You're spilling the sugar." She couldn't think of anything to say, but she couldn't listen to this kind of talk a minute longer.

"Well," Pat said, "I can truthfully say that I've never had any trouble with my children or my grandchildren. They're all good kids. Go to church, well, pretty often. They all have good jobs. I have no complaints."

Tiffany, the young woman with the new nose, glanced at Chrissie. Their mouths pursed as they tried to keep from smiling, then they looked at Pat. "How's Jeff?" Tiffany said. "What's he doing now?"

"Oh, he works for the state. He's the most considerate of all my grandchildren." Pat laughed, lifted her plastic-covered, jeweled hands like an old-time minstrel. "He's always dropping by. I'm so glad I never gave any of my old furniture away. He and his friend Tim just got a new apartment and they come by and go through the basement and take what they want. It's so much fun to watch them. They're like newlyweds!" Pat laughed gaily and suddenly stopped. Her face reddened and a look of surprise bulged out her eyes. She looked down at the blue paper fillers and quickly began working and said not another word.

The women were silent. Someone banged on a pan. "Lunch is ready," Irene called. "Come on, ladies."

Slowly the women stood up. Vassi said, "I'll bring your plate, Mrs. Tsourakis."

Mrs. Tsourakis watched them walk toward a line that was forming. At one end of the long table filled with bowls and platters, men were heaping their plates. She didn't know what the word *newlyweds* meant or why Panaghiota was for once silent. She wondered if the food would lay heavy in her stomach and if Mrs. Leloudis got home all right.

NEITHER
NOSE
NOR
ASS

Manny's and Greg's fathers had met in the Paradise Coffeehouse in 1910. They had a great deal in common. By the time the two sat down at a scarred table, they had washed dishes, worked on railroad gangs and in coal mines, and knew many of the same sojourners through their incessant search for work. They had much to talk about, but they would not agree on Greek politics. On their first meeting they drank demitasses of Turkish coffee and shouted at each other.

By that year, 1910, each had saved a small sum of money and set up shop in Greek Town near the railyards. Greg's father opened a saloon and Manny's father a coal, hay, feed, and grain store. They did well enough with their sisters' dowry installments that two years later they asked their families to choose village girls to come as their brides. Whenever they quarreled over politics, they made disparaging remarks about each other to their wives. Greg's father said Manny's father probably had Albanian or Serbian blood in his veins. Manny's father called Greg's father "a gypsy for all his fine airs. He went to school one year more than me. I know I'm a peasant, but he doesn't know he's one." In 1913 their wives gave birth to sons. By the time the boys were toddlers it was obvious who their fathers were. Greg was dark and thin; Manny was stocky, with a wide forehead, and light hair and eyes.

As their children grew, the families' businesses went through changes. The Prohibition amendment in 1918 forced Greg's father to change from selling beer to soft drinks. When more automobiles than wagons began to appear on the street, Manny's father stopped selling hay, feed, and grain and dealt only in coal. In the early 'twenties he sold his horse and buckboard and bought a small truck. In the middle 'twenties the man from whom he leased the coal store sold him his house cheaply, because he wanted to move to California to grow oranges. Manny's family became the first to move out of Greek Town. In the basement, Manny's mother kept a still going and burned a rubber tire in the backyard to camouflage the smell of the mash. When Prohibition was repealed in 1933, Greg's father began selling 3.2 beer. Regularly the two fathers argued vehemently over politics.

Throughout the years their wives reminded them that they had daughters to marry off someday and there weren't many eligible young men in this *ksenitia,* this foreign land. The women visited each other constantly and were inordinately polite to show that they had breeding and it would be advantageous to marry into their families. By the time Manny's and Greg's sisters reached adolescence, their mothers had become complacent, so certain were they that each would have the other's son for a son-in-law. Then the unbelievable news came: Manny and Greg were going to marry sisters, the daughters of a woman who visited only on name days, who had never made any special effort to pave the way for finding husbands for her daughters. All their efforts had come to nothing, the mothers morosely confessed to each other.

Manny married Mary and Greg married Aphrodite, called Fro, in a double wedding in 1937, four years before Pearl Harbor. The double wedding was performed because of an old-country superstition held by Manny's and Greg's mothers: a year should pass between family weddings or bad luck would follow. The wedding photographs stood on the fireplace mantels of the young couples' houses. The brides and grooms were handsome, mainly because they were young. The sisters were round-faced with shoulder-length hair and ringlets on their foreheads, in imitation of movie actresses of the late 1930s. Although the sisters' family resemblance was obvious, Mary's eyes looked straight ahead; Fro's were dreamy. "Like she's bewitched," their annoyed mother said. Aphrodite, in her opinion, had been like this since a child.

Greg, Fro's husband, often made disparaging remarks about women: "She's a flat tire"; "She's a cold potato." The sisters' mother knew enough English to understand the slang expressions—they were transliterated in the Greek-language newspapers she read; she sensed Greg was comparing other women to Fro and she thought it unseemly. It was well she was unaware that in their first months of married life Greg told Fro she had a body like the Venus de Milo's.

In the photographs Manny and Greg were in their middle twenties, a few years older than their brides. Their oiled hair was parted in the middle and combed straight back. Mary's husband Manny—the family called the couple "The M's"—had heavy shoulders and was shorter than Fro's Gregory. When he was a boy at a lodge picnic race, someone in the watching crowd had called out in village Greek, "You, Manoli, give up! You can't win with those short Peloponnesian legs." In a childish rage he raced ahead and won.

Fro's husband was as slender as his father. He held his head high, unnecessarily high, giving the impression of solemn dignity until a person noticed his large feet with the toes turned inward. In grade school he had been called "Pigeon Toes." His parents had come from a hamlet near the village Gramatikon, a few miles north of the plain of Marathon. When he was eight years old he had listened, eyes wide open, as the Greek school teacher orated on the great defeat at Marathon, where the betrayed Greeks fell to the Persians. Greg had raised his hand and said that his parents came from there and when he was grown up he would go back and walk right where the battle had taken place. "We've all come from famous places," the teacher drily remarked.

Although Manny and Greg had known each other since childhood, they had not been special friends. Gregory had remained in the old Greek immigrant district around the Union Pacific railroad yards, Manny's family lived ten blocks east. They had gone to different schools and played with their own neighborhood friends. Sometimes they sat by each other in Greek school, which was held after public school, but Manny was usually late. He dawdled on the long blocks to the church basement, watched all kinds of trucks go by, and gazed at ants carrying winter supplies to their little sand hills in tumbleweeded lots. Often he played in the city park until he thought it was time to go home. The big-bellied, bald teacher, who chanted sonorously during Sunday liturgies, never thought to ask Manny's father, whom he saw regularly in the Stadium Cafe, why Manny was absent so much.

Manny and Greg had one experience in common. Just before Greek school one day, they had traded marbles. Suddenly, at the door of the church basement, Greg decided he wanted his marbles back. Inside they continued the argument behind propped-up grammar books to shield themselves from the teacher. "You're a two-by-four Indian trader," Manny whispered, narrowing his eyes. "And you're a dumb *vlahos,*" Greg hissed, using the Greek word for peasant. The teacher ordered them to the front of the class, and following standard routine, they put out their hands, palms down. The teacher then whacked their hands hard with a thick ruler. When the class was let out into the darkening evening, they looked at each other, snickered, then burst into guffaws and imitated the teacher. Once in a while after that they played kick the can in front of the church.

After the double wedding the two couples were together constantly. The brothers-in-law began referring to themselves as *bajanakia,* a Greek word for men who had married sisters. They managed to buy small brick houses built in the 1920s, not far from each other. The sisters' father had given them the down payments; otherwise, in the Depression, they would not have been able to afford them. Mary immediately went to a secondhand store and looked for a bureau she could refinish. The oak one she liked had a deeply pitted top. She asked the owner if he had a piece of marble to place over it, and he showed her several slabs of old marble hearths. A gray one with a brownish stain near one of the edges was the least damaged. Following instructions in a manual, Mary removed the old finish, and sanded and stained the bureau with a light varnish. Manny took the marble to a monument company and had it cut to fit the top. The bureau was then placed against a livingroom wall under three small windows. On it Mary arranged a row of books and hid the brown stain with a pot of basil, one of many her mother grew for fragrance and good luck.

The mother and Fro admired it. "It makes the room so, so, I don't know, so *nice,*" Fro said.

"It's aristocratic," their mother said.

Fro looked at the bureau from all sides. "I'd really like one too," she sighed.

"'You've got fingernails, scratch yourself,'" their mother said proverbially. "Don't stand around wanting, get busy. Mary will help you."

"We'll go together, and Manny can send one of his trucks to pick it up."

"Oh, good!"

The next day Mary asked Fro about going to the secondhand store. "Oh," Fro said lightly, "Greg said he wouldn't want someone else's used furniture in the house."

"Too bad." Mary lifted her shoulders. She noticed that whenever Fro sat in the room, her gaze often rested on the bureau.

Almost every day the sisters spent the afternoons at their mother's house, drinking coffee and eating honey-nut pastries. While single they had pined for the day when they would have homes of their own and be free from their mother's constant advice, criticism, and proverbs. As soon as they married, their childhood home drew them like a magnet to their mother's kitchen. In the living room their identical twin brothers read comic books and sometimes, almost noiselessly, took the part of the characters in them. They were ten years younger than their sisters and had been partially raised by them. Their father called them the *benaria,* twin lambs.

Even though the mother and her daughters saw each other daily and spoke on the telephone in the mornings and often in the evenings, they still had so much to say—about relatives, the priest, the current Greek school teacher, other people's illnesses and foolishness. At least once or twice a week the sisters helped their mother cook the evening meal, set the table, and afterwards washed and put away the dishes.

Once a week the sisters took turns cooking frugal foods for their two families: spaghetti, bean soup, or chili. They ate in each other's kitchen and afterward played card games like steal the pile and seven up, which Manny complained good humoredly were ladies' games. Usually they ate popcorn and listened to the radio: Amos and Andy, Fibber McGee and Molly, Eddie Cantor, Edgar Bergen, and for a while "Information Please," but Greg often disagreed with the answers and said he would check them out at the public library. Always on Sundays they ate at the mother's heavy oak table in the dining room.

In summer Manny and Greg worked together, put in cement walks, and did small jobs around their houses. "'They're as close as ass and underpants,'" their wives' father said. The brothers-in-law bought the needed supplies from Sears and before they began a job, Greg read the directions carefully. "Come on, Greg," Manny would say. "You're wasting time. Just use common sense." One of their big projects was sanding and painting wooden window frames. Greg was meticulous about keeping the paint off the glass and used a watercolor brush on the adjoining wood. "It's going to be winter before we finish," Manny said. "Just paint them and use a razor blade after. If you have to."

Greg shook his head. "If you're going to do something, do it right. It's gotta be worth our salt."

The twin boys, their brothers-in-law, then in junior high school, watched them silently and followed them about, their eyes eager, as if they were watching a movie. They usually carried comic books with them and when Manny and Greg took time off and drank a beer, the twins sat close together on the porch or grass and read and discussed the comics in soft voices.

The lawnmower the brothers-in-law shared belonged to Greg, who always wiped the blades and oiled the parts after each use. In separate kitchen matchboxes, Greg kept a collection of screws, tap washers, rubber bands, paper clips, and nails separated as to size. He never threw anything away. Manny often drove the two blocks to Greg's house to rummage through the boxes. Greg also collected pennies in Mason jars; two full bottles and a partially filled third one were set on a top kitchen shelf. "You never know when they'll come in handy," he said and quoted a Greek proverb: "Bean by bean the sack is filled."

Greg made pronouncements that Manny told Mary to ignore. "Put the coffee grounds in the sink. They'll take the grease down with them." It was better, Greg said, to leave light globes burning, because more electricity is used up with the constant turning them on and off. "Where do you get these ideas?" Manny asked, laughing.

"Go ahead, laugh, but you'll see I'm right."

Saturdays were like parties. When work was finished and the heat of the day gave way to a balmy airiness touched with the fresh greenness of cut grass, they sat in backyard shade. From the house the scents of baking pastries and brewing coffee came and a front lawn sprinkler whirred pleasantly. The four ate, drank, and told anecdotes about Greek school days, practical jokes, bootlegging, and Greek immigrant buffoons. Greg knew a man who thought you could place orders for the women who modelled clothing in the Sears catalog. Manny had a collection of bootleg stories. He would never have had enough money to attend the university if his mother hadn't kept a still going in her cellar. Manny's mother had outwitted the Feds many times and he laughed long and loudly with each telling. "This one time she hid the whiskey bottles in the thunder jug and then lifted her skirts and sat on it. Boy! You should have seen those Feds make a beeline out of the house!" Greg told Fro that he could have finished college too if his mother had stooped to bootlegging, but thank God she hadn't. His father had sold bootleg whiskey in soda pop bottles, but Greg did not know this.

Mary half-listened to the stories, but she was content in the peacefulness of the backyard, the faint scent of flowers in the cool air, and the sense of well-being. Fro laughed appreciatively when it was Greg's turn to tell one of his anecdotes. In the waning day she gazed at him lovingly. Brilliant sunsets swept over the skies. The talk dwindled, and they sat in the lulling dusk until evening, then night, and unwillingly got up to leave.

On the days Manny and Greg pruned trees and bushes, they used a big truck to haul the cuttings to the dump. The old truck was one of two belonging to Manny's father, who owned the Superior Coal

Company. Manny's father employed two drivers who twice a week drove over a hundred miles south to a cluster of mining towns and returned with loads of coal for his store.

Manny had kept the books for his round, little father since he was a freshman in high school. When he graduated from the university, his father opened the store each morning and took a few bills out of the big, intricately carved cash register. He had bought it in the early twenties when business was good. He then hurried on his short legs out the front door to one of several coffeehouses in Greek Town. There he drank several demitasses of Turkish coffee, read Greek-language newspapers, and argued over the Metaxas dictatorship in Greece. He returned near closing time, opened the cash register to check the day's receipts, and continued his harangue as if Manny were as interested as he in Greek politics. He failed to see that Manny did not care at all about what went on in Greece and in fact kept working on the store's ledgers without once asking a question or acknowledging that he was listening.

Manny's father ate lunch in the Stadium Cafe and daily let everyone know that he did not like dictators: Hitler, Mussolini, or Metaxas. He always sat against a west wall where large pictures of old adversaries, King Constantine and Premier Venizelos, flanked a Class C Board of Health notice: the owner allowed patrons to lift the lids of pots before ordering. Everyone upstairs in the Dionysos Coffeehouse, where Manny's father spent the afternoon playing cards and the board game *barbout,* also knew he hated dictators. Manny's father played with gusto, knowing that the waiter carrying trays back and forth often glanced through the grimy windows with practiced eyes. Below, the city's vice detective patrolled the streets of Greek Town, his stomach bulging over a belt with a big tarnished silver buckle steering him forward. He wore a cowboy Stetson slanted over his right eye. Once in a while Manny's father walked two blocks south to Bill's Pastime Beer Parlor, which was owned by Greg's father. These incursions were instigated by something Manny's father had read in one of two Greek-language newspapers, the royalist *Atlantis* or the liberal *National Herald.*

Greg's gloomy father was a supporter of the dictator Metaxas and had to control himself whenever Manny's father came through the door. Times were hard and the two beers Manny's father drank while pushing his face into Bill's had to be considered. "You're lucky," he told Manny's father once. "People can go without beer, but everyone needs coal to cook." At each parting Manny's father gave his usual judgment of Greece's doom as long as Metaxas was head of the government. "The Greeks need the king," he warned in a thick village dialect with a wag of his index finger. "Otherwise there's chaos!" Greg's father turned a reddish purple and one evening he shouted at his wife, "Greece needs a benevolent dictator! The Greeks need Metaxas to keep order!" He then fell forward, dead, onto the dinner table, overturning a bowl of bean soup.

Greg had hated the beer parlor. "My dad," he said, "never intended to hold on to it. But it was quick money. He had to send money for his sisters' dowries and keep his brother in medical school in Athens. Then one day his partner drew out all the money from the bank and disappeared. Left my dad without a cent. My dad just wasn't lucky."

Greg's father had not owned his store, only leased it, and the beer inventory barely covered his burial expenses. Greg asked Manny to help him get a job. Just before the past election, Manny had given a county commissioner a low bid on coal for the general hospital. This squelched rumors of the commissioner's incompetence and helped him win re-election. At the time Manny knew it was good business; someday the favor would be returned. Fortunately, the bookkeeper for the commissioner's family warehouse had just been caught embezzling funds and Greg got the job keeping books. "Hell o' mighty," Greg said, "those warehousemen are low class and the commissioner isn't much better. He's buddy-buddy with them. This one guy's got him buffaloed." "Well, would you rather be back in your dad's saloon?" Manny asked.

At that time Manny and Greg joined the Kiwanis and met at their Wednesday luncheon meetings. They repeated little stories about the members to Mary and Fro. Greg liked the meetings. "The people are a better type," he said. He was so polite to the president that Manny nudged him after a meeting. "Why are you licking his boots?" he asked. "Don't get the idea they'll ever elect a Greek president or even vice-president of the Kiwanis."

The president put Greg on the committee for the annual Christmas dance. "He likes me," Greg told Fro. Greg never missed a Wednesday meeting but Manny attended less often. When Greg confronted him in a testy voice, Manny said, "I joined thinking it would be good for business. They can't do me any good. Me on the west side, right smack in the middle of those poor families." Manny eventually stopped attending the meetings.

The sisters' orderly, predictable life was disrupted by their giving birth at almost the same time. They cooked double portions of food, the extra one for whichever sister was not well or was up nights with a sick child. They helped their twin brothers with their lessons and tended each other's child when they had doctor's and dentist's appointments. Two years later they again gave birth.

The couples went on as before spending most of their free time together. While Manny and Greg worked on their books during the week, their wives jointly made jam for the children and Greek pastries for their husbands' name days and the great church feast days. On Friday evenings they brought the children to their mother's house, where for two hours she struggled to keep them from annoying her husband. The four ate in an inexpensive Mexican restaurant and once or twice a month Manny's teenage sister cared for all the children while they attended a movie. For these outings the sisters wore their best dresses, inexpensive ones they bought at a Mode o' Day store. Mary removed the chunky buttons and the cloth belt on her beige, long-sleeved coat dress, sewed on flat gray oyster shell buttons, and added a narrow patent leather belt. Fro looked unhappily across the table at Mary's dress.

On Saturdays the brothers-in-law continued to work together on their yards, cutting grass, pruning, planting a few eggplants, zucchini, tomatoes, cucumbers, and several grapevines. About two times a month they met at the Stadium Cafe and ordered the special of the day. This was a change for Greg, whose lunch never varied: roast beef sandwich, apple pie, and a cup of coffee. He sat up stiffly when someone they both knew from Greek school days pulled out a chair and joined them without asking permission or being invited. One wore shirts that were frayed at the sleeves. "I feel sorry for him," Manny said, "trying to sell insurance in this Depression." He always called the agent over and paid for his meal. An attorney who made out wills for the immigrants came in, scanned the room for potential clients, and sometimes sat with them. Several others from the railyards nearby looked happy to see them. Greg was affronted by their black finger-nails. "Hell o' mighty, what's to keep them from cleaning their nails," he grumbled. "Well, don't look at them," Manny said.

"I wish someone in the Kiwanis would offer Greg a good job." Fro shook her head sadly one afternoon and sighed between sips of coffee. "The people in the warehouse are so low class. You know what the secretary said to Greg the other day? She said she wouldn't have an-other child in this Depression and Greg told her, 'You can never be sure about that,' and she said, 'Oh, I'm sure all right. We do it through the rectum.' Can you imagine! A woman talking like that!"

"I was speechless," Mary said to Manny. "It didn't even occur to her that Greg started it."

Sunday was the most important day of the week. The two families ate enormous meals in the wives' childhood home. The house was fresh from Saturday's cleaning, with the lingering sharpness of frank-incense burned the night before to clean out obvious or hidden sins. The mother expected the entire family to sit around her dining room table every Sunday. "Like families should," she often said, appalled at some families who were picking up American ways and taking their children on Sunday excursions. She ordered her daughters about briskly and now they did not seem to mind: "Maria, stir the sauce. Aphrodite," she would not accept the Americanized "Fro," "see that the children don't go near the icon." Their children were more like brothers and sisters than cousins, quarreling, hitting, screaming, but wanting to be together. The twin brothers, the *benaria,* smiled on first seeing their nieces and nephews, then ignored them.

The family dinners suited Manny and Greg. Their own mothers cooked village food, stews and pastas, except on the feast days of the church, when they prepared the traditional specialties: rice and meat wrapped in grape leaves, eggplant *mousaka,* and custard-topped squares of pasta and ground meat. On holidays the young couples often ate two dinners to appease the husbands' families. Greg went grudgingly to his mother's house because he did not like his brothers' wives or his sisters' husbands. Manny saw his father every day, and spoke to his mother several times a week, when she called him about a prophetic dream or some gossip that could blacken the family name. He had been born into a family of sisters and they bored him.

Even though they were living through the Depression Mary and Fro's mother lavished her cooking with butter, the best grade olive oil, and choice meat. It never occurred to the brothers-in-law that she skimped all week to serve the bountiful Sunday dinners. They ate with relish and camaraderie. The parents looked pleased: they knew families with combative brothers-in-law. The father liked to say, "Ask your *bajanakia* about that" or "You *bajanakia* can handle it." After eating, they sat in the living room with their father-in-law, the women bustled about, and the twins played checkers on the carpet, then locked their bedroom door to read their comic books. The children noisily tried to get inside, wanting to point to the cartoon characters with sticky fingers and ask questions.

Manny had a keen memory for details of his childhood and he recalled a scene in his mother's kitchen when he was about fourteen. His mother and a neighbor were drinking coffee and with raised eyebrows and insinuating voices mentioned the birth of the twins and how embarrassed the babies' mother was: "Tsk, tsk, at their age carrying on." Manny had early learned the import of the bed springs' rhythmic squeaking in his parents' bedroom. "Yes, twins happen when there's too much bedroom *daravelli,*" the neighbor said and the two women laughed carefully because Manny was at the sink getting a drink of water. He knew *daravelli* meant too much carousing.

When war intensified in Europe, the men listened to the news on the radio, even while eating. "I hope Roosevelt won't get us into the war," the father said. Manny said Roosevelt was at least doing something for the unemployed. Greg said, "I don't like him. I can't trust any rich guy who inherits money." Manny said lightly, "No, but you'd trust some hide-bound Republican in the Kiwanis who doesn't know his ass from a hole in the ground." The twins sitting on a piano bench nudged each other. By their middle-teen years they were already as handsome as the dark, glossy-haired movie actors who seduced blonde starlets in movies. Leisurely the men smoked, the older man cigars, Manny and Greg cigarettes.

The sisters cleared the table, took squawling babies into back bedrooms in futile attempts to make them take naps, washed dishes, and set the kitchen in order. Mary and Fro left bedraggled, their mother satisfied that she had done her duty to feed and keep the family together. The father retired to his bedroom to take a nap; and Manny and Greg went to one or the other of their houses to listen to the radio or attend a baseball game. Greg did not like sports, but it was an opportunity to get away from the house and the whining children.

Twice they took the twins with them at the prodding of their wives, who in turn had been prevailed upon by their mother: "They've got to do something besides listen to the radio and read those silly comedy books." She had never been successful in forcing them to attend Sunday School or to join the choir, as their sisters had done.

Manny sat between the boys and exhausted himself trying to explain the game to them as they gazed off. He gave them a dollar to get cokes and popcorn. "You're wasting your breath," Greg said. When the twins returned they sat next to each other, at a little distance from Manny and Greg, and after finishing their popcorn took out their comic books.

With the bombing of Pearl Harbor the city came alive. Mary thought of it as a pod of seeds bursting open under the sun. Fro's eyes shone; it was exciting, she said. An arms plant west of the city and several army depots were built. Hungry-looking people moved into town, lived in trailers, filled the streetcars and stores. Troop trains sped into and out of the city. Freight trains chugged past, loaded with army materiel. Butter, sugar, and meat were rationed but the Sunday dinners continued to be lavish. The mother saved her coupons and used a little less meat and more rice in the *dolmadhes*.

The father talked about the military draft. His sons-in-law listened. Mary and Fro looked worried. They were pregnant for the third time. Their father said having three children would keep them safe and the war would be over in a matter of months anyway. He recalled that during the First World War, when he had just received his citizenship papers, he was about to be drafted even though he had three children at the time. It was different then. The United States was now bigger, stronger.

"Well, I'll tell you one thing," Greg said, "soon as the war's over, I'm going to Greece. I'm going to walk all over Marathon."

"Bravo," the mother said.

One Saturday the brothers-in-law were listening to a baseball game and their wives were mediating a quarrel that had errupted among the children in a back bedroom. Manny told Greg about an idea he had. He hadn't mentioned it to Mary yet. "I've been thinking, Greg, we can make a lot of dough with this war going on. The army's going to need the railroads for itself. If we mortgage our houses and cars, we could buy one of those big refrigerated trucks, drive it to California, and bring back fruit and vegetables for the army base and the arms plants. It's a big opportunity."

Greg looked at him, startled. His face turned red. "I wouldn't think of it. I wouldn't jeopardize *my* family. The business goes down the drain and our families are out on the street. No, sir, not me. I think too much of my family's security."

"You'd still have your bookkeeping job to fall back on. This is a real opportunity, Greg."

"No, I can't do it. Hell o' mighty, *no.*"

"Well, I'll go it alone then." Manny had counted on going to the bank with Greg for the loan. His heart gave an extra beat as he thought of walking toward some man seated at a desk looking at papers.

On the front porch steps, later, he wondered where he could get information on putting in a bid at the army base. Probably the best way, he decided, would be to find the quartermaster, who would show him the ropes. Manny went over the scene with Greg several times in his mind. It pricked him: Greg's startled face, the words *I think too much of my family's security* — as if Manny were a prize fool who didn't give a damn about his own wife and children. He thought of the scene often, especially on the long drives to southern California. It was as if it were a special document, folded many times and put away in a decorative box, that he would take out from time to time and look at anew.

For two years Manny and a driver drove the refrigerated truck. His first two bids had been so low he hardly made enough to pay for the gas. But Manny learned quickly. He had a hard time getting sufficient gas coupons at first, but once his proposal and low bids at the army base were accepted, his worries were over. Just as he expected, the railroads' priorities were moving troops and army equipment. He bought a mower and found a neighborhood high school kid to cut the lawn. Manny and Greg were able to see two baseball games together the first summer and none the next. Baseball players had been drafted and women were playing the game. Manny could seldom spare the time even to have lunch with Greg at the Stadium Cafe.

One afternoon Mary and Fro, each with a baby on her lap, were drinking coffee and eating pastries in Mary's kitchen. The older children played Indians and cowboys in the small living room. Fro said, "I don't know how you can stand to have Manny away so much. Don't you miss him?"

Mary thought: she didn't miss Manny at all. He needed as much attention as the children with his old Greek ideas of wives having to wait on husbands. She said, "No, I'm too busy with the children and the house and the yard."

"Aren't you afraid to be alone?"

Mary would not confess that every strange sound kept her awake at night for fear Fro would tell their mother and she would arrive to spend the nights at her house.

"And the children hardly see Manny at all."

"When he's home, we take a lunch up to the canyon. Things like that." Manny would have preferred lounging in his big chair and listening to the radio, but she was insistent.

Fro sighed. "Well, I'm different. I couldn't stand it. Of course, Greg is more the romantic type."

Mary looked at Fro with her mouth slightly open. "I guess," she said to Fro's shy, smiling face, "he takes the name Aphrodite seriously." They both laughed, Fro blushing.

After Mary had settled the children for the night, she sat in a chair next to the radio and listened to the war news. She did not hear much of it because she thought of what she would have liked to have said to Fro: Greg never paid much attention to his children when he was home. Fro had them ready for bed when Greg got home so that the two *romantic types* could spend the evening together in peace. There was a tone of criticism in Fro's words that Mary did not like. Fro used to be complacent, but every now and then some of Greg's manner came out. Greg was angrily critical of people, even of his father-in-law, but in a guarded way: "Well, you know the old man, he's not only from the old school, but the old school from Greece." Then he laughed as if he had made a joke. Mary hoarded Fro's remarks.

In 1943 Manny bought another refrigerated truck and to celebrate took the four of them to the roof of the Hotel Utah. They had an expensive dinner: shrimp cocktails, steaks, and baked Alaska. Black waiters in formal wear and white gloves waited on them. Manny laughed and talked loudly. Mary shushed him several times. "It's a wonderful feeling to be able to celebrate like that," Manny told Mary afterwards at home. "Even having to put up with Fro's silly talk," and he mimicked, "'Mary, do you want to go to the little girls' room?' and that Greg turning to me and saying, 'Well if they're going to the little girls' room, let's go to the little boys' room.' Where do they hear that kind of talk?"

As he undressed, Greg said, "I don't know about 'The M's.' Mary should tell Manny to go slow. He's jumping the gun. Expanding too fast. He should have been satisfied with that one truck. At least waited until he'd paid off the loan on it. He's lucky. So far it's worked out." Fro murmured in agreement with Greg's wisdom.

Manny and Greg happened to meet in the bank one day. Greg was depositing business receipts and Manny was talking to a vice-president. That evening Greg said, "You should have seen Manny. He was wearing a rumpled pair of pants and a shirt without a tie. He looked more like one of his truck drivers than a *big* business man. Could hardly take the time to say hello." Fro pressed Greg's navy blue striped suit more carefully than usual that night.

"I can't believe that Greg," Manny said to Mary. "He was depositing receipts. Something a secretary could do on her lunch hour. He'd just bought a book on some ancient Greek thing and wanted to tell me about it. Hell, you'd think he'd have the sense to know I can't take the time to shoot the bull."

The next day Fro brought her children to Mary's house to play. As they drank coffee, Fro laughed falsely. "Greg said he saw Manny at the bank yesterday. He just smiled and shook his head at Manny's pants."

"Manny doesn't care about clothes."

"Well, you'd think if he's going to the bank—"

"No," Mary interrupted, "Manny doesn't care about clothes."

"Well, Greg always has to look just right. He matches his neckties to his shirts and suits."

"Yes, I've noticed."

A long silence followed. "It's too quiet." Fro jumped up. "We better see what the children are doing."

Mary told Manny about the conversation. "Yeah," Manny snorted, "Greg needs to be dressed up to sit in that warehouse office."

"You could be more careful."

The following year Manny bought another truck and had five by the time Japan surrendered. "Manny's sure been lucky," Fro said.

"Lucky?" Mary repeated. "Manny asked Greg to go in with him and he said no."

Fro moved her shoulders about, a righteous mannerism Mary disliked. "Yes, but he didn't want to take a chance on losing our house and car. Manny was just born lucky I guess and it worked out for him."

"Well, if that's what you think," Mary said and Fro looked off, another new mannerism, of denial, and changed the subject abruptly.

"Why the hell didn't you tell her the romantic Greg couldn't see beyond a nine-to-five job? The goddamn sonofabitch."

Fro complained: "We don't get together like we used to. We used to have so much fun."

Mary said, "Well, Manny doesn't have a nine-to-five job."

Still, the mother's Sunday dinners continued. At the table Greg talked at length on the latest books on ancient Greece he had found during his lunch hour. He had begun speaking precisely and no longer said "hell o' mighty." One Sunday he showed the father a book of ancient Greek sculptures. "Look at them. Beautiful people. Not like the Greeks of today. Look at those faces, those bodies."

"You ever see that head of Socrates?" Manny said. "I'll show it to you. It's in one of my college books. If I can find it. Ugliest mug you ever saw."

The father laughed and lighted a cigar. The twins, in their late teens, no longer called the *benaria* by their father, looked from Manny to Greg with grinning delight. In their bedroom they had stacks of comic books neatly lined on top a chest of drawers. Their favorites were kept in a separate pile. The mother had come to hate the comics, and would have liked to burn them, but she did not dare. She folded her arms across her waist and looked worriedly at Greg's red face. With a show of enthusiasm, she said, "Why don't you leave the book for the boys to look at?" Greg said nothing and took the book with him. He never let one of his books out of his sight.

The twins showed a little interest in a diorama Greg was making. He extended the dining room table with the extra leaves, covered it with newspapers, and began to construct a scale model of the Acropolis and the marketplace, the *agora,* at its base. He had seen a drawing in the *National Geographic* and using it for a model began a year-long project of building the Parthenon on top of a clay hill. On the desert west of the city, he gathered pieces of rocks and bits of sagebrush in imitation of thyme and pushed them carefully into the clay. He then sifted a fine dirt lightly over the clay.

At the family dinners Greg dotted his talk with words that left everyone, including his children, looking at the ceiling and walls. Fro listened attentively, smiling as the words came out: Ionic, Doric, propylaea, metopes, tympanum. He sighed and shook his head: if only he could have real Pentelic and blue Eleusian marble, but someday, when he went to Greece, he could bring some back and redo the diorama. His face turned a dark red as he castigated Lord Elgin for taking whatever he wanted from the Acropolis to England.

Greg detailed each step of his construction. For the columns of the propylaea, the entrances leading to the Acropolis, he bought a small slab of marble from a tile company and had it cut into lengths. He treated the marble with acids to age them. The twins watched for a while, but Greg's sullen silence and the Mozart filling the house were too much for them and they escaped to the front porch with their comic books. Two months later Greg was ready to begin on the Parthenon. He cut pieces of white construction cardboard and carved wooden dowels into columns. All this time the dining room table could not be used. The family dinners were eaten in the kitchen and when guests were present, Fro set up card tables in the crowded living room. "I'll be glad when Greg's finished with his project," Fro said and smiled, shaking her head.

"So when he's finished," Mary said, "where's he going to put it?"

"I don't know." Fro frowned and looked at the dining room table with the white cardboard, glue, scissors, exacto knives, the half-finished Parthenon on top of the Acropolis, all carefully laid out and taking up the entire space of the table. "And he still has to do the marketplace." Suddenly she raised her head and laughed liltingly, as if to dispel any thoughts of displeasure Mary might have noticed. "But he loves doing it so much. No matter how grouchy he comes home from work, he turns on his record player and goes to work as happy as can be."

While Greg was working on his diorama, which he decided would include the Temple of Athena Nike, the Erechtheum, and the Theater of Dionysos, Manny bought land in a wooded area far out of the city and hired an architect to draw plans for a house. Fro told Greg she wished they had the money for a bigger house in a better neighborhood now that the children were older and bringing friends home. Greg pointed his finger at Fro. "You know what's going to happen to them?" He no longer called Mary and Manny "The M's." "Pretty soon their kids will grow up and be gone and the two of them'll be stuck in a great big barn."

"We don't have room for anything, not even bookcases."

It was true. On either side of the brick fireplace in the living room the shelves were crammed tightly with Greg's books on ancient Greece. "As soon as I finish my project," Greg said, "I'll build a playroom." The diorama took another year to complete. Greg was not satisfied with leaving it unadorned. He hired a sculptor from the university's art department to carve miniature figures on the metopes and tympanum and to carve the caryatids, the maidens who supported the roof of the Erechtheum.

Two years later he was ready to build the playroom. The diorama would be set up there. With the help of the warehouse electrician and plumber, Greg built a narrow room across the back of the house. He was so meticulous that it took almost as long as making his diorama.

On one wall he built bookshelves that over the months began to fill up with books about ancient Greeks and his new interest, classical music recordings. When the room was finished, he was appalled to find that for all his careful measurements, his diorama was slightly too wide and the dining room door and casings had to be removed first. One-fourth of the playroom was taken up by the table on which the diorama was placed. Next, Greg had a square glass case made for what he called his masterpiece and warned the children against throwing anything in the room. The glass could break and ruin his Acropolis. After a while the children played in their bedrooms as they had before the playroom was built.

When the war ended, the church resumed its Twenty-Fifth of March celebrations on the anniversary of the Greek revolution of 1821 that freed most of Greece from the Turks. Greg was appointed chairman of the dinner, which surprised the family. "One of two things," Manny said. "He's taken everybody's ears off with his ancient Greek talk, or no one else wants the job." Greg worked on the arrangements with uncharacteristic enthusiasm. He had always criticized anything connected with the church. Although the women's church organization, the Philoptochos, was as usual in charge of table decorations, flowers, menu, and the program, Greg held several meetings with their committee to tell them what he wanted. He bought a new suit for the occasion.

"Who's the speaker?" Manny asked Greg at a Sunday dinner.

"I got in touch with that professor at the University. Dr. Harkinson. He teaches ancient Greek."

Manny groaned. "What's he going to tell us? The same old crap about how great the ancient Greeks were?"

Greg bristled. "Just sit there and you'll learn something."

"Yeah? Me and the bananas who just came over? Well," he conceded, "You have to hand it to them. They worked like donkeys when they first got here and now they've got restaurants and *souvlaki* places all over town." Greg looked away, his face stonily set, as if Manny were telling him in a sly way that he was a failure.

"They're all money hungry," Fro said petulantly. "Not only them, but the Tsandourises and the Paliotakises, all that clique making money for the first time in their lives. Living it up. Las Vegas. Designer dresses."

The mother hurriedly asked what would be served.

"The Philoptochos women wanted the usual, roast lamb, pilafi, *pites,* but I told them no, let's do something different."

The mother frowned, looking puzzled. "But, Gregory, those are our foods. We always serve them at our gatherings."

"Not this time. I decided on steak, baked potato, green beans, and salad."

"No baklava?"

"Cake and ice cream. We're in a rut, and I'm getting us out of it."

"Well, good luck," Manny said with a sardonic smirk.

"It'll be something to remember," Greg said, looking at Manny with a long, dark stare. "I told that new priest to keep his prayer short."

"If you attended church affairs you'd know he does," Mary said.

"Well, there's something about him I don't like," Greg said. "I just don't trust him. Why would anyone in his right mind want to be a priest?"

Manny said, in a low voice so that he would not shock the father and mother, "You're practically an atheist, so what do you care?" Greg leaned far across the table, "When was the last time you went to church? At least I go to funerals."

Manny snorted. The twins looked at each other archly and smiled. "The priest doesn't even know where Marathon is," Greg said huffily. "He thought it was close to Sparta."

As was his custom, the father bought banquet tickets for the family. The youngest children were left at home with sitters; the mother, father, the twins, Mary, Manny, and the four older grandchildren sat at one long table. Greg and Fro sat at the head table with the guest speaker and his orchid-decorated wife, the priest, and the committee members with their wives. Greg had learned that the guest speaker's wife was always given a corsage and ordered one for Fro. Smiling, eyes sparkling, Fro looked over the crowd, her orchid corsage identical to the one worn by the speaker's wife.

The hall was crowded with parents, children, and grandchildren. Many were new immigrants who had come from Greece after the war.

Even though the men had almost uniformly shaved off their manly mustaches and their wives had had their salon-styled hair teased and puffed, like the women in the musical *My Fair Lady,* they were easily recognizable as immigrants. Several worked for Manny and according to their old-country custom, came over to greet him.

Greek and American flags stood upright in stands on either side of a small stage. Between them a poster of the Parthenon and a large picture of the current Greek school students were displayed on easels. In the din, layers of blue tobacco smoke floated above the tables. The scents of meat cooking, wine, and tobacco were pungent. Children fled the tables, ran around, and were brought back by older brothers and sisters. The priest, one of the American-born from the first graduating class of the theological school in Pomfret, Connecticut, gave the prayer and wished them good appetite in both English and Greek.

All heads at the father and mother's table turned toward the young priest, who delved into his plate with the good appetite he had wished for the gathering. The mother thought of asking him to get the twins involved in church activities; the father thought that he would set him straight as to the various church factions and let him know which one he should side with—his; the sisters would tell him what was wrong with the Sunday school; and Manny that he had connections who could sell him a house cheap.

Blue smoke billowed out of the kitchen into the hall. Greg and the committee members hurried into it and after a few minutes returned. The smoke hovered over the tables and women began touching their stiffly set hair and mumbling. The young people's organizations began serving the dinners.

Flakes of char had settled on the steaks. At some tables people were finished eating while others had not yet been served. The steaks were tough. Mary and her mother cut the meat into small pieces for the children. The baked potatoes in gold foil were not cooked enough, and the green beans were unsalted. Murmurs began and increased into complaints. A portly man with his napkin trailing from a pudgy hand walked over to the church president and, scowling, said something. The president lifted his shoulders to signify he had had nothing to do with the food. The dessert came eventually, cake soaked in melted ice cream. Manny said, loudly, to a young man serving the dessert, "I'll give you two dollars if you'll bring us hot coffee now." Mary told him to be quiet.

The president of the church stood up and after hitting his water glass ten or more times got the gathering's attention. Several immigrant mothers in black went on hissing their gossip. The president was a handsome attorney in his forties. He introduced everyone at the head table. He called the professor's wife a lovely lady while she preened, gray-haired, blue eyes glinting behind harlequin eyeglasses. He then lauded the speaker and said he wished he'd had the opportunity to take the professor's course when he was a student. He'd heard from others what a great class it was. "Boring as hell," someone at the table behind the family said. The president pointedly mentioned that Greg had headed the dinner committee.

The professor gave the usual speech about ancient Greece, the age of Pericles, beacon of civilization, the basis of Western culture, and so on. They should be proud, the professor said, to be descended from that glorious, noble race. Manny grew increasingly restless, drank his water and Mary's, and whispered to his oldest child, a boy who was just as restless as he was. From across the hall Greg frowned at him.

The applause shook the windows. When it subsided, Manny said in Greek to his father-in-law, "We're supposed to be celebrating the Greek revolution against the Turks. Every year those fools at the head table bring in some outsider to tell us how great the ancient Greeks were. We should just dance the old songs of the revolution and forget about these Americans who don't know a damn thing about what we're celebrating."

His father-in-law nodded, but said, "It's a way of showing respect for the Americans."

"Bull shit," Manny said, but not too loud.

Boys and young men in the pleated kilts of the *evzones* then danced in a circle, jumping, twisting, stamping. The professor's wife laughed so hard the orchid on her lace-covered shoulder shook precariously.

On their way out of the hall, the mother said to her old husband, "Why does Gregory have to be so stubborn? He's a crooked stick. We should have had *dolmadhes* and lamb like always."

"Everything he says and does has 'neither nose nor ass,'" the father said as he turned on the car's ignition.

Greg caught up with Manny. "What did you think of the speech? Satisfied now?"

"This is the last time I'm coming to these so-called March Twenty-Fifth celebrations!"

"Well, maybe it was a little slow getting the plates on the table."

"Yeah, the food couldn't have been worse. But I'm talking about that ancient Greek crap!"

"Now, see here, Manny, you heard the clapping. Everybody loved it."

"Tell it to my elbow."

Manny never sat through another March Twenty-Fifth celebration and Greg, who continued to criticize every church activity, did not miss a single one the rest of his life.

Greg and Fro did not attend the next family dinner. The mother called Fro again and again until she agreed that they would come the following Sunday. They came, Greg eating eagerly, as if he had long been deprived of nourishing food. Manny, half-forgetting his outburst after the church celebration, talked throughout the dinner and only remembered it when he directed a remark to Greg and was answered stiffly.

Not long after the celebration, Manny took his estimator to a Greek restaurant owned by an immigrant. The walls were painted a bright sky-blue, the color of the Greek flag. Pictures of the Acropolis, the Parthenon, the Temple of Zeus, and Delphi were placed about the walls. They sat in a shiny new red vinyl booth. Manny ordered for both of them: lamb *kampana* and Greek salad.

"Maybe I should have a sandwich," the small, bald estimator said.

"It's lamb in tomato sauce. It won't kill you to try it. And if you don't like the feta cheese in the salad, I'll eat it." Manny was pleased to see that the booths were filled.

The estimator scraped most of the tomato sauce from the lamb and took tentative bites of it. Manny stopped eating and listened. In the noise was a familiar voice—Greg's. He moved to the edge of the booth and looked toward the front of the restaurant, where Greg was talking to the owner who stood behind the cash register. Manny had noticed the first time he had eaten in the restaurant that the pudgy owner kept the nails of his little fingers long. Mary had read a folklore account that said this was a Greek provincial custom among men to show they did not work with their hands. The owner was listening with a patient nodding while Greg talked fast in Greek. Manny heard the words *Marathon* and *ancient Greece*. Later he told Mary about it. "What do you make of that Greg? He won't give the guys we went to Greek school with the time of day and he sits and talks to this import about ancient Greece. Talks the ears off this character who runs to Las Vegas every chance he gets."

"You figure him out."

The house Manny built became the center of the family's activities. The mother was forced to admit she could no longer cook the Sunday dinners and in comparison with Manny's wide, two-story house hers now looked shrunken. The children ran over the sweeps of lawn and into the encircling woods screaming in delight and fear. Greg in his immaculate suit always brought a bottle of *retsina,* which the women refused to drink, always lighted the barbecue pit, and offered to carve the meat. He performed all these tasks with authority, yet since the March Twenty-Fifth fiasco, he continued to be aloof and cool to Manny. At the table he argued with the children over the correct meaning and pronunciation of words. He had begun using the dictionary a lot, his children said.

In old khaki pants and a sportshirt that was unbuttoned at the neck and showed his undershirt, Manny sat with the old father and talked business and politics. The twins, now college students, looked about expectantly, waiting. They whispered to each other often. Mary and Fro sometimes talked about their never having shown any interest in girls. They had no friends. They went everywhere together, which helped because they then needed only one car. The mother was beginning to press her daughters about finding them wives. She brought the subject up to Manny, who patted her on the back and said, "If they don't have the urge, no one can give it to them." To Mary he said, "They should go to a monastery." The twins, though, had never been interested in attending church, even though the current youthful priest had dutifully invited them to a slide lecture on his visit to Saint Catherine's monastery on Mount Sinai. They had a new consuming interest; they went to garage sales and bought old comic books. They looked in newspaper want ads for the addresses and cruised through neighborhoods for signs taped to light posts. Finding a Captain Midnight and Mr. Ming among the junk made them giddy.

As soon as they finished eating, Manny stacked several records on his new phonograph console. The records were Greek folk songs, most of them from the era of the Greek revolt against the Turks. The mother and father leaned back in comfortable, soft-cushioned chairs and listened, thinking of their villages.

"Mary, doesn't Manny have any classical records?" Fro said in the kitchen.

"Yes, but he prefers the old Greek songs."

Manny had a sizeable collection of operas, but Mary would not say so. Manny had played the clarinet in his high school band and liked all kinds of music: jazz, hillbilly, western, and Caruso records his mother had ordered from the Atlas company in New York many years ago.

"Why is it when the family comes to dinner, you dress more sloppy than usual?" Mary asked Manny.

At one family dinner, Greg expounded on olive oils. "I wouldn't buy any olive oil except the first pressing. You can tell it by the dark green color."

"Aaa," Manny said, "it's too strong. I don't like it." From then on he insisted that Mary buy only light-colored olive oil.

When the children were in high school, Mary went back to the university to get a Masters degree in English. Fro got work as a secretary. She wanted to buy her children a car. All of the children in both families had small jobs in summer and on Saturdays, Manny's three and Greg's oldest at the trucking company and Greg's other two at McDonalds.

"You're lucky you don't have to work and can do what you want," Fro said.

"You never cared about school. You never cared enough to finish."

"Well, if I had the money, there are other things I'd do."

"I'm sick of that self-pitying talk of hers," Mary told Manny. "Every conversation we have turns into I have money and she doesn't. The next time she brings it up, I'm going to tell her it's not my fault."

"Don't waste your time. It'll go in one ear and out the other. She's like Greg's echo. They've both got that same look on their faces. You know what I mean?"

"Yes, petulant."

Greg and Fro's children complained to their parents: their cousins had new cars, not secondhand ones; they had new outfits all the time. The complaint of new outfits was untrue. Fro knew it, but she spent all her paycheck on her children. When the late 'fifties fad for circular skirts was in vogue, she sewed ten of them for her oldest daughter to wear over bouffant petticoats.

Greg talked a great deal at the family dinners about his father, how well read he had been, that he had loved classical music and had a big collection of books—although these had somehow disappeared. Neither Manny nor Mary could remember seeing these signs of culture. Mary did recall that after Greg's father had died, his mother brought her mother a letter from Greece to read and had written a reply for her. Her mother had said afterward that Greg's mother had been secretive about it. "Why wouldn't she have her own children write the letter?" Mary's mother had marvelled at the mystery.

"Would such a cultured man marry a village woman who couldn't read or write?" Manny said. "Some more of Greg's bull."

Something unspoken, like the stale remains of tobacco smoke after the smokers were long gone, took root in Greg's family: Manny's family had the money, but they had the culture. Manny was successful because he was lucky. There was even a slight, almost imperceptible tone that the money had come not quite honestly. The mother and father felt it too. The father looked bored when Greg talked about the philosophers. Greg quoted Aristotle often. Complaining about a warehouse man whose receipts he had untangled without thanks, he huffed: "Like Aristotle said, 'What grows old? Gratitude.'"

Afterwards, Manny told Mary, "He never did thank me for getting the commissioner to give him a job."

Mary wondered if she should tell Manny something she had recently read. After a moment she said, "I read an article that listed mistakes Aristotle had made. He even thought men had more teeth than women."

Manny mused on this. "Hmm," he said and again, "hmm."

At the next family dinner Greg said, "There's no one to equal Aristotle. Everything he said has been proved later by scientists."

"Oh, yeah." Manny looked at Greg without smiling. "He said men had more teeth than women. Why didn't he count them before saying something so asinine?"

Greg glared at Manny, said nothing more, and never again mentioned Aristotle at the family dinners. There were few family gatherings after that. The sisters' children were in college and were involved with their own friends and seldom saw each other. The mother and father stepped into a foggy terrain, into doctor's and dentist's appointments, surgeries, and failing eyesight. Mary and Fro took turns taking their parents to their appointments, talked with doctors, boiled chicken and meat for soups. Their days began with telephone conversations about the day's schedule—who would take food, who would drive the parents to their medical tests, and who would see that the twins, long out of college and bookkeepers for the state insurance fund, had clean and ironed clothing.

The couples had grayed and lost the last vestiges of youthfulness. Manny was completely bald, with a paunch, and looked like his father at the same age. Greg had kept his weight down, but arthritis forced him into a heavy, dogged walk. All had their own problems and were tired of hearing the mother talk about her twin sons.

She hated to die, the mother said, "and leave the boys unmarried. You must find brides to take care of them." The boys were now past forty and the mother was frantic at not having seen them with wedding crowns on their heads.

The parents died within the same year and left each of their children fifty thousand dollars. Manny put Mary's share into Treasury bills. He told Greg what he had done. "I think they're the safest investment," Manny said. Greg said nothing. "He's so secretive, I'd like to push his face in," Manny said.

The twins remained in the family house and the sisters spent Saturdays cleaning it while their brothers watched television. The twins had belatedly become interested in sports and this combined with their work in the state capitol and going to garage sales kept their days filled. They watched the football, baseball, and basketball games with wide-open eyes. The twins were now the sisters' main concern. Greg and Fro had gravitated to Greg's family and spent Thanksgiving, Christmas, and Easter with them. Mary and Manny kept the holidays for their children and the twins. "We'll eat with your family," they told Mary smilingly. They did not say aloud that Greg's family had too many unmarried distant nieces. It had always been interesting to Mary that the twins never seemed to discuss with each other what they would or would not do. One or the other would make a statement and the other would nod.

For all of Mary and Fro's attempts to find wives for them, the twins looked blankly at their suggestions: "Do you remember the Pappas sisters? They used to sing in the choir. Why don't you boys ask them out? Take them to a movie. Then you could come here after for cake and ice cream. Or you could take them to dinner somewhere nice." The twins merely stared and said nothing. Mary asked Fro to invite them to the church's Twenty-Fifth of March celebration and casually introduce them to the Pappas sisters and the daughter of their friend Kallie Gerondakis. The twins shook their heads. They started dropping off their laundry at a laundromat and their shirts at a cleaners. They found a cleaning woman. "They're getting more finicky," Mary told Manny. "The goddamn goofs," he said. Still, Mary and Fro watched over them. Every Sunday they ate at one or the other of their houses, then went home to watch *Sixty Minutes* and whatever followed.

In the middle 'seventies Manny and Mary made arrangements to go to Greece. Fro would keep an eye on the twins, although they no longer wanted to leave their house. They had a routine they did not want disturbed. "They're getting eccentric," Mary told Manny. "They were eccentric the day they were born," Manny said.

Manny was reluctant about leaving his business. With a pretense at humor, Fro said, "Greg's the one who should be going. *If* he had the money. He knows all about Greece. He's always wanted to go to all the famous places in ancient Greek history. He knows exactly how Marathon would look."

"Uh huh," Mary said.

"Why didn't you tell her Greg could be going just as well as us if he didn't spend all his money on those damn ancient Greek books and classical music? He spent a fortune on that Acropolis thing."

"And Fro spending every cent on her children. And their kids take it all for granted."

Greg spent every evening and his lunch hour going over the details of the Lion gate of the house of Atreus, their treasury, the Olympic stadium, the various oracles, and so forth, so that when the travelers returned he would contrive to corner Manny and show off his vast knowledge and Manny's ignorance. "I'll go there yet," he told Fro.

"We're just not a family anymore," Fro lamented to Mary, with a tinge of criticism in her sighing voice. "We don't get together anymore. The children bump into each other in restaurants or skiing. What would Mama say?"

Mary and Fro still telephoned each other often; together they cleaned their parents' graves, stopped at each other's house for coffee but never mentioned their husbands. The twins had begun going to the Little America restaurant every Sunday for turkey dinner. They took early retirement and spent their days puttering about their house and yard. Their hair had thinned and grayed. They were round shouldered and even though they were still slender, they had an identical roundish protrusion low on their abdomen, like a fallen womb.

Without the supervision of their brothers' house, the sisters had little to say to each other. They asked about the children, but hid their worries with smiles. Fro's oldest child had dropped out of college in his sophomore year, and her two daughters had made what to Fro seemed mediocre marriages. She often thought that if they had money, her daughters could have attracted better-off husbands. Mary kept quiet about her daughter's cancer, her one son's refusal to go into Manny's business, and the younger son's living with a divorcee and her two children.

"What'd Fro have to say?" Manny would ask after Mary put down the telephone receiver.

"Not a thing."

"He never did get elected an officer of the Kiwanis. Stayed in just to spite me."

"What'd Mary say about the tycoon?" Greg would ask.

"Not a thing."

"He was plain sloppy. Always borrowing things and then I'd have to go get them back." This had happened twice, once with a screwdriver and another time with a rake.

"I'll bet Greg invested that fifty thousand Fro got from her parents and lost his shirt," Manny said. "That's why he never got to walk all over the plain of Marathon. The goddamn fool. If he had put it in Treasury bills. Ah well."

"We weren't good enough for Manny after he made money," Greg said.

One morning a restlessness forced Mary to look about for something to do. Her cleaning woman would not be coming until the following morning; she decided to clean out the basement storage room. In a dusty cardboard box among battered stuffed animals and children's books, she found an old scrapbook she and Fro had kept when they were teenagers. It was filled with newspaper clippings of brides they had known and of lodge and church programs. The yellowed newspaper clippings reminded Mary of evenings in the 'thirties spent cutting, pasting, talking, laughing. Sixty-five years ago; with the muted surprise of the old, she thought of the number of years that had passed. She thought of Fro, probably alone, perhaps watching television, while Greg rummaged through his books on ancient Greece and gazed at his diorama. With the scrapbook in her arms she hurried up the basement stairs and telephoned Fro. The line was busy. Mary dusted off the scrapbook, forgot her cleaning, and drove to Fro's house.

After the children had grown up and no longer brought mud and dirt into their houses, the sisters used their front, rather than their back, doors when visiting. On that day branches of pruned rose bushes lay across the front sidewalk. Mary parked at the curb and walked up the driveway to the back of the house. She was startled to see the old grape arbor held up, not with old posts, but with marble columns, muddied at their bases. Immediately she remembered having seen on television years ago an old mansion of neo-classical design being torn down to make way for an insurance building. People were picking up whatever they could carry. Manny had said, "I'll bet Greg was the first one there." Mary gazed at the columns sadly. Fro had never said anything about them.

She rang the doorbell and Fro came to the door. Her drawn-down face pulled upward with a quick, happy smile and her eyes within their wrinkled lids looked at Mary excitedly. Mary felt a stab in her chest. Fro made coffee and they looked at the scrapbook and exclaimed over the past. Greg came in once, greeted Mary perfunctorily, and left the room. When she arrived home, Manny was watching a baseball game on television. Mary said nothing to him about the marble columns.

Greg died first. He left instructions that his body be taken to Greece for burial as close to the plain of Marathon as possible. "Yes," Manny said, "the dirt is better over there." Greg's body was kept in the funeral home, waiting for Fro or the children to take it to Greece. Two years passed and it still lay in the mortuary refrigerator. Fro often wanted to ask Mary if she would go with her to take Greg's body back. She wanted to vent her anger at Greg for putting such a demand on her and using up money that should have gone to the children. She could not do it and never gave a hint of her anger. She would not ask.

As soon as Greg died, Manny went back to using dark green olive oil.

IF
I
DON'T
PRAISE
MY
HOUSE

For the first time since her husband Bill died more than a year before, Anna Goursis sat on the king-sized bed they had shared until his last months. At one end of the room was a mirrored wall. About a decade ago she had had the mirror installed to make the room seem larger— although Bill had said it was plenty large and was just her usual piddling around the house. At the same time she had a wide opening made at the other end leading into the adjacent room, her daughter's until she had married. Anna called it her dressing room. In the 'thirties movies she had loved, actresses had just such dressing rooms filled with glamorous clothing. She and her friends would then come out of the exhilarating make-believe on the screen and have to walk past unemployed men shuffling along, spoiling the bliss. "You'll need that room when the kids come back for a visit," Bill had said, but she had insisted. Anna was remembering him more often lately. She looked at the silent telephone on the night stand next to the bed.

With a deep sigh she glanced at the Persian rug and then at the door leading into the hall. At one side of the door was an icon of John the Baptist wearing animal skins and holding a staff. Her decorator at the time had several icons on display and suggested that with Anna's Greek background it would be a good touch for the bedroom. No one on either side of the family was named John, but the icon went well with the beige and brown color scheme. Also, the decorator had pointed out, the blue of the icon's sky and the flowers in the Persian rug were the exact same shade.

Next to the icon were the closed folding doors of the closet where Bill's clothing had hung. She had given the suits, pants, coats, everything to the Disabled American Veterans: they had telephoned that their truck would be in her neighborhood. (She wondered later if they read the obituaries and called family members after a suitable period had passed.) Before the DAV called, she had thought of asking the church receptionist, an aging woman with black-lined eyelids, to send someone to pick up the clothing for the elderly parishioners living on Social Security. There had been talk about the program. When Anna was much younger, she had twice spoken with the secretary, when making arrangements for her parents' funerals. The secretary had annoyed her — talking, chewing gum, no respect for the dead. Thinking about the secretary and having to make an appointment with a church volunteer to come to the house — and of course she would have to offer him coffee or a Coke and listen to boring talk — no, it was too much bother, she had thought. She looked at the telephone on the bedside table, lifted the receiver, and heard the dial tone. The telephone had not rung for three days. She gave it a disgruntled look.

She looked again at the folding doors. They were built of pale birch; the grain of the wood made interesting patterns, long, feather-like, each centered with a swirling round nucleus. Suddenly two of them became eyes looking at her. Prickings chilled her cheeks. She stopped breathing, then jumped up, hurried into the yellow bathroom, and turned on the gold-plated spigots in the shape of flying dolphins. Her fingers shook slightly as she picked up a small brush and carefully probed her four-carat diamond ring. The brush was one Bill had used on his electric shaver. She had found it after emptying his drawers and thought it would be the right size to clean her rings. Her breathing now came steadily and she scoffed at herself for thinking she had seen eyes in the wood paneling.

After rinsing the ring and drying it, she placed it on her finger and lifted it toward the light. Bill had shrugged his shoulders, balked at buying such a large ring; her two-and-a-half carat was just fine — maybe a new setting. Mike Hatumbis had bought his wife a four carat, she had answered, and that settled it. She got the four-carat ring and had hoped Bill would not get close enough to Tessie Hatumbis to see that her diamond was really no more than a three carat, if that. Anna lowered her hand, thinking of Tessie and her husband, a cousin of Bill's, laughing together at something — Tessie, whose father, a limping, morose man who had worked for Anna's own father, now sporting a three-carat diamond ring.

She looked at the diamond again. Her daughter Christie had talked back to her once, about the ring: "Can't you leave Dad alone? You're always nagging him." Christie had immediately apologized, but still she had said it. Anna stood motionless for several seconds. A dryness, as if she had been in a dust storm, passed down her throat and settled in her chest.

She walked out of the bathroom, still examining her ring to see if she had cleaned it thoroughly, and past the birch doors without looking at them. Just as she was about to enter the dressing room, she stopped. Turning her head, she gazed at the telephone. Then quickly, afraid she might change her mind, she walked over to it and dialed Christie's number. She settled herself on the bed. The telephone rang once, twice, three times and she thought sadly: she's not home. Christie answered breathlessly. "Oh, hi, Mom. I was going to call you later."

"Oh? I thought I'd call *you* because I haven't heard a word from you in three days."

"Has it been three days? I've been spending so much time over at Debbie's. The new baby is so cute, but he's got colic really bad."

"I know all about colic. I remember it very well. Both you and Lee had it. I fed you bottles of chamomile." Anna's mother had brought the herb and brewed it. The truth was it hadn't helped at all, but she couldn't, of course, have told her mother that.

"Well, what I was going to tell you, Mom, is that with Debbie's new baby and the other two kids sick with colds, let's not have a big Easter dinner this year. Let's make it simple."

"What do you mean simple?"

"I mean I haven't the time to make *dolmadhes* and Easter bread and you shouldn't either."

"I don't know what kind of Easter that would be. Anyway Easter is forty days away. Things will settle down by then."

"I'm too tired. Just too tired, Mom."

For a moment Anna thought she should send her cleaning woman over to Debbie's house. She wouldn't offer. Debbie wasn't that appreciative of her grandmother, although she was nicer than her sister Samantha. "I just don't know what your grandmother would say—us having a simple Easter dinner like the Americans. We'll talk about it some other time. I've got an appointment." Anna didn't want Christie to know she had decided to attend the senior citizen's luncheon at the church. Christie had been trying to convince her to become active in the church programs for a long time.

Anna put down the receiver, but kept sitting on the bed. She looked at the telephone. The call had been short, unsatisfactory. Suddenly she did something she had never done before. She telephoned her son Lee at his office. She was afraid as she dialed that he would not be there. Washington, D.C. was two hours ahead in time. When his secretary said he was in his office, she felt buoyed. "What's up, Mom?" Lee said. "Is something wrong?"

"No. I just hadn't heard from you and I had a feeling I should call."

"I called last week."

"Yes, I know." He had never failed to make his weekly call, usually to advise her to go on a cruise: "Take trips. Spend the money while you can still get around," and Christie echoed him. "Well, it was just a feeling. How is everyone?" She always said *everyone,* which would include his wife, without having to speak her name. Almost thirty years ago the woman had told Anna she was bossy. After his brief recital of his children's and grandchildren's activities, they said goodbye. She thought: he hasn't invited me to visit his family for years. In department stores and restaurants, women she knew often mentioned visiting their children and she had to stand and listen in silence.

She stood up quickly and walked into the dressing room. Her clothing hung in meticulous order, at one side a row of blouses and shirts, next to them a row of skirts and suits, which she never failed to press as soon as she took them off, and across, separated by a wide, three-paneled, full-length mirror, a row of dresses and another of jackets and coats. Hat boxes lined a top shelf and several long, three-tiered metal frames held her collection of shoes, some as much as twenty years old. Her granddaughter Debbie had made a face over the shoes and asked why she kept the ones that were out of style. "You never know when they'll come back in style," she had said pointedly, trying to encourage Debbie to be frugal and at the same time criticize her for being a spendthrift, like all young people. They hadn't grown up in the Depression. Anna had been lucky: her family hadn't really suffered like Tessie's and other girls of their age.

She had already decided the night before what she would wear to Saint Basil's senior citizens' monthly luncheon. She had never attended any of the luncheons, had never given them the least attention, but in last week's church bulletin she read the notices she usually passed over. She read everything now that came in the mail, circulars, catalogs, charity requests, and postcards with pictures of lost or kidnapped children and, underneath, the words *Have you seen me?* The luncheon, the bulletin said, would signal the beginning of Lent and would be meatless; bingo would follow. It would be the last luncheon until after Easter.

She thought of Holy Week with an interest she had not felt for years. After her mother died, she attended only the Great Friday and Great Saturday services, but this Holy Week she would go to all the liturgies, day and evening. She might even go to the Friday evening Salutation liturgies of Lent. For forty days she would have something to do.

Now she was unsure of her choice for the luncheon, the black suit with beige silk blouse and tie that hid some of her wrinkled throat. She sniffed, annoyed with herself: she should have had a facelift while

Bill was still alive. He would have taken her to the hospital and home and seen that she had what she needed. It was also the money. Bill hadn't left as much as she had expected, and although she had more than enough with the bonds, his insurance, and her Social Security, the eight or ten thousand for a facelift now seemed an enormous amount. When Christie and Lee talked about cruises, she didn't want to tell them that she had become a little worried about spending so much money—she didn't know how much was enough. Also, it would hurt her pride if they knew that even thinking about taking a plane and going anywhere alone frightened her. She wasn't sure she would like being on a ship and getting too close to people anyway. On a cruise people would think of her the way she used to think of widows and divorced women—as injured, not quite whole without their men.

Anna took out the black suit. It was the right weight for early spring. She looked at it a few seconds and returned it to its allotted space. A dress would be better, she decided, then she could wear her mink coat. The mink always made her feel better. Lately it even gave her confidence; she had lost much of it after Bill died.

Anna thought of calling someone, perhaps Tessie. How could she put it? She could say, "Tessie, I have an appointment downtown at two and I thought I'd stop at church for the senior citizens' luncheon first. It'd be nice to see some of the old faces." She looked into the closet at the long mirror and saw her despairing face. She could not call Tessie. She hadn't had anything to do with her or any of the women in the Daughters of Penelope for a long time. She and Bill had become involved with people in their own business circles, only a few of them Greek Americans. The men Bill had kept up with since childhood, the ones he had gone with to public school and afterwards to Greek school and on to the university, had died, except for one who had Alzheimers, and another who never left his house. Yearly trips to Las Vegas and dinners at the country club had stopped and after a few luncheons, the widows drifted away to their children and grandchildren—and perhaps to other friends.

Anna buttoned on a dark blue silk dress and looked at herself in the mirror. As her doctor said, she was well preserved for a seventy-two-year-old woman. The dress was just a little tight at the waist, but she would be sitting down and no one would notice it. Her hair looked good. She'd had it freshly tinted and set the day before. She examined her face carefully: if she smiled a little the sagging on either side of her mouth was not so noticeable.

She closed the closet doors and opened the top dresser drawer where she kept her gloves, handkerchiefs, and jewelry box. At the back of the drawer was a framed picture turned face downward. She picked up a pair of lightweight, black kid gloves. She did not wear gloves anymore but carried them. "Ladies always carry gloves," she had told Christie, who laughed a little and said, "Samantha tells me no one says 'ladies' anymore. We're supposed to say 'women.'"

Anna reached for the picture and looked at it. It had been there since Christmas: Christie, seated, her husband next to her, and standing behind them their son and his wife, Debbie and her husband, and Samantha—snippy girl, not yet married and probably wouldn't be at the rate she was going. ("No one says 'ladies' anymore.") Sitting on the floor in a row were Christie's three grandchildren. Anna had been annoyed and hurt at the Christmas Eve family party when she opened the package containing the picture: why hadn't she been included? Her eyes looked unwaveringly on the oldest of the great-grandchildren, a ten-year-old who came into the house without greeting anybody. He was turned slightly toward the center, just enough so that his short ponytail showed. She would never display the picture. She hoped no one knew she had a great-grandson who wore a ponytail, like the hippies who were so terrible in the 'sixties and 'seventies.

She walked carefully down the stairs to the basement cedar closet. The mink coat smelled slightly of cedar. She stroked the black fur, breathing in with pleasure at the silky feel of it. Even though she had worn it on countless festive occasions, it looked new. She had taken good care of it. Cradling the coat in her arms, she went up the basement stairs with a lightness to her steps. Again in the dressing room she put on the coat, looked at herself in the mirror, and was content with what she saw. Next, she opened her eelskin purse and checked to see that her lipstick, compact, wallet, checkbook, car keys, and a fresh embroidered linen handkerchief were inside. She had two more things to do.

In the seldom-used guest bedroom, she had made room on a shelf holding a few books and set up an icon of the Virgin and Christ Child. A ruby red votive glass stood before it. On the thin layer of olive oil was a miniature taper set in a cork ring. The wick was black, burned out. "Oh, dear," she said aloud. She should have taken care of the icon before she dressed. She took off her coat, laid it on the bed, and leaned at an angle toward the votive glass to keep a chance drop of olive oil from staining her silk dress. With studied attention she pinched the burnt taper between her thumb and index finger and placed it in a whiskey shot glass hidden behind the icon. Then she meticulously poured olive oil from a small glass pitcher into the water in the votive glass. From behind the icon she picked out a new miniature taper from a small box, set it on the cork ring floating on the olive oil, and lighted it. She made the sign of the cross, whispered the Lord's Prayer, and for a few moments looked at the Byzantine Virgin.

She had only recently begun using the icon again. She could not remember how it had come about, but years ago the icon and votive glass had found their way to a basement cupboard. Two weeks ago she had opened the cupboard to store winter blankets, seen the icon and votive glass, and on impulse brought them upstairs. She cleaned them with a moist cloth and wiped them dry. Since then she made certain the icon light burned at night. With its faint glow and the burglar alarm turned on, Anna felt secure in her bed. She also began making the sign of the cross at the lighted icon when leaving the house and on returning, just as her mother had done.

Anna put on her coat and walked into the living room. On the grand piano was a silver-framed photograph of her parents. She walked slowly toward it, smiling. From the time they died she had begun a ritual of saying goodbye to them before leaving the house. When she returned she greeted them. The picture had been taken when her parents were in their early fifties, at the time of Anna's own wedding to Bill, fifty-one years ago. They were overweight, her mother in blue lace and her father in a tuxedo, the starched bib puffed out. They held their heads up with that dignity, that pride she knew from an early age made them different from other immigrant Greeks. She had always been proud of them, at church affairs, lodge conventions, baptisms, weddings. She knew people respected and admired her parents. When she was a very small girl, her father had been the president of Saint Basil's Church. Their family was also the first to move out of Greek Town, the neighborhood that had grown around the old church and into the east side residential area. That was about the time she stopped going to Greek school after public school. In the winter it was too dark by the time the angry old bachelor teacher let them out at six and when she got off the streetcar, it would be night.

She looked at her diamond wristwatch. There was plenty of time. In the small room that had been called Bill's den, she picked up a few pieces of mail that lay on the desk and read them again. She looked at her husband's picture, taken when he received the Chamber of Commerce award. She had been pleased as he spoke from the podium. "You looked so good," she said, talking to his picture, a man with thinned gray hair and deep folds on either side of his mouth, "not bald like most of the men, thank goodness." She stopped smiling. After the Chamber of Commerce banquet, they had had one of their best times in bed, but afterwards Bill turned surly: "Can't you just stay in bed? Do you have to jump up and get busy at some goddamn thing or other?"

Quickly she scanned the church bulletin: only the Friday evening service. "Oh, well," she said, then set the burglar alarm, and walked toward the rising garage door. She stopped and peered into the garage, first on one side of the black Cadillac and then on the other. The Cadillac was almost as new as on the day she and Bill had bought it, a year before he knew he would die. She kept the inside spotless as well.

She drove down the winding road, passing big houses with well-kept lawns and bushes. She didn't know the younger people who had bought the houses from their original owners. The old neighbors had moved to condominiums or to warmer places when their children were grown and gone. She was resentful when she saw the new owners walking breezily past her house, as if they didn't care to acknowledge that she had been there first.

She turned onto the main thoroughfare, but, before she realized it, she had passed the freeway ramp. It was just as well, she thought, as the car traveled through streets she had driven before the freeway was built. She drove slowly, smiling to herself, while passing the 1920 bungalows, like her childhood home, with greening grass, some with daffodils, crocuses, and hyacinths. Trees were beginning to bud.

As she neared the church, her heart gave a flutter. Who, she wondered, would be there? She thought of the stir she would cause when she came in. Of course she was older now but she was still elegant. People would remember how important her father had been in the Greek community. People had called him all the time about church and lodge politics, for work, for all kinds of reasons. And her mother was like a queen with women clustered about her on name-day visiting. She had a special, indelible memory of her mother. Anna must have been a very small child when it had happened. Her mother sat on a rocker on their porch in Greek Town and men on their way home from the railroad yards raised their hands in greeting as they passed the house. Her mother smiled and rocked. Everyone liked and respected her parents. Yes, she told herself, she felt good and, who knew? If she became active in the Philoptochos, she could even be asked to be president.

Anna drove into the church parking lot. As she locked the car door, she looked at the thirty or so cars already there. A Mercedes and a BMW were the only cars that could vie with her Cadillac. She wondered, as she walked to the hall adjoining the church, how much a Mercedes cost. She stood inside the entrance a moment, looking about at the women and a few men standing or sitting at tables talking, laughing. She breathed in pungent, appetizing food scents and thought how good it was to have a hot, substantial meal cooked by someone else instead of the sandwich she would have eaten while watching the noon news.

Her head held high, she went forward to a table near the door, where two women sat in deep conversation. She did not know either of them. One was in her sixties and looked vaguely familiar, a narrow face with a long nose; the other woman was probably an immigrant. Even though her tinted hair was salon styled, there was something about her. *Imports,* her generation had labeled the immigrants who had come to the country after the Second World War. The women greeted her politely. "Here is your ticket for the prizes," the woman with the salon hair style said with that slight separation of words that convinced Anna she had been right about her.

Anna smiled down at her and took the ticket. She walked slowly toward the groups of women and searched for familiar faces. Several women she had known all her life looked at her and nodded or said, "How've you been?" then went back to their conversations. Her heart beat faster. Then she saw Tessie Hatumbis and another woman sitting at a table with several empty seats. She went towards it. "Tessie! How nice to see you."

"Hi, Annie," Tessie said, the slightly popped eyes in her round face looking at Anna as if she saw her every day.

"Are these seats all taken?"

"No, sit down. This is Pete's sister Melpo, from Greece. She's visiting us."

Anna sat down with an angry pulling back of her shoulders. Tessie had called her "Annie," when from the time she was in junior high she had insisted on being called "Anna." She looked at Tessie's sister-in-law, who had light skin and pale hair with a few glistening gray strands through it. Speaking in the polite Greek her mother had always used, Anna said she was joyful at meeting her. She wondered why some women didn't wrinkle.

"Well, you're certainly dressed up," Tessie said. "Are you going some place special?"

Tessie was wearing a green jacket, the windbreaker kind women wore in shopping malls. Melpo, too, had on a similar kind in violet and blue. Anna realized that all the women in the hall were wearing skirts and shirts or cotton dresses. "I'm meeting a friend afterwards," she said and hurriedly added, "I had no idea it was so warm. When I got up this morning it looked like we'd have a cool day." She shrugged off the mink and arranged it on the back of the chair.

Tessie turned to her sister-in-law and translated Anna's words into Greek. Melpo looked at Anna quizzically, smiling slightly. "How long will you be visiting?" Anna asked her. She suddenly thought she could take her and Tessie to lunch. It would be something to do.

"I'm leaving next week. I've been here five weeks already."

Anna was unpleasantly surprised. Five weeks and she hadn't even known Tessie had a visitor from Greece. When Anna's friend Stella was alive, Anna had heard all the news from her. Stella's father and hers had been lifelong friends. They had come from the same Peloponnesian village, not far from Sparta. With three other village friends, one of them Bill's father, they made up a *parea*, a clique. Their families met at each other's houses for dinners, name-day visiting, and always on New Year's Eve for the traditional good luck card game. Stella had known all the gossip going on and she had unbelievable nerve. In high school she had cut classes and attended the court trial of the priest who had been sued for breach of promise by their Greek school teacher. In a back bedroom in Anna's house, she had whispered what their teacher wore, how she snapped at the defense attorney, and what the priest had written her—*my dove, my sun, I want you as you are*. They had giggled into hysteria at the thought of the priest with his pince-nez eyeglasses, his curly hair parted in the middle, writing these words to their flushed, overweight teacher.

Stella was dead, six years dead. Anna hesitated, then turned to Tessie. "I'd like to take you and Melpo out to lunch," she said in English.

Tessie translated into Greek for Melpo and said, "Thanks, but all of Melpo's time is taken up and Pete wants to take her to Las Vegas. Even back in the village they've heard about Las Vegas and so we're going over the weekend."

"Well, if I'd known sooner, I would have invited you before this." Anna turned to Melpo, smiled benevolently, and said in Greek, "The next time you come." She was envious; she had always complained that Las Vegas was glitzy, crude, and that she wouldn't go there except that Bill had insisted. Secretly she had enjoyed Las Vegas very much. She had always come back with a dress or suit from one of the expensive casino shops. She leaned forward, yearning for Tessie to say, "Why don't you come with us?"

"Eh, I won't be coming again," Melpo said, nodding. "My brother has made more than his bread in America. He sent money to help our parents, money for my dowry. That's enough. I won't let him pay for another trip."

Anna kept smiling. Tessie's husband had come after the Second World War and worked as a dishwasher. In a few years he and a friend had opened a small *souvlaki* place. Tessie had married him then, kept the books, and did much of the cooking. It had been a joke between Anna and Stella. Whenever they saw Tessie, they said, as soon as she walked past: "When two Greeks meet, they open a restaurant." Maybe it had been a decade or more, but it seemed to Anna that within a few years Tessie's husband had *souvlaki* places all over the city. Anna opened her purse and busied herself with going through it while Tessie and Melpo talked.

The thin, harried Philoptochos president approached a long table at one end of the room and said in Greek into a microphone, "Sit down, please. Father will give the prayer and then we will serve ourselves at the buffet table. As we always do, starting from the back tables."

Several women took seats about the table, nodded, and spoke pleasantries to Melpo, evidently already having met her. Two of the women were ninety years old; they had come from Greece as picture brides in 1918. "Well, Anna, where've you been all these years?" Mrs. Ghikas said, her thin hair puffed up in a vain attempt to hide her near baldness. Mrs. Karpetakis sat slumped in the chair next to her. Her eyes were blue veiled and her hands shook. "It's Anna Goursis, Roula. You remember the Dorakas girl." The veiled eyes gazed at Anna. "I've just gotten so forgetful," she said. "How are you, Anna?"

Anna saw herself talking animatedly to the two older women as if she could not stop. The priest walked to the microphone. He was a slight man with a thin, handsome face. He gave a short prayer of thanks in English, made the sign of the cross, and said, "Good appetite," in Greek. He then went from one table to another and greeted the women. Anna watched him with a quiet excitement. When he stopped at their table, he called each woman by name, spoke familiarly to Tessie, asked how Pete was, shook hands with Melpo, and said he had enjoyed seeing her at liturgies. He looked at Anna, who reached out her hand and said, "I'm Anna Goursis. My father was Gus Dorakas, one of the first presidents of the church." She smiled on. "But of course that was a long time ago and you wouldn't have known him."

The priest smiled pleasantly. "Yes, it was before my time. Glad to see you," he said and went to the next table.

Anna looked at Tessie, who was talking to Mrs. Karpetakis about cataract surgery. She was shocked that Tessie hadn't told the priest about her father, a patriarch of the church. After all the years Tessie's father had worked for hers. And her mother giving Tessie's mother clothes that Anna and her brother had outgrown. Anna looked at the women lined up at the buffet table. How fickle people were. Her father had been dead twenty years and no one remembered how good he had been.

It was now their table's turn to go to the buffet. Anna stood up, then looked down at Mrs. Karpetakis, thinking she should offer to bring her a plate. Tessie put her hand on the old woman's shoulder and said, "I'll bring you a plate." Mrs. Ghikas waved her thin, veined hand: "Someone always brings her a plate." And at that moment one of the few men in the room came out of the kitchen and to their table. In Greek he said, "Here you are, Auntie," and set a plate in front of her. "I'll bring you coffee and cookies in a minute."

Anna went forward with a backward glace at her mink coat, holding her stomach in, greeting women she had not seen for a long time. She joined the line and picked up a plastic plate and a knife and fork wrapped in a paper napkin. The Philoptochos president and several women stood behind the table to serve the food: salad, rice with shrimp, corn, potatoes and green beans in tomato sauce, *feta* cheese, Kalamata olives, and rolls. In a corner of the room on a long table a coffeemaker, cups, saucers, a pitcher of white wine, and another of red punch had been placed on one end and on the other various cookies, and *halva*.

As the lunch progressed, Anna ate with a good, warm nostalgia. The women talked about Lenten foods. Tessie had read a recipe in the *Greek Star* for cookies made without butter and eggs. Melpo said she fasted the entire forty days, just the way it had always been done, no eggs, milk, meat, fish, no, not even olive oil. Tessie said she only kept the fast for a week. Anna said nothing. On Great Friday and Saturday, she went without meat.

Tessie and Melpo brought coffee and a dish of cookies and *halva*. "You don't have to wait on me," Anna said. "We're waiting on everybody," Tessie said. Mrs. Ghikas was stacking the plates and Mrs. Karpetakis with palsied hands was placing all the knives and forks together. Efficiently Tessie picked up the plates and flatware and hurried to the kitchen. She had taken care of it before Anna had a chance to offer her help. Anna's bladder was uncomfortable. It was the excitement of being back in the hall after so many years away.

The women were moving about, making room for the bingo cards, and placing prizes on the cleared buffet table. Tessie had brought a package which she picked up from the floor and took to the table. Anna hurried to the restroom, through the sitting room, and reached a stall just in time. She hoped she was not getting another bladder infection. She was about to leave the stall when the outer door opened and Tessie's voice said, "Here's a pin. It'll keep the hem up until we get home."

"What a clod I am to put my heel through it," Melpo said, then, "Who is that woman with the fur coat?"

"That woman. I'll tell you about *that* woman. She came from a family of liars. My father hurt his leg on the railroad when I was a little girl and had to go to her father for a job. He was a labor agent and he used my father like a lackey. Once he made him go to the coffeehouses and give every bum in there twenty-five cents to vote for him to become president of the church. In those days lots of men died in the mines and in railroad accidents. The Church had to bury them. Most of them didn't have any money. Well, when her father was president he had the mortuary give him back twenty-five dollars for every man they buried. My father had to collect the money."

"Achh. Tsk-tsk."

"And her mother, with her nose up in the air, said her father was the mayor of Athens and didn't think that after the war we'd visit Greece and find out he was the mayor of a little town. She used to sit on her porch on payday and rock while the men coming from work threw silver dollars at her feet so they'd be sure to keep their jobs. Always praising herself, her house, her children, Agh!"

Anna's mother: *The proverb says: If I don't praise my house, who will?*

"What about her? Is she educated?"

"Not anymore than the rest of us. The man she married, his father had established a good business and left it to him."

"Eh, she sure uses old-fashioned Greek. And that mink coat in this weather."

The voices began to fade. Tessie said, "I had to wear her castoffs. And her mother used to hand them to my mother right in front of me. I had to play the games *she* wanted."

Anna stood in the stall while minutes passed. She stood there, her face, her hands wooden. She thought of ways she could get her purse and fur coat out of the room, but there was nothing to do but go back. She had to stay and play bingo. She could not let them know she had heard them.

She went back to the table, forcing her legs to be steady. The first bingo game had just finished. "We missed you," Mrs. Ghikas said. Tessie was frowning.

"I thought I had left my glasses in the car, but I just realized they were in my purse." She lifted her purse, took out the glasses, and put them on. The Philoptochos president called out the numbers. Game after game went on. Merriment followed each cry of "Bingo!" A man and his wife, ten years or so younger than Anna, brought the presents to the tables. Mrs. Karpetakis won a box of stationery. She pushed it toward Tessie. "Take it, Anastasia. I don't write letters anymore." Tessie leaned her head against Mrs. Karpetakis's fragile one.

Once Anna had a row of numbers, but she would not call out. Then she knew she had to get out or she would start screaming. She pretended to look at her watch. "I really have to go. I'm meeting a friend and I'm afraid I'll be late." She hurried out of the building and almost ran to her car.

She was not able to think clearly. Her first thought had been to telephone Tessie and call her a liar. Instead she stared at the telephone on Bill's desk until her shoulders lost their rigidity and slumped. She sat there until evening, then immensely fatigued walked into her bedroom and lay on the bed in her fur coat. She forced herself to look at the closet door, staring at it long enough to be certain no eyes were looking at her, but still her stomach was queasy.

One night when Bill had taken a codeine tablet and was quiet, his hand had reached over, taken hers, and slowly placed it between his thighs. She had let her hand remain there for a minute or so, then withdrew it. She got up, turned on the light in the dressing room, and tried to decide what she should wear the next day when she took Bill to his chemotherapy. She turned and the light behind her illuminated a ghastly, knowing look in Bill's eyes. A few nights later she began sleeping in her son's old room. "You'll rest better," she told Bill.

She pulled the bedspread tighter about her and began to cry, then sob, then whimper. She did not remember that she had not gone into the living room to greet her parents in the silver-framed picture.

Lent began. All week she thought of the Friday evening service, the first of the presanctified leading to Holy Week. The house was empty, cold, even though the heat was turned on. She huddled in the king-sized bed. The telephone rang once. Christie chattered about her new grandson and how exhausted she was helping to take care of him and see to the older grandchildren. Anna thought she should offer to send her cleaning woman over, but she wasn't quite listening to Christie, who whined, "I just don't know why we can't have Easter the same day like everyone else. It just causes confusion for the children. And we end up having two Easters. Double the work."

Anna hung up. As she dozed off, she thought of herself as a child going to the Petropoulos's Greek store to buy Lenten foods — Mr. Petropoulos in a stained white apron ladling out olives from big barrels, taking down cans of *halva,* crab, and shrimp. How quiet the house had been during Holy Week. Her mother would not let them turn on the radio because Christ was on his way to the cross. The church had been filled with incense, the candles glowed, the Lamentations were sung sorrowfully while the flowered bier of Christ was carried outside and three times around the church. Great Saturday, the light coming from the altar into the darkened church. The great joy and. . . . Oh, if she could only go back and be a little girl again and be different.

On Friday evening she put on a tweed suit, ate a dish of canned pears, and drove her car out of the garage. It was early evening; it would be dark soon. She drove to the church parking lot, put on dark glasses, and sat for a long time with her hand on the car handle.

THE
PEOPLE
GARDEN

It was early evening. From somewhere beyond the wide lawn bordered with immaculate flower beds, the faint scent of nicotiana came. Nina, a seventy-five-year-old woman seated on the patio, recognized the piquant scent and took deep breaths of it. The scent, the sky, the flowers blended into a tranquil prelude to night for her. Once such an evening would have been a small pleasure; now in her old age it was a great gift. As she gazed at the garden, her daughter Connie prattled on the telephone inside the house. Nina wished Connie would remain there and leave her free to contemplate her flowers.

She had been satisfied with her garden for the past ten or fifteen years. Until then she had given too little attention to the color and height of plants. Sometimes the garden had splashed with color all at once, then bloomed hardly at all for weeks; tall plants had often been too near the borders and shorter ones were hidden behind them. Now her garden was almost perfect.

Connie's voice had risen. She was talking to her sister Kathy as if Nina could not hear the conversation: "On the patio looking at her garden as usual." Connie's sardonic words made no impression on Nina. What Connie said and thought did not matter anymore to her. "You know," Connie continued, "how Dad used to think Ruffy was a person, not a dog? Well, I think Mom thinks her flowers are people not flowers." Connie laughed mirthlessly. Oh Connie, Nina thought, someday your children will laugh like that about you. She felt a small sadness for Connie and a faint pang for herself, for she would be gone by then.

The garden's early years had been the worst. She could hardly give it the time it needed. She would put the children down for naps, then listen at their doors for their even breathing. She would hurry outside to work before Tommy, her middle child, awakened. He seldom slept more than a half hour. Then she set to planting the haphazardly chosen perennials and annuals that she had picked up in nurseries on her way home from doctors' appointments and grocery shopping—the children left in the car with suckers to keep them quiet. Quickly she planted the few packs of snapdragons, petunias, and other flowers she knew nothing about—lobelia for example, only to find when they grew, dwarfed and shadowed along the base of tall flowers, that they were edging plants. She hadn't known enough about flowers then and had been too harried to read directions and space them properly. In the nurseries she passed by displays of plant food, insect sprays, sacks of iron and fertilizer and sometimes she juggled these in her arms, then stored them in the garage and forgot them.

She had become aware all through those early years of disorder that the garden was a miniature jungle. Days or more went by while she tended sick children or was involved with weddings, baptisms, and name-day dinners for both sides of the family and she had no time for weeding. Wild morning glory vines sprouted overnight, twined up the stalks, and strangled the flowers. Other weeds also grew alongside the wild morning glory, but they existed passively, taking up space, not choking the flowers. Still, they too had to be pulled up.

"Of course she shouldn't be puttering in the garden!" Connie burst out, her voice harsh. "Some day she's going to keel over tending her damn flowers! And you should see the dishes stacked in the sink."

Connie had a raw voice when she was angry. So unfeminine, Nina thought, with neither sadness nor annoyance. She was past all that. She tried, though, never to be caught kneeling in the garden when her daughters drove up the driveway. It was so hard to get to her feet. She had to keep a thick stake nearby that she would push into the earth and hold on to tightly to pull herself up. When she was caught, Kathy looked at her sadly; Connie spouted angry warnings and shook her head despairingly.

"She's as bad about that damn garden as *Yiayia* with her house! Mom's going to go out of her head just like *Yiayia* when she had to give up her house. That wonderful mansion," Connie said sarcastically about her grandmother's modest house.

Nina did no more than take note of Connie's disparaging her grandmother. Anger took too much exertion. She looked toward the left of the garden, where her children had played in a sandbox under an elm sapling. The elm was now taller than the roof of the house. Her mother used to sit in a folding chair next to the sandbox with Kathy on her lap and watch Connie and Tom. Nina had taken the opportunity to work in the flower beds. She had jerked out the morning glory and other weeds to give the garden some order. It was as if the garden had no dignity—overgrown in places, sparse in others. The weeding lasted but a few minutes. Connie and Tommy fought. Connie always wanted whatever toy shovel or bucket Tommy held protectively. Tommy was silent while their grandmother tried to mediate, but Connie glared at her and insisted on pulling the toy away from Tommy. It had never done any good to put Connie in her bedroom after her grandmother had gone. Connie misbehaved again and again. Nina resorted to taking her screaming into the house and into her bedroom. Her mother had been strict with her own children, but she looked sorrowful whenever her grandchildren were being punished.

"Oh, get with it, Kathy! You've always been a pushover. Look the facts in the face. The next thing we know she'll burn the house down with herself in it. And that stew you brought Monday? It's still in the refrigerator. She hasn't touched it."

The faint breeze brought again the scent of nicotiana. She had once had several nicotiana plants growing at the east end of the flower beds, but they had disappeared long ago. She had a moment's regret at having lost the plants and not replacing them. The flowers with their pointed petals had been pretty enough, but it was their ethereal evening scent she had breathed and valued while she hurried to complete the day's routine.

Later, when the children were in school, Nina had had more time to work in the garden, but she made mistakes continually. She tried transplanting flowers from the western mountains, Indian paintbrush, sego lilies, rose mallow, and others that had dazzled her as a child. They had not caught, had drooped no matter how carefully she had dug them up or how much water she had given them. She realized it was futile and stayed with seeds and nursery plants.

There, in the garden, with its moist dirt scent, the first green shoots, the buds, the flowers, she could face whatever the day brought: complaints from her mother-in-law over some supposed slight to her or her children; her mother's never-ending advice; John's bad temper and silences. When she took off her canvas garden gloves and replaced the tools in the shed, she was content; she felt her face had smoothed out. The restlessness of wanting something more and yet not knowing what it was vanished for a while.

Later, when the children were in their teen years, when Connie rebelled against even the smallest rules, when Tom began taking drugs, when Kathy shrank into herself, the garden was her oasis, her refuge. She would keep the turmoil at bay while turning the soil and pulling out weeds.

"Now listen, Kathy, and don't start with your two-cents worth of excuses for Mom. This new retirement home is really nice. The grounds are nice. They serve tea in the afternoon and women play bridge and . . . I know Mom doesn't play bridge! They have other things going on! She's got to get out of this house!"

Yes, she had to admit it, the flowers reminded her of people. As the nicotiana scent floated off, she thought it was like those who had come into her life, been important, and then were gone because she had been too busy and there was not the time, the energy to keep up with them

—those people who could have been lifelong friends instead of neighbors and relatives who eventually drifted off, unmissed, into their own middle and old age.

The lost nicotiana could have survived if she had tended it properly. Instead she had wasted time on flowers that had been unsuited to the climate, the altitude, the arid western air. They flowered not at all or briefly, dying out, like plans she had made, whimsical ones: working on an Indian reservation for a month in summer to do oral histories; or serious ones: going back to the university for a Master's degree after her children were in school. Her husband John had put on a disgruntled face; her mother and his couldn't understand it: "You're not lacking anything. Your husband's a good provider. Do you want people to think you have to work? And you'll neglect the children." She had given in too easily to old-country logic; she had connived with those around her to reject the desire. Her daughters, she had been determined, would not be bound and restricted as she had been. Yet they did not care about doing anything special at all. There were other times, too, when she had thought of doing something more, something different, but now she could not recall these dreams. They had died out like the wildflowers she had transplanted, like those from the nursery that she had not chosen well or taken care of properly.

A slight breeze brought a more pronounced scent of nicotiana and she was effortlessly remembering her three college friends, Diane, Katherine, and Melo. They had married about the same time, had their children together, went to Saint Catherine's for a while, until the suburban church was built and Nina began attending services there. Now she could not think how it had happened that they had stopped going to each other's houses for coffee. Gradually their visits tapered off and soon they seldom saw each other. It might have been their being too busy with children and their activities, or their husbands had not liked each other enough, and they all had those big family dinners at their mothers' houses for all occasions besides every Sunday. Like the nicotiana, her oldest friends were gone from her life. She didn't want to waste her time thinking over it.

Nina had learned over the years; she had experimented continually. The garden had now reached its final form. She uprooted flowers that attracted aphids and other insects: they required more attention than their prettiness warranted. They were like her two cousins. The three had had a ritual of meeting for lunch often and Nina had listened while her cousins excitedly talked about face-lifts, clothes, and possessions and she wondered why she was sitting there. What a revelation it had been when she not only did not miss them, but was relieved that she did not have to fritter away her time anymore. After her mother died, it seemed easy to put them out of her mind.

Her mother's favorite had been the pink roses in front of a clump of magnificent delphinium. The roses were a variety that was almost thornless. The old roses that had grown there for years had large thorns, which Nina thought of as the old-country ways her mother had brought with her. Her mouth moved soundlessly: *Mama. Mama.* Surrounding the roses, like chicks encircling a hen in a child's book, were iris—her sister Dena; a sprawl of miniature blue campanula—her sister Koula; and Icelandic poppies—perhaps herself.

The delphinium behind the roses was tall, the flowers so thick and heavy they did not have to be staked against breezes that would ordinarily bend flower stalks. Even before her father died she had begun to think of the delphinium as him in his prime. In previous years the delphinium had been scrawny, with fragile shoots growing sideways. Often some died during the winter and new ones had to be planted, but within the last few years the clump had grown tall and sturdy. It was so, she thought, because she finally knew that each evening her father had brought calm to the tempestuous house. Nina smiled: Why wouldn't he bring calm? His wife, her mother, had taken care of the day's unpleasantnesses.

The sideways shoots had been little glimpses of him: a story she'd heard about his life as an immigrant trying to keep from starving to death during his first year in America; giving help to fellow villagers, a hundred-dollar bill to one during the Depression years—the man's son had told her about it after a Sunday liturgy: "Your dad just gave it to him without even being asked." He found work for villagers' sons among his building leaseholders by promising an unwarranted benefit —repainting a building or cutting the rent. One twig was a horrendous scene with an employee who wanted him to sign a document for workmen's compensation by falsely attributing an automobile injury to a work accident. She had tied the offshoots and they had become strong and upright. Some offshoots escaped the ties and these she pruned: tight silences and sharp, whispered words while she and her sisters listened to the radio. Afterwards her mother had looked grim.

John used to say that Nina's mother had a one-track mind. He was right about that. When her mother wasn't cooking, she was inviting women guests or visiting them. She spent considerable time on name-day visiting. On the days when many young men bore the names of popular saints: Constantine, Demetrios, Nicholas, and John, she returned home pale with exhaustion. She had suffered visits from terrible bores, women who put on airs because in America they could wear hats instead of headscarves. It was unspoken and it was several years before Nina realized her mother was preparing the way for suitable marriages for her daughters. It worked well with her older sister Dena, now the circle of pale yellow iris. Dena had surreptitiously read *True Romances* and movie magazines and hid them under the mattress. Her mother and godmother had ingratiated themselves with a mother of five sons and the trio contrived to invite each other to dinners and picnics. Dena knew what was going on. It was easier, she said, having someone else find a husband for girls in the Greek way. "Just look at the American girls at school. They worry themselves sick if they don't have dates. Always afraid they'll be old maids."

Before each dinner party, their mother lectured Dena not to wear too much makeup, not to talk or laugh too loudly, to be modest, not to look at the boys boldly. For two months Dena crossed her ankles demurely, smiled sweetly, didn't look at her sisters because she was prone to laugh at everything and would certainly burst out if she met their eyes. When Zack, stocky, double-chinned, handed her the engagement ring without asking if she wanted to marry him, Dena flung herself on the bed afterwards, put a pillow over her head, and laughed hysterically—not because she was ecstatic, but because the pent-up laughter exploded and could not be stopped.

Her mother worried that finding a husband for Nina would be difficult. She feared that Nina might not be considered marriageable to Greek parents becase she was becoming too educated. Nina sat across from John in the university library one day and they walked out together, had a coke in the student union, and married after they graduated.

With the youngest, Koula, who called herself Kay, their mother had had different problems, harder ones than more girls being of marriageable age than young men. It also had nothing to do with Koula's looks. She was pretty. But there was something about her that warded people off, habits their mother had not been able to cure: making odd remarks, her eyebrows lifted in disdain. She was twenty-eight when their mother's sister matched her with a Greek immigrant who needed to marry an American citizen to remain in the country.

"You convinced Papa! That man is only marrying her so he can stay in the country." "Be quiet," Nina's mother hissed at her. "Do you want your sister to be unmarried all her life? No children for her old age? Be quiet." She would not be quiet. "That, that *gigolo!*" she shouted, an old-fashioned word her mother would not know. "That leech!" she shrilled in Greek. "Be quiet! The family has to find him work. That's what families do. It's everyone's responsibility."

"You mean my husband's responsibility!" A thick thorn had punctured Nina's arm that very afternoon and brought blood poisoning. She had been given massive doses of penicillin and had been allergic to it ever since. At the time she had felt she deserved the blood poisoning.

If she stared at the roses long enough, she became aware of her mother looking at her with a long, thoughtful gaze. She wondered if her own daughters would look at roses after she were gone and think of her.

She gazed at her family group, the delphinium, pink roses, yellow iris, the blue campanula. She was the only one still alive. The flowers were her memories. When the time came and she was separated from her garden, would her memories be lost? She had only to look at the pale yellow iris and remember Dena. When their mother could no longer manage the family dinners, Dena insisted they be held at her house. It was a tradition Dena kept until three years before she died and always Nina's flowers, often the pale yellow iris, were set in the center of the table. There were other irises, brilliant blues, pure white, butter yellows, purples, but Dena wanted the pale yellow ones. The two of them had telephoned or been with each other every day until Dena had children. Then she became consumed with them, their health, activities, clothes, their looks. A newspaper kept her husband Zack from seeing the children pass back and forth in front of him.

Arthritis eventually deformed Dena's hands and Nina took over the Easter dinners. She became even more conscious of keeping the family together after her parents, Dena, and Koula died. Between one Easter and another she did not hear from Dena's children, and Koula's preferred friends outside the family. Nina stopped cooking Easter dinners and heard one day that Dena's children did not gather in each other's houses for Easter. It was after Dena's burial that Nina looked at the pale yellow iris and remembered that her sister had once been vivacious but became pale like the iris years before she died. Nothing in the garden reminded Nina of her sisters' husbands. They were easy to forget.

Next to the pale yellow iris was the low blue campanula that was Koula. All her ideas and opinions came from the movies of the 'thirties and 'forties—men should be tall, dark, good looking; women should be soft, dreamy, nice, even though she was none of these. "The import," as John called Koula's husband Demo, short for Demosthenes, supplied other opinions for her, and most were about Greece's superiority over America. The blue flowers brought no other memories of Koula. They had hardly ever had family dinners at her house.

Next to the delphinium old-fashioned hollyhocks grew. When they were children she and her sisters, and sometimes their cousins, would cut off the flowers and pretend they were ballerina dolls. Nina started telling her granddaughter Melanie about the ballerina dolls one day and suddenly forgot what she was talking about. Her heart thumped with fear and with a great will of concentration she recalled what she was saying. Melanie had looked at her with watchful eyes.

Hollyhocks, pansies, morning glory climbing up the elm, bachelor buttons, Nina and her mother had liked these old-fashioned flowers most gardeners would not bother with. Nina had also liked yellow and orange nasturtiums, but she had not grown them because they made her father sneeze. She had thought of planting them after he died, she had even bought the seeds, but never had done anything with them. It seemed she would be breaking a pattern.

The garden now was almost perfect in her eyes. When they had moved into the house, new then over forty years ago, the dirt was clay in places, rocky in others. It took years of turning the soil, removing every pebble, mixing in fertilizer and peat moss until the dirt became soft, rich, and dark, a foot deep. She did it herself, not wanting to be in the house with John during those stormy first years. Her mother caught her one evening swinging a small pick into the hard dirt. "We didn't come to America to have our daughters work with dirt." Nina smiled at the memory and looked at the pink roses. Despite her words, her mother had always worked with her hands, throwing carpets over clothes lines and beating them with a heavy stick until she got used to the vacuum cleaner, and she had always planted a vegetable garden and a profusion of flowers. Those immigrant days; she shook her head.

Slowly Nina turned her gaze to a group of pinks, giant red Oriental poppies, and white columbines. Behind them, almost to the edge of the bed where little water reached, a low bush produced small pink flowers that lasted a few days in spring. The green of the leaves was dull, except for a few sprigs that were strangely glossy. The shrub had been in the garden from the time the dirt had been clay and rock, but because it had taken root she had done nothing more with it. She did not know its name; she had seen the shrub in a nursery and threw the tag away even before she planted it. Each spring it was there, leafless at first, then the green appeared followed by the small flowers. A frown made two vertical lines between her eyes. She had no idea why the bush reminded her of her husband John.

She gazed at the grouping she had come to think of as representing her family, not that she had actually planted them with that idea in mind. It had merely occurred to her after years had gone by that they were her family.

"If this keeps up, she's gonna become a recluse," Connie was saying, her voice rising to a shrill as it did when she was contradicted. "Oh, no, cutting down isn't the right thing for old people. They should get out even more. It keeps them from getting senile. I've told her I'd take her to the senior citizens' luncheons at church, but she only wants to go once in a while. What? Well, so now she's only got two friends to her name. No! Two friends are *not* enough. So what? You don't have to have something in common with people to enjoy being with them. It's to get her out! Don't you get what I'm telling you?"

Nina began to raise her eyebrows, but looked calmly at her garden. *Friends* did Connie say? No, she would not allow herself to think about Connie. She had spent years wondering if it were her fault that Connie couldn't keep friends. Her first enthusiasms petered out after a few months or a year, then she acquired new friends and the cycle began again.

Nina looked at a small cluster of pinks. Year after year it came up with only a few insignificant flowers on thick gnarled stems. Its faint cinnamon scent had almost vanished long ago, just as her son Tom had. She used to think back to her children's young years to see if there were clues to Tom's life. It had seemed to her that perhaps Connie had overpowered him, but she no longer wanted to think about it, nor look at the pinks with anguish and wonder where he was. She had thought he would survive the 'sixties and come back, get off drugs, finish the university, be like most young men his age. He came back, but only for money, for a few days, then he would be off, looking ragged, unkempt. In twenty years they had not received even one postcard. John had telephoned embassies in Mexico and India while she looked on at him, astounded. He wrote letters and sat in front of the television, his jowls pulled down in defeat, one hand on his old dog Ruffy's head.

She kept her gaze on the pinks, not asking herself the old, haunting questions: How did Tom live? Where was he? Was he dead? Now she merely gazed. Every spring she tried without much success to hide the thick stems with a planting of white or purple pansies. She had thought at times she would dig up the thick root, but decided she would let it die out. Yet it was tenacious; it survived the below-zero weather and each spring it was there with a few thin leaves and later the small pink flowers with little scent.

Her eyes gazed unwaveringly on the pinks until they blurred. She had quarreled with John, demanded that he spend time with Tommy, take him to baseball games. Sometimes the two went together; once she went with them and John spent the entire time talking about the game with the man sitting next to him, whom he evidently didn't know. "Nice to meet you," John said as they filed out. She looked at the green bush steadily. She had become aware during the past few months that she had not known John very well, had never known him deeply. People always said they liked him. He had been good to the children, except during their adolescences, when he would flare up at them and stamp out of the house. He had still stamped out of the house, almost to the day he died. She had hated him for it and too late came to know something else was always at the bottom of it, something in his business, or with his parents, brothers, and sisters, or with himself. She thought of all this as if from a great distance.

On one side of the pinks was the spectacular circle of tall red poppies, flamboyant like her bossy Connie, still on the telephone, now saying, "Well, *you* try to convince her to get someone to take care of her flowers. She shouldn't even be in this house at all. She should be in a . . ." She heard Connie, but placidly, and did not muse over her, thinking: Is it my fault that she's so bossy with me, her husband, her children? No one could quite put her in her place. Her dead father had. He'd shut her up with an old Greek proverb: Whoever pisses in the sea, eats it in the salt. Tom and Kathy didn't want to play with her when they were children. "She always wants her own way," Tom would say tearfully. Kathy had not minded when just she and Connie played together; she would docilely follow Connie's demands: "Now, you're gonna be my maid." When the three of them played together, though, Kathy had stood next to Tom and sometimes defied Connie.

At one end of the garden under a staghorn tree the white columbine were blooming. It was a perfect place for them, shaded by the tree, the matted leaves on the ground retaining moisture. They were truly Kathy, shy with people until she had known them a long time, feeling guilt too easily, calling her every day, sometimes twice a day. "I will never live in the same house with my daughters," Nina told Kathy, sensing that she wanted her there but that her husband was balking. She would never live with either Connie or Kathy; John had left her more than well off. At least he had done that. She had given up calling him a workaholic several years before he died. It took energy to use words.

Again she looked at the green plant. No, the garden was not perfect after all; it was not quite balanced; the dark green bush that had always been there was not tall enough, She should have planted a flow-ering bush of some kind, one that did not grow too large. Then she re-membered that she had planted a hibiscus near it, the Hawaiian plant with the large red flowers. After the snows melted one early spring, she thought it winter killed; the twigs broke off easily. Then she thought it might come up from the roots, as often happened with bushes. It remained, its brown branches without a leaf and she had dug it up, intending to plant another one with big, showy flowers, be-cause the green bush did not have enough color, but she kept forget-ting about it.

Her gaze slowly went over the width of the garden, lingering on the white daisies and bluebells. The daisies were her granddaughters; the bluebells her grandsons. She realized she was whispering to the daisies and bluebells, telling them how she would make the garden easier. She would have about two feet of the borders dug up and have sod put down. Narrowing the flowers beds would make much less work. She would forego planting annuals, the petunias, pansies, zin-nias, and marigolds that gave so much color to a garden. That would also make less work. She would stay with perennials, which came up every year, those that did not spread and require constant digging up and separating; she would concentrate on delphinium and phlox. She would have to dig up the iris. How beautiful they were, but they had to be divided every three years. But then what would remind her of Dena? She remembered that pulling the iris roots apart had brought on tendonitis of the elbow the last time she divided them. "Oh," she said softly.

A smaller garden would be all right, not so many beautiful colors; there would be times when not much would be blooming, but it would have to do. Just keeping the garden free of the wild morning glory weed was trouble enough. It was obstinate: when leaves fell and flowers faded and turned brown, the wild morning glory was still green, even under the first snows. It had to be pulled out and killed at the roots. It was what she had learned to do with annoyances and grievances: pull them out and forget them so they would not fester. She thought mildly how much easier her life would have been if she had learned this lesson early.

She looked at the dark green bush. She would think about it. There had been clues all along that could have shown her what John was really like. She had been blind to the deep wounds still inside him when he told humorous anecdotes of having been humiliated or wronged in his early years and then laughed uproariously. She had misunderstood the laughing; she had thought it showed he was at ease with himself if he could laugh like that.

She would think about it all. She had done all her other thinking and no longer dwelled on scenes, regrets, and angers, but she had not thought about him enough. She would. She would finally know what he had been like inside.

She gazed at the dark green plant. She began thinking. She would start with the first time she had met him. She tried. Again she tried. Then effortlessly images came to her of her mother, pleasant, warm ones—her mother lighting the icon and crossing herself before she left the house; kneading the communion bread and stamping it with the marks of Christ; sitting on the sofa with two old, black-dressed friends, watching a soap opera they didn't quite comprehend; smiling as her husband related a village anecdote.

Connie walked heavily out of the house. Nina sighed at being interrupted with her garden. She looked at the Icelandic poppies, pale orange, pink, white, delicate on their slender stems. She smiled ruefully. She had wanted life to be like them, with a quiet beauty, blooming year after year, with no interruptions.

THE

APPLE

FALLS

FROM

THE

APPLE

TREE

Part One

1950

The wine-colored Studebaker sped, churning up the dust on the long road that led to granite-tipped mountains. The child Athena was standing against the dashboard; her sisters, Tula and Katherine, and their children were in the back of the car. Athena was the youngest in her family, born twenty years after her oldest sister, Tula.

The three children in the back seat, a few years younger than Athena, had fallen asleep during the monotonous drive from eastern Utah toward the Colorado border. Athena was tired but too excited to sleep. The previous year she had been given the job of feeding the bummers, the lambs that were orphaned or rejected by their mothers.

Her mother gave her large-nippled bottles of milk and she sat in the shade of the house and tightly held the squirming lambs. She was afraid there might not be a single lamb for her to take care of that summer.

Athena's brother Danny was driving the truck behind them. Tula's older son was sitting between him and the scrawny little man who had come from the same Greek mountain village as her father. *Tsimblis* he was called, someone with sleep granules in his eyes. Athena did not know it was a nickname. Sometimes in the evening Tsimblis would be dancing outside of the bunkhouse all by himself, twirling slowly, eyes closed, singing the laments of guerrilla fighters facing torture and death if they were caught by the Turks.

Athena wished she were allowed to ride with Danny. He was fifteen, nine years older than she. There had been an even older brother. Her mother carried a snapshot in her purse and once in a while took it out and looked at it. Athena knew she should not ask her mother who the person in the picture was. She asked Tula. "That's our brother Ted. He was killed flyin' a bomber over Germany in World War II. You was only two years old. She forgits what he looks like and takes out the picture to remind her." Athena knew it was because of him that her mother wore black dresses and stockings.

Athena often looked at this dead brother's face in family pictures. On the Day of Souls, her mother took her by the hand and they walked to church. Her mother carried two round loaves of bread she had stamped with symbols of Jesus before baking. At the left door of the icon screen, her mother knocked and handed the cantor the bread and a list of family names to be recited by the priest during liturgy.

Her mother never spoke about this son. Two village friends, dressed in black for sons killed in the war, talked and cried over them between sips of Turkish coffee, but her mother only shook her head slowly. "Mama used to talk too and laugh a lot before Ted died," Katherine had said. Whenever her sisters' children visited and sometimes stayed overnight, her mother, their grandmother, would once in a while burst into laughter over some foolishness they had been doing. Her face then would change and look young and different for the moment. She did anything they wanted, took them on the streetcar to movies, to the

Liberty Park, and to Woolworth's. Only once did she get angry with them. Tula's sons kept blowing out the lighted taper before the icon of Christ and His Mother, kept in Ted's old bedroom. Their grandmother lighted it several times and each time the boys blew it out when she left the room. When she caught them, she stung them with rebukes: "It's bad. It's not nice. These holy things! Jesus and His Mother. It's sin."

She always had Greek pastries for them and if they wanted something special, she immediately went into the kitchen and cooked it. Once, when they giggled late into the night, Athena in her room and the four boys across the hall in Ted's old room, her mother had told them to be quiet. "You'll wake up *Papou,* wake up Grandpa." She had given up speaking Greek to them. "Your mothers and fathers should speak Greek to you," she said to them when she was frustrated because she could not make them understand what she was trying to say. Athena knew they understood, but they liked to play tricks on their grandmother, and then smothered their laughter. They did not dare try it on their grandfather.

As the silver-green sagebrush flashed by endlessly, Athena sensed her mother sitting behind her, silent, her hands folded on her black cotton dress. Her hands were brown from working in the garden. Her face looked smooth as a satin ribbon when she came in afterwards. Behind in the truck Athena knew Danny would be singing folksongs from the Burl Ives phonograph record he had given her: *Jimmy crack corn and I don't care.*

"Isn't that the Nielsen's Hudson ahead of us?" Tula asked in Greek and Katherine answered in English, "We'll probably see them in Grand Junction." Their father called them the "Nielsoons"; their mother, the "Mormonoi."

The Studebaker followed the Hudson and the half-ton truck ahead of it for another fifty miles. The caravan slowed as it entered the small town and parked in front of a grocery store. The dusty Hudson and green Studebaker parked next to each other. Doors sprung open and the squealing children ran into the store. The fathers shook hands. They were dressed in the uniform of stockmen: laced, high-top boots, breeches, plaid wool shirts, and western Stetsons. Athena's father was bigger than Mr. Nielsen, who was thin yet ruddy-faced, the kind of

Danish face that reddens and peels under the sun. Mrs. Nielsen took hold of her youngest son Rob by the hand. As he stepped onto the sidewalk, he looked at Athena and the other children disappearing into the grocery store and pulled his hand from her grasp. Mrs. Nielsen's grandmother sat on the back seat of the car talking to herself.

Inside the grocery store the families bought sacks of ice, lunch meats, eggs, and milk. "My God," Danny said to Tula and Katherine, "that Tsimblis sang those"—and he made a high-pitched *eeee* sound —"old Greek village songs all the way. I had to listen to him for almost a hundred miles. At least if he had *some* kind of voice."

Athena took a long time deciding which candy bars she wanted from the low shelves by the cash register. The other children had quickly grabbed several candy bars and were running around the small store. "Hurry up!" Tula said to Athena. "We haven't got all day." Rob Nielsen walked over to the shelves and with the solemn authority of an older child chose his candy bars, a Baby Ruth, a Snickers, and a Milky Way, and took them to the check-out stand.

Mrs. Nielsen stopped in the aisle to visit with Tula and her mother. Tula said she was surprised at how tall Robbie had grown and Mrs. Nielsen said the same about Athena. Mrs. Nielsen laughed, crinkling her weathered skin. "Yes, the change-of-life babies," she said. Tula said she wished Eliza could have come. They'd had a lot of fun out to sheep when they were kids.

"Well," Mrs. Nielsen said, adjusting a hairnet over her short gray hair, "my girls are all scattered now and have their own families to look after. I'm just surprised you and Katherine still come."

"It's a tradition," Tula said and Athena admired her much older sister, plump, pretty, with short permanented brown hair. She thought Tula was superior to Mrs. Nielsen, and Katherine, slender and not really pretty, taking out orange sodas and Cokes from the refrigerator, even more superior.

Back in the car Tula and Katherine admonished the children not to eat all the candy at once. "It's not like we're in town and you can go to the corner grocery store any time you feel like it," Tula said.

Athena sat on her mother's lap to eat her candy. Soon the car began climbing into foothills of scrub oak, green with spring, yellow flowering currant bushes, rabbit brush and sage. The car shook and chugged as her father changed gears again and again. "Watch the children," their mother said. "They'll hit their heads."

The road turned dry, rutted. Up the car went following curves, jogging over ruts, swerving to avoid rocks. The white frame house was ahead, the meadow grass at one side sweeping to pines that rose dense and acridly fragrant into the blue sky. The car jerked to a stop and the children jumped out. Athena's father took off his Stetson, dark stained above the band from years of sweat and wiped first his pale forehead where the sun never reached, and then his brown cheeks and chin. The mother, Tula, and Katherine were carrying out big pans of food tied with dishtowels from the truck bed. Danny and bowlegged Tsimblis brought out scuffed suitcases. Tsimblis still hummed the eerie songs of fate. The boys flew to the corral next to the sheepherder's log bunkhouse, and Athena ran to the stream to look at the clear water flowing over speckled pebbles. Sheep bells tinkled far off.

1951

The next year the boy, Rob Nielsen, did not go to the mountains with his family. Instead he sat on the back seat of the Hudson with the great grandmother. Boxes of food, pots and pans she had packed herself were wedged on the floor. Rob's father drove and when he turned his head slightly to glance at Rob's mother, who kept looking out the window, the muscles of his jaw moved. No one spoke during the two-hour drive. A stiff silence between his parents was commonplace. It was usually preceded by his father's coming home from town smelling of beer and tobacco. His mother followed the Mormon Word of Wisdom and ranted at him for going against it. Then the silence came and everyone in the house, except old Great Granny, was mute.

There had been a great commotion in the clapboard farmhouse. Great Granny said she would not go out to sheep. She would spend the summer on her old homestead. The family brought the Mormon bishop and the stake president, but she would not budge. She said she had lived eighty years alone, still did her own cooking, baking, and putting up fruit, and she didn't need a single soul out there with her. She forgot she had been living with Rob's family for twenty years. Before that she had lived in the same farmhouse with her daughter, Rob's grandmother and grandfather, but they had moved to Salt Lake City to be near a lung specialist. They had no sooner bought a house when Rob's grandfather was put in the tuberculosis ward in the county hospital. He died a few weeks later. Often Rob heard his mother tell visitors that her father, Rob's grandfather, had died from weak lungs and his grandmother soon after from a broken heart. Rob's Uncle Ed, who came home only for funerals, and sometimes for family reunions, said Great Granny would never die, that she was a sly old biddy.

The car veered off the highway and bumped along a narrow trail of wagon wheel ruts that had been reclaimed by sagebrush in places. Rob's father swore softly. The trail ended at the back of a decayed log house. Rob's mother tried to help Great Granny put her supplies away and sweep out the cobwebs and mouse droppings, but Great Granny chased her out with a broom. "Now git," she said.

Rob's mother told him to climb the roof of the low root cellar. She pointed to the base of a mountain and said there was a house there. "See, there's smoke comin' up from the chimney. If Great Granny gits sick or won't wake up, climb under the barbed wire fence and walk over there and tell them."

Rob watched the Hudson disappear in dust and then sat on the roof of the cellar. He kept his eyes on the road thinking the car would come back and take him away. He stayed there until the stars came out. At intervals Great Granny went in and out to whip a dust cloth against the log walls. He heard sounds in the blackness. He had to go in. Great Granny pointed to a slice of bread on a paper plate next to a jar of honey. Then she pointed to a cot at the side of the black wood stove.

Sometimes his great-grandmother forgot him, even though he was there before her eyes. Hunger pangs twisted his stomach. Every morning he walked a long way off to an irrigation stream and filled a pail with water, then came back and sat in the sagebrush. He gazed with infinite despair at insects hopping and fluttering about, knowing his family at that very moment were with the sheep, or in Grand Junction or Basalt buying supplies and not giving him a thought.

Great Granny talked about her son Robert, who had died, but not to Rob. She looked at the caulked ceiling as if she were talking to God. Robert, she said, went straight to the Celestial Kingdom, because he was only eight years old. "I didn't grieve as much for him as I should have because I knew from the time he was born that when he was a teenager he'd git stranded on Fool's Hill and never git to the top. Yes, Lard, I know You saw somethin' in him I didn't that You could use. Like teachin' the Gospel up there. Robert was hard like my mother, Lard. She'd git on her horse and ride into the sagebrush to do her midwifin'. And she'd leave me all alone with the young ones and I was only a little girl myself. My Pa was on a mission or doin' church work and sometimes I was left all alone with the little ones two-three days at a time."

Once Great Granny did talk to Rob. They were at the table eating biscuits and canned-milk gravy. She looked straight at him and said, "I hate polygamy. Joseph Smith must have got the revelation all mixed up or God made a mistake."

Rob was so surprised that God could make a mistake that he said in a crackly, unused voice, "Could God make a mistake?"

"God makes mistakes because He is still learnin' and gittin' better all the time."

At the end of August Rob's parents came to the homestead and took Great Granny and Rob home to get him ready for school. Great Granny did not know what was happening because Rob's mother had mixed a tranquilizer into a rice pudding she had brought. Great Granny liked rice pudding. The minute they arrived at the farm, his mother gave Rob a bath and washed his hair. He had not used soap and water all summer. The next day she took him into town to the dentist, who cleaned his teeth.

1954

Athena and her best friend Effie Pappas came out of the fifth grade class, each carrying a Greek school book and tablet they kept hidden from taunting schoolmates in a looseleaf notebook. They clasped hands because they were friends that day. The yellow school bus was parked in front of the school and farm children were waiting for the doors to open. One of them was Rob Nielsen, whose family ran their sheep across the mountain draw from Athena's family, the Demopouloses. Rob Nielsen was three years ahead of Athena in school. He did not look like his sisters, who had white hair and eyebrows and blue eyes. His eyes were hazel with eyelids that pulled up a little at the outer corners and his hair was a light brown.

Athena and Effie walked down Main Street of the small western town. Ahead of them Mary Ellen Martin swung hands with a girl who had just moved into town. Mary Ellen turned to look at them, then whispered loudly to the new girl. "They're Greeks. They wear crosses."

"I hate her," Effie said, narrowing her eyes. "Thinks she's better'n us."

They stopped at the bakery and looked avidly into the windows, then walked on to the Palace Candy Store and gazed at the display of chocolate riches. It was Holy Week and they could eat neither meat nor dairy foods in remembrance of Christ's blood. "Six more days," Effie sighed. On the Resurrection on Great Saturday midnight, they would be able to eat all the foods forbidden during Lent.

They came to the small Byzantine church and clattered down the basement steps. About twenty students were noisily wandering about; a few of them, like Athena and Effie, were the youngest of large families with immigrant parents. Several others were grandchildren of immigrants, but most had come from Greece after the Second World War or had been born soon after their parents' arrival.

The church had been newly renovated and smelled of fresh plaster and paint. The postwar economy had made the improvements possible. The mahogany altar screen had been painted white and the icons cleaned. The massive crystal chandelier, bought in 1915 by Greek immigrants working in the Black Hawk coal mine, was taken down and washed of decades of dirt, and the dark wooden floor, spotted with countless candle drippings, was covered with beige mosaic tile.

The basement walls and ceiling were also painted; the wooden floor as darkly stained as the one above, but from roasted lamb grease, was covered with linoleum; the restrooms were tiled and new fixtures installed. "Stop complaining about going to Greek school," their older sisters said. "You should have seen how it was when we had to go." "And the goofs we had for teachers, too," Tula always finished.

Athena and Effie sat next to each other at long tables used both for Greek school and the communal celebrations of the Dormition of the Virgin on the Fifteenth of August, weddings, baptisms, the fish dinners following burials, and, most important, the Agape feast on Easter Sunday—the roast lamb, the eggs dyed a dark red for Christ's blood.

At one end of the basement on a miniature stage, a portable green blackboard with the declensions of a noun and a spelling list showed the diligence of teacher and students. Next to the blackboard was an old scarred table and a kitchen chair, where the teacher sat on school days the better to see them.

Their first teacher was tired, old-country, soon to die of cancer. He did not shout insults at them or scorch them with stinging proverbs or tell didactic myths, as their sisters said he used to. He no longer caused scenes in the Liberty Coffeehouse, where a few old-timers drank demitasses of Turkish coffee and listened to centuries-old guerrilla songs on a hand-cranked phonograph. The teacher was no storyteller and, from a people who told of their bondage to the Turks as if it had happened a year or so previously, he received not even a nod of respect.

When he died the priest taught them, one of the last of the Greek-born, hurling sarcasms and apocalyptic predictions. "The Siberia for Greek priests in America," Athena's father and his friends called their western community. A few months later the reason for the priest's sentence to their Siberia was uncovered: a scandalous accusation by a married woman.

For another few months a young, American-born priest intoned above and taught below, then was spirited away to a midwestern community by an offer of more money. After him came a series of young men from Greece who were recruited as teachers even though few had finished high school there. They had arrived after the Second World War, some sincere and inept, the last of them arrogant and angry that he had not been awarded an important position on arrival. His uncle bellowed in the coffeehouse, "I slaved eighteen hours a day to establish my business and he thinks he should take over!"

While the arrogant young man with a great head of shiny hair and black cold eyes listened to recitations, Athena and Effie surreptitiously wrote notes to each other and drew pictures of figures that were supposed to represent their favorite movie actors. Athena drew a cartoon of the teacher that Effie said looked just like him.

After four years of Greek school, they succeeded in learning the alphabet and reading two primers. They also memorized poems for the archbishop's visitation on Mother's Day. For the program Tula sewed them identical dresses of sky-blue shiny cotton percale with white eyelet collars, blue and white, the colors of the Greek flag. The sisters tied big red satin bows on top their heads. Before leaving for the church basement, Athena's mother lighted the icon and together they gazed at the Mother and Son, crossed themselves three times, and recited the Lord's Prayer.

On the small stage the children stood in a row and one after another spoke their patriotic poems. As their turns neared, Athena and Effie clutched hands tightly and breathed quickly. They quaked out their mercifully short poems, and the parents, sitting on folding chairs, clapped and looked at each other benignly.

Afterwards Katherine, Tula and her husband Gus, the lithe, handsome man she had married on her seventeenth birthday, came over smiling and praising. Gus looked like an American, but he spoke with an accent: he had come to America as a boy of fourteen. He picked up Athena and lifted her high in the air. Athena was embarrassed and pleased. Gus put her down, lifted Effie, and then gave them each a silver dollar for good luck. Gus was twenty years older than Tula, the best dancer, people said, in the community. Leading the folk dances, he jumped high, slapped his ankles, twisted about the handkerchief held by the second dancer. Women clapped and men whistled. Through thumb and forefinger, they blew as if they were still boys whistling for goats on the rocky, thyme-brushed mountains of their villages.

1955

Rob's father had fallen off the tractor and injured his back. For a year he hobbled about and a hired man came to work the farm. Their sheep dwindled. There were not enough to trail up the mountains in spring and down again in fall. Synthetics had almost demolished the demand for wool. Rob's father grew worse; his legs swelled until he could barely walk. Then his kidneys failed. He knew he would die and he shamed the family by telling them often that he would not have his funeral service in the Mormon ward. He didn't want anyone getting up and talking about him either.

Rob's mother took out the last postcard she had received from her twin brother, Rob's Uncle Ed, and asked Information if he had a telephone. It had been discontinued, a voice told her. "It's just as well," she said, surrounded by her daughters and Rob in the mortuary, all looking at the open coffin. Several wreaths and sprays were placed on stands around it. "He's another one who doesn't know where up is."

The mortuary was filled with sheep-raising families. A small man with one leg shorter than the other who once worked for Rob's father said, "Well, my old friend didn't want no words spoke, but I gotta say I'm gonna miss the honest old bugger." Rob's oldest sister, Eliza, who lived on a farm eighty miles north, sang her father's favorite song, "Lonesome Valley." Then the funeral was over. "You're in charge now," the Mormon bishop said to Rob. Rob's mother had apologized profusely to the bishop when he had come to the house. "It's all right, Clara. They'll get him up there," and he looked upwards. Mr. Demopoulos shook Rob's hand. Whenever Rob saw him, he remembered the terrible row his parents had had over him.

Rob was almost grown before he realized his father was not keeping the Word of Wisdom. His parents had such quarrels he was glad to go outside and do chores. The last one was the worst. His father had gone into town and seen Jim Demopoulos in the feed store. They talked about going to the sheep raisers convention in Salt Lake City and then Jim Demopoulos told him to come by his house for venison stew. When Rob's father came home, he tried to joke about it. No, he said, it was the wine in the stew with lots of bay leaves and cloves that went to his head. Rob's mother screamed and screamed. It was terrible and from then on whenever Rob saw any of the Demopoulos children, he saw his mother's screaming face.

Uncle Ed appeared a month after the funeral. He had just learned that Rob's father had died. By then Rob had become accustomed to his father being gone, accustomed to the heavy voice no longer heard, accustomed to his parents no longer quarreling while he lay in bed and wished they would stop. Rob and Uncle Ed walked outside and stood looking at a field of alfalfa, ready for its third cutting. Rob's white and black sheepdog Jack stayed close to them.

Rob's Uncle Ed had the slender, wiry kind of body a person often saw in the West. Such men had deep rays at the corners of their eyes from years of peering under the hot sun and they took stretched-out, easy steps whether their legs were long or not. Rob liked such men.

He and his uncle stood by two parallel rows of sawed-off tree stumps. There had been a row of poplars lining the irrigation stream when Rob had been very small. They had already been scraggly then. The bark had peeled off in strips; the leaves vanished permanently; and the poplars stood, skeletal proof of decay. Rob's father sawed them down, leaving a row of stumps parallel to earlier gray ones and did not plant others. "Poplars give out too soon," he had said. "Twenty years is their limit." The clapboard house then lay exposed, with no shade in summer, nothing to keep snow from piling in drifts against it or dust from rising and pinging it with bits of rock when the wind howled.

Uncle Ed sat down on one of the tree stumps and Rob sat on the adjacent one. Uncle Ed looked at the alfalfa and shook his head. "I used to stick my bare feet in the irrigation stream under the poplars when it got too hot in the fields. But I couldn't do it for more'n a minute or two with your grandpa on the lookout. Yeah, my old dad never spared the rod. He sent me into the potato fields as soon as I was big enough to handle a hoe. I'd look down them long rows comin' to a point and I felt like a darkie on a chain gang. Course he had weak lungs. Couldn't do much work hisself.

"Then the Depression hit. I couldn't finish high school 'cause we didn't have the six dollars a year tuition. And your ma couldn't go neither so she up and got married. We damn near starved. We loaded the sheep on the freight cars and went to Denver. Couldn't find no buyers. Lambs had gone from eighteen dollars a head to three and we still couldn't find no buyers. We went on to Kansas City. Same thing. Went on to Chicago. Nothin' doin' there neither. We left them in the stockyards, just left them. Couldn't feed them. Come home empty-handed.

"Me and two other farm boys. We was about sixteen. We took off and hitchhiked up to Washington and picked cherries. Then we worked down the coast in the fish canneries. We'd stay up all night waitin' at the gates to git in. And there was plenty others with the same idea I c'n tell you. Got so we could gut a fish in nothin' fast.

"We was tight with the little money they paid us. People was starvin'. I mean *starvin'!* Then we heard this old guy, this wino, say — it was in a flophouse — said he used to make good money ropin' wild horses and sellin' them. This outfit shipped them to the Dakotas for dog meat. Well, hell, we all knew how to wrangle so we hightailed it back home and we was never hungry again, all through them last years of the Depression. Just before the war. I hate farms. I hate farm towns.

"That's what I told them when my dad, your granpa, got TB and had to move to Salt Lake to be near the hospital. Everyone expected me to come back and run the farm, but I wouldn't. I couldn't see myself locked up in this here farmhouse with Great Granny especially. So I offered my share of the farm to your ma and dad. You know they was tryin' to raise a few sheep and cattle on salt grass out in the sagebrush. Scrawniest cattle you ever saw."

So, Rob thought, this is how he came to be living with his parents, five sisters, and frail, tart-tongued Great Granny in one cramped house. He had a quick image of himself, not yet in school, and his dog Jack riding to town with his Uncle Ed. Jack stood on the truck bed, his head stretched as far as it could go facing the direction of town, his tongue hanging out sideways, his eyes blinking. In town Rob sat on the truck bed, rubbing Jack's ears, waiting for Uncle Ed to come out of Pete's Billiards. His mother sniffed his hair when they got home. The next day Uncle Ed put two scruffy suitcases in the back of his pickup truck and waved goodby to the family. Rob's mother stayed inside.

His mother called them to come in for supper. Rob could see it was a special dinner, fried chicken, mashed potatoes, peas, cherry pie, but suddenly his mother and Uncle Ed were quarreling.

"I'm not comin' back and take over this here farm!"

"Then what's gonna happen to the farm and what sheep we've got left? The girls and their families are better off where they are!"

"I'll bet you tried to git one of them to come back and they wouldn't give you a tumble. Well, it's not gonna be me. I hate farms."

"Oh, you're just talkin' about hatin' farms. So what you been doin'?" she said in a loud voice. "Breathin' gasoline fumes and forgittin' your religion. I'm glad Rob hasn't taken after you or his dad." She began to cry and wipe her eyes from the corner of her apron. "It's all goin' down the drain. Our dad's and Big Rob's work." She turned to Rob. "Your dad killed himself gittin' a flock together after the Depression. That's when he started havin' all kinds of trouble."

"Don't think you're gonna make me feel guilty," Uncle Ed said. "'Cause it won't work. Sell the goddamn sheep! Raise enough vegetables for your kitchen and live off your Social Security. 'Cause I'm not comin' back!"

When Uncle Ed drove off in an old dark blue Chevrolet that had lost its shine, Rob stood looking at the clouds of dust. Then he looked at the alfalfa and potato fields. They were surrounded by stunted scraggly sagebrush growing in patches of grayed earth. They were like something trying to be pretty in the wrong place. He had seen tall, silver-green sagebrush in other parts of Utah, but that good kind was not for his people, as if they didn't deserve it. Uncle Ed hated the green fields and stunted sagebrush and so did Rob. He was going to leave some day and never come back.

1957

Athena and her parents were on their way to the small town they had left two years earlier, after her father had sold his flocks and become a sheep broker. She sat on the back seat while her parents talked about the handsome young priest of the Salt Lake City church. He was insisting that parishioners pay their yearly dues before expecting wedding, baptismal, and funeral services. Athena's mother said, "But there might be people who can't afford it."

"In America everyone can afford it," her father answered angrily as he sped down the canyon road. "Thirty dollars a year, anyone can afford it."

"Eh, for some widows, even that is too much."

"Their children should pay it! The Mormons pay ten percent of what they make and we act like we're still back in Greece."

Athena had a flat, open box at her side. Charcoal and pastel chalks lay in its compartments. She had propped a tablet of art paper on her knees and was drawing the rearing mountains of the canyon. On the slopes among boulders and scrub junipers were charred skeletal trunks, remnants of trees that had caught fire when a mine had exploded and sent flames leaping from tree to tree. It had happened more than a quarter of a century ago.

The tablet was almost filled. She had drawn winter skies: in the distance snow-filled crevices of granite-tipped mountains; snow over the black cedars on the slopes; snow covering wide fields in hamlets, golden wheat stubble pushing through. She had drawn rows of ragged, leafless poplars lining unseen irrigation ditches, gray skies and mists hiding the earth and mountains, faintly visible red willows on the banks of streams, narrow houses far from each other: stuccoed-over pioneer adobe, old frame houses, occasionally brick, and, nearby, fences of weathered planks, saplings, or barbed wire enclosing empty stock pens.

She had sketched the seasons: spring skies: fresh gray sprouting on winter-dulled sagebrush; snow melting over winter wheat fields uncovering a velvety green; water running down irrigation streams; poplars turning green; flocks of sheep on their way to summer in the mountains; dogs running to keep them contained; men on horseback whistling to the dogs.

Summer skies filled pages: luminous blue with great cumulus clouds, birds flying toward the horizon; mountain and desert flowers: red Indian paintbrush, white and blue columbines; rose mallow, pine cones of all kinds.

Under hazy autumn skies she had caught with her brush fields of yellow; browns of different hues, deeply dark, burnished, umber, and fallow black; sheep down from the high mountains where they summered, moving gray masses, sentinel dogs speeding around and around them; farther south the red earth terrain, table-topped mountains, mesas layered with shades from brown to red.

Pages of the notebook were of sunsets in all seasons: blazing, rolling clouds; striated reds, oranges, magentas, and violets. On many pages coal towns stood out starkly, with their tall black tipples filling railroad cars; great heaps of glistening coal dust encroaching on company houses; a graveyard with a turnstile gate—a few weathered granite and marble headstones and many small black metal crosses with faded names on cardboard encased in brownish celluloid—the explosion dead; against the wire fence weeds and sagebrush.

For one long period she had drawn from memory people of her childhood: Ute Indians, Mormons, immigrants, miners, railroaders, sheepmen, store owners, their wives; a Serbian miner coming out of the post office, his blue eyes stark in his coal-smudged face; her father's friend from his same mountain village—sheepman, bootlegger, folkhealer; a miniature Italian woman who had outlived all ten of her children.

Athena worked quickly while her parents talked, mostly her mother, about family affairs. Tula had four sons; Katherine two; her brother Danny two daughters. Danny had married Joyce, a blonde woman, whom Athena's mother called the *Amerikanidha*. She would not believe he would marry the blonde woman until Danny actually stood in an Episcopal church and exchanged rings with her. "That *Ntose*," her mother said; she had never been able to pronounce the name *Joyce*, "I told her we would have Easter dinner, everyone, the girls, the children, but she had her excuses ready."

Athena's father said nothing. "What got into his head to marry her?" her mother sing-songed, her voice lowered as if this would insure Athena's not hearing. "There were so many nice Greek girls. He could have—"

Athena's father cut in with a proverb to stop her litany: "Even God gets tired of too much *Kyrie, eleison*."

They reached the floor of the canyon and passed through patches of farmland, then came to the first of the coal towns. Athena put away her notebook and chalks. She thought of seeing Effie; they would walk down Main Street to the Palace Candy for a Coke.

A massive pale rock mountain stood guard over the town. Many stores were vacant, paint peeling, their plate glass windows boarded up: machines had taken over the pick-and-shovel work in the mines. "They buried him like a dog," her father snorted, looking toward the graveyard on a small rise. "Nielsen! A few words and down in the hole. He was a man not a dog!"

Athena remembered the Nielsen boy who was ahead of her in school. She wondered what he was doing, if he were running the family farm, and what he looked like.

1959

Rob had to watch his money carefully while on his mission. His mother had embarrassed him at a family reunion by hinting that he didn't have much to take with him. She went up to the patriarch of the family, Great Granny's brother, whom she was fond of telling people "was high up in the Church," folded her hands over her apron, and smiled as if she had something special to say to the rickety, immaculately dressed and dignified old man. "Uncle Whitney, Robbie's taken after you. He's at the top of his class. He's always been frisky about catchin' the school bus." Rob took a step backward. "He saves every penny he gits workin' at the Artic Circle for his mission." His mother shook her head. "It's not easy, but he wants to do Heavenly Father's work."

Uncle Whitney had smiled kindly, patted her shoulder, and moved off. Rob's mother sold the rest of the sheep and Rob went to Brigham Young University and into the Missionary Training Center. He learned Dutch for his assignment to the Holland mission field.

During the first few months in Holland he felt dizzy at times, and several mornings a stab of ice in his chest awakened him. His companion was a farm boy like himself, but could not carry on a conversation about anything except the Book of Mormon, or the B.O.M, as he called it. Rob asked him once who the president of the United States was and the boy had to think about it for a minute before his eyes lit up and he said, "Eisenhower!"

There was not much time for conversation anyway. Their mission president kept after them, goading them on, telling them they had not made enough conversions. Their routine began with morning prayers, then a skimpy breakfast, followed by studying their materials, then out to knock on doors. Rob would watch his companion, Wilson Leonard, with interest. Sitting on the edge of a worn sofa, Wilson's big gray eyes looked at the listeners, usually two old people, with something like amazement. It was as if he had never before heard the story of Joseph Smith being visited by a celestial being who directed him to the buried gold plates, the Book of Mormon.

On the street people looked at the two of them, Rob and Wilson, wherever they went. People knew they were Mormon missionaries by their black suits, white shirts, and black ties, each carrying a Book of Mormon and tracts. Wilson would stare at the girls open-mouthed. He had a girl waiting for him in Idaho, but he always turned his head when a pretty girl smiled at them.

Each time the mission president harangued them about not having made enough converts, Wilson went out with renewed energy. In the evening, while cooking their meal of potatoes and onions and sometimes a little meat, Wilson could not stop talking. He was certain that the people they had visited that day would come to embrace the restored Gospel of Jesus Christ. "Did you see how their ears pricked up when I explained God's plan of progression, Rob? Did you notice how she glanced at her husband, then looked straight at me and didn't take her eyes off me?"

Rob wanted to say something biting, like "That's because you talk like a jerk," but he didn't because he thought there was something wrong with him, that he didn't have it in him to enter the house of strangers and tell them that what they had believed all their lives was stupid.

He made several converts, however, among a group of carpenters just by giving the history of the Latter-day Saints. One family prepared to leave for Utah and wanted Rob to remember them. They wanted to get away, they said; they had suffered so much during the war and had never got back to where they had been before it started.

During the last six months of his mission, Rob thought about his father often, just as he was falling asleep, tired and feeling a floating kind of unhappiness. He seldom had to listen to Wilson's reed-like snore for more than a few minutes because the moment he put his head on the pillow he began falling asleep. Then the images came: his father home from town and his mother screaming at him because he smelled of wine. His father trying to make a joke of it: Jim Demopoulos saw him on the street and took him home for dinner. She still screamed.

He was twelve years old, in a new J. C. Penney suit, his mother giving his hair a last brush. He was to be ordained a priest that day. His father standing next to the car, looking at them evasively. "If you think you're comin' to see your son ordained, you've got another think comin'! You're not gonna embarrass me! A worthy man will put his hand on Rob's head!" "Aw, go to hell," his father said and walked away.

One hot day Rob and Wilson sat on a park bench to rest. An elderly man was sitting at the other end and immediately began talking to them. He could tell, he said, by their clothes that they were Mormon missionaries. His voice was thin, with a bullying tone. Wilson imediately plunged in with the polite spiel they had been taught. He did not get far. The old man exploded, "Your Joseph Smith he saw God and Jesus Christ! My cousin Hedrick saw Them all the time but no one believed the poor fool!" Wilson's face turned red, but he went on in his poor, fervid Dutch. "It's not the same. It's—" The sneering old man stood up and hobbled off. Rob had begun to wonder himself if Joseph Smith had really seen Them or just imagined that he had.

1962

Athena was in her senior year at the university when she asked a work student at the reference desk for some help. He had light brown hair and eyes and was somewhat gangly. He looked at her as he stooped and brought out a book from under the counter. He then helped another student and when she left the book on the counter, he glanced at her again.

It seemed to Athena that she had seen the work student somewhere else, but she could not remember him in any of her classes. She made her way through a group of Vietnam war protesters in the hall and walked up to the second floor. At a study table, she opened her book and began reading. She lifted her head and, frustrated, tried to remember where she had seen the student.

Two young men stood at her side. "Found you at last," one of them said. His dark curly hair was almost to his shoulders and his thick eyebrows rose in peaks above large, deeply brown eyes. "What classes are you taking this quarter?" He sat down heavily and faced her.

"Oh, hi, Greg, Mark. Mostly art classes."

"What can you do with art classes after you graduate?" the other student, overweight and wearing faddish sloppy clothing, asked in a derogatory tone. "Are you gonna design things or teach or what?" He took a seat across from Athena.

Athena looked at him as if he were an annoying brother or cousin, criticizing her mainly because she was a girl. The two students were almost like cousins to her. They had all gone to Greek Orthodox Sunday school from the time they were children until their teen years, when they had joined the choir. The choirmaster had stopped practice often and glared at Greg and Mark for whispering and nudging each other. Athena was constantly angry at them. She knew they had joined the choir to have access to their fathers' cars. After choir practice they would take out girls—and not the girls in the choir.

"Athy," Greg said, a whine in his voice, "look at my paper will you and correct the grammar?"

Athena tightened her lips and read rapidly through the paper, making corrections in grammar and spelling. Greg and Mark whispered, looked at a blonde girl at the next table, and whispered again. Athena finished with the paper and pushed it toward Greg. "Why don't you get a steady girlfriend to correct your papers?" she said without smiling.

"You're a good kid," Greg said and gave his head a toss that caught the shine of his hair. Preening, Athena thought, and if he were sent to

Vietnam, they'll shave it all off. Athena watched the two walk away, their heads turned to the blonde student who glanced at them with a coquettish smile. To Athena they were just ordinary boys, spoiled by mothers and sisters, like so many young men in her church.

Greg's and Mark's mothers sought Athena out at church functions. Greg's mother gushed over her, complimenting her hair, her dress, told her Greg mentioned seeing her on campus. Mark's mother never failed to visit her parents on her father's and brother Danny's name days. Athena tried to avoid the mothers: they thought of her as a potential daughter-in-law and she could barely tolerate their sons.

On her way out of the library, Athena glanced toward the reference desk, but the work student was not there. She was disappointed: if she had another glimpse of him, she might remember where she had seen him. Every day she looked for him in the library. When he was there, she felt light, almost happy; when he was not, she felt heavy, disgruntled with herself.

One late afternoon she stayed longer than usual in the library. She was procrastinating because her mother had invited friends for lunch and she knew propriety would expect her to visit with them while they scrutinized her. She opened a card catalog drawer and was going through it when someone came to her side. She looked up. The work student was standing there, blushing, smiling a little uncertainly. "Are you from the Demopoulos family?"

Athena's heart beat in her ears; heat rushed to her head. "You're," she said, her lips stiff, "the Nielsen boy?"

He nodded, his eyes looking into hers with bright interest. "Yeah, the Nielsen boy. Rob. I wasn't sure who you were until the second time I saw you."

Athena was afraid to look at him and thought *I must say something.* "Does your family still own sheep?"

"No, it got too hectic after my dad died." He reddened, hesitated. "Would you like a Coke or something?"

Athena nodded, closed the card drawer, and walked at Rob's side across the campus toward the Union building. A Vietnam protest rally with jumping signs and sing-song shouting blocked the entrance of the library, but Rob pushed through, his head turned to make certain

Athena was following him. She held her books tightly against her chest. She could not believe what was happening. She was careful walking over the cement path, fearful she would trip or do something that would make her look ridiculous. She glanced at Rob fleetingly. He was looking up at the sky; the blue was rapidly fading into the grays of dusk. He was smiling slightly. Athena knew she could not go on, mute and dumb-looking. "What about your sisters? What's happened to them?"

Rob recited the family history of his five sisters, three had married ranchers, two lived in Salt Lake City, Marilynn married to a surgeon, Wanda to a social worker. "Eliza and my sister Tula were good friends," Athena said.

Rod gave a short laugh. "One day when the family was out to sheep, my mother found a *True Story* magazine under Eliza's mattress and had a fit. It turned out Liza and Tula passed those love story magazines back and forth."

Athena's stiffness vanished: *out to sheep,* sheepmen's language; Eliza and Tula exchanging contraband magazines and his saying Tula's name so naturally. In a corner of the Union Building they drank Cokes; Athena wondered about it. "Didn't you go on a mission?"

Rob laughed, his face flushing. "You mean how come I'm drinking a Coke? Well, I did go on a mission to Holland, but one of the first things I did when I got back was buy a bottle of Coke and drink it when my mother wasn't looking."

"My father has this old saying: 'Religion is like a fish. Eat the flesh and leave the bones.'"

"Well, that's sure different," Rob said.

They talked easily then about their grade school, going to the Colorado mountains as soon as school was out and returning in early September when the sheep were driven to winter grounds, about their fathers. "My dad thought a lot of your dad," Rob said, and Athena remembered her father returning home from the funeral and hitting the kitchen table with his fist.

"How often do you go back to the farm?"

"I haven't been down to stay for three years. Sometimes on the weekend I drive down for a day. I've been going to school year round.

I have to make up time for the two years I was away on my mission." He said he was in his second year of law school and asked what her major was. When she answered that she was in art, he asked if she would teach.

Athena sighed. "I guess so." She glimpsed a fine, intent look in his eyes, as if he liked her! Her skin shimmered. "I just wish I could paint all the time." She laughed apologetically. "Of course, it's just a fantasy." She fingered her glass, empty except for a few bits of melting ice. Fluorescent lights went on and Athena hoped they didn't make her skin look yellowish.

They lingered, fell into silence, and Athena was afraid Rob was becoming bored with her. She looked at him. He was gazing off with that same kind of smile as when he looked at the sky. "I guess I better go home. My mother invited some of her friends over and I'm sure the kitchen is a mess." She was instantly angry with herself. Her mother's kitchen was never a mess.

"How are you getting home? I'll walk a ways with you."

"My dad gave me his old car when he bought a new one." Now that she was not so worried about herself, she noticed his faded wash-and-wear pants and shirt. Students passed them wearing bright sweaters and shiny loafers. She knew he must be living cheaply and probably stayed up late to study after leaving the library.

They passed the war protesters. Athena often thought she should join them, but she was afraid it would be dramatizing herself if she did. She argued with her father about the war. He said it was every young man's patriotic duty to fight for his country. She looked down at the grass. "Do you think you'll have to go to Vietnam?"

"That'll be the day. Two years on a mission and off to Southeast Asia? No, they'll take the young kids first. By the time they get to me, it'll be over."

Athena smiled at the sky. In the parking lot Rob looked at the four-door Mercury, adjacent to a gleaming blue Porsche, and said, "Well, if you think this car's old, you should see mine." They laughed. As she got into the car, he said, just before closing the door, "Come by the desk when you can."

They began seeing each other at the Union Building and when the weather was warm, they ate sandwiches on a secluded grassy spot. It was far enough from the antiwar chanting and the vociferous responses—"Love it or leave it!"—that the commotion came like a distant, joyous celebration. "I don't think it's coming out like I thought it would," Rob said. "You know, about the Vietnam war. I just don't know what to think about it. They tell us it's to stop the spread of communism and then on television we see what our bombs are doing to that little country."

Several Friday evenings they ate in a Mexican restaurant. Athena met Rob at the library and allowed her mother to think she was meeting Effie. In the El Charro they sat in the small room in the smell of grease and blue fumes and held hands.

Athena was watchful of herself at home. She was afraid the miraculous happiness in her would show. At school she had to force her wandering thoughts back to her books and papers. Her entire day focused on seeing Rob, being close to him.

Her mother looked at her sadly when Athena decided she must tell her something about it. Rob had asked her out to dinner, she said. "There are so many nice Greek boys, why go with a *kseno?*" her mother said. Her father looked back at his Greek newspaper and said nothing. She had expected anger and a lecture on following her sisters' example. "American ways have worn them down," Katherine said when Athena related the scene to her.

Tula had married in her last year of high school. Until the wedding crowns were placed on their heads, she and Gus had spoken only a few words to each other. Gus had sent his friends to her father with the proposal. Athena had been about ten years old when Tula told her how it had come about and how happy she had been to be Gus's bride. Gus, she said, was good looking, not an inch of fat on him, the best dancer there was. He had come from Greece at the age of fourteen, worked in coal mines until he had saved enough to open a fruit and vegetable stand in Salt Lake City's west side, and in a few years he had a wholesale business in the farmers market.

Katherine had met Chris at the university and her parents had begrudged her a few dates evasively, unhappily giving in to the American custom of dating. Danny, being male, married Joyce without much of a confrontation with his parents. Only his godfather made dark predictions: his bill o' fare would be out of tin cans.

When Rob came to the house, he shook hands heartily with Athena's father, then more reservedly with her mother. His face was pink and he put his right hand into his pocket in a self-conscious manner Athena had not seen before. Her father motioned him to sit on the sofa, recently upholstered in gold brocade. He asked Rob about his mother and if she still lived on the farm. Her mother nervously twisted her hands in a washing motion and asked, "You drink Coca Cola, ice tea, coffee?"

"Oh, no thanks," Rob said quickly. "I wouldn't care for anything. We'll be getting along." When they got out to the front walk, their eyes met and they simultaneously spurted out with relieved laughter.

Her mother still hoped Athena would marry one of the Greek Orthodox university students and she criticized her friends' sons and daughters who had married *ksenoi,* foreigners, as she called Americans. "You forget Danny married Joyce," Athena said, and her mother answered, "We spoiled him and he did what he wanted." The second time Athena said she was going out with Rob, her mother said, "He'll try to make a Mormon out of you," and her father said, "Eh, at least he'll be a lawyer, not like" — and he looked at his wife over his glasses, — "that tramp son of your friend Mrs. Kazakas."

In the Mexican restaurant they talked about marrying after Rob graduated from law school. He was on the *Law Review* and an old, established firm had offered him a job. Athena did not tell her parents immediately about the marriage plans. Her mother did not know about the hurried minutes on campus, the quick paper-sack lunches, the whispers over the reference counter. Her mother said darkly, "He took you out once, twice, the third time he should come with a ring."

"We could have the bishop marry us in the ward," Rob said. His eyebrows came together in a frown, as if he were uncertain about this himself.

Athena felt she had been pulled into icy water. "I couldn't."

"We'll get some judge to do it."

One night in the back seat of Rob's car, they let themselves go beyond the nebulous boundary that had been unspoken but understood could not be crossed. As she put her clothes in order, Athena was appalled at what she had allowed to happen and, even with Rob holding her tightly, her mother's stern face flashed before her. What, she thought, if Rob would not want to marry her now?

Only one light was on in her parents' house. Her old father was asleep in a back bedroom, her mother was watching television with stupified eyes. Athena hurried through the living room, fearing her mother's eyes could instinctively know what had happened. She was sticky with blood and semen that had to be washed off quietly to keep from awakening her father.

The next day Rob was exuberant, even kissed her quickly while two students were looking through the card catalog. "My mother and Great Granny are visiting my sister Wanda," he whispered, "and I want to take you over there and tell them about us getting married."

Athena stood still and a little spark of fear burst through her heart. Rob laughed. "What's wrong? They won't bite."

Wanda's house was a squat brown brick 1920s bungalow. A buckled cement walk led to three steps, the top one pulled away from the foundation of the house. Scraggly pfitzer bushes grew on either side of the steps. In a corner of the porch rusted aluminum folding chairs leaned against the brick wall. While Rob rang the doorbell, Athena stood on the wooden porch feeling cold.

Wanda opened the door and squealed. "Rob! And you're little Athena!" Her doughy face beamed. She had the Nielsen family's white hair, eyelashes, and eyebrows.

On a lumpy green sofa, tarnished from sun and years of wear, the great-grandmother sat. "Hi, Great Granny," Rob said and reached down to kiss her softly puckered cheek.

"Is this your girl?" Great Granny said in a surprisingly low, strong voice.

"Yes, you bet!" Rob put his arm around Athena's shoulders. "We'll be getting married as soon as I graduate."

Great Granny kept her eyes on Athena while Rob's mother came in and filled the room with cries and questions. Like her daughter Wanda, she was wearing polyester pants and a short-sleeved top, hers in pale green, Wanda's in pink. Wanda's pants were lighter than the top from many washings. Rob's mother had a small roundness pushing out her pants in front; Wanda, like Tula, had gained a chunky kind of weight.

Athena sat in a straight-back chair next to the sofa. Family photographs in cheap black and brown frames stood on the end table, on the mantel of the brown brick fireplace, and on an old phonograph console. On the console next to a bouquet of plastic bachelor buttons was a small lamp with a parchment shade. On the walls were ancestral pictures from the pioneer Mormon matriarch and patriarch to their great-great-grandchildren. Athena thought she would like to sketch the room.

Rob's mother asked Athena about her parents. Her gray-white hair was permanented and rinsed with blue. Her eyes looked off with nostalgia. "Oh, we had a good life out to sheep. It was hard work and we didn't have any conveniences. That privy! Rob was scared out of his wits to go in it. Thought the devil lived there. But there were good things about bein' in the mountains."

The great-grandmother did not take her eyes off Athena. Rob stood up. "We've got to get going. I'm studying all hours for my finals." He reached over and, taking Athena's hand, pulled her up. As they said goodby at the door, Great Granny said from her seat on the sofa, "So, Wanda, we're gonna have a foreigner in the family."

"Shh. She's not a foreigner. She was born in this country."

"Well, if the cat has kittens in the oven, I don't call them biscuits."

Outside, Rob put his arm about Athena's waist. "Great Granny's a character," he said and laughed artificially, his face red.

Athena wanted to cry, now that the tension was gone, but she did not. She had never seen her mother cry. Her mother frowned on tears. After Rob left her in the parking lot and she got into her own car, she realized Wanda had not served anything, drinks, cookies, nothing. She looked in the rearview mirror with a nod of her head. Tula said of her next door neighbors, "Those Mormons wouldn't give you a glass of water if you were chokin' to death."

Athena's sisters gave a big dinner in Katherine's house for the two families. The house was a decade old but looked as new as on the day it was built. In the marble entrance an enormous bouquet of flowers fanned out on a table of inlaid wood. In the dining room on a table covered with embroidered linen were great platters of traditional Greek foods, several kinds of roasted meats, shrimp and crab, vegetables, spaghetti and rice dishes, and a giant bowl of strawberries and tropical fruit. On the marble-topped buffet silver trays held various kinds of Greek honey-and-nut pastries. In the family room and at one end of the spacious living room, tables were covered with exquisite family linens, and set with sterling, fine goblets for water and wine, and Lenox dishes. In the center of each table were bouquets of early summer flowers.

Rob's family exclaimed as they entered. "You shouldn't have gone to so much trouble," Rob's mother said, wearing her church dress, a flowered washable print, and holding Great Granny's hand to keep her from walking away.

Wanda and Tula, stolid matrons now, hugged and were tearful about the years they had not seen each other. Tula asked about Wanda's sister Eliza. "I learned to speak English from her," Tula said and they laughed.

After the guests had gone, Tula's husband Gus said, "Athinoula, he's nize boy." Athena smiled and decided not to remind him that when he heard she and Rob were planning to marry, he asked her, "Can't you find a nice Grik boy?"

Katherine's husband, already thick in the middle and prosperous-looking, said, "I'll give him some work. See if I like a Mormon handling my legal stuff."

The wedding took place two weeks after graduation in a mezzanine room of the Hotel Utah. All of Athena's family were there, her parents, her mother wearing a gray silk dress for the day instead of her customary black, Tula and Gus with their four college-age sons; Katherine and Chris with their teenage boys; and her brother Danny with his blonde wife Joyce and two daughters, also blonde. Most of Rob's family arrived from towns north and south of Salt Lake City. Some were teenagers looking on intently and making comments to one another. "More would have come," Rob's mother said, "but Robbie told us we couldn't bring the youngsters and it's so hard to git baby-tenders. Eliza wanted to come so bad, but they were right in the middle of their first alfalfa cuttin'." Rob's sister Marilynn and her husband stood out, expensively dressed and, though smiling continuously, looking at their watches several times. Someone had told Rob he should provide corsages for the women, and Athena's sisters and mother and Rob's sisters and mother and Great Granny all wore small corsages of carnations in various colors. Rob introduced the young people of both families; he left them and they tried to carry on conversations without success. Then each family formed its own circle and lively talk echoed in the room about Vietnam, missions, finals, basketball teams, and fraternity and sorority happenings

The mezzanine room gave an impression of bareness. Yet Katherine had ordered two large arrangements of white gladioli, which were placed against the satin draped and swagged windows, and a centerpiece of white roses and stephanotis for the long table. A juvenile court judge Rob knew put on steel-framed glasses and waited for quiet. He stood between the tall gladioli wearing a dark blue business suit with a small black book in his hands.

Athena wore a flared, ankle-length white organza dress and a veil that came to her shoulders. When she and Katherine had shopped for a wedding dress, Athena insisted on the simple, modestly priced dress. Katherine wanted her to have a more traditional satin and lace gown. "If I were getting married in the Greek church with all that ritual and everything that goes with it, I wouldn't mind Dad paying for a fancy wedding gown, but not for a two-minute ceremony."

In a few minutes it was over and Athena's family looked at each other expectantly. Then the families sat down to a seven-course prime rib dinner, at one end of the table the Nielsens, at the other end the Demopouloses. Chris made toasts. "You don't have to drink the wine," he said laughingly to Rob's family, "there'll be just that much more for us." He raised his wine glass: "Good luck to the bride and groom," then in Greek the traditional words, "May they live long."

Rob's family looked about the table and lifted their water glasses. "Well, just this once," Wanda's husband LaMar said, smiling, like a twin to his wife Wanda with white hair and white eyelashes. "As long as it's for good luck." He stood up, holding a wine glass, and said sonorously, "Our side of the family wants to wish the kids a long, good life, and to live by the highest principles of the faith and have children who will continue to uphold the principles of Heavenly Father." He took a deep breath and Chris, taking advantage of the moment, lifted his glass and said, "Again, to the bride and groom."

Athena hardly ate. She wanted the dinner to be over, to be rid of the tightness in her. She glanced at her parents, eating steadily, their heads bent, looking sad. The dinner went on and on, each family talking and laughing about their own affairs. Great Granny would not take her eyes off Tula. "Who did you say she was, Clara?" and then, "If God had dipped her in once more, she'd a come out black."

When they were finally on their way, Rob said they would drive straight through to southern Utah, to save the cost of a motel room. In her purse Athena had five one-hundred dollar bills her father had given her, but Rob said they should use it to furnish their apartment better. No other cars were on the straight desert road through Indian country. Against the night sky, black mesas rose, stolid, massive, converging in the distance. An ominous dread pressed against the car window. Athena tried not to think of the wedding, of the judge, the quick ceremony, the barrenness of the room. Something, she thought, irrevocably wrong had taken place there, but as soon as Rob reached over to put his hand on her thigh and started talking, the blackness outside the window enveloped them in intimate wonder.

Part II

1985

I

Athena was seated in the Relief Society room of the Mormon ward trying to remember if she had locked the front door of her house. Staring at the dark blue draperies printed with a bird-of-paradise motif, she could see herself trying the knob and yet she could not be certain she had locked the door. She wondered how she could rest without seeming to while the meeting went on. Giving a quick glance about, she was relieved that Rob's sister Wanda was not in the room.

Then she realized that she was sitting in the same place as on the day of her first Relief Society meeting, almost fifteen years ago. A few women had half-smiled at her that day. Several had given her curious glances and she had thought that she looked ethnic to them and that they might be wondering about it. Seated in front of her, two women had been making little cries: they had found that they had a common pioneer ancestor, a patriarch with several wives.

After a few seconds, while latecomers found seats and several mothers busied themselves with babies, diaper bags, and purses, and put pacifiers into waiting mouths, the Relief Society president smilingly asked an elderly woman to give the prayer. In a red polyester skirt and a white, long-sleeved top, her gray hair curled tightly, the old woman stood up readily, folded her hands one on top of the other, bowed her head, and began. "Heavenly Father, we thank You for the opportunity to be together in Your house and to hear the lesson today. We ask that you open our minds and hearts that we can receive the lesson and profit from it. We ask that Sister Merrill be inspired to give of her knowledge. We ask this in the name of Jesus Christ. Amen."

"Amen," the women said in unison.

"Amen," Athena whispered. Her sisters Tula and Katherine were lighting candles, crossing themselves before the icons while the priest swung the incense burner in front of the icon screen. Vigil flames burned in wine red glasses above the icons. Blue, acrid frankincense ascended to the dome where the great painting of Christ, the Ruler of all, looked down with piercing eyes.

The Relief Society president turned the meeting over to Sister Merrill, who, she said, would give the lesson on the joy of the Sabbath. Neat in blue linen that artfully concealed her thick waist, Joleen Merrill pulled a portable blackboard from between the draperies and spread out papers and charts on a table at the front of the room: she was a convert of ten years and tried harder with lessons than most Relief Society members.

Athena slowly slumped in her chair and leaned to one side so that she was hidden from Sister Merrill by the large head of fluffy hair in front of her. She did not want to be called upon, to remind the women that she came from Greek immigrant people. The old feeling that she did not belong had returned recently, as sharply as it had in the early years of her marriage. She gazed at the head before her and remembered how silky and shiny the woman's hair had been in years past.

One after another the women told of the Sabbath in their young years. The most elderly among them smiled eagerly, deepening the wrinkles on their faces. They didn't have television of course, one said, and were not allowed to listen to the radio on Sundays. Another with blue-tinted hair said they had to do chores that couldn't be put off, like milking the cows. A woman raised her hand and said they always had a special meal. Sunday was different, a small fluttery woman said: they got ready and went to church. No two ways about it. No whining. Athena turned her head in that direction, thinking her childhood friend Effie had spoken. She often thought, wrongly, that she had glimpsed Effie or heard her voice.

Athena remembered when they were girls, when their names were Athena Demopoulos and Effie Papakostas—Pappas in English. Athena's family moved to Salt Lake City and although they returned to the mining town for weddings, lodge meetings, and sometimes for funerals, Effie and Athena did not see each other often until they were students at the university. Effie then boarded with her mother's cousin, a widow who watched her every move. She and Athena studied together in the library until the day when Effie's father died and she went back to the mining town. When Athena heard Effie had married a Mormon in the Temple, she thought of Effie as having gone away, as if to a foreign country. Several years after Athena married Rob, she saw Effie in the ward. She had cut her long, wavy hair over the years ever shorter until it looked now like a cap.

A voice from the other end of the room said in a dispirited voice that her children always wanted to go to a movie all their friends were going to or watch a television program. It caused problems. Her father, a woman with a sad, tired face said, always read from the Scriptures in the evening and she was sorry they didn't in her own family. One of the younger women said she'd like Sunday to be a day of rest for her too, but her family liked a big meal so she spent all day Sunday in church and in the kitchen.

"Then do your cookin' on Saturday. That's what we use to do," the elderly woman who had given the prayer said. "Cook a pot roast. That's the easiest kind of meal. It can be cookin' in the oven while you're sittin' here."

Athena smiled: it was exactly what Tula would have said. Smartly dressed women with the latest hair styles gave each other amused looks. Their hair was permanented and unset, with strands streaked in lighter shades. They had little interest for Athena, but she had a liking for the older women, with their dated, polyester clothes and tightly curled hair. They reminded her of Tula and her friends. She hung her head, remembering herself in her child's Sunday dress, a bow on top of her head, leaning against her mother's warm, black silken arm. On the other side of her were Tula and Katherine in their grown-up dresses. Slowly she looked up to the dome, to Christ's hypnotic Semitic eyes. Each time the congregation rose, her father stood straight and tall on the right side, the men's side.

A young woman was saying she didn't mind the cooking if she could get her children to come to church without complaining, and a very old woman with a hard voice said, "My brother didn't like to go to church and my mother just said to him, 'Well, all right, we'll go to church and you can stay home with the devil.'" Good-natured laughter followed.

Sister Merrill pointed a piece of chalk at the women and began her schoolteacherish questioning on what could be done to bring the joy back into the Sabbath. "Now, what would you say brings about willing, joyful church attendance?" Hands were raised and those chosen gave their opinions: the parents' attitudes, cheerful expectations, lack of tension, having the bishop speak to recalcitrant young people. Athena thought of Stacy, who often made excuses to stay home from the ward, and several times lately had adamantly refused to go. Rob went red in the face and argued with her. Jim dawdled, but got into the car while Rob glared.

The first bell rang. Athena looked about the small room, at the bird-of-paradise flowered drapes. It seemed now warm, inviting, a place of rest. The Relief Society president laughingly thanked Sister Merrill for her excellent lesson and asked if anyone would like to give her testimony. A young mother said the Relief Society was so important to her. No matter how she felt when she came into the room, she always left feeling better, like the Lord had been with them.

"Anyone else?" the president asked with a chuckle. "Then I'd like to say that this past month my counselors and I have visited every home in the ward and, oh, what a wonderful experience it has been. When I think," her voice cracked and tears filled her eyes, "of the love that poured through those doors at us. Well, from most of those doors. I just want you to know I love each and every one of you and I feel privileged to be your president." She smiled sweetly as she looked about the room. "Sister Madsen, will you give the prayer?"

A heavy woman rose with difficulty and gave thanks to the Lord for the lesson they had been given, for the beautiful day and fine weather, and asked that they keep their minds open for Sunday school and for sacrament meeting and return safely to their homes. "We ask this in the name of Jesus Christ. Amen."

Athena absently lifted her hand to cross herself, then, opening her eyes wide, she remembered where she was and lowered it. She was afraid. "Amen," the women said, and the second bell rang.

Athena did not want to go into the hall used for Sunday school. She exhaled deeply to release the boredom masking as fatigue in her lungs. The hall was a dimly lighted basketball court where wedding receptions and programs were held until the new chapel would be built. Athena was always aware that there were no windows in it. She stopped at the water fountain and took several drinks, then, knowing she could delay no longer, walked into the hall and sat next to Rob.

The Sunday school teacher, Dr. Harrington, a gynecologist, nodded and waited for silence. Although he was nearing sixty, his sleek black hair had not a touch of gray. His patients complained that he never offered information; a person had to ask him outright to get it.

A retired professor began sparring with Dr. Harrington, who stared at him coldly. Athena looked above the doctor's head. On one side of her the woman in charge of the last ward dinner murmured, "Did you hear any complaints about the ward dinner?" Athena shook her head, though Rob had said that several men didn't think cold cuts, salads, cookies, and ice cream were their idea of a ward dinner. "I got Doug Slater's approval. No one said one word about the men expecting a hot dish."

In the row in front of them a young mother tried to keep a small child on her lap; with slippery twisting he was on the floor. After his third smiling success, she picked him up and carried him to the back of the hall where behind enclosed panels children babbled and a baby cried.

On the other side of Athena a neighbor was whispering to her about the tumors on her daughter-in-law's ovaries. Athena's eyes wandered while she said silently over and over *stop talking, stop talking to me.* To her left a few seats away Effie sat, her black hair severely cut, like a boy's. Her thin-faced optometrist husband sat next to her. His mouth had a downward pull and his long neck with its aberrantly sized Adam's apple craned forward. Athena and Effie nodded and made perfunctory remarks when they met. It took Athena a long time to recognize their drifting away from each other as shame for straying from the ways of their people. She kept looking now at Dr. Harrington but not hearing him. His mouth kept moving, moving soundlessly.

People were standing up. Rob was looking down on her, frowning. Athena got up, not meeting his eyes, and followed him into the chapel. She searched her memory to find something to think about in sacrament meeting. What had she read that she could think about? She looked around her, looked everywhere for distraction. On the first row, next to two white-haired widows whose space was unofficially reserved for them because they were nearly deaf, a returned missionary was holding hands with a pretty girl. He had been inspired, the missionary had said on his return, to go back to a house he had visited the night before and "you guessed it! I converted them!"

Athena sat down and looked at the back of the missionary's head. Paul had written that he expected the entire family to meet him in Canada at the end of his mission "and have a real vacation before coming home." Athena tried to get air into her lungs; she thought she would suffocate.

Marilynn, flawlessly pretty, and her two closest friends, all waiting for their missionaries to return, were singing in the choir. The woman at the organ had a pink plastic flower over her ear. On the dais the youngish bishop and his two counselors were smiling, legs crossed. Behind them on a wall of vertical strips of mahogany was the only religious symbol in the chapel, a large painting of Christ—flowing light brown hair, a small neat beard, and big theatrical eyes looking passively into the distance. The picture had been placed there about fifteen years before, when the Mormon church was becoming well known and was accused of being un-Christian. Before this the wall had been lined with pictures of the church presidents, from young, clean-shaven Joseph Smith, gray-bearded Brigham Young, and on.

> Great King of heav'n, our hearts we raise
> To thee in prayer, to thee in praise
> The vales exult, the hills acclaim
> And all thy words revere thy name.

A square, big-headed man gave a prayer of gratefulness to Heavenly Father for the fine weather, for peace in the world, for President Benson's quick recovery. He asked that the leaders of the Church be blessed to carry on their burdens. He asked blessings on the missionaries toiling far away. He asked that everyone's mind and heart be open to hear the testimonies that would be given. Several children toddled up and down the aisles.

Athena's gaze blurred. Tula and Katherine were sitting on the third pew, where their mother had always sat. The liturgy would have begun. The priest intones the supplications, the choir and the cantor sing the amens, *Kyrie, eleisons,* and the "we beseech Thee, o Lord." Altar boys in white and gold robes file out of the left side door of the altar screen holding tall ceremonial candles. The priest in rose brocade chasuble follows, lifting the gold embossed Bible high, calling out to Christ for salvation.

The bishop, a wealthy architect, made several announcements. For five years he had been their bishop, one of the best they'd had, everyone agreed, hurrying to help in deaths and accidents, smoothing family upheavals, seeing to the elderly and the indigent. He was also the youngest bishop they had had. To Athena his boyish, even features, his bright eyes reminded her of actors who were not quite stars. He was wearing his usual tweed suit; he may have had many, but they all looked the same.

Athena glanced over her shoulder at the door. The bishop went on about choir practice that evening at five o'clock; the day and time for the Relief Society sisters and their daughters' fashion show and refreshments; a Fireside meeting the following Sunday to hear a Brigham Young professor speak on emotional crises; a fundraising project by the young men and women of the ward for the proposed chapel—they would take orders for family portraits; the fathers and sons' outing postponed because of rain in the Uinta mountains. Then, as an afterthought, he thanked the sisters lukewarmly for the ward dinner they had prepared.

Smiling, the bishop took in the entire congregation with a long glance and said they appreciated their wives, their eternal partners. Athena restlessly brushed against Rob. The head of the dinner committee smiled at the bishop, grateful for his absolution.

Two girls were given the young women's recognition award. Athena leaned slightly forward expecting to see a disparaging look on Stacy's face. She had been named Anastasia, after Athena's mother, but she had the wide, pale face of Rob's Danish people. Athena often felt sad when she glanced at her: Stacy walking with heavy, awkward steps, annoying her father with remarks about conservatives, and staying for hours in her room reading. Sometimes she flared up over trivial remarks made at the dinner table. Athena thought it was her fault. She hadn't known how to talk with her and too late realized that Stacy kept important thoughts to herself. At that moment Stacy had a look Athena recognized, of gazing deeply into her own world.

Athena closed her tired eyes: they had been happy little children, Paul shyly and self-consciously taking charge of Family Home Evenings when he was ten; Marilynn playing dress-up with her friends and sometimes with Stacy; Jim struggling with his school work. Marilynn and Stacy helped him write themes; Paul showed him an easy way to remember the multiplication tables. Jim jumped on his bicycle and pedaled up and down the road shouting the times tables in a loud, high voice. "I still hate school," he told them later.

Several babies were blessed, the bishop, his counselors, the father, and male members of each baby's family forming a circle about the child while a short prayer was given. The mothers sat smiling among the congregation. Several eight-year-olds who had been baptized had hands placed on their heads and were told to remember the Scriptures, refrain from sinful companions, listen to their parents and teachers, work hard in school, and help with chores. The bishop asked for further blessings on a little girl, who, the bishop said, was having trouble with her learning skills.

Athena raised her eyes above the eight-year-olds. Not long after their marriage Rob had asked her to be baptised and go through the Temple with him to be married for time and eternity. She could not remember how she had answered him.

They were singing the sacrament song. Rob looked at Athena and she remembered to smile. They heard Marilynn's clear, high voice above the rest.

> O God th' Eternal Father, Who dwells amid the sky,
> In Jesus name we ask thee To bless and sanctify,
> If we are pure before thee, This bread and cup of wine,
> That we may all remember That offering divine.

Athena smiled at Marilynn's beauty, remembering her running into the bathroom to put wet washcloths over her red, puffed eyes. Marilynn cried easily over lost dogs, abused children, and old people pushing grocery baskets that carried the paltry food of the elderly poor. Athena kept puzzled eyes on her: Why was she so accepting? Why hadn't she, her mother, helped her to think? A fine coldness passed over her forehead. Girls were always getting pregnant. Or getting married too early and to the wrong person, just to be married. Marilynn would get into something or other without thinking. There were times when she looked at Marilynn and she seemed a stranger.

Rob pressed her arm as the choir sat down. "What's wrong?" he asked. Athena shook her head. The twelve-year-old deacons were coming by with white trays holding miniature paper cups of water and torn bits of supermarket bread.

Nothing bread, her mother had called such bread. Her mother had often baked bread for the Holy Trinity communion. She shaped the dough into round loaves, then pressed a wooden stamp of the cross on it; a letter was carved between each arm: I C X C: Jesus Christ Conquers. The bread was thick, chewy. Athena thought of the last time she had taken communion in Holy Trinity, the priest holding the silver chalice, the icons gleaming darkly. It had not mattered to her then that she could never again take communion because she had not married in the church. Since that day she had gone there only for family weddings and baptisms.

A round-faced deacon stood before her holding the white tray by the handle. She took a piece of bread and the miniature paper cup of water.

"Take, eat," the priest is calling out, "this is my body, which is broken for you, for the remission of sins. Drink of this ye all. This is my blood of the New Testament which is shed for you and for many in the remission of sins." Tula stands before him, having fasted and prayed that her husband Gus would die peacefully. She takes the red silk cloth the priest holds, places it under her sagging chin, and opens her mouth for a spoonful of wine and bit of bread.

Testimony began. Athena had to think of something quickly. She would think of Tula's house, of driving there that evening in the pink-gray dusk to see Gus. A boy of nine was at the side of the lectern, his lips moving as if he were chirping: he loved his parents, teachers, sisters, and President Benson. This was his testimony. She would drive through the half-empty Sunday streets past Liberty Park with its rows of great cottonwoods to the purple brick house. She had taken the nostalgia and sadness of her mother's house, now owned by strangers, and brought it to Tula's. She hung her head in humiliation: for years after she married, she had been ashamed of Tula and Gus. She had wanted to forget her Greekness.

A handsome, well-dressed man in his forties was giving his testimony, his face contorted with tears. The men on the stage were smiling benevolently. Then a young mother said she must have done something very special in pre-existence to be blessed in this life with a wonderful husband who loved her and was supportive of her and the children, who were such a joy. They made it possible for her to carry on all her church assignments. Athena had heard the young husband called a saint: he watched the children on Saturdays while his wife took her easel and paint box and drove off to paint old barns. Athena thought of the tubes in her paint box, in the basement somewhere, probably dried up. The young mother stepped down and Athena gazed at her serene, beautiful face.

The missionary was speaking, looking fondly from time to time at his fiancée. Athena thought of her son Paul standing at a door, waiting. The door opens. He begins to speak. The door slams. Another house and he sits in a small, shabby living room, the Book of Mormon on his knees, speaking seriously to two people. Suddenly Paul turned into Jim. She looked across the aisle. Jim was staring sleepily at the missionary. She kept her eyes on him. Someday his face would be a weathered brown like her father's. With sudden awe she saw how much he resembled his grandfather when he had been out in the wind and rain with the sheep. That's what Jim wanted — to be a sheepman as his grandfathers had been, to have a dog like his father's Jack. "Why did they have to sell the sheep?" he complained.

The returned missionary was telling a story about times on his mission when he had been discouraged, but his faith had pulled him through.

Athena's shoulders shook. She tightened her lips to keep the mirth inside. There was no reason for her to be laughing she told herself. It had nothing to do with the missionary. She must stop it. Quickly she took a handkerchief from her purse and covered her mouth. The mirth escaped. She hoped it sounded like a cough. She bit the inside of her mouth until it bled. Rob pressed against her. The mirth came out again, disguised as a cough. Several times she pretended to cough and then steeled herself.

A woman with a wrinkled, grieving face said her son was lost to drugs and she would be lost too if her faith had not been so strong. She still had not given up. She still had faith that he could be saved. A sudden stillness came over the chapel as if even the fidgeting children knew they must be quiet. Athena closed her eyes.

Then before them was Rob's sister Wanda. Athena felt she was wilting, as if she were standing under a blazing sun. Rob moved about. "Where'd she come from?" he whispered angrily. Wanda was wearing a full black skirt she had had since the 'fifties and a white blouse with a girlish collar edged in narrow lace. Through the thin fabric the V neckline and cap sleeves of her Mormon garments showed. Her mouth quivered. The congregation moved restlessly, except for the two shrunken widows on the front pew. Pushing their wrinkled necks forward, they kept their faded eyes on Wanda with grave curiosity at this newest recital of grief and succor of faith.

Wanda's two-year-old grandson wandered down the aisle followed by an older sister with pinched lips. Bossily the girl tugged his arm. He protested and tried to wiggle out of her grasp. Firmly she lifted him. Wanda merely raised her voice. The boy continued to complain while his sister carried her heavy burden back to their grandfather LaMar, who sat with folded arms high up on his chest, the buttons of his faded navy blue suit jacket straining over his big stomach. Across the aisle Stacy looked at Athena with a roll of her eyes.

Wanda had stood at countless testimony meeetings and expounded, weepy and fulfilled, on how her belief in the restored gospel had helped her repudiate sin and overcome adversity. Now her grandchildren were her cross to bear.

Athena silently repeated the words *cross to bear.* No cross adorned the wardhouse; except for the picture of Christ the walls were as plain as a high school auditorium. She took a deep breath, audibly, and Rob turned to her.

Wanda said Heavenly Father knew them all by their first names, about prayer giving her the strength to go on. The congregation leaned back at her finish, except for the two elderly widows who looked disappointed. But no, Wanda with a fresh rush of tears wavered on.

Athena heard no more, thought no more. She closed her eyes. When she opened them a tall old man was at the lectern. He had been their neighbor when they lived in the subdivision house built on the old farmland. The old neighbor wore pink hearing aids on his horn-rimmed glasses and his bent-over wife no longer recognized Athena in the grocery store. His heavy voice shook as he spoke of knowing Jesus was the Christ. Athena smiled to give him encouragement. His old gray suit hung on him in drapes as her father's clothes had for several years before he died. Her father had lost weight but would not buy a new suit or overcoat. "Send my clothes back to the village when I die," he had said.

People were leaving. Rob was standing, looking down at Athena. She glanced at him, then at the people leaving the chapel. She stood up.

2

Throughout priesthood meeting, while Bud Duckworth held sway on the lesson taken from *Doctrines and Covenants,* Rob was aware of the letter from Paul in the breast pocket of his coat. He had not yet spoken to Athena about it. The letter had come to his office rather than to the house and, at seeing the familiar handwriting on the envelope, Rob had felt suddenly unhappy.

He thought of getting away for a few days. He was tired of everything and lately Athy had dark circles under her eyes. It was the routine, doing the same things day after day. Uncle Ed had said on his last visit a few weeks ago, "What's wrong with Athy?" It had startled Rob, but then he knew there was something going on with her, though it could be she was just tired.

It was a perfect time of year, he thought, to go to San Francisco. Just the name of the city brought memories of brief visits there when the children were grown enough that Athena did not have to worry about their being left behind. The children had in fact enjoyed their Aunt Katherine's big house, the swimming pool, and the excursions she arranged. Completely at ease, he and Athena had slept late in the St. Francis. Some mornings they had breakfast brought to the room, although it took some getting used to after watching their money carefully the previous ten years or more. They agreed that the few days were a rare, deserved time of flight from responsibility. They had laughed: their sheep-raising families would have been aghast at the extravagance that they would never know about.

The San Francisco skies had been clear blue, the air cool—at least it had always seemed so to Rob. Athena delighted in the displays on vendors' carts: gladioli in brilliant reds and yellows, daisies, blue flowers like the old-fashioned bachelor buttons, and others that she said did not grow in their part of the West. They saw plays, ate in touted restaurants, and after a few days it was enough and they were ready to return to their desert state.

Rob unbuttoned his suit coat and with his index finger felt for the folded letter in the breast pocket. After reading the one page inside, he had dropped the envelope into the wastebasket. He would keep the letter in his pocket, he thought, until he found the right time to talk with Athena about the Church. They had not said anything about it since the San Francisco trip, when they were having dinner in the Cliff House. Athena had looked over the bay. "There are too many things you have to believe in, things I can't even feature." He had said nothing more: he had jarred the tranquil mood of the evening.

Bud Duckworth droned on while Rob sorted out the things that were bothering him: Paul's letter; his friend Kimball Parks, who would surely be their next bishop and had something to say to him; and the tension in his law office, now that the last of the old men who had established the firm was about to retire.

Rob settled back and looked behind him to make sure Jim had found a seat. As he expected, Jim had sat next to a scrawny, unhappy-looking boy. Freckled Bud Duckworth, who owned a drycleaning store, began the lesson. The new dark blue suit with football shoulders he had bought when he had been assigned to teach the class made him look even more short and squat. He was taking the class seriously and refrained from telling any of the folksy stories that he used to entertain people in other settings. He wanted to make his mark as a devout, learned teacher. He told them to turn to page 134 of *Doctrines and Covenants* and then he leaned his head back, his chins looking like two thick pink sausages. With the resonance that speakers used in church conferences, he intoned, "Now we have this revelation given to the Prophet because there were some elders who balked at their assignments. We can learn from it."

Rob felt he was being stared at and, turning his head, saw Kimball Parks a few seats away smiling at him with the same youngish look he had had since their university days. Rob nodded solemnly and looked back at Bud Duckworth. Rob had become uncomfortable around Kimball Parks in the past year or so. Kimball was now exuberantly zealous; he could quote passages from the Book of Mormon to prove anything of the moment. In times past Rob could bring up incongruities and anachronisms and Kimball would answer pleasantly in that patient manner they had been taught as missionaries. But no more; Kimball had climbed above discussions to a high plain of certitude, from which he could look down on ordinary, confused people. Rob remembered the first time he had noticed it. He had forgotten what they were talking about, but Kimball had smiled condescendingly, almost, it seemed to him, secretly. It was the smile Rob remembered.

Rob looked at Bud Duckworth trying to be earnest and intellectual, but hardly heard his voice. Rob knew Kimball thought he was responsible for his becoming a regular churchgoer again. But it was Paul who had done it and Rob again remembered the letter in his breast pocket. Paul had been such a nuisance almost from the time he started going to Primary with his friends after school. It was part of grade-school fun for him: running to the chapel after school was out, chasing and playing tricks on each other. Rob himself had looked forward to Primary when he was in grade school. For Paul it was all fun: Primary and getting baptized along with the same friends when he was eight. Marilynn, Stacy, and Jim had followed his lead.

Then Paul began to complain that he didn't like being picked up by neighbors for church. One night he sobbed when he saw a six-pack of beer in the refrigerator. Until then he had only stared accusingly at the brown bottles while holding open the refrigerator door longer than necessary. That evening Athena had prepared tacos and enchiladas for Rob's birthday and had bought the Mexican beer to make it special. Paul sobbed on and on about the gospel, gulping air, crying afresh.

Rob self-consciously drank a little of the beer, then took the bottle to the sink. Now, years later, he wondered how he should have handled Paul. It was the last time he ever drank beer at home. From then on, when he had a craving for it along with Mexican food, he and Athena went to a restaurant far from their neighborhood, where he could drink a bottle of beer in peace.

Before he and Athena had married, they had eaten Mexican food because it was the only kind he could afford. He had really learned to like it while he was in law school. Every once in a while a group of students would go down to El Charro on Second South. The food was filling and cheap and Rob had finally got to taste beer. Kimball went with them a few times, but he looked dismal sitting at a table with beer bottles on it. Occasionally during the first ten years of their marriage, they ate there on Friday nights. Even now, he still liked going into a dim cafe that smelled of hot grease.

After the failed birthday dinner, Rob began going to church more often and Athena sometimes went with him. He knew she went to keep Paul from being miserable. Paul wanted them to be like other parents, he kept saying, and go to church all the time and go to the Temple and get sealed with him and Marilynn and Jim and Stacy so they could all be together in the Celestial Kingdom. Don't keep saying it, Rob told him. It'll come. Don't push it.

When Paul became a deacon at twelve, Rob and Athena began going to the ward almost every Sunday. How could they not, Rob told Athena, with their son carrying the sacrament tray? Now, no matter how he would have liked to sleep late and leisurely read the Sunday newspaper, he got up and went. Afterwards he felt contented with himself, even if he sometimes didn't like what he heard. It was the chapel itself, where he sat with people like his own, who had come from pioneer stock, suffered to cultivate the desert, fought with the federal government over polygamy, made the church wealthy and powerful, the chapel that gave him feelings of security and, yes, pride. Mormons were everywhere in high finance and in government, the FBI, CIA, Congress, heads of bureaus. Yes, he thought, it was something to be proud of.

A retired history professor was saying in his laconic manner, "Well, Brother Duckworth, all that makes God sound like the neighbor next door."

Bud Duckworth was sputtering, "This is revelation. This is, this is —." The bell rang and Bud Duckworth's dangerously red face began to return to its pale freckled normalcy. Rob hurried out, leaving Kimball Parks talking soothingly to Bud Duckworth. In the dimly lighted basketball court he sat toward the back of the room. He placed his *Doctrine and Covenants* book on the folding chair next to his and kept his eyes on the door. The seats were almost all taken when Athena came in, looked about slowly, and then walked toward him. He was beginning to become used to the sad, thoughtful look on her face. He wondered if it was just that she was getting older. He squirmed and did not know why.

The Sunday school teacher, Dr. Harrington, who always let his listeners know he came from English-Welsh stock, nodded and waited for silence before he began. Just looking at him reminded Rob that his great-grandmother, Great Granny, had hated the English: "They thought they was better than us Danish pioneers. They had fits if a Dane was married into the family. Treated her like dirt."

"Maybe," the retired history professor said, sitting in his usual place on the front row, "we should look at the Book of Mormon more as a literary history of Lehi bringing his people out of Israel to America. Maybe we should look at it more as a symbolic history."

"No. No," Dr. Harrington said, amid sudden movings of bodies and feet in the wake of the professor's expectedly unorthodox remarks.

"I think you've been influenced by those biblical historians who want to rewrite the Bible," Dr. Harrington said icily.

The professor lifted his hands and let them drop. "Okay," he said and folded his arms as if he would patiently endure the lesson.

It was possible, Rob was thinking, that Great Granny could have known Dr. Harrington's people. Both had homesteaded in Spring City. Dr. Harrington now pointed to a fat young man with raised hand. "I think we're just as stiff-necked as the Israelites. Well, maybe not that stiff-necked, according to our Scriptures."

Woodenly Dr. Harrington was completing the lesson. When he retired, Rob thought, he would no doubt be sent as a mission president, where he would bedevil the missionaries and expect absolute obedience. *Obedience,* the word that always came up in the ward; it bothered him. Then one of those sharp, frightening episodes struck him: What should he do? Keep on going and not think of his faith's inconsistencies? Keep going and raise questions and be silenced? Leave? His heart gave a turn. Everything was connected to the Church for him, his family, friends, even his firm. Leave Kimball Parks and men he had known for almost thirty years, because certainly they would have nothing to do with him if he renounced his faith? He would have to resign from the firm. Go out as if he were a recent law school graduate and open an office in a shabby building. Come down in income. His children would be shaken. Paul would never look at him honestly, never trust him again. Should he just stay and look at only the good the Church did? His lungs felt bruised. He didn't know. Then he realized that Athena was so still she might be sleeping. He moved his head a little; she was sitting straight, looking above Dr. Harrington's head, her thoughts somewhere else. The bell rang.

Except for Wanda's testimony, it was better in sacrament meeting. He liked hearing Marilynn's sweet high voice in the choir. But he grew tired of listening to people standing at the microphone and giving their testimony. Some of them reminded him of maudlin people called to the witness stand. There was something going on with Athena. Twice he had to nudge her.

On his way out of the wardhouse, Kimball Parks pulled at his elbow. "Rob, you old sonofagun, I've looked for you in Lamb's Grill. Where've you been keeping yourself?"

Athena was standing nearby, also caught. Wanda was talking into her face about the grandchildren Family Services had put in her care. Marilynn, Jim, and Stacy were in a group clustered about the returned missionary and his pretty fiancée, who bounced on high heels and clutched his arm. The returned missionary was asking about Paul. "Boy, we sure lucked out not getting sent to some banana republic!" He ran his forefinger across his throat and laughed. "When do you expect to get the call, Jim?" Jim blushed deeply. Athena was looking at him instead of at Wanda.

Rob looked back to Kimball, disconcerted. "I've hardly stepped out of the office," he said. "That water case in Sandy."

"Don't overdo. Take time out," Kimball said in his smooth, paternalistic tone.

Already the bishop, Rob thought, as he turned away. Kimball reached out and touched his arm. Rob disliked the way Kimball had begun talking. But he had to concede that Kimball would be a good bishop. He would be competent, look to professionals when people came to him with hard problems, and he certainly might not be sentimental, grin at the women, and talk about cherishing wives. Rob thought, though, of another bishop, Bishop Murdock, a big, stooped man with white hair like the proverbial mane of a lion, almost a legend now. When people talked of someone being Christ-like, Rob thought of Bishop Murdock, always counseling forgiveness, putting human concerns first, bending the rules for them. Kimball, yes, Rob thought, would be all right, but he would never be another Bishop

Murdock. If he had gone to that good old man when he and Athena were planning to marry, Rob knew he could have helped him out, maybe even talked to Athena, and he wouldn't be worrying now about the Church, the Temple, any of it.

Rob hurried past a group of people circled around a gray-haired couple ready to leave on a mission to the eastern states. "It's something we've always dreamed of," the slender woman said. Her abdomen had fallen; Stacy had said it looked like a basketball. "Now the children have left the nest, we're off to work for the Lord!" She laughed. "Well," her husband said, "I wish they'd given me a month or two to enjoy my retirement."

Ahead of Rob, Wanda was rapidly explaining to Athena that they were late for ward because she couldn't get the grandchildren ready in time. Athena helped the children into Wanda's dirty red van. They were thin, all five needing a haircut, their clothes faded. A legend on the van's bumper sticker said HAPPINESS IS FAMILY HOME EVENING. Paul had taken charge of the Monday Family Home Evenings from the time he was little. He read stories of miraculous appearances of the Three Nephites; Marilynn played the piano; Stacy read school themes on the Anasazi and other Indians; Jim told sheep stories he had heard from his grandfathers and tried to blow on a harmonica that Athena had bought him. "Why did they have to sell?" he always asked.

As Athena reached for the handle of the car door, Effie Whitman and her husband went by. "Good morning, Sister Nielsen," the optometrist said. Effie and Athena said hello. Rob thought: not even "Hello, Effie," "Hello, Athy." He got into the car. He wished he had made a point long ago of becoming friends with Effie and her husband, not for himself—the optometrist was a stick-in-the-mud, as his Uncle Ed would have said—but for Athena's sake. She and Effie should have stayed close. Now they acted as if they were strangers, even worse, as if they'd had a feud, which he knew they hadn't.

Stacy and Jim got into the car while Marilynn walked daintily toward it. Rob could see why Athena worried about her. She was always conscious of being looked at and ended up acting unnaturally.

Rob felt uncomfortably warm: obviously Kimball was starting on a campaign to get him and Athena married in the Temple so he could have him as one of his counselors—which he didn't deserve: he had always managed to get out of church work. Then this letter from Paul. He had expected to talk with Athy about Paul's letter in the afternoon in the quiet house, but it wasn't the right time: she seemed not quite— he didn't know a word for her inattention. He put a hand on his chest where Paul's bothersome letter lay underneath the tweed fabric.

> I just don't understand it, Dad. Here I'm bringing the Gospel to people and telling them to go through the Temple and my own parents haven't gone through it. How do you think it made me feel when I was getting my endowments before my mission and my parents weren't there with me. You said you'd talk to Mom that day and here it is almost two years later and you haven't. How are we going to be together in the Celestial Kingdom if you and Mom don't go through the Temple. How do you think that makes me feel?

If he had waited until he and Athena were married to become intimate, this would not be coming up to make him miserable now. If he had controlled himself and converted Athena first, it would have all been taken care of. He hadn't had the courage to tell Bishop Murdock that he and Athena had been immoral in the back seat of his old car, hear his lecture, but get the recommend for the Temple. It had been easier to tell his family that Athena was not yet ready to be converted.

He looked into the rearview mirror at his children. What did they know about their parents anyway? What did Paul know about his feelings, about the law office, about the strange worry he sometimes had when he looked at Athena, about Jim's poor grades? Children didn't know. Rob twisted his lips in annoyance. When talk came up about the struggles his and Athena's parents had had, worst of all in the Depression, losing everything, both fathers doing repair work for the WPA until the Second World War got them on their feet again, it just sort of passed over the children's heads.

Then the office—he could not possibly say to the children how much he wanted to be head of the firm. If Dick Sheffield got it instead, he would be ashamed to face them.

All but one of the attorneys who had founded his staid Mormon firm had died within the past three years. Thatcher Bailey, kindly, always helpful, now ready to retire, had warned him once, no, not warned, more just giving him advice. He'd told him: "You ought to be more active in the Church, Robert." Rob was next in line to become head of the firm, but Dick was more active—the word was everywhere—in the Church. Dick's family had been prominent since pioneer days, colonizing, important in business, in the Church hierarchy, in politics. Dick had four generations of college people behind him and Rob had not a single university graduate paving his way. His Uncle Ed hadn't even finished high school. Dick also had season tickets to the symphony and knew when the music was played especially well; he took a half-day off last week to see an exhibit in the university's Fine Arts Museum. He always looked composed, at ease; he had a good vocabulary. He drove a Mercedes. Whenever Rob saw the Mercedes, he remembered that Dick had inherited wealth and that he himself had not inherited anything. He had got where he was all by himself. His envy was tempered somewhat; Athena's father had left her a modest inheritance. They had put it into government bonds, held jointly. He still thought of the money as belonging to Athena's father, the big sheepman summering his sheep on the range next to his father's. Nostalgia passed through him softly. That's where he and Athena should go, not to San Francisco, but to the Colorado mountains, walk all over their fathers' range land, take the trails to the sheepherders' camps, carry a lunch and eat it in the cool air among the quaking aspen and the columbines. Yet he knew they could not go without taking Jim with them. Stacy might want to come. Then it would not be the quiet rest he and Athena needed.

Rob drove down the winding road of their neighborhood thinking he had probably made a mistake in staying with the firm, but he had been grateful to be taken in right after graduation. One of the first cases he had been given was a *pro bono,* a young Ute Indian who couldn't get into the carpenters union. He had felt intensely excited talking with the long-haired Ute, preparing the brief, and the exhilaration when he'd won. Like a wonderful feeling of being cleansed. He had a few more cases that left him with this same clean, good feeling and he came home happy with his day, happy he was a lawyer.

Then the firm began giving him corporate law cases. A newer member of the practice, a pale redhead, was doing the *pro bono* cases. Rob had passed his crowded little office one day and looked at him, his reddish head a few inches from a law book, other thick volumes open on the messy desk. A swift thought—he should go out on his own—had streaked into and out of his head. He was a married man with a baby coming. No, children didn't know what it was like to be a responsible adult.

Rob brought the car to a stop. The children jumped out, Marilynn as awkwardly as Stacy, now that no one was watching. They were suddenly in high spirits. Rob turned to Athena. "Is something wrong, Athy? You seemed to be daydreaming or something." Then, remembering his own wandering thoughts, he said, "Well, I had a hard time keeping my mind on what was going on."

At the back door she passed him, her eyes on his, wide open, a soft look in them he did not understand, a look reminding him of the young Athy of their university days. He was struck, as he had not been for a long while, at the lustrous strands in her light brown hair, the deep brown of her eyes, and even more her skin, still with that golden color seeming to come from within. A wondrous desire burst in him; he had not felt such passion in years, a flashback to the marvelous first days of his love for her.

Now, in the moment she passed by to enter the house, he had a presentiment of her beautiful skin with the fine rays at the outer edges of her eyelids thickening, becoming expressionless. He felt terribly cold, as if he had grabbed a giant icicle.

3

Athena drove down Seventh East in the fading day. Toward the west, vestiges of a red sunset brushed over the sky in feathery pink clouds. She was at peace driving to Tula's house: like a reprieve, she thought, from the agitation that had taken hold of her. She smiled as she drove past Liberty Park where her children had ridden the merry-go-round, watched ducks and geese swim in the man-made lake, and eaten hot dogs and syrupy, brilliant red and purple ice cones. Afterwards they crossed the street to Tula's 1920s purple brick bungalow and sat at her dining room table. Platters and bowls steamed with fragrances. Tula's house was her refuge.

Athena parked at the curb, walked up the narrow cement path and up the steps to the door. She turned the doorknob and shook her head. Rob, whom Tula and Gus respected as an attorney, a man of learning, had tried to change Gus's old village custom and Tula's small-town habit of leaving doors unlocked. "What can you expect," he had said, but with an affection that had taken years to develop, "of someone who calls her refrigerator an icebox and her basement a cellar?" The door opened to muted Greek folk music and the scents of cinnamon and hot honey. Athena remembered the warm sweetness when she was a child in her mother's house.

Tula and Katherine were sitting in the dining room at the massive oak table covered with a beige crocheted cloth made by their mother for Tula's trousseau. In the center was a cut glass bowl filled with past Christmas and Easter cards. "Sit down, honey," Tula said, as if Athena were one of the family's children instead of a sister. "We're sittin' here instead of the kitchen so Gus won't hear us."

"I'll say hello to him first." Athena walked through the room, comforted by its bulky oak furniture, the glass cabinet with Tula's best glassware and demitasse cups, the buffet top filled with photographs of varied sizes: wedding, baptismal, graduation, and family pictures of canyon picnics, and Christmas, Easter, and Dormition of the Virgin celebrations. Beyond the immaculate kitchen of oldfashioned, white glass-fronted cabinets and hexagonal-tiled drainboard, a family room had been added. It had been a playroom when Tula and Gus's sons were small.

Gus sat on a worn sofa, his old man's freckled head with a few gray hairs carefully combed across it hung down; the loose flesh of his face drooped. Several Greek records lay stacked on the metal arm of a record player awaiting their turn to fall into place and begin spinning. A singer sang that he would send a boat with golden sails to return the girl from Samos to her island; he would strew pomegranates on the seashore.

Slowly the old man opened one defiant eye sideways. Then both reddened eyes opened wide. "Athinoula," he said. She kissed him. "Tell Tula I'm sleep. She make me take medicine. She make me tired."

Athena nodded; something stuck in her throat and she could not speak. She returned to the dining room and sat down. "He's gone down hill, Athy," Tula sighed. "These last few months, he's gone down hill."

Tula sat, a shapeless, sorrowing mound. Her short gray hair was held in place by a hairnet. She always wore one while cooking. Athena looked at her and Gus's wedding picture in the center of the buffet's display. They had been slender, handsome, Gus twenty years older than his bride, renowned for leading the circle of dancers at church celebrations. A miniature cardboard icon of the Virgin and Child was inserted into the corner of the frame.

Athena glanced over her shoulder. Through the door that led to a short hall a faint golden light came. As Katherine poured her a cup of coffee and Tula served her three kinds of pastries, Athena turned to the doorway again.

"It's decaf," Katherine said. Her hair too was gray and short, but brushed back over her ears. Athena was proud of her; except for a slightly thickened waist, Katherine's body had retained its youthful shape. Clothing hid the signs of aging. "We're talking about the priest's sermon," she said. "How insensitive can he be? He called women who'd had abortions and lesbians and gays sinners? Just think what that would do to women who've had an abortion and—"

"They shouldn't a had one," Tula interrupted.

"Oh, Tula, you think everything is black and white. And telling homosexuals they're sinners. Didn't it occur to him there might be one sitting listening to him?"

"Well," Tula pushed out her lips, "he did say that one time that we shouldn't hate them, only hate what they did."

"Oh, of course, it's all right for straight people to know the warmth of another person, but he would deny it to a homosexual. As if they wanted to be the way they are."

"I just don't know why you go to church at all, Kay," Tula said shaking her head at Katherine. "You haven't taken communion since I don't know when. Sometimes I wonder what you believe."

"I certainly don't believe everything the Church says."

"What are you talkin' about?" Tula hissed. "If the Church says somethin', then you've got to believe it."

"What do you know what our church believes? You probably think God's an old man with a long beard sitting on a cloud up in the sky."

Tula sputtered, "Well, I guess. I —" She didn't finish and looked at the coffee cup in front of her in bewilderment. Then with a lift of her head she straightened up and folded her arms over her enormous breasts. "I have no idea what you're talkin' about," she said. "I can't believe what I'm hearin'. You always could upset me. Just because you went to the university."

"I used to think about those things all the time. Years ago. Then I realized my problem wasn't that at all. My problem was I didn't know if there was a God."

"My good God!"

"Then I stopped thinking about it and only hoped."

Tula tapped the table with a demanding index finger. "Then why did you kill yourself takin' your kids and then your grandkids to church every Sunday and Holy Week and stuff? Hmm?"

"Because I thought they should have the memory of churchgoing. To give them some order to their lives." She looked away. "Besides, it's our culture."

"What is this world comin' to?" Tula raised her eyes and made the sign of the cross three times. Then she looked back at Katherine. "You know what's gonna happen to you? You're gonna be like poor Gus in there. He never went to church. Hardly ever took communion. And then he got old."

"Who knows," Katherine said, lifting her shoulders, and smiled at Athena.

Suddenly Tula brushed her hand across her eyes as if to discard what had been said. "Another thing, Kay, let's not start complainin' about this priest we got or the archbishop'll send us some kook and we've had enough of them."

Tula and Katherine began talking about priests. Father Mark, one of the first priests born in America, had gone to seminary to get out of being drafted in the Second World War. "He should have run a restaurant," Tula said. Katherine said that when they did have a good priest, like Father Anthony, people didn't like it that he was on community boards. So he left and they got Father Ted, with oil spots on his robes and white socks showing under his robes.

Athena said, laughing, feeling part of them, "Remember how Papa swore at him because he was so sloppy making the sign of the cross. Papa said he touched his nose, his appendix, his collarbone, and his *paidhakia*," the Greek word for an animal's small ribs.

Tula and Katherine laughed with her. "He was a gossip too," Tula said, her face pink with happiness at seeing Athena animated. "What's worse than a gossipy priest?"

"And what was it Papa said about Father Philip?" Athena asked eagerly. "The one from Greece who rang a little bell and his wife would come running."

A nostalgic look came into Katherine's eyes. "Papa said he wanted to put a sheep bell around his neck."

Tula glanced at her sisters sadly. "We was lucky to have him for our dad."

"Why didn't we have Mama's and Papa's funerals in the old church?" Athena asked suddenly. "That was their church. Why did we have the services in Prophet Elias?"

Tula flared up. "What do you care what church they had their funerals in! You're supposed to be a Mormon." She folded her arms over her breasts again as their mother had when she had said her final word. But Tula had more to say. "You was born Greek Orthodox and as far as I'm concerned that's what you'll always be!" She pushed out her lips.

"Oh, for heaven's sake, Tula," Katherine said.

"I was never baptized a Mormon! I only go to the ward because of the children."

Tula swayed sideways, her face squashed with remorse. "Oh, I didn't mean it, Athy. I'm just so tired. Up all night with Gus. And my Sammy is having trouble with his kids." She breathed rapidly. "The reason we didn't take them to Holy Trinity was because of my legs. Those steps kill me. The old-timers like Gus, when they built the church, none of them had old folks around. They didn't think they'd ever git old and have a hard time climbin' the steps."

"It's okay," Athena said and Tula plied her plate with several more pastries and ordered Katherine to refill her cup with coffee. They began talking about the children and grandchildren of the family, then about people, some of whom Athena knew, and others she did not. Tula explained who they were, what business they were in, and how many children and grandchildren they had.

Athena looked at the golden haze coming from the hall. "I should wash my hands," she said and walked slowly toward it. At one end of the hall was a linen closet; the doors of the central cabinet had been removed and in the recess was an icon of the Virgin and young Christ. In front of it was a glass of water with a layer of shiny, yellow olive oil. A small burning taper floated on it.

The mellow light spread over the Byzantine Virgin, over her grieving eyes; the boy-Christ smiled faintly, his thumb and middle finger held together in the ancient sign of blessing. At one side of the icon lay a dried palm from Palm Sunday, twisted into the form of a cross; on the other side a withered carnation from the Good Friday tomb of Christ, its red now turned to brown. A small bouquet of yellow crocus, white alyssum, and a few violets were placed next to the carnation. Athena looked at the Mother and Son. The talk from the dining room, the folk song from the television room receded back, back into a profound silence. In the golden light and silence she gazed. Then the thumb, index and middle fingers of her right hand came together and with their own volition made the sign of the cross.

After a few moments, her sisters' voices reached her and she went into the spotless, hospital-white bathroom, rinsed her hands, and returned to the dining room.

4

Rob sat at his desk, his back against the ceiling-to-floor windows. His office was uncomfortably bright from the sun reflecting on the white walls and he had put on a pair of dark glasses. Yet he felt chilled. On his desk was a pile of documents, but he had not gone through them.

He gazed at the oil painting on the wall facing him. It was a western scene of sheep being trailed through sagebrush. Athena had painted it the first year of their marriage, before Paul had been born. Like a plaintive child, he thought: why couldn't Paul let things be until he came home? Why did he always have to have his own way? He had enough worries at the moment.

With a cold heaviness in his chest, which he feared was a prelude to bronchitis, he thought of the previous night. Athena had always looked forward to the Hackett's neighborhood party—the house filled with great arrangements of flowers, the pioneer furniture and pewter, the buffet table crowded with bowls and platters of plain, abundant food, a small bouquet of flowers on each blue linen-covered table.

They had sat at one of the tables with Dr. Harrington and his pretty little wife, and the old farmer who had sold the land that now made up the neighborhood, and his wife, whose face was crisscrossed with wrinkles. The light party talk turned suddenly to the murder of a young woman and her baby. The old farmer said he didn't believe in waiting for the Lard to git around to giving murderers the business and murmurs of assent passed through the room. Then, to Rob's horror, he heard Athena's shaky voice: "I don't believe in capital punishment. It's un-Christian." A silence settled like an unheard thud over the room and although within a few moments the talk and laughter began again, the former gaiety was gone.

"You didn't have to say it there," Rob told her when they reached their house. For answer she went to their bedroom and closed the door. Later she came into the kitchen where the children were eating pizza and took two aspirin.

The telephone rang. "Your sister-in-law," his secretary said. He didn't want to pick up the receiver. Tula spoke in the harsh tones she used when she was worried. "Something's wrong with Athy, Rob. She should see a doctor. She's not herself. I'm just so worried. You just gotta force her to go to a doctor. She won't listen to me or Kay."

He had barely hung up the receiver when another call came through, from Wanda's husband LaMar. Now what? he thought. All his sisters lived ordinary lives with the highs and lows of everyday crises, but Wanda and LaMar's house was in constant chaos. When he first started with the law firm, he was pleased to be looked to for help. Now he wished he would be left alone to solve his own problems.

"I'm sorry Athy was so upset this morning," LaMar said in an apologetic voice. "I know we just lean on both of you too much. You know we have Darla Kay's children with us until the court decides if she can have them back. Athy was so nice to bring a bucket of chicken from Harmon's and ice cream and soda pop. The kids were in seventh heaven."

Rob waited, tapping his pen against the polished wood of his desk. "Darla Kay is in no condition to have her kids back yet." He knew his voice was cold, but he did not care. He was sick of their crises.

"It was just that she was so tired, Rob. She hadn't slept nights, with Courtney's colic and then little Dave got the earache he gets all the time and it just got too much for her with the kids needing their breakfast and Verl working nights. Of course he's not much good when he *is* home. She didn't mean to hurt the baby. I told Athy if the court called and asked questions about Darla Kay, she could tell them Darla Kay was really a good mother. Athy just blew up, Rob. She said they better not ask her. She'd tell them Darla Kay's got no business having all those children."

"Anyone can see that."

"Rob, please. Talk to Athy. This investigation they're doing could just bring their whole family down."

"Hmf," Rob said as he hung up. He tried to imagine Athena losing her temper with LaMar. She had liked him from the start, smiled at his farmerish pronunciations: *Lard* for Lord, *carn* for corn. What's happening? What's happening to us? he repeated silently.

When Rob returned home that evening, Athena was in the bedroom with the draperies drawn. That night he awoke in dense blackness, his face clammy. He had dreamed of himself, the small boy in the blackness of his great-grandmother's homestead cabin. He was curled up on the cot, his head covered except for a narrow slash through which one eye peered out with horrible fear. His heart beat wildly against his thin chest. His great-grandmother could have died in the next room and he was alone, alone forever in the icy blackness.

5

After the Hacketts' party, Athena could think only of hurrying to the sanctuary of her bedroom. As she went by Rob, standing at the door of their house, she saw a strange staring in his eyes. She walked quickly through the living room and down the hall to her bedroom. Carefully she closed the door and sat on the wide bed.

She kept her eyes on the door. Muted sounds came through it: voices, footsteps, the clink of dishes, knives, and forks. A frightening vision bloomed malignantly: Dr. Harrington and the old farmer stood among a great throng on a wide plain, smiling, nodding, and under their feet the earth was fed by roots of blood, the blood of the Old Testament, of Revelation, of the Book of Mormon, the blood of retribution.

She trembled, afraid of something terrible expanding in her head. Rob's heavy footsteps came toward the door and stopped. She waited. Her heart beat in staccato. She placed a hand over her mouth to keep the words inside and her other hand clenched into a fist against her breastbone to stave off the horrible pounding that would come. Rob's footsteps turned back. In hazy relief she exhaled.

After a few minutes she stood up, caught a determined look on her face as she passed by the dresser mirror and walked into the kitchen. Marilynn was sitting at one end of the table, where Athena always sat, and serving pizza to Stacy and Jim. Rob was at the sink filling a glass with water. "Is your headache better?" he asked and she understood he had made this excuse to the children.

"I'll be glad to drive you to Brighton or Snowbird," Jim said. "It'll still be light for a while. Mountain air always clears my head."

Athena gazed at him sadly for the need at his age to clear his head. "Poor little ones," her mother used to say when her grandchildren were small, "what they have to go through." Athena shook her head and, aware that Stacy was watching her, turned slowly to face her. Stacy glanced about and leaned over her plate, but Athena did not reprimand her.

While the children were at the table, Rob nodded to Athena to follow him into the television room. For a few minutes they sat in silence, then Rob got up and shut the door to the kitchen. Athena took a deep breath and said, "I'll never believe in killing no matter what anyone says."

Rob's face flushed. "You made everyone uncomfortable. It wasn't the right place."

"I had to." Athena was amazed how it had come out without her thinking of saying it. She felt buoyed: after all, it wasn't hard to be true to oneself.

"There's a time and place for everything," Rob said.

Athena did not answer. She knew even one word might bring on a bad quarrel and she would not allow it; she was not ready. She went to her desk and began her weekly letter to Paul, trying to convince herself that what happened at the party was not as bad as it seemed. If she said anything more to Rob now, it would swell and swell. Her fingers shook as she held the pen. She tightened her fingers about it and wrote a longer letter than usual. She named friends of Paul's she had seen at the grocery store and the gas pumps; she repeated a remark Gus had made that she thought he would find amusing—although Paul didn't have the fondness for him that Jim had. She had hidden too much Greekness from Paul, the oldest child, and from Marilynn as well.

She stopped writing and looked at the paneled wall. She had let her children be steeped in Mormon family history and lore and had said little to them about her own parents and their life as despised immigrants. She had been ashamed not too many years back when Tula and Gus had been around Rob's family. She had made them out to be funny, "characters," because of Gus's heavy accent and blunt honesty ("What you mean the wine in Bible is grape juice? That's Mormon talk") and of Tula's Greek words mixed in with her poor English and her dark looks. Athena had come to her senses with Jim and Stacy. She frowned because she was not sure of Stacy. But then she was writing a paper on Greek proverbs for her anthropology class. The first proverb Tula gave her was: "A crow is born white, turns gray, then becomes black like its parents."

"Do you want to say anything to Paul before I close," Athena asked Rob, her voice gentle, knowing she had shamed him at the Hacketts. He was reading the lesson which he and an elderly man, Brother Mitchell, would use when they went ward teaching the next day. Athena looked at Rob's open book. She felt helpless, alone, like the time when she was a child, lost in the pines at sheep camp.

"Hm, let's see," Rob said and Athena felt sorry for him trying to be pleasant. "Tell him I'm thinking of trading in your Taurus for an

Oldsmobile. I saw Bob Durham on the street day before yesterday and he told me he knows someone who would take it. Oh, and tell him I'm starting on my first day of ward teaching."

The next morning Athena put the letter into the porch mailbox for the postman. Several hours later she heard the familiar rattle of mail being deposited. Among the advertisements and bills was a brown envelope in Paul's handwriting. Happily surprised because his letters usually came in the middle of the week, she hurried with the mail into the television room. As she sat down at the desk, her face prickled: the letter was addressed only to her. She tore open the envelope.

> Dear Mom,
>
> I think you ought to just read the Book of Mormon and *Doctrine and Covenants* again. It's all there, the Truth, the answers to all questions. And some questions that aren't will be answered at the right time. We have the Truth. Why do you think I'm here? To bring people the divine plan of salvation. We are God's Church. I can't believe you're acting so strangely. And I'll never understand why you and Dad haven't gone through the Temple. How do you think it made me feel when I got my endowments before I left for my mission and my own parents weren't in the Temple with me?.

Athena hurried to the end of the letter holding the tip by her thumb and index finger. Her hand shook as she opened her stationery box.

> Dear Paul,
>
> I'm your mother. What do you mean writing to me as if I were a child? When you were twelve, your church gave you the priesthood, making you think you were superior to your mother and every other female. Well, to me you're my son and you still have a lot to learn.

As she wrote she dabbed tears from her cheeks. Her anger collapsed and she leaned back against the chair. After a moment, looking at the wall without hope, she tore the two pages and Paul's letter into shreds. The pieces fell onto her lap; slowly she made a ball of them and let it drop into the wastepaper basket.

Almost an hour passed while she stared and wondered who had written Paul and what that person had said. Not Jim, she thought, unless he had scribbled a lighthearted comment about something she had said. No, someone had accused her. She thought of Marilynn—could she be the one thinking in some distorted way to get Paul's support for her and Arnie's marrying when he returned from his mission, or Stacy in bad temper, or Rob out of perplexity?

She tried to recall what she might have said; what whoever had written the letter had discerned in her words. She thought of each one of them again, Marilynn, Jim, Stacy, Rob. If they were there at that moment she would lash out that they were tattlers, that they didn't have the courtesy to talk with her about it, that they wanted her to be a puppet, to nod like Wanda when told to nod. They had taken away her privacy.

She prepared her words for them, for him, for her, for whomever it was. Then she knew she would not say anything, because it might lead to talk she did not want to hear. She would not mention Paul's letter. She would let the betrayer wonder. She would look for signs.

Several days later the Relief Society president telephoned to ask Athena to be in charge of salads for the widows' dinner. Athena said she was not feeling well. When she hung up, she was angry with herself for not having been quick enough to give a better excuse. She would be getting telephone calls; she would have to do her grocery shopping beyond the neighborhood to avoid being seen; and Rob might meet a committee member's husband and be asked about her.

Something bad she knew was happening to her and she had to do something about it quickly. She had to think about Stacy and Jim. Her outburst at LaMar—how had she let it happen? She had to occupy herself differently.

She was standing motionless in the center of their sons' room when Rob returned from work. He came to her side and put his arm about her waist. "You okay?" he asked. They stood in silence. A blue and white Brigham Young University pennant was nailed above Paul's bed. He had transferred from the University of Utah in his junior year, even though Athena and Rob had not wanted him to. His side of the room was neat. On his otherwise empty desk were photographs of his basketball team, made up of church friends; his high school graduating class; and a girl in a prom dress. Above, his books were lined on shelves, textbooks, a few mysteries, and biographies of Mormon church leaders. Athena touched the worn *Catcher in the Rye* that had excited him when he was about thirteen. Jim had asked about it before Paul had left on his mission. Paul had considered and then said it wouldn't interest him. He suggested other books which Athena bought and Jim said were dopey.

Jim's side of the room was a mess, the bedspread thrown over to hide rumpled blankets, magazines and books placed in slipshod manner on his shelves along with his harmonica, an old sheep bell, and a dirty soccer ball. He had been a champion little league player. "Why are you crying?" Rob asked.

Athena blinked and, carrying the university catalog, returned to her desk and went over the list of classes for the summer quarter. She wrote down several, hoping to find one that had not been filled. She told the family at dinner, "I'm thinking of taking a class at the U this summer quarter." She had a compulsion to jump up, get into her car, and drive away. Stacy and Jim looked at her with interest, Marilynn frowned. Athena avoided their eyes.

The following week she registered for the contemporary literature class. She walked across the rolling campus to the bookstore and felt a slow-motion lightness lifting her. The grass on either side of the paths was brilliantly green. She was aware of a smile on her face and students smiling back at her. She thought how beautiful the trees would be in autumn, yellow against the blue sky. By then life would be better.

In class the students treated the professor as if he were their peer, but Athena looked at him with sadness. He was thin, gray at the temples with a sparse white and black beard that made him look older than he was. He wore metal-rimmed glasses, which had been faddish in the 'sixties, and Levi's with heavy cotton pullover sweaters in grays and browns. He often looked at her with an encouraging smile. At first she stiffened, afraid he would ask her a question or for a comment, but he merely gave a nod of acknowledgment and went on in a lifeless, automatic tone that showed no interest in the books and authors he was discussing. She had seen him on campus when she had been a student and knew he was repeating the same lectures he had given then, year after year the same talks, all outlined in an old green leather notebook.

She tried but could not keep her thoughts on what the professor was saying. While he talked about John Updike and the Rabbit novels, she was thinking he reminded her of Rob's father. He also had become a gray man early. Until he died, he wore breeches, plaid shirts, and high-top boots laced to his calves that signified what he had once been, a sheepman.

The bell rang and, embarrassed, Athena realized she had daydreamed the class away. Every day her attention effortlesssly left the thin, gray professor. She was determined to listen, to learn, but a sickish feeling in her stomach prevented it. Without her knowing it, she would be recalling other days and the sickness in her stomach would vanish. At times she saw bright images between herself and the professor, sheep moving down to winter grounds, snow-covered fields, red-earth plateaus.

Athena looked through the windows of the classroom. She looked about. She was alone in the room. She wondered how long she had sat there. At the next class she noticed that the professor had not once glanced her way. Her face flamed. She would pay attention, she lectured herself sternly, and she must even ask questions to let the professor know she was alert, listening to his bored repetition of old lectures.

She tried and failed. By Friday pain beat above her right eye. When she got into her car to drive home, sunlight stabbed through her eyes into her brain. She drove fast, thinking that she must get to her house quickly.

At the door she dropped her books and ran into the dark bedroom, drew the draperies, and fell on the bed. An hour later Stacy cautiously opened the door. Stacy's worried face was large, larger, growing ever larger. "What can I get you, Mom? Don't get sick, Mom."

Over the weekend she stayed in her room, taking aspirin, drinking juices, unable to eat. The family drove to church without her. By Monday she was well enough to attend class even though her thoughts still wandered and she had a strange sensation of something fomenting inside her. By Friday her head was pounding and she lay with eyes closed against the diminished, but still too-bright light of the draped bedroom window. The following week repeated the cycle.

"There's somethin' wrong," Tula told her.

"It's migraine," Katherine said. "I know. I had the same symptoms twenty years ago."

"Make an appointment with the doctor right now," Tula ordered. "This has gone on long enough."

"Will you make the appointment or shall I?" Rob said in the hard voice he used at times with the children.

After the doctor's examination, Athena dressed hurriedly and went into the doctor's office of brownish walls, orange seat covers, and a reproduction of orange marigolds on one wall. She sat on the edge of the chair next to the rolltop desk and looked above it to family photographs on the wall. In the past the picture of the doctor's wife had been replaced every few years, but for at least ten years the same one remained in a gilt-flowered frame: a smiling woman nearing fifty, crinkles around her eyes, her hair in an outdated bouffant. The family picture taken every Christmas was on the desktop: each year the children had grown taller; now they were wives and husbands with children. Next to the photograph was a piece of wood with a motto burned into it: HOME IS WHERE THE HEART IS, the boy scout work done years past by one of the doctor's sons. Athena swallowed a sob.

"Your heart is good," the doctor said as he opened her twenty-year-old file and wrote in it. He glanced at several slips of paper and said her blood count, triglycerides, cholesterol were all right. He faced her and Athena felt odd: his blue eyes began to fade as he spoke to her. "Now, your main complaints are the migraines and feeling fatigued?"

"Yes." His eyes were now as pale as a white sky before dusk. Athena saw his mouth move: she was to stop at the laboratory and make an appointment for a thyroid test.

She stood up and suddenly forgot his name. It rattled around in her head and would not be still long enough. "Thank you, Doctor," she said and hurried down the hall, past the laboratory, through the waiting room, and to the parking lot. She got into her car and drove off through streets that led onto a boulevard. She had driven for nearly twenty minutes, but when she turned off the ignition, she had no memory of streets, cars, people, shopping centers.

6

The buzzer sounded. "Your sister-in-law," his secretary said. Rob lifted the receiver: "Tula? Katherine?" he said quickly, hopefully.

"It's me." Tula breathed heavily into the receiver. "Rob, what are we gonna do about Athy? Kay and I are real worried about her."

Rob lowered his voice. "The doctor said there's nothing wrong with her physically. He said it's fatigue."

"Well, I don't know about that. In the first place she shouldn't of decided to go to the university and tax her brain any more than it is. And how come she's fatigued? I think she should see another doctor."

"Maybe you're right, Tula. We'll see. You've got enough to worry about with Gus. We'll take care of it. Don't worry."

Tula's voice hit his ear drum. "Of course, I'm gonna worry! She's my baby sister!"

Just before noon Chris telephoned asking to meet him for lunch, but Rob knew these invitations, knew by the tone of Chris's voice that they were more a command that boded a finger-pointing monologue. He said he had an appointment. "Goddamn it, Rob, don't put me off! Kay's been telling you all along something's wrong with Athy."

"She'll be okay. She—"

"Don't give me any of that bullshit! Don't be so damn optimistic. You Mormons are even cheerful at your funerals."

Rob hung up. "Damn Greeks!" he whispered. "Always putting their nose in other people's business." He felt guilty. He owed being a partner in the firm to Chris. A few months after he and Athena married, Chris gave him the bulk of his legal work. He left only a little for his elderly lawyer. "Can't drop him like a hot potato just because he got old," Chris had said.

Rob watched Athena more closely. She had always been up and fully dressed with his breakfast ready the moment he sat down at the kitchen table. Now she sat on the edge of the bed, still in her nightgown, her face heavy from sleep. She had begun to sleep even throughout the day. On weekends he followed her motions; she made beds, put clothing into the washer, prepared meals. He had a shaky sensation that he was photographing a slow underwater documentary for television. Athena seemed to be following a deeply learned routine that needed no thinking. He did not want to mention anything about it to her. Everything was wrong, different. He was especially disturbed by a new habit. With each lift of her arms, she stopped to breathe. "What's wrong?" he forced himself to ask. Her voice came slowly as if with great effort: "My arms are so tired." The childish tone in her voice first affronted then frightened him. He went into the children's bedrooms and told each one, "Your mother needs help. She's very tired and you've all got to help more than you've been doing."

She did not want to see anyone. She stared at the telephone when it rang. Rob would not pick up the receiver even if he were near it. He thought it would keep her aware of everyday life if she had to answer it. She made excuses for lunch invitations.

"Well, for hell's sake you're not going to have any friends if you keep this up."

A smile came to Athena's lips. For a moment a brightness was in her eyes. "My father had a Greek proverb about that," another long pause, then panic struck her face. Her mouth twisted as she tried to remember what the proverb was.

The next day Rob made a decision as he drove to his office: he would forget all about talking to Athena about Paul's letter. She was not being logical. When she came out of this moodiness, he would convince her that she was veering away from the Church and family because of muddled thoughts. She had to put them out of her head. Then she would feel better. He felt his heart snag on something.

Early the next morning a garbage truck awoke them as it lumbered to a stop in front of their house. With a bound Athena ran to the bathroom and the sound of vomiting and toilet flushings began. "What is it?" he asked on her return. She shook her head, but Rob felt a little surge of relief: maybe her trouble was really physical; the doctor had overlooked something.

Athena sat on the bed, squinting with abhorrence. "Tell me," he insisted: he had to get to the bottom of this, this terrible problem that was upsetting him, his work, the whole house. Like a child long used to obeying, she told him haltingly, searching for words, about an incident years ago. He had been away on two-week army reserve training. Paul had recovered from a sore throat when Marilynn, only six months old, had become sick and refused all liquids. Athena held her night and day. Tula and Katherine brought food, tried to take Paul with them, but he clung to her legs.

She had forgotten the garbage can standing in the sun. Twice the garbage truck passed by and the trash container under the kitchen sink had filled up and begun to smell. On the third pickup day she heard the garbage truck down the street. Marilynn was drowsy. Athena put her next to Paul, who was asleep in his crib, ran to the kitchen, picked up the trash container, and hurried outside. The sun blinded her; heat rushed at her as if from a giant, open oven. She lifted the garbage can lid. A mass of thick pink worms buzzed and rolled furiously. She dropped the lid and ran back into the house to vomit. "The sound of the garbage truck made me remember."

Rob did not know what to say. "These things that are happening," he ventured, not looking at Athena, "I think we better see a psychiatrist about them." He raised his eyes. She was not listening to him. He sensed she was listening to something else. He left the room with a heavy fear of disaster waiting just ahead.

The Relief Society president telephoned him. She had brought a casserole, she said, rang the doorbell again and again, and was about to leave when the door opened. She handed Athena the bowl and while she was talking, Athena closed the door. "She looked so bad. What can we do to help, Brother Nielsen?" He said he would call if there was something the Relief Society could do. When he returned home, he saw the casserole on the drainboard and wondered if they should eat it. It should have been refrigerated. He glanced at Athena, ready to say something about refrigerating food, but such a situation had never happened before and he said nothing.

Athena stopped cooking. Marilynn prepared the meals with Stacy's help. After the food was on the table, either Jim or Stacy went into the bedroom where Athena sat on the edge of the bed and led her to the kitchen. Methodically she ate a small amount of the food Rob placed on her plate, staring at it the entire time. "We should act normally," Rob told the children. "She'll come out of it." He looked at them; they nodded, looking miserable, perplexed, and he felt the burden of having to instigate conversations that he did not want to think about at the moment.

He asked Marilynn about Arnie, who was still on his Mexican mission. Although she merely answered that she had had a letter, it occurred to Rob that if he brought up the subject of her wanting to marry when Arnie returned, Athena would come to her senses and speak her mind. "I hope you've given up the idea of getting married when he comes back. Don't say anything. Let me finish. Trying to go to school, babies coming along, penny-pinching. It doesn't work."

"Oh, Dad, it won't be like that at all," Marilynn said softly with a glance at her mother, who went on eating small bits of food. Rob would not look at Athena. Her face was becoming skeletal; her shiny hair dull; her short fingernails grown long. In their bedroom at night, he begged her to tell him what was wrong. "I don't know," she said.

Jim said he did not want to go to seminary classes. "I didn't go to seminary myself, Jim, but if you'd go, you'll learn more about your faith," then angrily, "You've got to pay more attention to your school work." Stacy said she wouldn't go to Fireside. At the last meeting a woman had talked about miracles in pioneer days. "I won't insist on it," Rob told her. "Oh, do what you like." He tried to care, but he did not want to think of anything at the moment but Athena eating the little dabs of food while tears fell down her cheeks. The tears exasperated and frightened him.

Athena got up from the table abruptly. She hurried through the kitchen, her eyes astonished. The family stared and stopped eating while her footsteps sounded down the basement stairs. When she did not immediately return, they began eating, one after another, surreptitiously looking toward the open kitchen door that led to the basement. Several minutes passed. In the cold silence Rob strained to hear her returning footsteps. A tightness reached up to his throat. He put down his napkin and walked with deliberately unhurried steps out of the kitchen and down to the basement.

At the foot of the stairs he listened. There was no sound in the unlighted hall. He opened the door to the cemented room where bottled water, flour, dried foods, and other survival items were neatly stored according to the Mormon church directive. He closed the door quietly and slowly opened the adjacent one to the furnace room. Athena was kneeling at the foot of shelves Paul had built as a teenager. Shoe boxes and cardboard containers had been opened and were in disarray. On a center shelf children's books and stacks of manila envelopes, bulky with bank statements and tax records were in place. Three big boxes had been pulled from the bottom shelf. One held the children's once-cherished stuffed animals, matted, an eye, an ear, a paw missing. He had been ready to throw them out, but Athena had said the children might want to see them some day. The second box holding the children's early school drawings had been rifled through. The third box had fallen on its side and out of it crocheted lace, white embroidered doilies, small hemstitched napkins had spilled. He remembered Athena saying her mother and Tula had made them for her trousseau, but they required ironing and she had stopped using them. At Athena's side was an open shoebox filled with Paul's British-made knights of armor. He had played with them for hours at a time when he was in grade school. In front of Athena was a shoebox with small tubes of flattened, used oil paints. Rob squatted at her side. After a few seconds he said in a low voice, "What are you looking for?"

Athena lifted her head and looked at the shelves. After an interminably long time she said, her voice weak, despairing, "My book of charcoal sketches. I made when my father took me. Sometimes. When he was buying sheep." Her voice went on in a monotone, "They were in a green book." Rob remembered only a brown hawk. Athena had used water colors to paint it, sitting imperiously on a fence post, its eye a menacing black bead. He had told Athena he would frame it for his office but had never gotten around to it.

Athena picked up a flattened tube of paint and looked at it. "I'm dried up. Like this tube."

"You can paint again. There's no reason why you can't."

"I've lost years of my life."

"Don't say that. Just think of all the good things in your life. Come on now. Don't let the children see you like this." He stood and lifted

Athena to her feet. Taking her hand he led her up the stairs. When they entered the kitchen, the children's faces were turned to the door, their eyes frozen.

That night Rob had a dark, unpleasant dream. His father was in it, but on its periphery, moving slowly about, his shoulders pulled down, his face unshaven, like the derelicts near the railyards.

Athena stopped speaking. At first the family kept up the pretense that she was listening and taking part in their talk. Then they began to carry on conversations as if she were not in the room. Marilynn said Rob should talk to the bishop about what to do. Stacy shrieked. Rob said, "Bishops aren't educated in these things." Marilynn insisted. "If the bishop and his counselors would only come and lay hands on her head, she'll get better. It happens all the time." No one answered her.

Katherine came every day and sometimes Tula, when she was able to make arrangements with her grandchildren to stay with Gus for a short time. They wanted to take her to lunch, shopping; they brought food to last for days. Katherine said Chris insisted that she take Athena to San Francisco for as long as she wanted to stay. Athena shook her head while tears washed down her face.

One Saturday the three sisters sat on the patio while Rob was at the desk paying bills, a job that Athena had always taken care of. Tula's brusque voice came through the open windows. When he and Athena were first married, he had mistaken the tone for anger and learned later that her voice took on a coarseness when she was worried or afraid. "Athy, there's a Greek psychiatrist in town now. He's from back east, born in Boston. Mary Likakis said she knows someone who goes to him, and I'll bet it's her sister. And she says the good thing about him is he knows our customs and all, everythin', and you don't have to explain every little thing. He knows."

Rob sat up straight. Although he had come to like Athena's sisters, after becoming used to them, he bristled now, his face hot: what was this nonsense about "customs and all"?

Katherine said, "I'll make the arrangements." Athena did not answer. Rob went into the kitchen for a drink of water. He let the water run a long time; he wanted it to be cold, to cool his face. On the drainboard Tula had placed Athena's favorite foods: *moussaka;* artichokes cooked in olive oil, lemon juice, and onions; and apple pie. Katherine had set the table. As he lifted the water glass, Athena slowly walked into the kitchen, tears running down her face, and went into her bedroom.

Tula was crying on the patio, "My baby sister. What's gonna become of her?" They were walking now to the gate, then to the car parked in the driveway. Their voices came back to him through the open windows. "I've been thinkin', Katina," she said. "It's got to be one of two things, either the LDS church or somethin' about sex."

"Lower your voice!"

"Well, maybe Rob's too demandin'."

"Oh, for heaven's sake, Tula!"

The car backed down the driveway. Rob lifted his arms and dropped them. "I'm at the end of my rope," he said aloud and his eyes stung. That night he had one of the dark, chaotic dreams that he had come to expect after being sleepless for hours. He awoke in the stark blackness, the dream forgotten, but leaving him with an intense longing for a glass of cold beer.

7

One morning Athena sat on the bed gazing out the wide window. A far-off thought of someone crying in the night struggled in her memory, Marilynn's voice crying and calling, "Oh, Mom, Mom." The memory vanished.

Beyond a low hedge a figure, a neighbor, was kneeling and digging about a weeping willow trunk. A thought came: was it time for spring planting? Blinking tears away, she got into her car for the first time in two months and drove to a nursery. She bought the same spring plants she had every year: zinnias, marigolds, snapdragons, and petunias; tomatoes, green peppers, and zucchini. They were scraggly leftovers. She was unaware that the planting should have been done weeks earlier.

As she pushed the filled cart toward the checkout counter, she saw on an otherwise empty wooden platform three small rusty cans with delicate green plants growing in them. By their leaves she recognized them as Icelandic poppies and put them in the crook of her elbow. She hoped at least one would be a bright red color. *Paparounia,* Christ's blood, her mother had called red poppies.

Inside the dark play house Chris had given Marilynn when she was small, she pulled on old canvas gloves and chose a trowel from a perforated wall board on which rows of tools hung. Tears spilling down her cheeks, she planted the flowers between perennials of iris, phlox, and delphinium; the vegetable plants between the play house and the small rose garden. She kneeled, dug into the dark earth, removed the plants, one after another from the square plastic containers, placed their packed roots into the holes, and tamped dirt around the stems. She was following long-remembered routine and still was unaware that it was almost too late for planting. The freshness of overturned earth, the pleasant coolness in the air did not reach her and the feelings of peace and lightness she had had in the past while working with plants were absent.

She returned the trowel and gloves to their proper places, a rule Rob had made when they were first married: everything in accustomed order. She then went to the kitchen, washed her hands, and opened the refrigerator. A white package lay on the second shelf. She picked it up and knew by its softness it was fish. She opened the package and put the halibut into a bowl of cold water to soak, as her mother had always done. She chopped an onion and a green pepper and opened a can of tomatoes. Fresh tears fell. While she was at the stove stirring the sauce, the children came home. They exchanged surprised looks. "Mm," Marilynn said with an exaggerated intake of breath, and Stacy mumbled, "Did you put basil in the sauce?" Jim, who preferred meat, said, "It looks good, Mom." Athena did not answer. Marilynn and Stacy quickly set the table.

As Athena washed lettuce leaves, Rob's car came up the driveway. Athena lifted her eyes. The car passed the window, Rob frowning, his lips pressed together. Moments later he came into the kitchen, stopped with a start, then put his hand on her shoulder. "Hi," he said and looked at the oven, profound relief passing over his face.

At the table the children carried on a lively conversation, spurred almost to hysteria. They glanced at Athena to see if she heard or cared. They could maintain it but a few minutes. Rob asked about their day, which had once been Athena's domain. His mouth turned downwards with disappointment.

"I'm going to write this paper on a contemporary author," Marilynn said, "so I'll have it ready for English 105 and won't have it hanging over my head during autumn quarter. Only I don't know who to choose."

Rob, Jim, and Stacy looked at her, at the incongruity of her studying during the summer. Marilynn kept her eyes on her mother as if expecting a sudden sign of interest.

Stacy snorted. "You don't know *whom* to choose. You don't know because you read bestseller trash."

Rob tapped his fork against his plate and gave a warning nod toward Athena: his family was falling apart. "How about Stephen King?" Jim said.

Stacy narrowed her eyes at him. "That junk," she said.

Her head down, Athena ate a small circle of halibut in the center of her plate and did not touch the salad. Then she stared above their heads at the wall. Rob looked at her, then at the plate, then again at her. The children were silent. "Eat some of your salad," Rob said quietly and mechanically she lifted her fork. The children began talking again, but quietly as if the sound of their voices would cause Athena to stop eating.

A few days later Rob brought out a bottle of tranquilizers. He waited until the children had left the room and said, "Athena, why don't you start taking these tranquilizers Dr. Burnham prescribed? They'll make you feel better. Then you can go to this psychiatrist he recommended. To find out why you're not happy, why you won't talk." Athena gazed at him and turned her head.

Summer passed. Athena weeded the garden. Each day she accomplished the necessary household tasks. Almost every evening Rob, and sometimes Jim, took her by the arm and opened the car door. She got in docilely and gazed out the window at the passing green, granite-tipped mountains of Brighton and Alta. The family noticed that she no longer wept. She heard their whispered words at times, but they passed through her and away. "Why don't you call Dr. Burnham again, Dad," Jim's voice. "I've called him so often, I feel like a fool. If she'd only take those pills he prescribed."

Tula and Katherine brought food, led her to the patio, served pastries and coffee from a thermos. They talked about priests, the church festival, Tula wondering about going to the memorial hall early in the mornings to supervise the making of the *dolmadhes* and then on to the nursing home to see Gus. Katherine told Tula that her feet wouldn't take it. She should give it up. When Athena walked through the house to her bedroom, she saw their secret looks. They were waiting for a sign of interest from her, but she did not have the energy. She heard them talk to Rob in the kitchen. "I think she's comin' out of it," Tula's voice. "I don't know when it started," Katherine's voice.

"Maybe it had to do with Mama and Papa dying."

"I don't know." Rob's voice. "Everything seemed to bother her and then she just lost interest, even in Paul's letters."

Paul ended his weekly letters: "I hope you're feeling better, Mom." Athena stared as his letters were read.

Toward the end of summer, she spoke three words, her voice rusty, unused. She handed Stacy a covered bowl and said, "In the refrigerator." Stacy looked at her, surprised, then happy. The next day Athena said to Jim, "Get peat moss."

On the third anniversary of her mother's death, she cut all the red roses, the last of summer, and drove to the graveyard. The Icelandic poppies had bloomed weeks earlier, yellow, white, and orange, but no reds. Tula called later to lecture her. "Katherine and I came to pick you up. Why, in God's name, did you go up there alone?"

"Oh, Tula," Athena said.

After a silence, as if Tula was trying to decipher what she had heard, she said, "How come just the red roses? Oh, Athy, Athy, you're makin' it so hard on me. I've got my Gus in a nursin' home now. I could hardly lift him after his last stroke and the kids made me put him in St. Joseph's. Me! I always said I wouldn't never let him go to a nursin' home! Oh. Oh. And I have to go every day to be sure they treat him right. He was too modest. He wouldn't let me take him to the bathroom. He said, 'No, I'll go to the nursin' home.' And now he sings that old song our Dad and old Tsimblis used to sing, the one about

Charos. You know. The man says the nightingales tricked him, told him he would never die. And then he sees Charos, all dressed in black, comin', ridin' over the valley on his black horse. And the nurses and aides make fun of him. Ach, ach."

Athena tried but could not answer for a few seconds. She was being pulled out, out into the world, out of that safe place. Then she took a deep breath and said, "I'll go see him—in a little while."

"But you've got to go with me! Don't go yourself. He can't use his hands and I feed him. It makes him ashamed. We'll go together and you wait outside until I see that he's okay." Tula began crying. "He understands. He knows what's happenin' to him. His pride is hurt. And Katherine thinks I'm just a hick the way I talk to the doctor. *She* went to college. I didn't."

Another two months passed. Rob saw sadness on Athena's face, instead of the blank, passive look. He did not know if it was a good sign or not. After dinner one evening she put on the brown tweed coat she wore on errands to the grocery store, the bank, and the cleaners. Rob looked up from the desk in the television room. "Are you going to the grocery store?'

"No."

"Oh, I thought I would go with you." He had never gone on errands with her; Athena never asked nor expected him to. She was like her mother and sisters. He had been amused at her mother, who had never understood American men going to stores with their wives: "Not men's business." Athena had laughed, telling of her mother's scorn for them, standing about in department stores, waiting for their wives to come out of the dressing rooms to ask their opinion on whatever dress, suit, or blouse they were contemplating buying, and holding their purses by the straps. He thought: if her mother were alive, all this wouldn't have happened. One Saturday, after he and Athena had moved into their first house in the subdivision, Tula and her mother came, laden down as always with pans of food. This closeness had taken him a few years to accept. The furniture had all been put in place and he was outside using a stiff, long-handled brush to wash the three cement steps leading to the backyard. Athena's mother mumbled angrily after saying, "Hallo, Robe," and went into the house.

"What's wrong?" he asked Tula, plump, still pretty then, smiling at him. "She's mad that your doin' what she thinks is women's work. She's gonna give Athy a lecture."

Athena was at the door now, hesitating. "I'm going to walk to the school and back."

As soon as the door closed, Rob got up and looked out the window. The leafless elm branches that divided the driveway from the neighbor's property reached into the grayness above. Athena lowered her head against the cold breeze. She was without a hat and pulled the coat collar about her neck, but it fell back in place when she put her hands into her pockets. He thought: why hadn't she put on a hat, a scarf, gloves? Then, that he would take them to her. He did not move from the window, knowing that by the time he found them, Athena would be out of sight.

He sat at the desk again, disturbed at the image of her lone figure under the barren branches walking against the wind. He began reading the lesson he and Brother Mitchell would give on their Sunday afternoon rounds. He was accustomed now to being questioned about Athena. One of the wrinkled little widows who sat on the front pew in the ward always asked, even before he got inside her house, "How is Sister Nielsen's troubles?" "She's getting along," he would answer, and peering deeply into his eyes she would sigh.

His thoughts floated away from the page before him. At first agitated, he began to feel encouraged at Athena's going for a walk; it was a good sign. At that time of year no one would be outside to stop her, to ask well-meaning questions. He leaned back in the swivel chair and rocked back and forth impatiently: it had gone on far too long.

The next morning while Rob and the children ate sweet rolls and drank orange juice, their Sunday breakfast habit, Athena prepared a roast for the oven. Rob was aware that the children were watching him, just as he was watching Athena. She was wearing a navy blue skirt and a white shirt, the kind of dress she wore at home. After putting the roast in the oven, she scraped carrots and peeled potatoes.

The children placed their glasses and plates in the dishwasher and left the kitchen. Rob lingered until he heard the children open the closet door for their coats. He stood up, waited a few seconds, then said, "I thought you might come to the ward with us this morning." Athena said nothing.

In late afternoon she wrote Paul, the first letter since her illness. She had no news for him as she once had had about the ward and the children's activities or something she had read in *Dialogue* or *Sunstone,* periodicals Paul disliked: "Liberal," he had said of them, "inappropriate." She wrote: "I'm thinking of you. It's colder than usual this year. The magnolia tree has been cut down. Love, Mom."

That night in bed, Rob said, "I'm glad you wrote Paul."

Athena inhaled deeply. "I don't know what," she said and breathed out heavily, "he'll think of me when he comes back."

Rob fumbled for her hand and patted it.

8

Rob lay in bed. Cool, caressing air came from the window that he had opened a few inches; the room was darkly protective. He thought he had lived just such a moment before, then remembered it. It was after his father had died and the death ritual had been completed: buying the cemetery plot and stone, ordering a wreath of carnations, sitting on a front pew at the funeral, feeling strangely ready to cry, eating the dinner prepared by the Relief Society, and the last act—going through his father's legal papers. After they had returned home and gone to bed, he lay awake in the blackness and the feeling had come, a euphoria that his father would no longer struggle with pain, that the frightening images he had seen were over. His father had been very near to having his dignity destroyed.

Rob reviewed the signs of Athena's coming out of it, the word *it* that he and Athena's sisters used because they had no other that was adequate: the letter to Paul after months of not having written; that night in bed confessing: "I don't know what he'll think of me when he comes back." He fell asleep quickly and when he awoke he knew he had dreamed something pleasant.

The following Sunday he heard the good sounds of kitchen noises before he opened his eyes. Athena was already up. He showered leisurely. When he went into the kitchen, he was pleased to see that the table was set with their usual Sunday breakfast: large pitchers of orange juice and milk and next to the microwave oven a tray of breakfast pastries. Athena was opening the oven and putting a roasting pan into it. She was wearing her navy blue skirt and white shirt. Fear turned in him. He stood for a few seconds and then forced himself to speak.

"Athena, you're coming to the ward aren't you?"

Athena shut the door and stood with her back to Rob. She faced him. "No," she said quietly.

"Why, what do you mean?"

Her voice fell into a whisper. "I gave up who I was."

Rob turned quickly and walked into the television room, opened the closet, and took out his coat. The children were looking at him, like statues with stunned eyes. "Let's go," he said, and from the corner of his eye he glimpsed a figure go into the kitchen and touch Athena's arm as she sat down at the table.

After they were seated in the car and Rob backed down the driveway, he said, "She's your mother. I don't want any of you making her more miserable. We'll talk about it some other time." Seated next to him, Marilynn dabbed at her eyes. In the rearview mirror he glimpsed Stacy with a fist pressed against her mouth and Jim looking out of the window as if for help. Juices turned in his empty stomach. He recalled a scene he had not thought of since the day it had happened and bile reached to his throat. The family had been sitting in the ward listening to a visiting member of the Seventy, aides to the Apostles, talk about the restoration of the early church through Joseph Smith. The speaker pontificated in a dreary monotone. Turning his head to rub his neck, which was prone to spasms when he sat too long, he glimpsed a dead hopelessness on Athena's face. A chill had passed over him and quickly he looked back to the speaker—and then forgot about it. He saw now that there had been clues to Athy's illness and that he should have paid attention to them—and even more—that he hadn't wanted to pay attention to them.

He had acted like a fool in the kitchen. Now he had to drive his children to a fast food restaurant for something to eat. He felt humiliated at how he must have looked and what the children thought of leaving the house and eating in a restaurant on Sunday morning. He stopped at a squat pseudo-cowboy place advertised as "the family restaurant."

He could hardly look at the children, Marilynn and Jim across from him and Stacy at his side. At several tables were younger fathers than he with grade school-age children eating the Sunday pancake special. Rob thought with nausea that he was like a divorced father taking his children out to eat on his weekend custody arrangement.

"Your mother's not over her illness yet. We'll have to give her more time."

The children nibbled at their English muffins and jam. "We'll just have to go to the ward without her for the time being," Rob said, lifting his eyes quickly and looking down at his food, which tasted like sawdust. When they got up to leave, Jim said in a tentative voice, "Well, at least Mom was honest." Rob's heart bumped against his ribs.

They drove without speaking to the ward and into their classrooms. Rob heard only snatches of the lesson and the announcements. Images came to him: Athena gazing dreamily while sitting next to him during Sunday school; when the children were recovering from an illness, she insisted they remain one more day inside—if the day were a Sunday.

He thought of the stillness in the house when they returned. How would they speak in the awful discomfort? His children would never forget this morning. And he wondered what Athena was doing at the moment. Then he thought they should have stayed home. He should have asked Athena to come into their bedroom to talk about it

No one spoke as they drove home with Jim at the wheel. They were silent and, when the car stopped, they got out slowly. Athena was in the kitchen taking out the roasting pan from the oven. Her chest was rising and falling rapidly. Rob thought he should say something but nothing came to him. Marilynn said, stiffly, "Hi, Mom." Jim gave Athena an embarrassed glance. "Hi, Mom," he said and quickly left the room. Stacy went close to her. "That smells good."

"Come on, kids, let's get the food on the table. Let me carve the chicken, Athena." His face flamed—calling Athy "Athena" and offering to carve the chicken. She had always done the carving, as her mother and sisters had. He felt there was a bone stuck in his throat.

"All right," Athena said and he exhaled softly, deeply relieved that she had spoken and they would not have to eat in silence. Athena finished preparing the lettuce salad. Marilynn and Stacy brought rolls, milk, and ice water to the table. Once seated, they began passing the bowls and platters around the table, then Rob remembered to give the blessing, which he had begun reciting again after years of omission. Paul had always given the prayer. Rob thanked God for the food set before them, thanked Athy for preparing it, asked that the day be peaceful. He reddened at the word *peaceful*.

Their usual Sunday table talk had centered around the ward, whom they had talked with, what news they had heard, and the announcements the bishop had made. They strained now for topics. "Jim," Rob said, "I want you to take your mother's car to the garage and see about that noise in the brake system."

Marilynn shrilled that one of her friends had been given a Honda for her birthday. Jim began talking about a newly released list of ratings comparing American with foreign cars and he and Rob talked at length about various makes. Marilynn asked about prices. Athena and Stacy took no part in the conversation. Stacy hunched over her food and ate doggedly. Rob noticed Athena looking at her pensively.

After dinner Athena sat down to write Paul. Rob sat in the cool leather chair and reviewed the lesson he would be giving later. He glanced furtively at Athena; she was wiping her eyes. He wondered unhappily what she was writing. Athena left the room quickly. After a few minutes he went to the desk to get a pencil. The letter was covered with an advertising brochure from a department store, but the last two lines were visible: "You believe we have to go through the Temple to be together in Heaven, but that has never concerned me. If there is life after death, I expect families would naturally be together. I will always love you."

He went back to his chair and read and reread the smoky printed words. Athena returned and stared at the wall. Marilynn came in and said peevishly—he would have to talk to her about this; she was incapable of sustaining the earlier cheerfulness—"If you're finished, I want to use the desk to write Arnie." Athena stood up, her shoulders sagging.

In the evening, after Rob returned from ward teaching, he met Athena in the hall off the bedroom wing. They looked at each other.

"Come into the bedroom a minute," Rob said in a low voice. They sat on the bed side by side but did not turn to each other. "We've got to stay together as a family, Athy."

"I know. I've thought about it. For years."

"Can't you just go and look at the good part? You're the one who told me that proverb of your dad's: 'Religion is like a fish. Eat the flesh and leave the bones.'"

Athena turned to Rob and looked at him sorrowfully. "People can do that with their own religion, Rob, but not with someone else's." She lowered her head. "Whatever happens, I have to go back to my church."

Rob glanced away.

"Do you want to talk about the future?"

"There's nothing to talk about."

Athena knew the nearly hidden sign of anger in his voice, but she thought she also heard something remote, indecipherable. "I have to go back."

9

Although Prophet Elias was closer to her house, on this first Sunday of her return, Athena wanted to hear the liturgy in Holy Trinity, the old immigrant church. The children and Rob left the house for the ward earlier than she for church. The children were noisier than usual, to cover their self-consciousness. From the door they called out goodbys loudly. "Well, goodbye," Rob said. At the corners of his eyes were small puffs of skin, an early sign of aging, more noticeable when he was not speaking or smiling and especially when he had not slept well. Athena answered an almost inaudible goodbye. For a brief moment their eyes met and Athena sensed in his a hope that she would suddenly pick up her purse and come with him. As he turned, she thought it was impossible for her to have married anyone else. She could not imagine it.

She got into her car wanting to drive to the church in peaceful unconcern about everything except the clear blue day, the church, the people inside, the people like her parents, like her sisters and their husbands. She thought, though, of the previous Sunday, after she had told

Rob she would not go to the ward again. She had let herself down on a chair, her knees weak, and one of the children had come into the kitchen and put a hand on her shoulder. Since then she had wondered which one it had been.

As she drove toward the three-domed, burnished brick church and into the asphalted parking lot, she willed thoughts of her family away. She walked toward the church and up the cement steps, a pulse beating at her temples. A middle-aged man ahead held the heavy door open for her. She entered the narthex. Her heart beat wildly with ecstatic relief. Once before she had felt such emotion; in her childhood, she had skipped at the side of railroad tracks, not hearing the train whistle, and then steam rushed past her bare legs.

She crossed herself while deeply inhaling the acrid incense, took a five-dollar bill she had ready in the pocket of her purse and placed it on the silver tray. A bald, smiling man behind the counter said, "Good morning." Athena smiled and picked up a white votive candle for Gus and lighted it from the flame of another. Several burning candles had already been pushed into the boxed, shallow bed of sand: a few people had arrived early while the Orthros was being chanted. Athena crossed herself again at the icon of the Holy Trinity. A rush of joy, of freedom, filled her head: no one was watching, she did not have to hurry.

A few immigrant widows and several people of Tula's generation sat near the front, two of them on the third pew, where Athena's mother had often led her and her sisters. For a moment Athena stood uncertainly, then took a seat behind it.

She looked at the icon screen. The middle door, the Royal Gate, was closed. At the cantor's lectern a dark young man with long hair in a knot, his beard, black and skimpy, was chanting melodiously about God, the Unapproachable Radiance. She remembered her sisters talking about him: a theology graduate who had refused to take a parish. He wanted to become a monk they had said.

Athena sat transfixed, unaware of the choir entering the balcony at the rear of the church with a rustling and settling into places, or the movement of the parishioners: the elderly seeking their accustomed pews; the new immigrants who had come after the Second World War and were older than she; and young couples and children of all ages. She did not feel strange, as she had been afraid she would. She thought of seeing Effie Pappas in the grocery store. She would not look away from her. She thought of the day Tula's husband Gus would be in his coffin and she would be there with them all, grieving, belonging.

The middle door of the altar screen slid open and the slender, dark priest in green brocade robes stepped out. The ancient liturgy began. For a few moments she thought of Rob and the children and remembered again her mother's words: "Poor humanity, what it has to endure."

While the choir sang the hymns of the day, Athena became aware of a smile on her lips. Across the aisle a three-year-old was sucking his thumb. Whenever the priest chanted "In the name of the Father, the Son, and the Holy Spirit," the child took out the thumb to make a jigsaw cross with inexpert fingers and transferred his other thumb to his mouth at the same time. His pretty, obese mother smiled down at him. She was wearing a dark blue dress patterned with large red flowers, a startling presence among the mundanely dressed parishioners.

An old woman's voice said loudly in Greek, "Father Markos had a better voice." Heads turned to Mrs. Karafoundis, a tyrant to girls of Tula and Katherine's generation. "Senile," Tula had said, "falls asleep in church and talks out loud when she wakes up."

The side doors of the icon screen opened and several acolytes came through them, holding tall brass candleholders with lighted tapers. The youngest, a boy of about nine, wearing a robe that dragged on the floor, almost tripped as he took his place before the middle altar door. The priest followed, lifting high the silver embossed Bible. He called out a long, sustained cry of proclamation and longing. Slowly he passed through the Holy Gate and glanced meaningfully at the head altar boy, who was returning the censer to its stand.

The doxology continued, priest, cantor, choir, calling, responding, and Athena's lips began moving. A fine hurt brought tears: no, she had not forgotten. She thought of Tula and Katherine sitting in Prophet Elias, not knowing she had come back to the church. She had wanted no commotion, no crisp remarks from Tula. She was right to have wanted to come alone, in peace.

She thought of Holy Week, the chanter and priest reciting the events from the New Testament as Christ came ever nearer to His Passion: Great Thursday, mournful, bleak, a pall of grief over the congregation; Great Friday, the people following the flower-decorated tomb of Christ and singing dirges; Great Saturday and the infinite joy of the Resurrection at midnight.

Many acolytes filed out of the left door of the icon screen, carrying heavy candleholders with lighted tapers and brass standards, the youngest now wearing a robe that fit him. The tall altar boy swung the smoking censer in the path of the priest, who held high the covered chalice and paten. The priest raised the Gifts and again called out long and poignantly, asking the Lord God to be ever mindful of all humanity. He returned to the altar and supplications began that the wine and bread become the Body and Blood of Christ.

Athena knelt. The choir sang softly while a soprano voice soared. Help us all, Athena prayed, and closed her hot eyes. When the long line of parishioners formed to take communion from the common spoon she had once spurned, she watched each one with infinite envy.

She looked at the children in their Sunday finery coming down the aisle to attend Sunday school, clutching pieces of consecrated bread. Little girls in frilly nylon dresses with ornamental clips in their hair held hands; little boys wearing suits, strutted, privileged to be males. The Greekness in some of the little faces had been modified by another strain of blood or by several, called "American." She gazed, smiling at the children as they dawdled or half-ran down the aisle.

She breathed in deeply of the incense-tinged air. She knew she could never take communion as long as she was married to Rob. The rules made by men would not let her. But she was there in the church of her people and someday perhaps the rules would be changed and she then could approach the priest holding the chalice and place the red silk cloth under her chin.

Epilogue

1995

Several years ago, Athena began inviting all of Rob's family for a family dinner on Easter by the Gregorian Calendar — American Easter as the Greek Orthodox called it. Over fifty guests had come the year before and this did not count Rob and Athy's own children and grandchildren. She used her finest embroidered cloths, which her mother and Tula had made for her, and each table was bright with spring daffodils, hyacinths, and tulips. Besides the traditional ham, she cooked her children's favorite foods, including stuffed grape leaves for Jim, who came for the day, driving down from Utah State University where he studied range management. He had gone back to school after several years herding sheep for the Papoulas family in the Colorado mountains, near his grandfathers' old homesteads. Stacy came from an archaeology dig in southern Utah, stocky, short, sunburned, and smiling. Paul and Marilynn spent considerable time chasing after their children — Paul had four and Marilynn three by then.

Paul's oldest was eight, a serious little girl, Anne, who had started drawing under Athena's tutelage when she was four. Sometimes Anne let her pencils or chalk remain idle in her hand and Athena would catch her granddaughter looking at her. Yes, she knew Rob's family thought her eccentric, beyond their Mormon world, but it mattered not at all to her. She was buoyed with happiness to see the children in their Easter finery and to know that her own Holy Week was coming.

Every evening she would attend the services that followed Christ ever nearer to His Passion, she would be part of the procession that walked behind his flowered tomb singing the Lamentations, and she would stand in the darkened church on Great Saturday midnight, until a lone candle appeared in the altar and moved forward to give light. Soon all the candles would be burning and the joyous song "Christ is arisen" would gain force and grow louder and louder, and more joyful with each repetition. She would be there for His Resurrection.